PRAISE FOR KIMBERLY G. GIARRATANO

"*Razor-tongued and whip-smart, Kimberly G. Giarratano's PI captivates in the second installment of the Billie Levine series. In* Devil in Profile, *Billie gets tangled in a case pulled straight from the zeitgeist. The plot is a matryoshka of love, betrayal, and murder that Billie peels open, her need for answers at odds with her loyalty to those she loves, proving that this series has serious staying power. I would follow Billie Levine anywhere.*"

Katrina Monroe, author *Graveyard of Lost Children*

"*If you enjoyed Kimberly Giarratano's adult debut,* Death of a Dancing Queen, *you're going to love her second book in the Billie Levine series,* Devil in Profile. *Giarratano does a masterful job of introducing us to Billie's quirky family and then leads us on a roller coaster ride of twists and turns worthy of a Jersey Shore boardwalk ride...Count me amongst Billie Levine's biggest fans. This is a must read!*"

Robyn Gigl, critically acclaimed author of *Survivor's Guilt*, one of TIME Magazine's *100 Best Mystery & Thriller Books of All Time*

"*What a joy to keep readerly company with Billie Levine, the newly-minted (and somewhat reluctant) private detective who takes her bow in* Death of a Dancing Queen."

New York Times Book Review on *Death of a Dancing Queen*

"*An appealing and resourceful protagonist with realistic personal problems complements an intricate plot filled with valid suspects and motives. Readers will want to see more of Billie.*"

Publishers Weekly on *Death of a Dancing Queen*

"*Giarratano capably keeps a plethora of balls in the air in the suspect-drenched, tangled plot, but the real draw here is Billie, her family, and the sundry, offbeat characte*[...] and filled with infectious spirit.*"

Bill Ott, Booklist on *Death of a I*

"A spunky take on hard-boiled detective drama."
Angel Caranna, Library Journal on *Death of a Dancing Queen*

"Billie displays some true grit and some impressive detective chops along the way; so tell those corner boys to stop making all that noise- there's a new Jersey Girl in town."
Deadly Pleasures Mystery Magazine on *Death of a Dancing Queen*

"An exciting mystery novel that connects the past and present of organized crime, all while showcasing the challenges of caring for a struggling family member."
Foreword Reviews on *Death of a Dancing Queen*

Kimberly G. Giarratano

DEVIL IN PROFILE

A BILLIE LEVINE NOVEL

DATURA

DATURA BOOKS
An imprint of Watkins Media Ltd

Unit 11, Shepperton House
89 Shepperton Road
London N1 3DF
UK

daturabooks.com
twitter.com/daturabooks
The devil is in the details

A Datura Books paperback original, 2024

Cover by Sarah O'Flaherty
Edited by Eleanor Teasdale and Desola Coker
Set in Meridien

ISBN 978 1 91552 329 7
Ebook ISBN 978 1 91552 330 3

Printed and bound in the United Kingdom by TJ Books Ltd.

9 8 7 6 5 4 3 2 1

MIX
Paper from
responsible sources
FSC® C013056

To my daughter, Paloma. May you never lose that feisty verve.

AUTHOR'S NOTE

I was inspired to write *Devil in Profile* after reading Sophie Gilbert's "The Persistent Crime of Nazi-looted Art" (*The Atlantic*, March 2018). In the piece, she chronicled the 2010 investigation into Cornelius Gurlitt, an elderly gentleman living in Munich. After German officials caught him on a Swiss train with a suspicious amount of cash, they dug into his finances. A search warrant on his apartment led to the discovery of over 1,500 hidden works of art from masters such as Picasso, Monet and Chagall. These works had been plundered by the Third Reich, particularly Cornelius's father, Hildebrand Gurlitt, and had not been seen since World War II. Cornelius had inherited his father's stolen collection, and would periodically sell off a piece when he needed money. Hence, the character of Karl Sauer was born.

Art is powerful. That's why Hitler went after it so hard. He censored the artists, burned the books, and looted the museums. He labeled modern art as degenerate and claimed it wasn't suitable for children. Sound familiar?

Art is meant to be shared, appreciated, displayed, even questioned. But to do that, we need to see it because if you silence the art, you silence the people. I suppose that was the point of authoritarian leaders like Hitler. But we know better now.

Don't we?

CHAPTER ONE

Karl Sauer was driving to his storage locker when he hit a kid on a bike. Rotten luck.

At least he hadn't picked up the Salomon yet. Immediately, he imagined being rear-ended while it laid nestled in the trunk, its gilded frame splintered on impact, and shuddered. He'd then have to sell the Egon Schiele sketch to cover his unpaid property taxes.

He thought he had perfectly timed this errand – after rush hour but before school dismissal. That golden hour when New Jersey traffic was most navigable and when police officers were likely slouched in their cruisers, a QuickChek sandwich in one hand, a cell phone in another. Eyes on a screen, and not on an old man driving a 1995 Buick with a suspended license and broken tail light.

Only, Karl did not expect a cobalt sky – not in November – so blue that Emil Nolde himself might've used it as inspiration to paint *Lake Lucerne*.

The guy was a genius. Who cared what Angela Merkel said publicly?

However, he should've anticipated that his eyes would adjust poorly to sunlight. The last time he had been outside was three months ago, when his money had run out, and he had to sell another one from his stash. The Gleizes. He was sad to let that one go.

Sighing, more in annoyance than acceptance, Karl eased himself out of the car and shuffled over to the boy.

He wasn't a young child, so he shouldn't have been crying so much. But the kid was practically sobbing as he hunched forward on skinned knees and cradled a limp wrist. The bike lay mangled in the gutter; its front tire was still spinning.

"Fuck," the kid whispered, stretching out the word like taffy, as he tilted forward, letting his forehead rest on the asphalt. His breath came out in pants. "Fuck."

His black hair hid some of his face, but not his dark skin.

Karl relaxed slightly. No one would care that he had just tapped some illegal with the bumper of his Buick.

Karl glanced down a street lined with gas stations, convenience stores, and a few houses with stained roofs and sagging porches – rentals most likely. A man in a turban eyed him suspiciously from his perch at the Exxon station.

Hearing police sirens, Karl began to sweat. He'd have to make this go away somehow. And fast.

Clapping his hands in rapid succession, Karl barked, "Get up. Walk it off." Then for good measure, "You don't want immigration to get ya."

The boy didn't move.

Fine. Maybe he was born here, but perhaps his parents weren't?

Reaching into his pocket, Karl withdrew a wallet and thumbed inside for big bills and tossed them at the kid's feet. "That should take care of it."

The boy said nothing.

"Do you speak English?" Karl asked, disgusted.

The boy then titled his face and then something changed in his expression. A resolve.

Smart. Take the money.

Besides, if not Karl, some other driver would've eventually hit the kid and not possibly be as generous. He should consider himself lucky.

As if coming to the same conclusion, the boy reached down and with his good arm swiped a cell phone with a cracked screen from the patch of grass that flanked the sidewalk. Wincing, but no longer crying, he steadied his floppy wrist against his sternum and squared his legs. Karl watched as a bloodstain blossomed on a patch of denim.

For a brief second he felt remorse. He must've hit this kid harder than he–

The boy kicked Karl in the gut, sending him stumbling back against the hood of his car. Arms flailing, Karl tried to find purchase, to keep himself from landing backwards, but it was no use. His spine connected with the hood ornament, snapping metal in the process. Karl screamed and rolled sideways; his shoes skated on the gravel as he fell onto his ass with legs splayed.

Now it was he who couldn't catch his breath. His hand clung to his chest as if trying to cinch his ribs together.

The boy lifted his chin and spat into the street, a glob of his phlegm landing an inch from Karl's crotch.

A crowd began to form. A Black woman emerged first, squinting at the spectacle from her front porch. The man in the turban still staring from the nearest diesel pump. Finally, a woman whose ethnicity Karl could not determine, carrying a plastic bag of goodies from the convenience store, yelled, "Are you all right, sir?" She was clearly talking to him.

He had to get out of there. He was becoming memorable. Scrambling to his feet, as quickly as an eighty-eight year-old man could scramble, Karl hobbled to the driver's side. He plopped into the front seat, the keys left in the ignition, the engine still rumbling, and slammed the door.

As he drove off, he heard the kid scream, "That's right, old man. Drive away! I got you, asshole! You won't get away with this!"

Karl glanced back in the rearview mirror to see the retreating figure of the boy holding his cell phone out from his body like a bayonet, recording Karl's departure, and more importantly, his license plate.

CHAPTER TWO

Billie Levine chewed a bite of soggy pizza and streamed an episode of Graham Norton on her cell phone while she watched the door for her mark.

She had concealed her Hyundai behind the building, lest the woman spot it, next to a dumpster where seagulls pecked at discarded pizza boxes for slips of crust. Absconding with their treasure, their wings had barely cast an outline against the overcast December sky.

If one went by the calendar, winter hadn't even started, and yet Billie already resented its presence. The constant chill. The gridlock heading into Manhattan. The traffic on Route 17 and Route 4 and Route 80 and the Garden State Parkway, although one could argue that never changed. The dirty slush. The bare trees.

The desolation.

Once the ambiance of the holidays was over, there was no point in snow – it just made for frustrating commutes.

Billie adjusted an earbud and turned her attention back to Graham Norton, hoping her phone wouldn't shut off for no reason at all (it had been doing that lately). She'd seen this episode before – Matt Damon, Bill Murray and Hugh Bonneville having way too much fun, clearly drunk after the premier of their movie – and it never failed to soothe her. Like jabbing a stick into the spoke of the hamster wheel that was her brain. Lately, all her worries and worst-case scenarios had been replaying inside her head like a film she couldn't turn off.

And yet things were steady. She had a new part-time gig with decent pay. Aaron was back in her life and he, too, had found a decent job – a *legal* job – at a local auction house. And thanks to Aaron's less-than-kosher connections, he had secured Billie's mother, Shari, a spot at Safe Horizons Day Program, a daily care facility for people with dementia. Every day a bus arrived to pick Shari up and take her to a swanky facility where she made art projects and flower arrangements, leaving Billie and David time to work, socialize, food shop, hell, even take a shit without worrying about whether Shari had left the house unnoticed. Billie felt like she and her brother were finally getting to be typical 20-somethings, although *typical* was a relative term.

Even Gramps was hanging in there. He'd stopped frequenting the Clam Bar – so he was slightly more sober – but that had more to do with him losing his best friend Ken Greenberg than it had to do with any sort of epiphany on his part. And David was content. He and Matty were officially a couple now, which should've made Billie happy, except David kept dropping hints about moving out. David was her anchor, and Billie wasn't sure she could handle their mother all by herself in the evenings.

Yet despite all this, Billie found herself clasping onto her life with an oily grip, desperate for the constants to stay constant. Why couldn't life be as sticky as this godforsaken floor? She tried lifting her Doc Marten from the tiles below.

Since it was a Sunday afternoon, the joint was teeming with small children. Billie counted three simultaneous birthday parties, the rooms so thoroughly packed with kids and confusion, no one had been alerted when she swiped a slice from a margarita pie.

None of the teenage workers seemed to take notice of the single, adult female sitting alone. She hadn't paid for a wristband since she wasn't going to climb the jungle gym or play laser tag. Perhaps she passed for a parent or older sister.

Most of the adults were clustered together, one hand

clutching their kid's winter coat, another holding a juice pouch. Every so often, they would glance through the giant windows to peek as their child crawled up the rope ladder or slid headfirst down the tube slide, but mostly they were just eager for adult conversation.

My property taxes went up again.

What's happening with that Amazon Fresh?

My kids' teacher wants another conference.

A toddler jostled Billie's arm, sending a drop of grease down her sweater. "Shit," she said loudly as she brushed a paper napkin over the stain. This was her favorite vintage cardigan – a rare find that she bought at the flea market in Englishtown from a man who looked like a ZZ Top caricature. She and Nicole had driven down there together for a fun girls' date, a way to patch up their tenuous relationship, made more fragile by Billie's carelessness with Nicole's feelings. That was the other thing about adulthood – Billie had such little personal time, she found it nearly impossible to nurture her friendships. They were neglected gardens.

Billie cursed again.

"Language," hissed a woman from a nearby table. "There are children present."

Clearly. The place was crawling with them. Like ants.

Rolling her eyes, Billie considered darting into the ladies' room for a minute to salvage her outfit, but she couldn't risk the mission. Esha would be so disappointed if she failed to deliver. Also, she had given Billie that whole *you're the only one I can trust with this* speech. Billie wasn't sure if it had been resignation or a pep talk.

Even so, she wouldn't screw up now. Thanks to Detective Doug Malley, she finally had a stable gig. At this rate, she could pay off her student loans before the next decade.

Another kid bumped her from behind, sloshing her soda and splashing her phone. Directly across, Billie watched as a little boy buried a knuckle in his nostril. Identical twins were running circles around a haggard woman who had to be their mother.

Billie didn't think she hated children, but this place could make a girl schedule a tubal ligation.

She glanced at the giant clock near the rock wall. Where was this woman? She was an hour late, and of course, Billie had arrived thirty minutes early. Because when she staked out a mark, she was nothing but professional and prompt.

Suddenly a luxury SUV skated past the window and stopped short in the fire lane.

Showtime.

Billie leaped to her feet and plucked an envelope out of her messenger bag.

A white woman with long dark hair and a designer purse slung over one shoulder gripped a little boy's hand. She stormed into the place like a hurricane and mouthed, *I'm in a hurry*, to a blonde woman in the back, but the blonde wasn't having it. She vehemently shook her head as she ran over. In an accent to rival Carmela Soprano, she bellowed, "You gotta sign a waiver, or he can't play."

Perfect.

Billie yanked an abandoned orange Play Palace cap off a table and plunked it over her ponytail. "Ma'am," she said, heading over, clicking a pen a few times. *Don't watch what the left hand is doing.* "I have that form for you. Won't take but a second."

The woman sighed, but visibly relaxed. She brushed her long hair off her shoulders and sent her son off to remove his shoes by the cubbies.

"Adrianna Greco?" Billie said to her.

"Yeah," she replied, slightly taken aback that Billie knew her full name. Then: "Oh, right. Because we're on the party list. Is he the last one to arrive?" And another realization, one of abject horror, probably at her own stupidity. She began to retreat but was stopped by a claw machine full of L.O.L. eggs.

Billie stepped forward and slapped the envelope into her hand. "Mrs Greco, you've been served."

Billie whirled around to dump the cap and gather her belongings. Unfortunately, Adrianna Greco wasn't done with her. "At a kid's birthday party?" she cried out. "Bitch! You fucking bitch!" She lurched forward, but Billie wasted no time in darting toward the rear exit.

"Take it up with your ex-husband!" she called over her shoulder.

Adrianna might've cursed at Billie again, but she was too far out of earshot to hear and too focused on unearthing car keys to unlock the Hyundai. So focused, in fact, that she almost didn't notice the bouquet of tiny red flowers – poppies? – resting against her windshield, a corner of the brown wrapping held firmly in place by her wiper blades.

Were they left for her as a gift? Or were they poisonous flowers? The petals having been spritzed with laced perfume? That was a thing outside of Batman, right?

She debated on chucking them into the dumpster beside the car until her more sensible side said, *Get over yourself.*

A voice screamed out, "Are you still here, bitch?"

Billie swiped the bouquet off the glass and dumped it on the passenger's seat. While she sped out of the parking lot, she reasoned that since tonight was the first night of Hanukkah, Aaron must've left them for her as a little present.

It would be just like him to surprise her in this weird way.

Except she had never told him where she would be this afternoon. And also, he had never asked.

CHAPTER THREE

When Billie arrived home, she found the electric menorah perched in the front windowsill with two orange bulbs glowing like harvest moons.

Juggling her bag and the bouquet of poppies, she shut the front door with the tip of her boot and cried out, "Who lit the menorah before sundown?"

"For Pete's sake," Gramps yelled back from the kitchen. "What are you? The Jewish holiday police?"

Rolling her eyes, she shrugged off her jacket and tossed it into the coat closet, followed by her messenger bag. Grabbing the flowers, she headed into the kitchen and set them by the sink. "Turning on the electric menorah is my job," she said while rummaging in the junk drawer for a pair of scissors.

"I didn't realize you were still eight years old," Gramps shot back. He stood hunched over the table, making adjustments to a pickle platter. "You can light the candles for the one in the dining room. I'll let you use matches and everything. Like a big girl."

"Funny," said Billie. She unearthed the scissors with a look of triumph and went to work freeing the poppies from their paper wrapping.

"Flowers, huh?" noted Gramps. Then, almost bitterly, he asked, "Aaron?"

When Billie didn't respond, he changed the subject. "How'd that stakeout go this afternoon?"

"I got her." Billie opened a cupboard and slid out a glass

vase. She blew off the dust, filled it with water, and dropped the poppies inside.

"That's my girl. I trained you well."

Billie shifted over the plate of pickles to make room for the arrangement.

"Weird choice," said Gramps, gesturing to the flowers. "You don't see those outside of Veterans' Day." Then, for good measure, he added, "In England."

"They're nice," she said, not really wanting to add fuel to whatever fire Gramps was setting ablaze.

He stepped back to admire the display of prepared foods. "Half sours, just like you like," he noted proudly. "I also got pastrami – the good kind – and Swiss. And the low-sodium turkey your brother goes on about. I also went to Nagel's for the latkes and coleslaw, and Butterflake for the rye bread and sufganiyot. I swear everyone has upped their prices again. 'Not my fault,' they say, 'inflation.'" He rolled his eyes. "Inflation my ass. Did Big Jelly suddenly hike the mark-up on preserves?"

"Probably," said Billie. She was suddenly aware that the house seemed quiet, too quiet. No television sounds emanated from the living room. "Is Ma napping?"

"Your brother took her to visit the yenta. Shari made her a gift in that program of hers, some ceramic piece so…" he trailed off with a shrug.

"Good. She needs fresh air," said Billie automatically, but without thinking she glanced at the time. Her mother got anxious in the evening, and more agitated, particularly when it came to her bag. *Where's my purse? Did I come with a purse?* But David knew how to handle her. Billie could argue that he was the only one who could handle her.

Her stomach quickly churned. If David moved in with Matty…*don't think about it.* She exhaled long and slow, a tip she learned from a shrink on YouTube that was supposed to help her calm down, but only worked thirty percent of the time.

"Do you think this is enough food?" Gramps scrutinized the spread. "I don't think this is enough food."

"You're spending too much time with Mrs D'Andrea." Billie waggled her eyebrows, but Gramps wasn't even looking at her. He was frowning at the cold cuts.

"Those Italians know how to feed people. Ugh. I should've sprung for the roast chicken, too."

"Matty and Aaron won't come empty-handed," she replied.

He grumbled, then huffed in annoyance. The Goffs would forever cement a place on Gramps's shit list. Aaron took the coveted number one spot.

"Since when do you care about quantities of food?" she began, but then a cacophony of voices cut through her question.

David had returned with Shari. And by the sounds of it, he brought Aaron and Matty with him.

"Be nice," Billie warned her grandfather.

He made a face but said nothing.

Matty entered first, hefting a shopping bag onto the counter. He pulled out treats – a six-pack of a fancy IPA, two quarts of soup, and a cheesecake – like a magician yanking colorful scarves from a top hat.

Gramps made a beeline for the beer.

David and Shari came in next. Shari still wore her coat, but was sporting a knitted hat that Billie had never seen before. "From Mrs Rodriguez," David explained.

The yenta.

And then finally Aaron squeezed into the already tight kitchen. He was dressed in a green button-down shirt and dark denim jeans, his leather bomber jacket draped over an arm. From behind his back, he revealed a small box wrapped in gold paper. Aaron beckoned her over with a flick of his chin.

Grinning, Billie pulled him into the empty living room. She glanced quickly behind her to make sure that Gramps wasn't spying, and then kissed Aaron deeply, her hands gripping the front of his shirt. He had been so busy with his new job, and she with hers. And as Aaron was crashing on Matty's couch, and Billie still slept above her grandfather's snores, sex had been relegated to the backseat of Aaron's car. Twice they had been caught: once by a cop and once by the security guard from the Paramus Park Mall. Billie had felt like a teenager again, and not in a good way.

Aaron smiled as he pulled away. "You can't get me all turned on when I'm two minutes away from saying Kiddush with your family."

In defeat of pragmatism, Billie rested her forehead against his chest. Aaron reached his arm around and tapped her shoulder with the edge of the box. "Happy Hanukkah," he said. "Open it."

She stepped back a bit and hesitated. "The sun hasn't set."

Aaron cocked a brow. "You worried about smiting God? Because let me tell you, I have done so much to smite God – I mean so much – and I'm still standing."

"What? No." Then: "Wait, you believe in God?" She shook her head. Not the point. "I like traditions," she explained. "Let's open gifts later."

Aaron pressed the box lightly into her shoulder. "Please."

"This and the flowers. It's too much," she said while ripping off the paper and revealing – "the Swatch."

"Circa 1995. Just what you wanted. You know who Jews should really worship? eBay."

Billie joked, "At Temple Beth-Bid." She laughed. "Now that's smiting God."

"Kids, come eat," Gramps called to them.

"Menorah first," Billie and David cried at the same time.

"Menorah first," Gramps repeated, somewhat resigned.

As she and Aaron made their way to the dining room, Billie whispered, "He's being so weird. Worrying about the food. Turning on the menorah early."

"Well, I imagine," Aaron said cautiously, "that it's still so hard with Ken being gone. Didn't Ken celebrate Hanukkah with you guys?"

Billie audibly sighed, but really she wanted to smack herself upside the head. "Crap. I wasn't thinking."

As they passed the kitchen table, Aaron stopped and stared at the bouquet of poppies. "Pretty," he said, almost to no one in particular.

Remembering Gramps's comment, she said, "Poppies are a weird choice. Do you think I'm a British solider from World War I? Did I die at the Somme? Am I a ghost?"

Aaron laughed.

"Where'd you buy 'em?" she asked, genuinely curious.

"Polish florist," he replied softly. "They're Poland's national flower."

"Poland?"

Aaron cleared his throat. "Yeah, you know, cuz my ancestors were Polish "

"I thought they were from Odessa."

"Mom's side," he said quickly. "That Pale of Settlement. Flowed like the tide."

Billie had more questions, but she felt like she was reading too much into this. She'd been given flowers and a vintage watch. As far as she was concerned, this was a damn good start to Hanukkah.

Then why wasn't she feeling good?

"Do you need an engraved invitation?" Gramps called to them.

"Coming," she said. She could forgive her grandfather's impatience and his fussing over the food, his grumpiness, and short temper. After all, his best friend had only been dead a month. Ken didn't even have his headstone yet; the unveiling hadn't been scheduled. Probably wouldn't happen until spring.

Billie could forgive Gramps for anything.

"Is that our, uh, old men-men? Candle thing?" Shari asked as they clustered around the dining room table.

"A new menorah," Billie replied automatically. "David broke the old one."

"I did not!" Adjusting his yarmulke, David handed Billie the matches.

She swatted them away. "You do it. It's your job."

David shrugged, struck the match, and recited the prayers. Then they returned to the kitchen to fill their plates in a buffet-style line.

"Two kinds of matzoh ball soup," David remarked. "We fancy now."

"I made mine," said Matty, feigning offense. "That's Bubbe's recipe. Homemade stock. Chives. The works."

"Our grandma's recipe came from the Manischewitz box," said David.

Gramps pointed at David with the prongs of his fork. "You loved your grandma's soup."

"It wasn't a criticism. Just stating a fact. Jeez."

They carried their meals back into the dining room and settled around the table. Gramps uncorked a bottle of merlot and poured everyone a glass. "David, you wanna recite the blessing?"

David began, "Baruch atah Adonai, Eloheinu melech ha'olam, borei p'ri hagafen."

"Amen," the table chimed in unison.

Gramps took a long sip, then said, "I'd ask you boys how work is going, but I'm sure it's nothing I should be hearing."

"Gramps," Billie and David hissed at the same time.

"I'm gonna ignore that," said Matty with a spoon half-way to his mouth.

David squeezed Matty's shoulder. "You shouldn't be ashamed of the Malta Club."

"It's not the dancers that I find shameful," muttered Gramps.

Matty made a choking sound. He mouthed help to his brother.

Gramps wouldn't let up. "And where are you working, Aaron? That chop shop in Paterson?"

Aaron twisted in his chair and stared at Billie with wide eyes. She shrugged helplessly.

Turning around, Aaron gulped down the wine. "I'm working at an auction house in Ridgewood."

Gramps's brows shot straight up. He dabbed at his chin with a napkin. "Mahmoud's?"

"You know it?" Aaron asked.

"Ammon Mahmoud and I go way back." His gaze narrowed. "What do you do for him?"

Billie dropped her spoon with exasperation; it clanged like a bell.

"I don't really work with him much. I mostly handle his daughter Fatima's business. She deals more in antiquities. I help her catalogue inventory, set up for auctions. Move boxes. Grunt work." Aaron scooped a dollop of sour cream onto his latkes. "Nothing too exciting."

"The Mahmouds are a good family," said Gramps. "You get me?"

"That's enough," said Billie.

Matty cleared his throat and darted a glance at David, but David was visibly shaking his head, the universal gesture for *read the goddamn room.*

For a minute nothing was said, and Billie relished the quiet. She exhaled and stabbed a bite of latke with her fork.

"So your father called today," said Gramps.

Billie dropped the latke in her water glass. "What?"

"Are you shitting me?" said David.

Shari blinked several times. "Samuel?"

"Not my father, the kids' father," Gramps explained. "Craig. My good-for-nothing son."

"Oh," said Shari. "Right. Craig. How is he?"

"Who cares?" Billie grumbled under her breath.

"He's fine," said Gramps.

"Does he want money?" David scoffed. "Last time he called, he hinted that we owed him money."

"No, he's getting married, and he wants you to save the date." Gramps sounded exhausted.

"Married? To the art teacher? The one he ran off with?" said Matty.

"Matty," hissed David.

"Save the date? Really?" Billie's voice hitched. "What's the opposite of saving the date? Losing the date? I'll lose the date, then." She folded her arms over her chest. She looked petulant but didn't care. He had some nerve calling the house and asking his grown kids, who he had abandoned after their mother's Alzheimer's diagnosis, to fly to Sedona for his wedding. "What did you tell him?"

"I told him not to hold his breath," said Gramps. "But you know your father."

Billie pushed her plate away. "Yeah. We know him."

Gramps raised his beer bottle as if in silent toast, then took a swig. "Happy Hanukkah."

"Happy Hanukkah," they mumbled, but any joy the holiday had held for them as children had been supplanted by harsh realities and obligations.

Adulthood was a bitch.

CHAPTER FOUR

Billie dropped a box wrapped in blue foil paper onto Aaron's lap, startling him.

Sitting on the Levines' cement stoop, a cup of coffee cradled in his palms, he glanced up at her, genuinely surprised. "What's this?"

"My turn." She sat down next to him, her hands thrust deep into her coat pockets. Her breath materialized into white puffs of cotton. At the end of the driveway stood Matty and David, their heads tilted in whispers. Billie could only guess what they were conspiring about. "It's a jet ski," she added, not taking her eyes off her brother.

Aaron set aside his mug and picked up the gift, tossing it lightly in the air as if trying to gauge its contents by weight. Billie figured that a guy who spent most of his life checking over his shoulder could not help but be suspicious of even the most innocuous things, like a Hanukkah present...from his girlfriend. "You didn't need to get me anything."

She chided, "Don't be insane. Open it."

David would definitely be moving out, just a question of when, not if. How far would he go? One town over? Two? Another county? South Jersey?!

"They'll stay close," said Aaron.

"Did I say something?" she asked, suddenly freaked that she might've verbalized her fears without knowing it.

"No, but I know how you think." Aaron unveiled a pair of brown leather gloves, leaving the remnants of tissue paper and cardboard discarded on the stair behind him. "Are they monogrammed too?" He slipped them on and held his hands out in front of him, noting the gold embossed letters, *A.G.*

"Two kinds of matzoh ball soup aren't the only things that are fancy in this house," said Billie. Then softer, she asked, "Do you like them?"

Aaron kissed her lips. "Love them. Nicest gift I've ever been given."

"That's bullshit. I know for a fact that your father bought you a 2010 Pontiac G6 when you turned seventeen."

Aaron snorted. "My dad *acquired* a Pontiac G6. Extorted it from a guy who owed him money. Not the same thing."

"Suppose not." She reached for Aaron's abandoned coffee and took a sip.

"I can't believe your dad called today," said Aaron. "When's the last time you heard from him?"

Aaron only meant well by asking, but Billie didn't want to discuss her father. "Don't remember."

It was just this past summer. He had sent her a mean text. *I did everything for you for 20 years and you couldn't even mail me a box of my things. What kind of daughter won't do a small favor for her father?*

Billie apparently.

Craig had left a few belongings when he had high-tailed it to Sedona to be with his mistress: an old Mets T-shirt, a ring his grandfather had left him (David had that now), dog tags from a buddy who died in the first Iraqi war (Billie sent those to the widow), and some other crap she could barely recall.

Billie had been going through a lot then – dealing with her parents' separation and starting college, and mailing her dad a box of junk didn't seem high on her priority list. Many years later and he was still resentful. Who held a petty grudge that long?

David suddenly laughed loudly, and Billie's focus whiplashed to more pressing matters. "You think they'll get married?"

"Pump the breaks, dear. You sound like every Jewish mother ever." Aaron wrapped his arm around her shoulders and brought her in for a squeeze. His proximity warmed her but did little to alleviate the rolling of her stomach. Even her intestines ached. What was wrong with her? One minute she was horny, the next she wanted to crawl into the bathroom and die.

She passed him back the cup of coffee.

"Speaking of weddings," Aaron began.

"Let's not."

"Jenn Herman."

Billie's stomach threatened to revisit the latkes.

"Saturday. I'm just reminding you."

"Ugh."

"We're invited."

"You're invited," corrected Billie.

Aaron hugged her playfully. "And you're my plus one."

Billie groaned.

Aaron sighed, the levity replaced with annoyance. "I told you about this a month ago. I'm going. Matty's going. David's going. So…"

"I'm going," she finished. Jenn Herman was no friend to Billie – not since tenth grade when Billie caught Jenn shoving her tongue down Aaron's throat. Now whenever Jenn's name was mentioned, all Billie could see was a hand wrapped around Aaron's neck, manicured fingernails glinting in the florescent lighting, as she yanked him toward her glossy lips.

Billie often found herself circling this memory like a Great White, if for no other reason than her brain wouldn't release it from her consciousness. *Just let it go.*

"It's free food and dancing," Aaron continued. "You might have fun."

She shifted her frozen ass on the concrete stair. "It's one night. I can handle anything for one night. Even Jenn Herman."

"That's the spirit." Aaron's phone buzzed with a text. Frowning, he got to his feet. "Yo, Matty, time to peace out."

Billie rose too and dusted off the bits of gravel stuck to her backside. "Everything ok?" She made her voice sound unaffected.

"Yeah," said Aaron. "Just Fatima texting me about work stuff."

"Cool," said Billie.

"Dinner tomorrow, remember? I got reservations for that Thai place."

"I remember," she said, except she hadn't remembered until now.

Billie needed to start using the reminder feature on her phone, except her cell, like an old lady, could not carry one more app or it would die.

Aaron kissed her goodbye and scuttled down the steps. He gently pulled Matty away from David and pushed him toward the passenger's side of their Acura.

David joined Billie on the stoop and said, "Aaron seemed in a hurry."

"He's got work tomorrow," said Billie automatically. "Besides, Gramps can exhaust anyone." She pointed to the window; the curtain suddenly shifted closed.

"Now who's a yenta?" David said with a frown.

"I heard that!" called Gramps from the living room.

Shaking his head, David went inside the house while Billie stood outside alone, hoping the frigid air would sting her skin raw so she couldn't feel the storm surging through her insides.

CHAPTER FIVE

The following morning Billie drove to a shoebox-shaped gray building in Paramus. It was three stories high and bordered by squat little trees that flowered in the spring, but for now were nothing more than matchsticks poking out of a frozen ground.

Esha Patel owned and operated EP Investigations out of a second-floor corner office, across from a podiatrist and upstairs from a reiki spa, whatever the hell that was. She employed half a dozen process servers, a small brigade of investigators, and one IT guy who was actually Esha's useless (her word) nephew.

Long ago Detective Malley and Esha had had a tryst (his word), although Esha claimed that they had only gone on one date, and she paid. To which Malley added, "But dessert was on me at my place." Billie had no interest in hearing the rest of that story; she was just thankful Malley secured her a gig that helped float her own PI firm while she waited for cases to magically drop in her lap. She'd gotten some inquiries from potential clients who had read about her in *The Bergen Record* last month, but she didn't return their calls, not that Gramps knew about that. Lately, Billie preferred taking orders from those more capable than herself, like Esha. The work was mindless in many ways, the Play Palace stakeout notwithstanding, and it gave Billie a much needed breather. Levine Investigations could wait until Billie had the mental bandwidth to devote fully to the firm.

Whenever that happened.

In the meantime, she was content serving papers. Not everyone was as slippery as the soon-to-be ex-Mrs Greco.

Billie arrived at the office, just as Derek Campbell swiveled around in his desk chair to greet her. He was the only one who didn't elect to work from home, mainly because he didn't have much of a home to speak of.

"Morning, Harriet the Spy," he quipped while straightening his tie over a yellow-tinged dress shirt that probably hadn't been yellow when he bought it.

Derek was Esha's principal investigator. He also epitomized the gumshoe cliche: mid-40s, out-of-shape, divorced, a drinker and a smoker, and living in a tiny, one-bedroom apartment he could barely afford. Billie heard him curse out his ex-wife over the phone multiple times, the call typically ending with a sigh and a grumbled, "You'll get your payment."

Billie had secretly nicknamed him *Dyson* because he sucked up all the overtime.

"You stained your tie," she pointed out.

Derek took notice and dropped his feet. He vigorously rubbed at a splotch with a napkin he unearthed from the mountain of trash on his desk.

Malley said that Derek had once tried for the police academy but dropped out before graduation. "The cadets used to call him 'Garbageman.' Said he belonged in sanitation." Malley shook his head. "If you can't hack immature ribbing, you can't hack this job."

Billie headed toward Esha's space in the back, the only spot that had a window. The blinds were open, and Billie glimpsed the scraped-up bumper of her Hyundai in the parking lot.

"You did good with the Greco woman," said Esha as she squinted at the computer monitor, reading glasses resting comfortably on top of her dark hair.

"Thanks," Billie replied, feeling antsy. Normally, she would pick up documents from the lawyer and not Esha's office, except Esha specifically had asked her to stop in. Billie couldn't help but wonder why. More like worry why.

She got her answer when Esha flung a manila envelope across the desk. "Told the paralegal at Goldstein and McCann that I had the girl for this job. She seemed skeptical, but I assured her that I would brief you before you went out."

Reaching for the papers, Billie cocked an eyebrow and plucked the post-it note off the envelope. An address in Elmwood Park was written in Esha's precise handwriting. "Tricky one?"

"Elderly man. Lives alone. No one has managed to get him," said Esha. "Other firms have failed, but we won't."

Billie lifted the flap on her messenger bag and dropped the documents inside. "What did he do?"

"Hit a kid on his bike. Broke the boy's arm. Much of it was recorded on a cell phone, including the old man leaving the scene. Local police picked him up, but his daughter bailed him out. Old white guy isn't going to face any consequences, so the parents are suing." Esha squinted again at the screen.

"Gotcha," said Billie as she tapped the top of her skull.

Esha glanced up and then slipped the eyeglass frames over her eyes. "It's going to require some creativity on your part. Like I said, no one has been able to get him. Thinking stakeout. Bring that boyfriend along for company."

"Might have to. We were supposed to go to dinner tonight."

To her credit, Esha appeared apologetic. "I'd ask Derek, but he's got his kid's basketball game."

Translation: *parenting shit is more important than boyfriend shit.*

"Don't sweat it," said Billie, already regretting having mentioned her date. She had seen Aaron last night. Reservations could be changed. It was local Thai food, not Nobu. "I'll be there."

Esha visibly relaxed. "Glad I can count on you."

Which was exactly what Billie wanted. Maybe if Esha made her full-time, Billie could put Levine Investigations on a long hiatus. It would be so much easier to work under someone else for a while, and not just anyone else, but a capable, strong woman like Esha. Also much of the investigative work was computer-based. Background checks and the like. Easy. Safe.

"I'll keep you posted," said Billie as she turned to go.

When she passed Derek's desk, he was hunched over, feet square on the floor, cell phone pressed to his cheek. His ex-wife stance. "I promise things will be better. Tell him that, will you? Did you give any thought to my idea?...Why does your dickhead boyfriend get a say?"

Without meaning to, Billie caught Derek's eye. He immediately sat up and faced his computer. She couldn't hear the rest of his phone call and she didn't want to – Derek reminded her of her father.

CHAPTER SIX

Karl Sauer lived on a dead-end street in Elmwood Park, a small borough that bumped up against the Passaic River and was within throwing distance of Esha's office in Paramus. Although with midday traffic, and an unscheduled stop at QuickChek, Billie thought it felt more like launching distance.

Small Cape Cods were lined up side by side, like green Monopoly pieces on the board. A few homes had been expanded – a roof blown out, a floor added, an extension built on the back – but most were tiny three-bedroom bungalows, post-war construction, when kids shared spaces and families considered one bathroom adequate. The lots were cramped, but many typically had lush green lawns, swing sets, and grills.

None of that in use now, though.

Any one of those houses could clear half a mil in today's market. Well, maybe not Karl's. It was a dump with a dingy brick exterior and a roof covered in black splotches. Decades of grime left sooty lines beneath the large bay window. On the other side of the door was an air conditioning unit pushed against a small square frame, and on the door itself, a large homemade sign that read *No Solicitors* in thick, black marker.

The whole facade reminded Billie of a woman's face, her mascara running after a fight with a man who swore he loved her. Even the grass was dry like straw and bleached like bone. Only a layer of snow could improve its appearance.

Billie drove past the house and parked her car near a copse of barren trees that marked the end of the block but still enabled her to keep the sight lines.

She cut the engine and twisted a telephoto lens onto her DSLR camera. Esha had said that the man was a recluse. Sighing, Billie wondered how long she would have to sit here. The last time she had conducted surveillance outside an old man's house, he shot at her. Then he shot himself.

She exhaled and recited a mantra she handpicked from another shrink on YouTube, "Stay present. The past is done; it can't get you."

Billie's cell vibrated. She swiped it off the seat and glanced at the screen. Catching sight of the sender, she immediately dropped the phone. Her father had messaged her.

We should talk.

Her stomach curled in on itself. The past couldn't get her, huh? Sure felt like it.

Craig Levine rarely contacted her, but when he did, it was mostly to chastise her about perceived slights.

You couldn't be bothered to call Emily for her birthday.

I fractured my wrist, did you know that?

I didn't hear from you for Father's Day.

But now he was getting hitched, and Billie didn't care enough to be bothered.

That's not true, she did care. She cared how much of a prick he had been.

She ignored the text, even though she wanted to throw her piece of shit phone out the window, and went back to staring at Karl's house. Except there was no way to suppress the current of rage that bubbled within her veins. Her father had some nerve contacting her. After all this time, the man had never once – not once – apologized to her or David for abandoning them.

Shari hadn't been properly diagnosed by the time Craig Levine made off with Billie's high school art teacher, but

Shari's behavior had become worrisome long before. She was forgetting to pay bills and messing up at work. She had become hostile and belligerent.

"I deserve to be happy, too," Craig had said before getting into the car with his mistress.

Sure, Dad. Your needs come first.

Unfortunately, his departure had ensured that no one would be happy except for him.

Billie's phone rang and she flinched – her cell was playing a strong man game with her blood pressure – until she saw Aaron's name on the screen. "Hey."

"Are you all right?"

She schooled her voice. "Yeah. Just some work stress."

"I'd be happy to relieve that stress later," he said.

Billie pictured him grinning over the line. She said, "I'll take you up on that."

A laugh, then a beat. "Wondering if I should pick you up or do you wanna meet at the restaurant?"

Reality settled in her chest, and she exhaled.

"Oh no."

"I'm on a stakeout in–" She sat up straighter. A middle-aged man had just exited his side door to toss out the trash. "Hey, I see a neighbor. I'll call you right back."

Billie scrambled out of the car. Her boot hit a slush puddle and drenched her sock. "Dammit."

She waved her hand above her head to signal to the guy who, in turn, made a big point of looking anywhere but at her face.

He was in his forties with dark hair, tan skin, and presumably a dad bod underneath a navy fleece. He wore a platinum wedding band. Christmas lights were strung around his door and windows. A blow-up Santa sat deflated on his front lawn.

"Hey, sir, can I ask you a question?" she said.

"You Mormon?" he said as he dropped a black contractor bag into the pail. "I don't talk to Mormons. Or Jehovah's. I don't wanna go to my own church let alone yours."

"No," she said, shaking her head. She handed him a business card, one of many Esha had insisted she carry. "I'm from EP Investigations. I wanted to ask you about your neighbor, Karl Sauer."

The man glanced next door before twisting around to look at his own house. "Is this gonna take long? I'm in the middle of cleanin.'"

"Honestly, Mr–"

"Amato," he said, tapping the white embroidery on his fleece that read *Amato's International Moving and Storage*. "Gary's fine, though, since you're not selling religion."

She continued, "I just need to know if Karl ever pops his head outside."

That elicited a snort. "No. Never."

"Not even to take out the recycling?"

That elicited an even bigger snort. "I've never once seen a garbage can at the curb in front of his house. His daughter used to come by every so often and remove a few trash bags, but she hasn't done that in years."

He must leave his house some time, Billie thought. After all, he had hit a kid with his car. What was the reason that drew him out then?

Billie briefly saw a woman's face appear in the Amatos' window and made a presumption. "Maybe your wife would know."

"My wife?"

Billie gestured at his wedding ring. He glanced at the band as if seeing it for the first time and frowned. "Doubtful. In the last five years, she's only spoken to him once and that was to give him an earful about the state of his yard. I wouldn't bring that man up to her if I were you. Anyway, we're moving next year, so he won't be our problem for much longer."

"How long has Karl lived here?" Billie asked.

Gary shrugged. "I wanna say, since the seventies, but you'd have to ask my mother-in-law. She lives with us. This was her house."

"Is she here?"

"She's at her son's place right now," he replied.

"Thanks for the help."

Gary nodded and watched as Billie headed over to Karl's front stoop. She raised her fist to knock.

"Wastin' your time," Gary called. "But you do you." He watched her for a moment, as if he needed to commit Billie's pathetic attempt to memory so he'd have a story to tell his wife later.

Futile but Billie decided to pummel the door with the side of her palm anyway. No one answered. She pressed her ear against the wood and listened.

A jet flew overheard, muffling any sound that Billie might've heard from inside. She smacked the door in frustration.

If Karl didn't leave, she wouldn't be able to get him. If she couldn't get him, she'd disappoint Esha. She also wanted a case; she'd get paid more if she was assigned a case.

Billie twisted the new Swatch on her wrist and noted the time. As she walked back to her car, she called Aaron back. "Listen, I'm gonna have to adjust our plans. This assignment is a lot harder than I thought it would be. Feels impossible to get access."

"Who are you staking out? Taylor Swift?"

"I wish. I'd have her sign my copy of *Midnights*." She grimaced. "No, just some old dude in Elmwood Park who hit a kid on his bike. A recluse."

"Go home, Billie. It's not worth it. Elmwood Park?" Then quieter, almost imploring, he said, "You're not superwoman. You can't get to everyone. Esha'll understand."

Maybe, she thought. But Billie liked the idea of working for someone who saw her potential and valued it. Also, Esha gave health benefits to her full-timers. Billie wanted those, too. But to get to full time, she needed to show Esha that she was as good an investigator as the Derek Campbells of the world – the divorced dads with unlimited amounts of time because they only parented two weekends a month, and in Derek's case, if that.

Billie climbed back inside her Hyundai to get out from the cold. "Give me tonight," she told Aaron. "I'll get him." But she didn't sound confident. She sounded weary.

She dropped her head back and closed her eyes for a moment. She'd skin a dog for a nap. Most nights, her brain couldn't slow down long enough for sleep to catch up. "The past is done; it can't hurt you," she recited. "It can't hurt you."

CHAPTER SEVEN

Billie awoke to knocking on the car window and a woman blinking at her.

Dark hair in a messy bun. Olive skin. Lululemon leggings and a Patagonia jacket. Recognizable face.

Fatima Mahmoud, Aaron's new boss and Billie's old classmate.

Fatima and Billie had never run in the same social circles, so it seemed weird that she should be outside Billie's car, peering at her as if examining a lizard in an aquarium.

"Alive," Fatima said cryptically to an even more recognizable face behind her – this one wearing a frown. Aaron.

Billie wiped drool from her mouth, lowered the window, and met a blast of cold air. "What are you doing here?"

Fatima leaned over. "Making sure you're not dead."

"The hell you talking about?" Billie shifted her neck back and forth, trying to dislodge the soreness from having slept on it funny. How long was she out? She glanced above Fatima's head to a salmon sky. A while, if the sun's descent was anything to go by.

"I was out for a run when I saw you in your car," said Fatima, nodding at the Hyundai. "Not gonna lie – freaked me out. You looked unconscious."

"You thought I was unconscious and so you called my boyfriend and not the paramedics?" Then to Aaron, she said, "How did you get here so fast?"

"I was already in the neighborhood." His hands were thrust inside his jacket pockets. "I called you; you didn't pick up."

She checked her phone. Dead.

Gesturing to Fatima, Aaron said, "She had me worried."

Nothing about this sounded likely, but Billie was too exhausted to argue. She could interrogate Aaron later, but for now, she grabbed the door handle. Fatima retreated a step to give Billie space to exit the vehicle and stretch her legs.

"It's not safe to sleep in your car at night," said Fatima.

"Says the girl jogging without a reflective vest," Billie retorted. "Might I remind you both that this isn't my first stakeout rodeo."

"I don't even know what that means." Fatima held up her hands, having surrendered to the point. "I'm just trying to look out for another woman."

"Do you live in Elmwood Park?" asked Billie.

"Fair Lawn. What difference does that make?"

Billie waved that away as she glanced up. The streetlights popped on one by one. She then peeked around Fatima's head to the exterior of Karl Sauer's house. "Again, I appreciate the concern but – shit."

Aaron whipped his head around. "What?"

Billie stabbed a finger at Karl's door. "The sign fell. He must've come outside."

"Huh?" said Fatima as she squinted into the distance.

"I fucking missed him," said Billie, nearly cringing at her own whininess. She reached into the open driver's-side window and retrieved the papers she was supposed to serve him. When she turned back to Karl's house, a figure darted out from behind the bushes. Covered in black from head to toe, he blinked at her from behind a ski mask and ran down the block, only to disappear around a corner.

Well, that couldn't have been Karl. Men edging toward ninety did not sprint. "Did you see him?" she cried, pointing into the dark. "That guy running away?"

Fatima and Aaron shook their heads. Fatima's gaze had

been on the neighbor's blinking Christmas lights while Aaron was staring at Billie.

"Nevermind," said Billie. Her Spidey-sense tingled, and she made a beeline toward the house.

"Billie, no," Aaron warned.

"I don't like this," Fatima nervously called from the street.

Billie ignored them both and swooped down to retrieve the handmade *No Solicitors* sign that had fallen to the concrete step.

She knocked loudly. "Mr Sauer?"

No answer.

Again Aaron grumbled, "Fatima's right; something is off."

Her gaze was drawn to splintered wood alongside the door molding. Damage that hadn't been there earlier. Something was definitely wrong. She reached for the knob, and it turned easily.

Aaron grabbed her elbow. "Bad feeling."

"Should we call the police?" she asked. If there had been one guy fleeing the scene, maybe there was another still inside the house?

He hesitated. "Sure, let's call the Bergen County Detectives Bureau and leave an anonymous tip right after we're a safe distance from this place."

But if Karl Sauer was inside, and he likely was, he could be hurt.

"I'm going in." Billie shrugged off Aaron's grip. Gingerly stepping over the threshold, she pushed the door wider, only to be met with an odor so foul it could rival the stench of Exit 13A on the New Jersey Turnpike. She stuck her head back outside and sucked in fresh air, desperately trying not to vomit.

"Jesus." Aaron turned his face away and hacked. "Stay here."

Unconvinced, Billie unwound her scarf and then tied it around her nose and mouth. She gave herself an internal pep talk. *You can do this without hurling.*

Sucking in a big breath of December air, she re-entered the house and nearly collided with a pile of moldy boxes that rose like a sentinel, blocking part of the foyer and the bottom of the stairs.

The living room was dark, the bay window covered up with canvases and framed prints.

Garbage bags sat on a sofa like walruses on a beachside cliff. Billie tried to maneuver down a tiny hallway carved out between see-through plastic bins filled with newspaper and old magazines. The smell grew stronger, even beneath her scarf. The fragrance of her Gain detergent wasn't going to save her now.

She emerged into a tiny and dismal kitchen. Empty cans littered what Billie could only assume was the countertop. Dirty dishes piled high in a sink. Rusted pots and pans were left scattered on the stove, the remnants of cooked food engraved inside. Empty packaging tiled the floor.

Billie stifled a gag.

This house was the literal interpretation of the expression, 'not enough room to swing a dead cat.'

Oh, God. Please don't let me find a dead cat.

She shuffled toward a dining room packed with art books, figurines, acrylic paint, glassware and – Billie stopped. The stench had grown so powerful, her eyes watered. She had reached the epicenter.

Crouching slightly, Billie identified the fuzzy material of a loosely draped argyle sweater vest. Her eyes trailed down until they connected with shriveled hands, and then back up to a ghoulish gray skull with skin so thin and stretched, it was as if someone took a vacuum to the old man's face and sucked out all his flesh.

Billie gasped before attempting to spin around. She stumbled back out the way she came, using the plastic bins as her guide, until she practically threw herself outside. She pushed down her scarf and puked up her guts.

So much for mantras.

When she righted herself, she found Aaron watching her, his expression unreadable. No, not unreadable, but blank as if none of this surprised him. Had he been so conditioned to the ghastly that watching his girlfriend puke up her lunch didn't warrant a "what ya see in there?"

Sirens wailed in the distance.

Aaron shifted uncomfortably. "I called the cops."

She spit out remaining acid. "That was responsible of you."

"I'm the most responsible," he replied with a hint of humor, but his smile dropped the minute the flashing lights of a police cruiser cast shadows on his face. "Fatima split, by the way."

"You could've split too," she said to him as she wiped her mouth with a crumbled napkin she'd swiped from one of her trips to Starbucks. "I would've handled it."

"I have no doubt, but I'm not an asshole," he said just as the officers exited their vehicle.

Something told Billie that even just being witnesses, they were going to pay dearly for this.

CHAPTER EIGHT

The Elmwood Park Police Department showed up first – two mustachioed cops who looked so much alike, they could've been brothers. Elmwood Park was a small town, maybe they were. After going inside to check out the body, one of the officers graciously gave Billie a Lysol wipe to clean her hands. She really wanted to douse herself in bleach.

Then the medical examiner arrived, and finally the Bergen County Detectives Bureau. Eventually, the press would get wind. Billie mouthed a silent prayer that the man assigned to the case would not be–

Detective Esteban Morales emerged from an unmarked cruiser, followed by his partner, Doug Malley.

"Oh, great," Aaron said under his breath, referring to Morales, "the ex."

"We never dated," Billie pointed out.

"Even worse," said Aaron, sulking with his hands in his coat pockets. "Since you had slept together."

"You didn't have to stay." Morales passed Billie by with a curt nod. Malley, on the other hand, gave her a fist bump.

"And leave you alone with a dead body? I don't think so. You shouldn't have gone in there to begin with."

Billie eyed him suspiciously. "Why'd you come here?"

"Fatima said you were alone in your car, unconscious."

"Fatima also rugby tackled me in the senior parking lot and told our class that she hooked up with Niall Horan, so maybe we shouldn't take everything she says at face value."

44

"Were you sleeping in your car? Alone? On a random street where you could've been assaulted?" Aaron asked without a hint of mirth.

Billie opened her mouth to answer but was interrupted by Malley who leaned a meaty hand against the door molding and grumbled, "I've officially seen everything."

"In your line of work, you haven't come across a hoarding situation before?" Billie asked, disbelieving.

"Hoarders, yes." Malley pulled down his mask. "Three-week old corpses, also yes. But together, no. New territory." He stepped off the stoop and fanned out his coat similar to how an elephant might fan out his ears. Malley was a large gentleman, more square-shaped than man-shaped, but he contained the confidence of Don Draper and a list of exes to back it up. "Wish I didn't wear my good trench; the smell won't come out for weeks." He then gave Aaron a cursory glance. "Goff."

Aaron nodded, also cursory. "Detective."

"Did the Elmwood boys take your statement?" Malley asked.

"Yes," said Billie as she made room for men in lab gear to enter the house.

Malley tilted his chin toward a mess on the lawn. "Your puke?"

Billie didn't even bother to look. "Also, yes."

"Gonna have to rule that out."

"So the body has been there for three weeks?" she said.

Malley jutted a thumb toward the front door. "Give or take, according to the lab rats inside. Probably natural causes."

"I don't know about that," Billie singsonged with a quirk of her brow. "I saw a dude run from the place a few minutes before I got inside. Wearing tactical-style boots."

Aaron balked, then turned green. "How could you even tell in the dark?"

"You ok?" Malley asked Aaron.

Aaron stepped back. "The smell."

"I assume the victim is Karl Sauer," Billie said, fishing.

"According to his suspended driver's license." Then to Aaron, Malley said, "What time did you show up?"

"Five-ish, I think." Aaron turned his face to the street and inhaled deeply.

Malley looked at Billie for confirmation. "Yeah, five," she said. "He woke me up from a nap in my car – I dozed off during a stakeout." She quickly realized how that sounded. If she had been napping, she hadn't had eyes on the house or Aaron. But if the old man had been dead for weeks, what was Malley's interest in Aaron's whereabouts?

"You didn't go inside?" Malley asked him.

"No," said Aaron. "Can we leave?"

"Just as soon as Morales clears you."

"Great," Aaron muttered.

As if on cue, Esteban Morales came outside and removed a mask. He wore a black suit under his coat. His dark hair was slightly disheveled, and he had stubble from a few days' growth. He was still ruggedly handsome, but no longer handsome enough to tempt Billie. She felt a bit of relief. Glancing over at Aaron, he didn't feel the same.

Morales said, "Where've you've been all day, Mr Goff?"

"Work," Aaron replied.

"At?"

"Mahmoud's Auction House."

"Can someone vouch for that?"

"Mr Mahmoud," Aaron shot back. "Feel free to call him."

Morales jotted down the name in a small notebook. "I will."

Malley gently patted Billie's shoulder. "All right, kiddo. You and Goff can head out now. Just stay local."

Billie made a face. "Where the hell would I go?"

"Not you," he said.

Oh, right. Aaron.

As Aaron escorted her back to her car, she spied a young officer talking to Gary Amato, whose arm was wrapped around a woman with bleached hair and dark roots. Billie presumed it was the wife. As the officer scribbled down notes, the woman's face began to crumble in on itself until tears emerged. This seemed like quite the emotional performance from a woman who hated the state of Karl's yard.

Billie fished her car keys from her bag and turned to Aaron. "Guess I'm free now for that dinner and movie."

"Billie," began Aaron as he watched the flurry of police and crime techs scurrying about Karl's house. "You just saw a really gross dead body. You threw up. I think we're going to have to put a pin in tonight's date."

"You're right," she said, sighing with the feeling that the universe was conspiring to keep them apart. "I probably should go home and scrub my eyeballs, try to unsee the corpse. If that's possible…"

Aaron brought her in for a hug. Inhaling his cologne, she buried her face in his chest. She pulled away and said, "Maybe I'll catch up on Bake Off–" Her thoughts were immediately interrupted by an intrusion.

Glancing down at Aaron's hands, she noticed that they were blue from the cold.

"Aaron, where are your gloves?"

CHAPTER NINE

The following morning, Billie sat at the kitchen table with a half-drained carafe of coffee. Her leg bobbed up and down uncontrollably as she scrolled through a paltry list of hits on her phone. She had googled Karl Sauer's name and come up dry. She managed to find a bearded man on Instagram with the same surname, but different spelling of Karl, and two Facebook accounts that seemed promising at first, until she noticed the Berlin address and the other belonged to a trucker in Omaha.

Unfortunately for Billie, the Karl Sauer that she had literally stumbled upon in that house of horrors in Elmwood Park did not exist as far as the internet was concerned. That Karl Sauer was a ghost. Maybe even a literal one, seeing as how he was dead and all.

He may not have an online presence, but he'd been around for almost nine decades. Abandoning her phone, she slid her laptop toward her and tried the newspapers archive. She paid $8 a month for North Jersey access, so it was time it produced dividends.

She entered Karl Sauer's name into the search bar and got one hit.

She'd take it.

The Bergen Record had published a piece on Karl in 1970. Apparently, he made news for selling a Pablo Picasso drawing for $250,000. Jesus. What was that in modern money? With inflation, a gazillion dollars, easy.

"My mother was friends with him," he'd told the reporter. "He gifted her the piece, and I've recently sold it to a collector."

There was a photo of Karl, substantially younger – dare Billie think it, handsome – standing beside the artwork which Billie could barely make out due to poor photo quality.

The article went on to mention that Karl's mother, an Austrian national, had met Picasso in her youth in Spain. Picasso was known for bedding women; Billie wondered if Karl's mother had been such a woman. The article also referred to Karl as an art appreciator, but didn't mention his profession or family. Perhaps, at the time, he had neither.

So the man sold one Picasso in 1970 for a quarter of a million dollars, and then did nothing after that?

Nothing that left an online trace.

Detective Malley suspected that Karl had died of natural causes, which seemed the most likely. An elderly man who lived alone among refuse and mold surely couldn't have been in the peak of health. And yet...she thought she spied a rust-colored stain beneath his shriveled skull. Not to mention the thief in the night who fled the scene.

And there was Aaron who hadn't been wearing his new gloves.

"Forgot them at home," he had said.

"Did you lose them?"

"No, just forgot."

Her leg jiggled faster.

Focus, Levine.

"Will you cut that out?" Gramps grumbled as he gripped the edge of the table. Dressed in his gray Kentwell College sweats, courtesy of last year's Hanukkah gift, he said, "You're rattling the china."

Billie pressed a hand to her thigh to stop its trembling. "Sorry."

Gramps then frowned at Wordle.

"You stuck?" Billie asked, before adding unhelpfully, "It's a word you know."

He shot back, "Despite what you think, Miss Smarty Pants, I do have a decent vocabulary."

"You didn't know aphid."

"Who knows what an aphid is?"

"I do." She leaned over to glance at his phone screen, and like a child, he pulled it from view.

"Let me see," she said.

"I don't want you judging me," said Gramps, tilting his body away. "I'm on my last turn."

"What letters do you have?" She pawed for the phone. "Seriously, let me look."

"No. I can do this on my own."

The doorbell rang, putting an end to both their ridiculousness, and Gramps rose to answer. "It's probably Mrs D'Andrea dropping off another casserole." He rolled his eyes, but a smile tugged at his lips. Like many straight men, Gramps enjoyed the attentions of a woman, particularly if she flirted with lasagna and chicken cacciatore.

Billie heard Gramps shuffle to the foyer and mumble to the visitor, "What do you think? The Y goes in the last spot?" But the response wasn't from a female admirer.

Gramps was still tapping on his phone when he returned to the kitchen with a grizzled Detective Malley in tow, last night's trench having been swapped for a navy peacoat with bright, gold buttons. Malley wiped his palm over his freshly shaven chin.

Billie silently gestured to the coffee carafe, her manners stolen by her preoccupation of the dust motes visible in the sunbeam stretching from the kitchen window to the grungy tile. She inhaled deeply, wondering if she could still catch a whiff of last night's kitchen odors. David only remembered this morning to take the trash out to the curb.

Malley, the clever detective that he was, understood Billie's wordless gesture, and thus responded with a wave of his hand and a simple, "I had a French press at home."

Billie wasn't even sure what she was so self-conscious about; if French presses were houses, then Malley lived in a Styrofoam cup half-filled with last night's decaf.

Malley pressed his heavy hands onto her shoulders before leaning back against the molding that separated the kitchen from the dining room. "Just came to check in on you, kiddo. See how you're doing. It's not every day that you stumble upon the crypt keeper, pickling for three weeks. And that smell. The dry cleaners rolled out a big bin and made me toss my coat inside. Wouldn't even touch it." He shuddered.

Gramps crossed his arms over his chest. "Oh really? A pickled corpse?" He shot a look at Billie. "You said you just encountered a hoarding situation."

"There might have been a dead body," she said dismissively. "Anyway, I'm fine. Last month, I had a run-in with not one, but two neo-Nazis, and a gun in my face for good measure. I think I can handle a mummy." She looked squarely at Malley. "By the way, I can't find much on your vic except he made a fortune in 1970. So was it natural causes or what?"

Please be natural causes.

Malley scoffed. "You know I can't comment on an ongoing investigation."

"You're the one who came to my house," she pointed out.

"Be nice," said Gramps.

"I am nice," she shot back.

"You sound grumpy."

"I'm not grumpy," but even as she said it, she said it in a *mood.*

"I wanted to see if you're all right," Malley answered defensively. "Esha explained, in a little more detail, why you were there, and what Karl Sauer was sued for."

"So?"

"So," he said, reaching into his pocket for his cell phone. His finger darted across the screen, stopping when it landed on a photo of a young kid. He set down the picture in front of Billie. "You mentioned seeing a figure in black last night."

"Really?!" said Gramps with a shake of his head.

"Could it have been this kid that you saw outside the house?" asked Malley, clearly ignoring Gramps's indignant outburst.

Despite Malley's overt concern, he was obviously here on official police business.

"I saw a grown man." Billie examined the photo — a school picture – but it was more for show than any real consideration. The boy was a teen. Thirteen years old, fourteen tops. His build was slight. He had narrow shoulders and spaghetti arms. Billie shook her head and laughed. "Definitely did not see a child."

Even Gramps scammed a look. "You think that boy could pass for an adult?"

"Didn't say that," said Malley, his tone skirting the edge of annoyance. "Just wanted to know if it was possible that she saw him?"

"That kid has a broken wrist," Billie pointed out. "The man I saw fleeing the scene was broad-shouldered, fast, wearing boots."

Malley took back his phone and squinted at the photo. "The kid's father maybe?" Although it sounded as if Malley was talking more to himself than to Billie or Gramps.

Billie sat back in the chair, feeling a bit smug. "So not natural causes?"

Malley slid the phone back into his pocket. "I didn't say that."

Billie got to her feet, her thoughts racing, swirling. She snagged on a thread and pulled. "You wouldn't be here asking me to rule out a line of inquiry if you thought this was a natural death. Or maybe the death was natural, but a crime occurred nonetheless?"

Again Malley patted Billie's shoulder, a little rat-a-tat-tat, the way a loving dad might say goodbye to his daughter. "I should get going. Oh, come by the precinct today, will ya? Before five, preferably. Morales has some questions for you."

Crime it is.

Then to Gramps, he said, "Walk me out to the cruiser."

Bille could feel the indignation swell inside her. She appreciated Malley's paternal concern but she would appreciate it more if he treated her like a peer and not a dependent. But like a kid, she ran to the living room window, once she heard the front door close. Through a gap in the curtains, she watched as Malley spoke. She couldn't hear anything, but whatever Malley was saying appeared to be throwing Gramps into an apoplectic fit.

Shit.

Malley drove away, and Gramps stomped toward the house, only stopping to retrieve an errant envelope that had been sticking out of the mailbox.

He came inside and stabbed the air accusingly. "You are not to see Aaron Goff anymore, got it?"

Gramps darted into the living room, circling the first floor of the house like a bull in an arena. Billie followed him. "What did Malley say?"

"Nevermind that. If he wanted you to know, he would've told you." He pressed the envelope to her chest. "Here. A holiday card." Gramps checked his watch. "Look at that. Time for my nap."

"Nap? You just woke up," she said, but Gramps was already making his way toward the stairs.

Billie was left alone in the living room, turning in a slow circle from the hurricane that was Gramps's emotions. And she was moody? What the hell just happened?

Surrendering with a sigh, she opened the envelope, a garish red that signified both Christmas and irate grandfathers, and noted the lack of a return address. That should've been her first clue. Her second was that the card was one of those charity freebies, a photo of a fluffy kitten in a Santa hat, sent from an organization the Levines had never donated to, and the third clue was the inclusion of a set of black and white photographs of Billie sleeping in her car.

Taken just yesterday.

Billie frantically fanned the card and skimmed the inside, trying to locate a signature, a hint of the sender. These were obviously snapped with a telephoto lens, and the message was clear: *we can get to you.*

Billie immediately ran through a mental list of people she pissed off on any given day, and while that list was long, not one of those asshats could be bothered to stake her out for photos.

So that meant new players were in town, and Billie had to look over her shoulder. The problem with glancing behind you all the time was that you couldn't see what was ahead.

CHAPTER TEN

Billie sat beside a desk in the Bergen County Detectives Bureau bullpen, trying to focus on the questions being asked of her while phones rang off the hook, and men in suits shifted around her. She spotted uniformed officers with handcuffs dangling from their waists and Glocks in their holsters. Several civilians shuffled past her, including an older woman, trailing a disinterested detective, as she described in detail the suspicious looking man who loitered outside her building.

Malley was nowhere to be seen, but Morales was flitting around here somewhere, taking statements. She grew restless as the cacophony of police business circled her like a swarm of wasps.

Just then a handsome Asian guy, wearing a sports coat over a Nike hoodie, plopped into the chair across from Billie. His black hair was freshly cut and molded into shape with a product that carried a hint of peppermint and rosemary. As she stared at him, trying to place his face, he cut her an annoyed look.

Billie glanced away, pretending to take an interest in a desk calendar while a beanpole of a detective – Riley? Rowan? Ross? Rumpelstiltskin? – tapped a pile of papers together to align their corners.

"Miss Levine," he said, before setting them down. "Carefully read the statement and then sign by the X."

Billie scanned the document, skimming her account of events, since she both wrote it and witnessed it, but she got

55

distracted by the Asian guy addressing a female detective. "I want to talk to someone about the Karl Sauer death. There's a connection between him and Roza Filipek that I think detectives should be made aware of."

Billie leaned over the desk, inching her ear closer to the man's voice. "Roza with a Z, by the way. Polish national."

There were responses of 'just a minute' and 'hang tight while I find someone to take down your information.'

The detective then left, and Billie rose from her chair.

"Miss Levine, you're not free to go yet," said Beanpole. "Detective Morales–"

She rolled her eyes and said nothing while his voice disappeared into the void of noise. Dropping into the desk chair next to Nike hoodie, she began, "Hello there, Mr–"

He narrowed his gaze. "Professor–"

"Doctor?" Then answering her own question, she shook her head.

"Professor Jeremy Yang," he said.

"Oh, so no, like, doctorate?"

"Working on it," he grumbled.

"We're getting off topic," she said. "What is it that you know about Karl Sauer?"

He smirked. "You're not a police detective."

"No."

"Well, then, it's not your business," he replied, crossing his arms over his chest.

She leaned in and dropped her voice. "But what if I make it my business?"

He sat back, his posture now a shield against her. "Is this your attempt at flirting?"

She pushed the chair away, hoping the distance would diffuse the heat blooming across her face and chest. "What? No."

Why did he think she was flirting with him when she was simply trying to manipulate him for information?

She bolted to her feet, hoping that if she was standing and indignant, he'd feel somewhat chastised. She opened her mouth to tell him off just as Morales said, "Don't disappear, Goff."

Billie whipped her head around to find Aaron, bomber jacket draped over his wrist, being led out of the precinct by a uniformed officer. Next to him was a middle-aged Black man in a suit. Aaron's lawyer.

Morales, clearly aggravated, gestured toward Billie. "You're next, Levine." Then he jerked his chin toward the interrogation rooms behind him.

"Looks like the only one who should be answering questions here is you," Jeremy Yang said with raised brows.

Billie moved toward him only to be tugged gently back by Aaron. He slipped his hand inside her coat pocket and kissed her cheek.

"Are you all right?" she whispered. "What's going on?"

"It's all good," he said, grinning. "I just invoked Gramps's Rule Number Five."

But before Billie could ask him a follow-up, Morales loudly barked to the young cop by Aaron's side, "Get him out of here, Officer."

"Come on, Aaron," said the lawyer, resigned. The man certainly earned that retainer. Probably could buy a yacht defending the Goffs' messes. But when would he get to sail that yacht if he was constantly at Neil Goff's beck-and-call? Crime was time consuming.

Billie watched Aaron and his counsel get escorted out of the precinct. Morales called her name again, and this time, she went toward him.

Whatever was in store for her couldn't be good.

CHAPTER ELEVEN

Billie found herself sitting in a gray folding chair, in front of a gray metal table, surrounded on three sides by gray cinderblock walls. If not for the ridiculously large, two-way mirror across from her, she would've felt like she'd been pressed inside an aluminum tray, ready for baking. Aside from the noxious fumes of cologne and stale coffee, the interrogation room was as hot as a hairy man's ass crack.

All done on purpose, of course. She briefly wondered which old-timer was asked to spray his aftershave on the walls in order to slowly torture the poor schmuck being questioned. In this case, the schmuck was Billie. And not long before her, Aaron.

She was shrugging off her coat when Morales entered, devoid of a smile and his suit jacket. He was all business as he set an iPad on the table. He wordlessly scraped a chair across the linoleum and sat down, adjusting his tie in the process.

These cops – everything had to be a performance.

Billie removed her beanie and tilted her head so that she had an unobstructed view of the mirror. Smoothing down her part, she tried to appear as unbothered as she could, despite being very bothered. Her coming in to sign a statement had all been a set-up, and Malley had been the messenger. She'd get him for that deception.

"How can I help you, Detective?" she said with more formality than was warranted. After all, they had seen each other naked. She was certain that their history made this interview an outright ethics violation, but to mention that might destroy her leverage. Billie felt the blackmail could be best utilized on another day.

Morales flicked his finger across the iPad screen to reveal a series of mugshots.

Billie joked, "Ooh, it's my favorite childhood game, *Guess Who.*" She pursed her lips. "Is the criminal wearing glasses? Does he have a tattoo on his face? Is he a domestic terrorist? Did he get radicalized in prison?"

Morales ignored her quips as he handed her the tablet. "You know the drill. Stop if anyone looks like the man you saw fleeing Karl Sauer's house."

"Know the drill? I could teach the drill." Billie slid her finger across the iPad screen, enlarging the image to see height and weight information. It had definitely been a man with a tall build, over six feet. Race? If she had to guess...white, but being that it had been evening and he'd been masked up, she couldn't be certain. Theoretically, she couldn't even swear it was a man. Gender was not a given. "This is all so pointless," she began innocently, before glancing up at him. "I didn't see the killer's face."

"The medical examiner has not drawn any conclusions about cause of death," recited Morales with a twinge of *nice try.* Then he checked his phone.

"My guess is that with the Christmas holidays coming up, you won't get cause of death until after the new year. And then, you know, it takes a while for people to get acclimated to being back to work, still writing the previous year on their autopsy reports."

"Death doesn't take vacations, Billie."

"Death, no, but medical examiners do, especially when they have a timeshare in Ft Lauderdale."

Morales sighed, likely finding her humor ill-placed. His phone buzzed with an incoming text and he rose to his feet. "Be right back. Keep scrolling."

She exhaled as her finger pushed aside photo after photo, stopping only when she landed on a familiar face. When Morales returned with Detective Beanpole in tow, she held up the screen showing Aaron's photo from a court hearing three years ago. "Is this your idea of a joke?"

"No." Morales jutted his chin at his clean-shaven counterpart. "Detective Ruiz will sit in with us."

"Ruiz!" Billie exclaimed, but her joy at rediscovering Beanpole's name was quickly displaced by internally freaking out as to why she forgot it in the first place.

"Focus, Billie. This isn't a game," said Morales.

No, it was not, although focusing often felt like a full-time job.

Sadly, Morales hadn't asked Billie here to sign a statement or peruse digitized photos. Not with Aaron having been in this same seat only minutes ago. Clearly, Morales had something cooking inside that handsome brain of his.

Billie's stomach sank under the weight of implications.

Detective Ruiz clicked a pen several times while Morales laid a plastic evidence bag with a piece of gold jewelry trapped inside. "You know what this is?" asked Morales.

"A chai?" she responded.

"Do you recognize it?"

"Yes, chai is a Hebrew word spelled with two letters: chet and yud. It means life." She playfully toasted the air with an invisible glass. "L'chaim. To life."

Morales cleared his throat. "Let me rephrase. Do you recognize this particular piece of jewelry? Do you know its owner?"

"It would be like identifying someone's crucifix," she said, nodding toward the gold cross entangled in Morales's tie. "It could belong to anyone."

Ruiz picked the iPad off the table's surface and tapped the screen to wake it up. Aaron's picture, complete with the adornment of a gold chai appeared like a betrayal. He displayed the screen for Billie's inspection. "Could this be the same necklace?"

Billie shrugged. "How should I know?"

Billie suspected that Morales was trying to rattle her, but it also felt to her that he was showing his hand on purpose, which she found even more disorienting.

Ruiz then laid another evidence bag on the table. This one had a leather glove inside. Without meaning to, Billie ran the side of her palm across her brow, removing a line of sweat from her skin.

"This is Aaron's chai. And this is Aaron's glove." Morales tapped the bag and smirked. "It has his initials on it. In gold. Macy's?"

Billie swallowed. The mounting evidence was there, presented to her like a gourmet dinner. But as Morales removed the domed lid, what sat on the plate had all the appearances of her boyfriend's last meal.

"I've been wondering where that went," she said, reaching for the bag.

Morales yanked it back. "Evidence."

"Oh, well, I must've dropped it," she continued. "I was wearing the gloves when I arrived at Mr Sauer's home."

Ruiz glanced at Morales who leaned back in the chair, his arms crossed over his chest. "A.G. are not your initials."

"Of course, not," she said. "I had borrowed them because my hands were cold."

"You borrowed your boyfriend's gloves?"

"My hands were cold," she repeated.

Morales clucked his tongue. "Well, then you must have the other glove?"

Mimicking the detective's posture, Billie gave it a few seconds before she thought to reach inside her coat pocket and slap the other leather glove on the table.

"Where'd you drop it?" Morales asked.

"Well, if I knew that, I would've gone back for it." A pause. Then quiet, followed by sputtering on behalf of the detectives. She said, "Anything else, or am I free to go?"

Morales dipped his chin so slightly she wasn't sure if he was actually allowing her to leave, until he cleared his throat and gestured toward the door with his hand.

Gathering her belongings, including the glove and hat, Billie made her way to the door, but then stopped. "He went legit. Try to cut him some slack, ok?"

Morales didn't even glance in her direction. "Detective, escort her out."

Ruiz nodded before silently leading Billie out of the interrogation room and into the hallway that filed into the bullpen. His cell must've rung because he halted and pressed his phone to his ear.

Spotting a man's broad back, she abandoned Ruiz and made a beeline for Doug Malley. He sat facing away from her, legs splayed, with the phone to his ear.

She stood next to his desk, pretending to wait for him to finish his call, while her fingers gently grazed a yellow legal pad. JEREMY YANG and a phone number were written in blue ink. But also, INTERPOL and RESTITUTION.

Hm. Yang had said 'Polish national.'

But *restitution*? What was that about?

Fingers gripped her forearm. "Time to go," said Ruiz.

"Yeah, yeah," she said as he led her away. The last thing she saw before being manhandled out the front door was Malley's bemused expression, and Morales's pissed one.

If only Morales knew Gramps's Rule Number Five: *When cornered, lie.*

And if Aaron, who normally spouted the arrogance of an untouchable politician when dealing with law enforcement, felt cornered, then something serious was going down. So serious, Morales called her into an interrogation room to sweat her out.

Billie would not be caught off guard again.

CHAPTER TWELVE

"Seriously? Shul?" said Aaron as Billie pulled him inside the temple's backdoor, peeking over his shoulder and into the dark parking lot as she did so. He tripped over the rubber mat – scattering rock salt onto the rug – and stumbled into a small vestibule. Righting himself, he asked, annoyed, "Why couldn't we have met at Nagel's?"

Rather than answer his question, Billie waved Aaron down the hall and into the dimly lit sanctuary, surrounded by stained glass Stars of David and menorahs (the six-stemmed ones, not the kind currently in the Levines' living room). On the wall closest to the entrance were plaques for all the dead congregants whose families paid to have them memorialized near the restroom.

There was a standard perfume trapped in the carpet of most houses of worship – a mixture of stale coffee, archaic books, and religious guilt.

For Billie, the guilt was as much a part of her Jewish identity as her small stature and sardonic wit. Millions of Jews died in the Holocaust, and she couldn't even be bothered to attend High Holy Days services.

Did she care for nothing?

Although to be fair, the last time she had attended temple services was her Bat Mitzvah. As soon at the Torah scroll was rolled up and tucked away, Shari Levine was thinking of all the money she would save on synagogue dues. Her Jewish obligation paid in full.

The Levines surely valued their Judaism, but why was it so expensive?

"Nagel's might be compromised," she said. "Too public."

"What are you? CIA?" Aaron plunked down into a chair and sighed, the joke dispersing with his obvious exhaustion. It must take a lot of energy to lie to her all the time.

Billie hesitated before sitting down herself and tugging off the knit cap Mrs Rodriguez had gifted Shari and that Billie had grabbed in her haste.

It felt eerie being here without a crowd of old folks kvetching about the traffic on the ride over.

"Who did you bribe to let you in?" he asked, turning around, the corner of his mouth quirked in such a way as to reveal the pride he must've felt at his girlfriend's underhandedness.

Billie was momentarily offended. "No one. The Sisterhood has its Hanukkah party tonight." Then she added, "And Rabbi Schechter owes Gramps a favour."

Translation: William Levine got rid of a few parking tickets.

"So what's with the secrecy?" asked Aaron, but his tone betrayed his indifference. He knew exactly what this was about, especially when Billie unveiled a single leather glove – its partner being held in the Bergen County Detectives Bureau evidence lock-up. "You slipped this into my pocket because you were in Karl Sauer's house." She did not address it as a question. "You invoked Gramps's Rule Number Five."

"What did you tell Morales?" asked Aaron.

"What do you think? I lied for you."

Aaron exhaled. Billie wasn't sure what was more troubling, that Aaron assumed she would tell the truth about the glove, or that she had to perjure herself to cover Aaron's crimes.

Definitely both.

"What were you doing in his house? Did you go there before or after I had fallen asleep in my car?"

"Before," said Aaron. "Night before."

"Why?"

Aaron rubbed his hands on his knees. Likely, trying to wipe the sweat he was producing from all his deception. "I really don't want you involved in this."

"Involved?!" She closed her eyes a beat and injected an eerie calm into her voice where there was none. "I lied to a detective on your behalf. I'm already involved. Now tell me why I'm involved."

A thought occurred to her. That smug professor – *Jeremy Whatshisface* – had said something about a Polish national.

And then the word INTERPOL in Malley's block handwriting.

Karl Sauer's Picasso. He had sold one; maybe there were more.

"Does Karl Sauer have anything to do with your stint in Israel?" she asked suddenly.

Aaron rounded his shoulders and rubbed the bridge of his nose. "How you figure this shit out is beyond me."

"Jesus, Aaron."

He jerked up his chin. "It's not what you think."

Her intestines clenched and she whispered, "Please tell me you didn't kill an old man for money."

He sputtered for a second. "N-no."

Billie supposed she should be glad for Aaron's indignation, but really she was just defeated. Why did all the men in her life cause her so much stomach upset?

"First, I did not kill anyone," he hissed while twisting around, in case an old lady from the Sisterhood came wandering by. "Second, that old man? Not a good guy."

Billie gestured for him to continue.

"That's all you need to know," he said, like that would suffice.

She slapped an envelope into his chest. Initial confusion stamped his features, followed by a harrowing realization when he examined the photos of Billie sleeping peacefully, and vulnerably, in her car. "Oh, fuck." He sank lower into the chair.

"Who took those pictures?" she asked. "The same guy I saw running from Sauer's house?"

Aaron shrugged, but that was probably because he wasn't sure, not because Billie was wrong. She didn't get much wrong lately.

"I swear that it will get so much worse for you if you don't explain everything," she said with such dead seriousness that Aaron momentarily looked afraid.

He also looked defeated, but Billie didn't feel like a victor. She hated reverting to threats, but this idea that Billie was somehow safer if she was kept in the dark was antithetical to everything she had been taught, not to mention witnessed. The more she knew, the better. Especially since her proximity to Aaron made her a target.

He began, "I initially went to Israel for a different kind of employment, but after that, uh, position didn't pan out, I got approached by a group to help out with some business."

"Enough of the euphemisms," she snapped.

He clarified, "I met an ex-Mossad agent who was running a group out of Haifa. He needed men, no wait there was Yaeli, she ran our communication ops – so people, with certain skills to pull off jobs."

Billie frowned.

"Heists."

She frowned even more.

"Recovering art, jewels, and Judaica stolen by the Nazis."

That shut her up. No, it didn't. "You were working on behalf of Holocaust victims?"

"Kinda. Tomer's team would identify heirlooms in the possession of others, mostly thieves and bad guys, really want to hammer that point, and we would go in and steal them back. We'd–"

"Robin Hood it," she finished.

"Basically."

"Roza Filipek," she whispered, remembering Jeremy's reason for even being at the police precinct. "How's she connected?"

"Roza's an art thief who got her start in black market antiquities; she worked her way up the ranks in several underworld organizations."

As he spoke, Billie took out a notebook and clicked a pen. Aaron gently put his hand over hers. "No paper trail."

"What if I don't remember all the details?"

"No," he said firmly.

Billie set down the pen and gestured for him to continue.

"Word is she took out a former boss with a paintbrush through the eye. Ok? That's not a woman we get on the wrong side of. Even me. So no documentation. Nothing that connects us."

"What kind of operation does she run?"

"For hire. She gets calls from all over the world, mostly billionaires and tycoons, oligarchs, who want an art piece – painting, statue, something off the radar, but valuable – and she sets up a team to fetch it."

"Was she responsible for that Van Gogh theft at the Singer Lauren Museum?"

"Doubtful. The people who call her are after the obscure shit. Shit that has been rumored to be missing. Stuff they can brag about owning when really it belongs with descendants or in the fucking Met."

"So what happened? Your team ran into Roza's? Collided on a job?"

"We got to the goods first. Cut them off at the knees. And once the Israelis got their hands on the stuff, no way Roza could touch it. But our last job, I messed up, and she…" he trailed, and then gestured to the scar along his neck. "I was lucky. Made it to Warsaw, then Tomer and the team life-flighted me to a hospital in Tel Aviv. I owe him big time."

"Sounds to me like he owes you," she said. "You almost died on his watch."

"I signed on for it."

Billie wondered if Aaron's misguided altruism had anything

to do with her. After all, she had broken his heart with this parting shot: *I can't be with a criminal.*

"So Karl Sauer," she continued. "He had the attention of both Roza and your Mossad connections."

"Karl's father was an art collector before the Nazis took over, but then he became an assistant to Hildebrand Gurlitt, one of Hitler's four art brokers. Gurlitt had, like, over a thousand pieces of art when he died. Guess his buddy, Sauer, had acquired some too."

"So you're saying Karl Sauer inherited a lot of valuable Nazi-looted art."

Aaron nodded.

Inherited this sketch from my mom, said Karl Sauer. Deceitful bastard.

"Who are we talking about here?" Billie asked.

"Name a famous artist."

"Matisse."

"I guarantee he has one."

"Uh, Klimt?"

"That too, I'm sure."

"Chagall? He was Jewish," she said. "Just watched a clip on YouTube about him."

"There's a list that Tomer's group has collected over the years. Chagall is most definitely on it."

"So why were you sent to Sauer's house?" Billie asked. "It's a mess inside; how were you to find anything?"

"Karl Sauer doesn't keep his art collection in his home. He has a storage unit somewhere. Tomer got wind of an old man who was selling some suspiciously valuable art in Jersey through super shady avenues."

"Roza?"

Aaron nodded. "At first, it was one art piece. A sculpture. Then, later, a sketch. Then a painting."

"Drips and drops."

"Like he was trying to stay off the radar, but got greedy. Soon, more works of art began flooding the underground market. Shit people hadn't seen since the 1930s. So Tomer hired me to look into it. He wanted me to tail Sauer for a bit, see if he was the guy. But since the old man is a recluse and barely leaves his house, I had resorted to putting a tracking device on his car. Weeks ago, I get a notification that Karl was on the move, but he never made it to his unit. He hit a kid on his bike and turned around. After that, he went silent. I mean now we know why – he was dead – but Tomer had thought the dude was laying low. He said we had to move since Roza's team was suddenly stateside. It was imperative we find the art stash first."

"Tomer asked you to break into Karl's house," she finished.

Aaron nodded. "Sauer supposedly wore the key to the unit around his neck. But when I saw him, he wasn't wearing it. And I had to check." He shuddered. "Roza's team must've gotten to him weeks ago, and Tomer's info was stale. I guarantee that storage unit has been cleaned out already."

"You think Roza's group killed Sauer?"

Aaron ran a hand through his hair, fluffing it up into little spikes – a known tell when he wasn't confident in his information. "Who else? Unless he really died of natural causes."

"Did you mention any of this to the Bergen County Detectives Bureau?" she asked. "Omit the Tomer/Mossad stuff, but tell them about Roza Filipek?"

Aaron shook his head. "I squeal, and it's a death sentence. Besides, the cops don't have anything on me."

"The glove–"

"Is circumstantial, at best. And you muddied the waters on that."

Billie slumped in her seat, pushed down by the weight of Aaron's involvement. "They suspect you were in the house. Morales. The BCDB. If the art is missing, they think you stole it. And if Karl Sauer did *not* die of natural causes, then they'll think you killed him. Either way, this is bad."

"*I'll* worry about it," he said emphatically.

"A man is dead. A Polish madwoman and her goons are making threats. No." She got to her feet. Decision made for her. "I'll handle this."

Aaron rose to meet her, his face ashen now. "Billie–"

"Don't." Billie fanned the photos, like showing off a losing hand of poker. "Look at these pictures. Roza is clearly sending me a message."

"A message? Now who is using euphemisms? Roza's dangerous. And she's mad at me, particularly. She'll happily take out everyone I love. Including you and your family."

Billie touched a line of skin that went from his jaw down to his neck.

Aaron grabbed her fingers and gently pulled them off his face. "Keep clear of her. I couldn't be more serious. This is like Colfer Dryden, but a thousand times worse. Plus, she's female and European – a goddamn chameleon."

"Aaron, I love you, but you're in a world of shit, and yet somehow I'm the one who stepped in it. No," her voice final, but determined. "I'll work this case. Because I see only two ways out – either we leave it up to the BCDB, and you get arrested and targeted in prison, or Roza gets to you, in which case you die in excruciating circumstances. In either scenario, you die." She made her way down the row of seats, still talking as much to herself as to Aaron. "I'm invoking Gramps's Rule Number Six."

"Which one is that?" Aaron called after her.

"Sometimes, you gotta clean up other people's messes." And then she was out the door.

CHAPTER THIRTEEN

That night, Billie sat cross-legged on the floor beside her bed with her laptop open and a pen tucked behind her ear. She had googled Roza's name, but not a ton came up. She did find a brief mention in *The Atlantic* about the unsolved theft of artwork from a woman's collection in the early 2000s. There was a footnote that authorities had looked into the movements of Roza Filipek, but Billie had her doubts Roza would be involved. According to Aaron, Roza dealt in rare pieces. She wasn't so much an art broker as a treasure hunter, attending to the fetishes of men with so much money, they spent it trying to perversely one up each other. After all, what did it mean when bazillionaires stole black market relics from each other for fun?

Billie kept searching and found a few photos of the woman. One was grainy, featuring a teenage Roza with puffy blonde bangs and a mole above her lip – an actual feature or a Madonna imitation? – standing with a group of students in front of a Soviet-style building. Another was Roza as an older woman, thirties maybe, dressed in sequins, standing next to a well-dressed man in front of a fireplace, surrounded by lush furnishings. She still had the mole. The caption mentioned a villa in Italy. Roza had certainly traded the Iron Curtain for velvet drapes, hadn't she?

Billie continued digging around until she came to a citation for an article from the *American Journal of International Law* written by Finkel, A., et al.

Art heists, criminology, and the Soviet-era upbringing of Roza Filipek.

Well, I'll be damned, she thought.

Also, Billie was actually damned. Stupid article had a paywall.

She texted Nicole, and within seconds, her phone rang.

"You want my Kentwell library login?"

Billie winced. Nicole had been her college roommate and best friend for years. If David was her rock at home, Nic was a boulder firmly planted in the outside world to shield Billie from a life of harsh loneliness. And how did Billie repay such kindness? By constantly hitting Nic up for help with her cases.

Billie had been making an effort to repair the damage. Just last week, she went over to Nicole's house to set her up with a new video security system. Not exactly a Girls' Night Out, especially when the old man across the way yelled at Billie for being "too damn loud in the hallway."

Billie replied sheepishly, "I can't get into the databases without one." Then she grumbled, "I spent a fortune on tuition and I'm not entitled to access Lexus-Nexus. What gives?"

There was a big exhalation, and then a text. "There. It's been sent," said Nicole. "Whatcha working on?" It sounded like she was talking between sips of merlot, which she probably was.

"Trying to do research on an international criminal enterprise. A woman-led enterprise to be exact."

"That's a change of pace. If anyone could be in charge of large-scale crime, it's a chick."

"Preach. Except, I'm stuck. I found some articles on BBC, and a few in German that the translation software butchered to death, but nothing that helps."

"What's the gist?"

"Art thief working on behalf of men with insane amounts of money and no shame. Mostly after their personal collections. Secret art."

"Pornographic?"

"No, but controversial nonetheless. Think Jewish art, stolen by the Nazis, and reacquired illegally. Should be in a museum or with descendants, but isn't."

Sip. "Hmmm." A swallow. "Have you considered talking to Jeremy Yang? He's a doctoral student in the criminal justice department."

That gave her considerable pause. The guy from the precinct? "I actually met him briefly. He was…"

"A prick."

"Ish. Prick-ish."

"Prick or ish, he's a teaching assistant who works under Dr Finkel. Supposed to be pretty brilliant. Anyway, he's working on a dissertation about international crime organizations, or something like that."

"Really?"

"Yeah. He might be worth hitting up, if you can spare some of your pride. Cuz he'll take it from you."

"I don't know…" She'd had her fill of dealing with arrogant, annoying men.

"My coworker ran into him at a fundraising event. Begging alumni to fund the new science building. Yang had a bit to drink…he's difficult. Also, kind of a troublemaker."

"Good trouble or bad trouble?"

"Hard to say, but I'll text you that tea."

Billie's cell phone beeped. "Nic, I gotta another call. My boss."

"Go." Then: "You owe me lunch."

"I always owe you lunch. Catch ya later." Billie switched calls. "Hey, Esha."

"Billie, dear, glad I caught you. I'd like you to come in tomorrow morning and meet with a prospective client."

Billie sat up, pressing the phone into her ear, to be sure she didn't mishear. "A client? You want me to work a case?"

"Yes," said Esha. "The woman asked for you."

"By name?"

"Yes. And to be honest, I wasn't ready to give you this responsibility, but she insisted on you, and you're available."

Not a testimonial Billie would publish on her website, if she had a website.

"What's the case about?"

"Not sure," said Esha. "I assume we'll find out together, tomorrow."

For weeks, Billie had been hoping Esha would entrust her with a proper investigation, one that would lead to full-time employment, stable hours, and even dental insurance. The only obstacle right now was Roza Filipek and her hell-bent revenge on Aaron.

She shouldn't agree to this. Not if Aaron was to survive the next few days.

Billie opened her mouth to protest, to make her apologies, but the mouse-like noises must've sounded like acquiescence because Esha simply said, "Great. See you tomorrow," and disconnected the call.

Billie closed her eyes, took a deep breath, and counted backwards from ten. Then she reread Nicole's text with the library login information and pulled up the journal article by Finkel et al.

It was going to be a long night.

CHAPTER FOURTEEN

Flurries arrived at the exact moment Billie got to the entrance of the office building. Seriously, Mother Nature was barely even trying, most likely saving her rage for nor'easter season, just as New Jerseyans grew complacent. The minute some man in Leonia said, *it's been such a mild winter* – bam! – a foot of snow, followed by a week without on-street parking. No, thank you.

Billie spotted a mound of cigarette butts below an unlucky shrub.

Derek.

When she entered Esha's firm, and strode past his desk, his jacket emitted a stench of nicotine and ash. Maybe he wouldn't have such money troubles if he didn't smoke like a chimney.

The minute Esha spied Billie she hurriedly waved her inside the office. A woman was already seated, and Billie glanced at her Swatch, the fluttering of panic rising through her belly. Esha specifically said nine o'clock, and it wasn't even ten minutes to.

"You're on time," Esha said soothingly.

"I'm early," said a woman with a benign smile. She was in her late forties or early fifties, a bottled red. She wore a paisley scarf over a lavender sweater and jeans. Tidy, but not professional. A work-from-home type.

"Billie, this is Mrs Cantor." Esha rose from her desk and leaned over slightly, pointing to the remaining empty chair. Billie took that as a cue to sit. "It's rude to stand while the clients are seated," Esha told her once. "Makes it seem like you're in a hurry to leave."

In a hurry to leave should be Billie's epitaph.

"Christina," the woman clarified as she extended her hand in greeting.

"Nice to meet you," replied Billie cautiously, still not sure why she had been summoned here. Stakeouts and Play Palace notwithstanding, she was merely a glorified mail carrier. She'd been hinting that she wanted a case for weeks, so why now? Esha had other female investigators on her staff. Granted, it was the holiday season. Maybe they all begged off the work.

"How can we help you today?" Esha asked Christina.

The woman stared at her handbag for a second. "I'm here, in part, because of my father…Karl Sauer."

Hold the phone.

Esha immediately jumped in to say, "Before we begin, I must tell you, Mrs Cantor – Christina – that Billie had been assigned to serve your father papers for the lawsuit. She was at his house and discovered his body. She's been in contact with the police."

What was Esha doing? Trying to get her tossed off the case before they even heard the details?

Christina, however, was not fazed. "Oh, I know. That's *why* I'm here. Detective Malley spoke highly of Billie."

"Malley told you about me?" asked Billie.

"Yes. Said you were the one to help me. That you'd reserve judgment."

Did Malley even know Billie?

Seeing an opportunity, Billie quickly tried to mold her face into something that resembled sympathy. Act sorry. *She doesn't know you know her grandfather was Hitler's art broker. She may not know that either.* "My condolences."

That elicited a snort from Christina.

So she probably knew.

"We weren't close," said Christina. "Like at all."

Billie wasn't sure how much to reveal here. She had just learned that Karl Sauer came from a rather icky pedigree.

said, because that was all she could think to say,
·ecause she lost the vocabulary to describe the
ad never seen pinks and reds with this level of
·ewhere flowers were drained of their pigment to
vork.

instinctively traced the two little initials in the

· anything. Just two tiny letters as if the artist
· diminish the work with their own identity.
·se from her crouch, she wasn't clear on what
·ed of her, and she wasn't motivated by tales of a
·with Nazi leanings, mentally ill or not. What was
·ng her up to do?

·y," said Christina, wistfully. "It's also the only
· ever gave me. Even my mom was surprised he
·ith it; he'd been a stingy bastard his whole life.
· that the Picasso money wouldn't last forever.
· be careful. My mother just wanted to be able
· summer camp." She frowned. "Unfortunately,
·n people are more concerned with getting
·galls and Kandinskys. This little piece isn't on
·d I can't hold onto it without knowing where
·. I also can't just throw the artwork away.
·eant something to someone. To end up in a
·that is equally tragic." She looked at Billie, as
·olution. "Maybe there's more of my dad in me

·," said Billie, "you want me to locate the artist

·dded. "Or the original owner? What if there's
·ily out there that sold this painting to my
·der duress? Or what if it was looted?"
·searched the canvas. If it did come from pre-war
·nagined it originated with a novice. The work
· exquisite really, but that stemmed from the

And she didn't exactly learn that from official sources. Except, "Cantor is a Jewish name." Without thinking, Billie had revealed her hand.

Esha gave her an odd look.

But if Christina had guessed at Billie's insinuation, she didn't say. She stroked the finger where a gold band would normally sit, a band that was suspiciously absent. "I converted. It's one of the reasons my dad and I barely spoke."

Based on what Billie had garnered, that tracked. It suddenly occurred to her how serendipitous this meeting was. "I have to ask, um, did the medical examiner mention cause of death?"

Esha furrowed her brow. "I don't know if that's relevant, Billie."

"Right," she said quickly. "Not important."

Esha continued, "I believe that Christina would like you to locate someone for her." She smiled benevolently. "Is that correct? Why don't you explain to both of us exactly what you would like our firm to do for you?"

"This is all confidential?" Christina asked. "Nothing will be said to anyone else? No newspapers or social media posts."

"Of course," said Esha. "My staff exemplifies professionalism." She looked at Billie.

"Absolutely," Billie reassured her. "One hundred percent." Then for good measure: "I abhor Facebook."

"It's just, I don't know what I'd do if this got out. It's so embarrassing. I think my boys would – and the rabbi," Christina stopped, her cheeks coloring to match her hair.

Billie knew what was coming, even if Christina didn't.

"To be honest, I'm shocked myself, although my husband thinks I should've known. But who would've ever thought…?" Her voice trailed. She stopped, exhaled, and began again. "Apparently, my father had earned a living – if you could call it that – selling Nazi-looted art, an inheritance from his father, who I just found out was an assistant to one of Hitler's art brokers."

Quite a mouthful to the unsuspecting, which Billie was not. She checked to gauge Esha's reaction, but her professionalism amounted to a poker face that could rival anything seen in Vegas. Turning to Billie, she said, "Did you know this?"

"No," replied Billie, aiming for utmost sincerity but probably landing shy of bullshit. She should lobby for an Oscar for the restraint in her performance just then.

Christina rubbed a red mark into her palm. "My father certainly didn't live like a man with millions of dollars' worth of art. He barely paid his property taxes on time. He never even gave my mom child support. However," she said, composing herself, "I'm now working with Detective Malley and a restitution group so these priceless works can be returned to the original families or museums. Only," her voice broke. "I can't even do that because his storage unit was burglarized. Everything was taken."

So Aaron was right. Roza's crew had gotten there already.

"The Bergen County Detectives Bureau is looking into the theft," said Christina as she pressed a tissue to her cheek. "I found the list in his shoe."

"The list?" Esha asked at the same time Billie said, "Which storage place?"

"My father kept a meticulous inventory of his art. Kinda funny when you think about the state of his house. Well, not funny, really." She sighed and turned her body so she was facing Billie. "He kept a detailed list of his art collection. Painter. Title of the work if there was one, if not, subject. Place of origin. Most of the art he had kept, except for a few pieces that he crossed off. I assume those are the ones he sold. There are also some that are circled in pencil, but I don't know what that's about. And yes, he kept this list in his shoe."

"Are there invoices?" asked Billie. "Who did he sell the paintings to?"

Christina shrugged. "I can't find that information. The inventory sheet is handwritten. When a piece was sold, he simply crossed it off the list. Out of sight, out of mind, I guess."

Billie wondered if the goon was looking for the ot house? Possibly.

Christina said, "My mo art collection was just a f emigrated. He claimed that that she was an art student that was a lie." She exhal sorrow of deception. "As Babbling about a storage but I tuned it out. You kn Christina's voice grew soft suspicious, asked to see the two-and-two together, but him. You know? He wasn'

Billie sympathized. The place?"

"Paretsky's," said Christ Billie knew it, but prete Meanwhile, Esha gestu abstract design, propped one of the artworks?"

"No." Christina twiste herself to the item she ha ill, clearly. He hoarded art to eat or keep the lights me for some reason."

Derek began hacking u "Can I take a closer loo "Of course," said Chris Billie got up from the It wasn't large, maybe blotter, but it was striki a kaleidoscope. Or if so window and scattered t

"Lovely," she particularly colors. She vibrancy; sor make this ar

Her finger corner: AS

No date c didn't want t

As Billie was being as deadbeat dad Christina set

"It is love thing my dac had parted He often sai He needed t to send me t the restituti back the Ch their radar, a it came fron It must've n landfill, well if wanting ab than I'd like.

"To be clea of this piece?

Christina r a Jewish fa grandfather u

Billie's eye Europe, she was beautiful

colors and not mastery. Not that she had a lot of knowledge on the subject. She did take one art history class, but there was something about the piece that screamed imitation, and not originality.

"Is this an insane request?" asked Christina.

Yes.

"No," said Esha. "It's doable."

Was it? Billie didn't think so. She found herself stuttering, "I-I d-don't...I don't know if I have the foundational knowledge for this."

Christina leaned forward and said kindly, "I'm not expecting you to pore over books, but you're resourceful, right?"

She was, but there was a limit to her capabilities.

Esha didn't look sure either. "Mrs Cantor – Christina – if Billie isn't confident, perhaps we should look to my principal investigator, Derek Campbell. He really does excellent work, and if I may say so, has decades of experience. Just this past summer, he worked on a case for the Montclair Art Museum. He would be perfect for this particular investigation."

As if on cue, Derek hacked loudly.

"Frankly, I'd prefer a woman right now," said Christina. "Men – how do I put this? – are currently on my shit list." Then to Billie, she said, "I just need someone smarter than me to try. That's all. And Malley trusts you."

Sure, someone smart, but let's be real, also someone Jewish. Somehow this request stopped being about art and morphed into exculpation. Billie always thought that Jewish guilt was passed down via genes, but she supposed it made its way to the converts too.

"Ok, sure," said Billie, thinking that it might not be a bad idea to get close to this case. After all, once the medical examiner ruled on Karl's death, all Billie needed to do was ask Christina about the results. "I'll do it; I'll get started."

Esha beamed. "Excellent. I'll have my admin send over the retainer agreement and contract."

"May I keep the painting?" Billie said before quickly adding, "Just temporarily."

"Yes! Please. I can't bear to look at it, to be honest. It no longer feels like a gift, for a million reasons."

"And the inventory list, too, if you have it," said Billie.

"I have a copy at home; BCDB has the original. I'll bring that in."

Christina suddenly looked twenty pounds lighter, while Billie felt the weight of this case sink into her socks.

She rose, almost dazed, and shook Christina's hand. She carried the artwork out of the office while Esha rambled on about expenses and per diems.

Billie passed Derek at his desk. His eyes traveled all over the canvas, probably sizing up the magnitude of the task, maybe considering this bullet aptly dodged. "First big case, huh?"

"For Esha? Yes. In life? No."

Whirling around in his desk chair, he then eyed her up and down. "No offense, Nancy Drew, but I'm surprised Esha didn't assign it to me. I have more experience. I did settle that museum thing–"

"I know. I know." Billie stared him down and without a hint of empathy said, "You just weren't wanted."

Derek's smirk quickly disappeared, as did Billie.

CHAPTER FIFTEEN

Billie carefully placed the painting in the backseat, and then went to work on removing the thin layer of snow that had settled on the windshield. With a gloved hand, she shoved the powder off the glass containing all the annoyance of an old lady waiting in line at a supermarket deli. Billie wouldn't make it to spring, not without a huge dose of Vitamin D and a major attitude adjustment.

Aaron was being targeted by a criminal mastermind and law enforcement. Danger was coming for him from both ends, and yet, Billie was the one anticipating bullets. She considered turning around and marching right back into Esha's office, declaring loudly, "I can't do this!" But everyone was counting on her.

Billie shook the wetness off her glove, but really she was trying to shake off the increasing uneasiness that she suddenly was being watched.

Phantoms, Gramps would call them. *Every PI senses them from time to time.*

"Real or imaginary?" she had asked him.

His response was a shrug and a "depends."

Not exactly helpful, but with his wizened voice in her head, Billie scanned the parking lot, trying to decipher which vehicle might not belong outside a concrete gray office building in a compressed suburb. A beige Corolla? A white Mercedes? A cobalt Alfa Romeo with a dented fender? They were all fair game.

Except...there.

A black Suburban, shiny, freshly washed, the exterior devoid of salt residue, idling on the far end of the lot. It was as out of place as a hookah in a tuberculosis ward.

Also missing was the front license plate, a tell-tale sign that the vehicle was out-of-state, a rental perhaps. New Jersey had a two-plate system, front and back. New York and Connecticut too. Cops liked to be able to clock you coming and going.

Billie darted to the driver's side and had her key in the ignition before she even closed the door. Her tires slipped on wet slush as she peeled out of the parking spot and headed toward the complex's rear exit.

Palming the wheel, she begrudgingly stopped at a red light and checked the rear-view mirror. The Suburban sat three car-lengths behind her.

That phantom was materializing right before her eyes; it might as well have been her passenger for all it mattered.

The light changed and Billie turned left, heading for the nearest off-ramp, cutting off the driver behind her, and getting the middle finger in return.

"Whatever, dude," she grumbled as she drove deeper into a residential area. The lower speed zone would make it harder to shake the Suburban, but easier to monitor if she was still being followed.

Which she was.

The SUV was now two car-lengths behind, riding the bumper of an elderly woman doing the speed limit.

Billie passed the sign for Kentwell College. She could easily disappear on campus if she could get to the entrance before her pursuers caught up.

Turning left into the college's gate, Billie raced toward the visitor parking deck, nearly taking out an undergrad in the process.

"Sorry!" she screamed through her closed window as she made a sharp swing into the deck. Stopping abruptly at the booth, she snatched a ticket from the machine. The mechanical arm lifted with all the urgency of a French waiter, and Billie found herself slapping her steering wheel in frustration.

Zipping through, she scoped a tight space by the stairwell and squeezed her little Hyundai into the narrow spot. Billie grabbed a Kentwell Lions baseball cap and her bag from the backseat before flinging open the driver's-side door and scratching a Volkswagen's paint.

"Shit!"

She darted for the stairwell and caught her breath. Some students in puffy jackets passed her on the stairs, eyeing her labored breathing with quirks of the brow and pursed lips.

Billie turned her attention to the small window that looked into the parking deck. The black Suburban had stopped in the middle of the driveway.

She fumbled for her phone to snap a photo of the car and its driver.

A hefty blond man emerged from the passenger's side and came around the front of the car, slapping a crowbar against the palm of his hand.

Well, this didn't bode well for her Hyundai or the deductible.

She took photos of him as well. Then switched to video so she needn't worry how she would explain to the insurance agent that a European brute totaled her car with his bare hands.

She couldn't look, so she held her phone up to the window while cowering by the door. She waited for the sound of broken glass, followed by the crunch of metal. What she heard was the short wail of a siren.

Never in a billion years did Billie think campus police would rescue her, and yet now she'd probably have to eat the hat she was wearing. Worth it to save her car. And her life, of course, but mostly the car because without wheels, Billie was categorically useless.

Through the window, she watched as an officer stuck his head out the window and hollered, "you're blocking traffic," at the tawny mercenary. The edge of the crowbar peeked out from beneath the Volkswagen.

The Suburban quickly took off and circled around, seeking the exit.

Mission to kill Billie now officially abandoned...for the moment.

Billie caught the plate, though. She missed the digits, but recognized the state ID. Pennsylvania.

She collapsed onto the stair, gripping the handrail like it was the only thing saving her from a thousand-foot drop. She exhaled, the sound of her breath funneling into a hysterical laugh. She'd been through worse, so the damn near hysterics seemed more unsettling than the near-hit.

When she could finally get to her feet, she dialed Nicole Mercier, who was no doubt sitting in her cubicle, a hundred yards away, typing furiously at a computer and not imagining her best friend being nearly done in by hired hitmen. On second thought, Nic was rarely surprised by anything Billie did anymore.

Nicole answered curtly on the first ring, "Can't talk. Got a staff meeting in five."

Billie leaned her head against the stairwell's cold, cinderblock wall. "Remember that criminology professor you mentioned?"

"Jeremy Yang, the TA? I gave you his digits."

"God, no. Not him. The professor who wrote that paper? Finkel, et al? I think he can help me out." A pause. "Where's his office?"

CHAPTER SIXTEEN

According to Nicole, Dr Finkel was finishing up a lecture in the Paul B Schwing Jr Humanities Building – which the undergrad only ever said with the thrust of their hips – on the far side of campus. If Billie hauled ass, she might reach him before he headed home for the day.

The adrenaline fueled her legs, until she stumbled out of breath into a nearly empty classroom, skidding only when she saw an unfortunately familiar face.

Jeremy Yang. He stood next to a student, a lanky guy with bleached hair and half a dozen piercings.

"Did Dr Finkel leave? Did I just miss him?" Billie asked breathlessly.

"If by *just* you mean an hour ago, then yes, you just missed him," said Jeremy.

Billie checked her watch. "When are his office hours?"

That got a laugh out of the lanky guy who tried to smooth it over with a fake cough.

Jeremy, however, was examining Billie with a narrowed gaze and irritated expression. "You're not a student, so what do you want with him? You can't audit the class. Finkel hates that, calls it freeloading." Then he considered something. "On second thought, you're his type, so he'd probably make an exception."

"I'm not sure what to be offended by first," she replied.

"Why not both?" said the kid. An exchange student by the sound of his accent which would have been nearly imperceptible if Billie hadn't spent hours watching YouTube clips of academics discussing criminality in a post-Soviet Eastern Europe.

"Poland?" she asked him, but it was hardly a question if Billie suspected the answer.

He hesitated. "Warsaw. How did you know?"

She shrugged. "Long story."

"That's enough," said Jeremy. "Stop interrogating him like a psycho." To the guy, he said, "See you next week, Tytus."

Tytus nodded, adjusted his backpack, and left, casting Billie a wary gaze in his retreat.

Jeremy waited for him to be out of earshot before he turned on Billie. "You."

"Me," she said.

"Do you always go around asking people where they're from? It's rude, not to mention creepy."

"It's for work," she replied defensively. Although now she could see how that conversation sounded.

"What do you want?" Again with the sigh. The man was full of annoyance, and it leaked out of him like helium from a balloon.

Billie gave him a hard stare. "I read Dr Finkel's piece in the *American Journal of International Crime*. The one on Roza Filipek, and I wanted to discuss it with him. Is that ok with you? What are you, his handler?"

"I'm his teaching assistant, so in theory, yes, I handle things. All things in fact. That kid who just left. He's practically my TA because Finkel does fucking dinkel."

"Funny," she said.

"I remember you from the precinct. I got the impression that you were in trouble, so what do you need my help for?"

"*Work*," she said. "And I'm not in trouble."

"Uh huh. Who are you?" Staring at her, he rattled off the alphabet. "FBI? CIA? DOJ?"

She smiled. "NYB. Not your business."

"Now *you're* being funny." Jeremy slipped a laptop into a black leather backpack and slung it onto his shoulder. "Suit yourself, but Finkel knows shit about Roza Filipek."

"That article–"

"Finkel et al; Tytus and I are the et al. Tytus, being from Poland as you so artfully established, knows a lot about Roza – the woman's crime syndicate wreaked havoc on his country for years – and together we wrote the damn piece; Finkel just took credit for it."

"Sounds like Tytus should get all the credit."

"Sure. Not like I've never spent several semesters in Polish archives or anything." Jeremy brushed past her and out the door.

Billie gave herself a moment of self-castigation, knowing she was going to have to swallow her pride like bitter greens, before hurrying after him into the hallway. His long legs carried him at a faster clip than she could manage, and she found herself annoyingly jogging after him. This whole ordeal would count as her run for the day.

"Hey, dude," she called after him. "Jeremy. Doctor... Professor. Think we got off on the wrong foot."

He stopped in front of a closed door and turned around to field a coquettish wave from a dark-haired beauty. Dr Finkel perhaps wasn't the only professor with a type.

She couldn't help herself and asked snidely, "Student of yours?"

Jeremy ignored that and unlocked the office door. A paper sign written in Sharpie was taped beneath a placard with Dr Finkel's name in embossed gold. Ah, the lowly TA. So lowly, he's not entitled to a proper label.

Jeremy attempted to close the door in Billie's face, but was thwarted by the tip of her Doc Marten.

He easily surrendered and dropped his backpack beside a cluttered desk that sat in front of a window with a view to the next academic building. He shuffled some papers around, and Billie wondered if he actually had office hours or if he had simply come here to escape her.

Either way that plan was foiled.

"Listen," he said, his eyes searching the desk, his fingertips dancing over folders, pens, and paperweights. "I have work to do, so..." he waved her on as if shooing a stray cat.

"So do I, dude. I'm balancing two cases, and I don't have the time for–"

He cut her off. "Cases?" Arms crossed, he stared at her. "You're an investigator."

Billie didn't much appreciate the heavy implication of disbelief in his voice.

"Yes," she said drily.

"For whom?"

"Well," she began, somewhat defensively, "I run my own firm, Levine Investigations, and I consult–" (sure, why not?) "–for Esha Patel."

Jeremy smirked. "Oh, you're Billie Levine. I've heard about you." He let that hang in the air for a moment. "Is that why you were at the precinct the other day? For a case?"

"Yes," she lied. "That's exactly why I was there." Then: "Why were you?"

"In my circles of research, you hear chatter."

"You heard about Karl Sauer's death?"

He nodded. "One of the detectives called the department and asked for a consultant."

Billie scoffed. "They asked for Dr Finkel, didn't they?"

"I went in his stead. He would've never shown up anyway."

Billie crossed her arms over her chest, matching his stance. "What did you tell the detect–?"

Jeremy cut her off, "Why does your current case revolve around Roza Filipek?"

She leaned against a tall bookshelf and uncrossed her arms, pretending she was an open book, in a language he couldn't read. "Again, that is not something you need to know."

He challenged her. "Esha Patel does local work – process serving, insurance fraud, cheating spouses..."

All the kinds of cases Billie wished she had.

"What sort of investigation is Esha covering that involves an international art thief on the run from the FBI, CIA, and Interpol?"

"Who said this was for Esha?"

He cocked a beautifully manicured eyebrow.

"Help me or don't. I don't care anymore." She made for the door just as her cell phone rang, displaying an unknown number. Spam. Of all the times.

Jeremy gave another performative sigh, but this one stopped Billie. "Listen, I don't want to be responsible for your gruesome death, which knowing Roza would involve some kind of impaling by an instrument you value. A fountain pen, perhaps."

"The hell–"

"The woman loves irony, but the point is she's no one you want to get on the wrong side of."

Billie could argue it was too late for that. "Go on."

"She got her start in forgeries until she realized it was more lucrative to cut out the middle man, literally, and deal in the real thing."

Billie mimed stabbing her eyeball with a paintbrush. "I know, she's a scary bitch."

That got a bemused laugh out of him. "Scary doesn't even begin to scratch the surface. She'll not just kill a man, she'll make his life a living hell first. Drain his bank accounts. Get him on the no-fly lists."

"Why?"

He shrugged. "She's a sociopath."

"How does she do all this?"

"Aliases, disguises, and connections. She employs a team and moves her art through the ports, some through the freaking US mail, some through shady businesses. It's rumored she has warehouses in France, Brazil, South Africa. The industry isn't regulated the way you think it is. Art dealers hate paperwork and prefer to trade in secrecy. The secrecy also helps with tax evasion."

"Could Roza be here?"

"Last reported, she was on St Barts. She's still in hiding, ever since she got busted for flipping art works and charging a huge mark-up. She screwed over a Russian oligarch. Heard about it?"

Billie shook her head.

"Powerful, rich, and one of the few Putin hasn't tossed out of a window."

"Yet," she said, suddenly feeling buoyant.

"Why are you smiling?" said Jeremy.

"Because Roza messes up. She burns bridges and has weaknesses. Greed. Herself." Feeling satisfied, she combed through her bag for a business card which she set on a stack of books on the desk. "Thanks for the info. I know it hurt you to give it. If you can think of anything else, or you need an investigator, call me."

Laughing, Jeremy shook his head. "That'll never happen."

And Dr Finkel had the reputation of being an asshole.

Billie frowned. "Suit yourself." But before she left, she had one last bit of inquiry she needed verified.

"Oh, dude, one last thing."

He took out his laptop and began clacking away. "What?"

"Karl Sauer. When he had to sell his paintings to pay bills, who helped broker those deals?"

He immediately stopped typing. "Ever hear of Mahmoud's Auction House?"

CHAPTER SEVENTEEN

Billie arrived at Mahmoud's Auction House a little after two, although it might've been dusk as far as anyone could tell. Daylight in winter was shorn like a buzzcut.

The auction house was located in Ridgewood in a large rectangular building that resembled a Lego brick. The entrance to the facility was along the side, identifiable by its narrow green awning. And of course, the door wouldn't budge. Billie tugged on the handle several times, rattling the lock, until a Black man with broad shoulders swung it open, unperturbed. His entire aura screamed hired muscle. "Yeah?" he said curtly.

"Hey," she said, just as curt. "I'm here to see Fatima. She's expecting me." She wasn't, but it wasn't like this guy would know. He was protection, not a secretary.

"You're not on the calendar." Ok so he had guessed, but Billie was let in anyway. Then, more gruffly, the guy said, "Second door on the left. You lead."

Billie walked down a tight hallway, feeling self-conscious as he trailed her.

"There," he said as he sidled past her and knocked. "Fatima, you got a visitor."

"Come in," she said, followed by a sniffle.

The man opened the door and jerked his chin at Billie. "Friend?"

"Thanks, Marcus," she said, giving Billie only the most cursory of glances. "It's fine."

Fatima's eyes, normally outlined in black, were rimmed in red.

Marcus gave Fatima a dubious look, sensing that whatever drama she was going through wouldn't improve with unexpected visitors, but he let Billie into the room regardless.

The space reminded her of Matty's office at the Malta Club in that they were both small, cramped, and full of boxes of indeterminate objects. The difference was that Fatima's floor held books, stacks of them. *Antiquities of Ancient Egypt. Mesopotamia and its Artifacts. The Rosetta Stone and Other Looted Treasures.* Matty's desk was mostly surrounded by sequined costumes and boxes of tampons. Fatima's trashcan held brochures for European museums and London realty companies. Matty's contained dirty makeup wipes and false eyelashes. Each space made sense in context.

Billie didn't even have a desk; she had a booth at a deli, and Bernice insisted she take all her *crap* with her when she left for the day.

Fatima rubbed at her nose before clacking away at her computer. "If you're here to see Aaron, he doesn't take a break for another hour."

"No," Billie replied, somewhat indignantly, as if she were some high school chick showing up to her boyfriend's shift at Wendy's to score a free Baconator. "This is business-related."

Fatima stopped typing on her laptop. "Detective Morales told me not to talk to you."

"Oh, really?" said Billie, not even trying to hide her surprise.

Fatima's proud shoulders dipped. She had slipped up, her mind clearly on other things. But what things?

"He spoke to my dad about your dead guy," Fatima added quickly.

"A dead guy whose house you happened to be outside of the other night. You know? Before you split."

"Totally random," said Fatima. "I was out for a run."

Billie scoffed: the international noise for *I don't think so.*

"If Morales had been here, he must've had a reason. Did

Mahmoud's ever do business with the dead guy, Karl Sauer? And if so, how could you *not* have known where he lived?"

"First, we lead a ton of auctions with thousands of pieces, and I don't know the addresses of every client. And second, more importantly, we never did business with Karl Whatever. We are a legitimate company and my father would never deal works of art with shady provenance."

"That didn't sound rehearsed at all." Billie plopped into the chair and unzipped her coat. "Let's pretend for a second that I believe you. How would you know if a work of art had a questionable history?"

Fatima blinked several times. "You want me to sum up my entire art history degree for you in five minutes?"

"I mean no, but yes."

There was a great sigh, followed by a shaky inhalation. "We require a paper trail. Certificates of authenticity. Signatures that can be verified."

Billie reclined slightly. "We seem concerned about two different things. Your issue is authenticating the art, and mine is making sure it's yours to authenticate. Karl's collection was made up of stolen works. Pieces that rightfully belong in museums or to Jewish families that owned them."

Fatima scoffed. "Newsflash: most museum art is stolen. The entire British Museum belongs to Egypt."

Billie held up her hands, placating. She couldn't argue the point. Again, she only ever took that one art history class. Fatima, despite her flippant high school experiment in moving from the cheerleading clique to the goth group to the rugby team and back again, grew up around this stuff. She had a bachelor's degree in art history from Rutgers and even did an internship in Cairo before coming back to Jersey to help her father run the auction house. Billie had to give deference where deference was due.

Even if it was due to Fatima Mahmoud, who suddenly looked like she could be dismantled by a gust of wind.

"You never did business with Karl Sauer?" Billie asked.

"No."

"Did he ever try and sell you a painting? Would you have a record of that?"

Fatima dropped her chin, probably realizing that the quickest way to get Billie out of her hair was to go along with whatever scheme Billie had concocted. If only all people would realize that, it would save her so much time and aggravation.

Fatima called out, "Papa!"

Marcus dipped his head in.

"Can you get my father?" Fatima asked him. "Tell him that Billie Levine is asking questions."

Marcus disappeared, and Fatima grabbed some Visine from inside a drawer. She held the bottle to bloodshot eyes and squeezed. "You didn't mention why you're really here. You're not police."

"I can't tell you how many times people remind me of that," said Billie. "I'm working a case."

She removed her cell phone from her pocket and slid it across the desk; the photos app had been opened earlier and Billie imagined this moment going much more smoothly, but now her cell twitched like a dying roach. She tapped the screen several times, then groaned, then pressed the side button, waking it from whatever self-imposed death spiral it craved.

"I've been hired by Karl Sauer's daughter to find out about this art piece. Hold onto your butt, it's a painting, so just try your best. He gave it to her as a gift, but as you so eloquently pointed out, it was likely stolen from someone. She wants to return it."

Fatima leaned over Billie's phone and pursed her lips. Her fingers danced over the screen, enlarging the image, twisting it, turning it, curiosity getting the better of her. "Reminds me of Fahrelnissa Zeid. Ever heard of her?"

Billie shook her head.

"Of course, not. She was a Turkish painter, born at the turn of the 20ᵗʰ century, who produced vibrant, abstract work. It's got that vibe, but it's obviously not her. It's not a forgery; more like–"

"Flattery."

Fatima abruptly stopped and pushed the phone away. "Hand the work off to one of those art restitution organizations."

"They're not equipped," said Billie. "Small potatoes anyway."

"You got a date, a name?"

"I've got initials."

Fatima chuckled, the first sign of joy that Billie had witnessed since she'd been here, even if it was at her expense. "You're S-O-L."

"Shit out of luck? Thanks."

Fatima turned in her chair and went back to typing on the laptop. "If fangirling was a painting, it would be that."

Billie turned the phone toward her and frowned. Then, because she couldn't help herself, she asked, "Did someone die? I mean other than Karl Sauer, but I can't see you being sad about that."

Fatima laughed, cackled really, and then shook her head. "Heartache."

"Breakup?"

Aaron popped his head in, a dolly in his grip, boxes piled precariously like a Jenga game gone on too long. "Where do you want these?" He spotted Billie, surprised, then smiled. "Hey."

"Hey," she replied.

He looked good. Arms at an angle, biceps pumped from the heavy lifting, a slight flush to his skin from the exertion. Manual labor was sexy.

She pointed at her phone, answering a question he didn't ask. "Here for work."

Nodding at Billie, Aaron addressed Fatima, "Stuff came in from the Robeson collection. Where do you want it?"

"Main room. It can sit there until Thursday's auction."

"Ok." To Billie he said, "What's going on?"

"*Art stuff,*" she said, hoping her tone would communicate what she could not.

Aaron took the hint. "Gotcha." He hesitated slightly before giving her an awkward kiss on the cheek, and then whispered, "We'll talk about this later."

Billie nodded, and he left, casting her only a cursory glance as he wheeled the dolly around the corner.

A man's voice called out. Old, raspy and with a hint of Cairo. Fatima closed her eyes for the briefest of seconds before responding in Arabic.

There was the sound of shuffling feet, and Mr Mahmoud appeared in the doorway. Billie rose to greet him.

Ammon Mahmoud was slim, bony, with thinning hair that was still remarkably dark for his age. He wore brown slacks and a tan dress shirt.

Fatima rambled off more in Arabic, and not for the first time Billie wished her superpower was understanding world languages.

Mr Mahmoud smiled and outstretched his hand to greet Billie. "How's your grandfather?"

"Good. Good," she said. "Retired."

Nodding, Mr Mahmoud looked past Billie at his daughter.

"She's asking about Karl Sauer."

So Fatima does know his surname after all. *Mr Whatever, my ass.*

Mr Mahmoud sighed as if this entire conversation was an unwelcome nuisance in his day. He grumbled something to Fatima, that Billie could only guess was Arabic for: *why am I being bothered?* After all, if Morales had come by, Ammon Mahmoud was the first man he would want to speak with. Billie was redundant.

Shaking his head, Mr Mahmoud said, "I did not do business with that man. Not trustworthy. He wouldn't let me bring in experts, wouldn't let me examine the collection. He wouldn't show me documentation. I said, no."

He raised thick brows and looked expectantly at Billie.

"Thank you, Mr Mahmoud. I appreciate your time."

He grumbled again to Fatima, which sounded like admonishment, and disappeared down the hallway.

Fatima waited for him to leave before dropping into the desk chair. "Morales mentioned that he was talking to other auction houses. It's possible that Sauer went somewhere else. Somewhere less reputable."

"Like where?" Billie asked, testing her.

"Anywhere. Most don't know their ass from their artifact, but they'll do business with anyone." She batted those thick Middle Eastern lashes, all innocence, her eyes brighter with the help of drops. "Now, I got shit to do, so if you don't mind."

It suddenly occurred to Billie how often she was asked to leave places. First, Jeremy. Now, Fatima. Except Jeremy just found her annoying; Fatima, on the other hand, was likely hiding something.

Billie sat back, making it obvious she wasn't going anywhere. "The name Roza Filipek mean anything to you?"

"No. Should it?" She answered too fast. Like the negation was a marble rolling around in her mouth, waiting to be spit out. Impatience growing, Fatima said, "Anything else?"

Mr Mahmoud's voice rang out from another room.

Fatima rolled her eyes.

"Coming, Papa," she said before turning to Billie. "You gotta go."

"Can you come by?" Billie asked as she shucked on her coat.

"Huh?"

"To see the artwork. The Zeid knock-off. It'll be in my house. Maybe if you see it in person, you can get something from it that I can't." Billie rose from the chair and plucked a shiny, black business card from a metal container on the desk. A cell phone number was printed in gold lettering beneath Fatima's name. "I'll text you."

Fatima waved her away. "Yeah, sure." But beneath that outward ambivalence, Billie thought she spied a hint of curiosity.

On her way out the door, Billie waved goodbye to Marcus who was shucking on a navy fleece.

"Leaving?" she noted.

"Second job," he replied as Fatima called him to escort Billie outside.

Her phone buzzed with a voicemail. She flinched, fearing she'd hear her father's voice on the other end, telling her what a shitty daughter she was.

I raised you, and you can't call me?

She debated on just deleting the message, but the practical side of her – the what if it's a prospective client calling, or better yet, the fantastical offering of money to do nothing – won out.

She stood in the glow of the building's exterior light and listened as a shaky voice said, "It's Desiree from Safe Horizons. Would you be able to come to our offices right away? There's an–"

The message suddenly cut off. Billie clamped down the panic rising in her throat and quickly dialed Safe Horizon's phone number, the one saved in her contacts, but was met with a busy signal.

She ran straight to her car.

CHAPTER EIGHTEEN

By the time Billie had arrived at the Safe Horizons Day Campus, campus being a stretch since it was nothing more than a one-story building near River Dell High School, she was drenched in stress sweat and her stomach had twisted itself into the shape of a wrung-out washcloth.

She parked her Hyundai in the fire lane outside the building, giving no shits to the gray-haired security guard yelling at her to move the *damn car*, and darted inside.

Stopping breathlessly at the front desk, Billie practically attacked the first person she saw – a middle-aged woman in a Christmas sweater – and blurted out, "Is Shari Levine all right?"

"Shari Levine?" the woman repeated.

"Yes!" Billie snapped. "My height-ish. My face-ish. She's a client here."

The woman visibly relaxed, giving Billie the same expression Billie often gave people she thought were stupider than herself. "I know who you mean, and of course, she's all right. What made you think–"

"That would be me." A woman emerged from a back office. She was Black, petite, with close cropped hair and dangly, gold earrings. She had style for days, something Billie admired, but doubted she could pull off without consulting magazines and a subreddit thread. "I'm afraid I'm responsible for scaring the crap out of Ms Levine, pardon my language."

Billie had met the woman once before, but she still needed the name tag to jog her memory, something the manager observed.

"Desiree Hamilton," the woman said, pointing to the large pin on her chest. "Program director."

Desiree. The woman on the voicemail had said her name. Billie should've remembered.

"Of course," Billie said, as if she had never forgotten a face. She was two seconds from uttering an *I'd remember you anywhere*, but decided not to embarrass herself further. This woman worked with dementia patients all day long.

"I take it you didn't hear the rest of my message?"

"My phone is dying," said Billie. "And I didn't recognize the number, so I didn't pick up, and then I had...a work meeting." She stopped and took a breath. "I got freaked out that something happened to my mom."

"She's fine," said Desiree, "and I should've led with that. I should also let you know that it's being handled. If you follow me into the back office, we can discuss the matter."

Billie sighed, feeling both confused and slightly put out, before trailing Desiree down a carpeted hallway and into a spacious room with a desk, computer, and windows that looked onto the busy street out front. The walls were painted a buttery yellow. On one side hung a child's handprint in bright red. The name Kareem and a year written underneath in black marker. Desiree's son, Billie assumed.

"If this isn't about my mom, what is it about?" Billie asked.

"Well, it is, but then it became something else."

That didn't make things any clearer.

A familiar voice entered the sphere, followed by his evermore familiar gait. "You need more cameras, Ms Hamilton. I'd also suggest a proper safe."

"Gramps?"

He grinned, an expression Billie hadn't seen on his face in some time. "Oh, hey," he said.

"What are you doing here?" she asked, sounding far more accusatory than was probably warranted, but what the hell?

Desiree pointed to a Queen Anne-style chair, indicating Billie should sit. Which she did, as she was both emotionally and physically drained. Gramps joined her and let out a pleased exhalation. He was enjoying himself.

"So I called you first, but then I phoned your house because your mother had a bit of a panic attack today–"

"Oh God."

"Regarding her purse," Desiree finished.

"Her purse?" Bille asked before closing her eyes. "Yes, her purse. She's been so preoccupied with it. Always wondering where it is."

"Right, and today it got so bad, we thought we should call you, see if you could bring it by."

"Which I did," said Gramps as he raised his arm with Shari's handbag dangling like a giant bass from a fishing line.

"But then I started to talk to your grandfather here about an issue we're having."

"Another issue with my mother?" asked Billie, not sure how many more problems she could handle right now.

But Desiree shook her head. "My office was burglarized." She vaguely gestured around. Billie swirled in her chair to get a look at the space.

The desk was huge with a computer centered on it and surrounded by files and stacks of binders. Painted ceramics, either belonging to clients or Ms Hamilton's child, collected dust on bookshelves.

Billie turned back around. "Uh, I can't tell what might've been taken."

Ms Hamilton ruefully shook her head. "Of course, not." She rummaged in her pocket and withdrew a piece of paper. "I made a list."

This office, like every office she had seen today, was a mess best described as *shit only the person who sits here can find.*

Billie read the items aloud. "Petty cash box." She glanced up. "The whole box?"

"It was locked, which is why I imagine they took the whole thing."

"How much?"

"Five hundred dollars."

"All right," said Billie. "Next, laptop."

"Chromebook," Gramps interjected.

"Ok," said Billie.

"Keyboard."

Ms Hamilton nodded. "Yes. External keyboard with an ergonomic design. Better for my carpal tunnel."

"What would you say that is worth?"

"I think I ordered it from the office catalog for $85."

Billie glanced down at the paper, which grew moist in her hands. "Three paint brushes–"

"Brand new."

"Brand new paintbrushes, gold earrings." She glanced up.

"Ten carat," said Ms Hamilton.

"And noise-cancelling headphones."

"Bose. Those were expensive."

"I see." Except Billie did not see. What a weird pile of crap to steal. Nothing worth much.

"I'd love to hire Levine Investigations to look into this," said Ms Hamilton. "But on the down-low, if you get my drift."

"I don't actually. It doesn't seem like the thief got away with anything valuable."

"It's not the items I'm concerned with here. It's the–"

"Theft itself, Billie," said Gramps cutting in, and condescendingly, too.

"I wonder if it's an–"

"Employee," Billie and Gramps said together.

Billie set the list of stolen items on the desk and pushed the paper back. "I'm so sorry, Ms Hamilton, but I can't take this case. I already have two–" she caught herself "–one big case on my plate right now."

Ms Hamilton pushed the paper toward her. "I'm willing to

pay. I simply don't want upper management to know. They will see it as negligence on my part. To be honest, this isn't my preference, seeing as how your mother is a client here, but then your grandfather came to the rescue with the handbag and said we really shouldn't let this go. So serendipitous."

"Quite," said Billie, and this time, everything became crystal. She cupped her hand around her mouth and whispered so only he could hear, "This wouldn't have anything to do with you not wanting to clean out Ken's house, would it?"

Gramps leaned forward and addressed Ms Hamilton directly, "Levine Investigations would be delighted to take your case. And you needn't worry; we are the epitome of discretion and we would certainly never judge your establishment for being the victim of a bad actor."

That was some speech. Had he been practicing it?

"Since my granddaughter is busy at the moment, I will take the lead on this." Gramps elbowed Billie gently, his unspoken cue for her to produce the retainer agreement.

For the briefest of seconds, Ms Hamilton looked unsure until Gramps said, "Email me a list of all your employees, both recent and those who have been fired or quit in the past year. I'd also like copies of any incident reports with clients and visitors."

"So you're certain that it's an employee?" Ms Hamilton paled. "My God."

"It's a start," said Gramps. "But honestly, it could be anyone. Maybe someone came in off the street and hunted for drug money. Send me your security footage."

"I'll have Jim get that to you." She glanced at Billie who now felt extraneous to this meeting.

Gramps had this covered. She said to him, "I gotta go."

He waved her off. "I'll keep you posted."

She laid the contract on the desk and gestured with her chin to the hallway. "May I check in on my mother?"

Frowning, Ms Hamilton said, "I'd prefer you didn't. It might confuse her, even upset her."

"Fine." Billie swung her bag over her shoulder and went outside to her car, which thankfully had not been towed. The security guard grumbled, "About time."

As Billie opened the driver's-side door, she spied a black Benz with heavily tinted windows parked across the street. The headlights were off, and Billie couldn't make out the driver, but it was obvious from the white plume snaking out of the exhaust pipe that the car was idling, not parked. Billie shivered against the December chill. She imagined the driver did too. If he wanted to look inconspicuous, he shouldn't have turned on his heat.

She had a tail she needed to shake. Second time today. This was getting ridiculous, but she supposed she was getting in the practice.

She'd have to lose him between here and Paretsky's. And then she'd need a new set of wheels.

CHAPTER NINETEEN

Billie drove to Paretsky's Storage off Route 17 in Rochelle Park and left the car in the fire lane while she popped into the office. Brian Paretsky, who graduated high school with David and who Billie had wrongfully assumed had some kind of thing for her, stood at the counter, wearing earbuds and singing Taylor Swift.

He wore a pink polo shirt, a black hoodie, and khakis – not a work uniform as he was the owner's son – which struck Billie as an odd style choice. But everything about Paretsky's was odd. Brian's father had converted an old parking garage into a storage facility, and he mostly catered to those looking for a cheap solution to the ever-growing pile of shit they owned.

Cheap storage meant cheap facilities: no cameras, lax security, and an indifference to theft.

So Karl Sauer renting a unit made little sense. Why would a man with millions of dollars of priceless art risk its safety in a place like Paretsky's?

That was a question for Junior.

Billie sauntered up to the counter with a smile that was not reciprocated.

Brian frowned, more like grimaced, before popping out an earbud. He eyed a door in the back, and Billie wondered if he was going to call for his father.

Or make a run for it.

"I was told not to tell you anything," Brian said, his hands up in the air as if he could stop her by the sheer force of his will.

Her will was stronger.

"Who?" Billie asked, wondering if she should be flattered by how many people were being advised against associating with her. "Was it Detective Morales or Malley?"

"My dad, actually."

Dammit. The elder Paretsky was arguably the scarier of the authority figures Billie had to sidestep.

"Besides, the police have already been here, collected everything, and swabbed the unit for God knows what," Brian added.

"All right," Billie cooed as if talking down a wild animal. "So, then, what's the big deal if I look around? I assume the BCDB cleared the scene, right?"

Brian said nothing. He wouldn't even make eye contact. It was amazing how many people supplied answers without admitting to anything at all.

Billie wasn't even sure why she felt this desperate need to see inside an empty concrete box, but she was hoping beyond hope that there was something visible that would either exonerate Aaron or finger Roza Filipek. Of course for the crime scene unit to have missed a flashing arrow pointing to a clue seemed as likely as Billie getting Brian to show her video cam footage.

Then again, desperate people did stupid things.

Billie tapped a rhythm on the counter. "What will it take for you to let me into Karl Sauer's storage unit?"

Brian shook his head like a Labrador retriever. "Nothing. Nothing is worth getting into it with my old man."

She pursed her lips, batted her eyelashes. "Come on, Bri. You must want something. Fifty bucks?"

He cackled so hard, she jumped.

Frustrated, she stood up straight and stared him down. "There's always something."

He looked like he was just about to push her out the door when his face registered an opportunity. "There is one thing."

She was afraid to ask.

"You're going to Jenn Herman's wedding, right?"

"Yeah," she said cautiously.

"So am I."

"Ok."

"And so is Fatima Mahmoud. She's a bridesmaid."

"All right."

"I think she might have a thing for me, but I'm not sure. Can you talk to her? At the wedding?"

Billie pressed her hands on the counter and stretched her back. Popping back up, she said, "What are we? In fifth grade?"

"You asked."

"Why can't you just invite her out to dinner like a grown-up?"

"I have no read on her," he said. "And I'm afraid of making a fool out of myself. She's cold one minute, friendly the next."

"And yet, you want to go out with her?"

He nodded, then replied, almost moony. "She's so beautiful... and exotic."

"She's not a parrot, Brian."

"I know."

Because she was naturally suspicious of everything, she asked, "Why now, though? When's the last time you spoke to her?"

"She came here a few weeks ago. Mid-November, I think."

That could line up with Karl's death. "Are you sure?"

"Pretty sure."

"What was she here for?"

"To rent a unit," he said. "Asked me to show her around, so I did. She's thinking of moving, and she needed to store her stuff in between places."

Moving, huh? More like she knew Karl was dead and realized his storage unit was suddenly unguarded and up for grabs.

Mr Mahmoud had begged off dealing with Karl. Yet for Fatima, Karl's demise was too big a payday to ignore, and she wouldn't have to work with the man if he was dead.

"Deal," she told him.

Billie went outside to her idling car, and he followed. "The unit key, Brian."

He scurried back to the counter and retrieved a master set from a desk drawer. Once he got inside the Hyundai, he directed her on where to go.

"How did she seem to you? Fatima?" Billie asked.

"Like I said, she was super nice to me when she arrived, asked which first floor units were available, so I went back to the office to check. When I returned, she was yelling into her cell phone, and then she just bounced." He pointed. "Stop there."

They got out of the car, and Billie scanned the premises while Brian jimmied the key in the lock. He hoisted the garage door open. Billie decided she needed a flashlight and retrieved one from her center console.

"Had she ever been here before that day?" Billie asked.

"Yeah, but we didn't talk then. I'd been checking on the bird cams, and she didn't see me."

"What did she do?" Billie waved the beam around the cavernous space. It was, as promised, completely empty.

"Walked around, then left."

Billie halted. "That's weird, right?"

"Guess so," he said, and Billie wondered if Brian had fantasized that maybe Fatima had come to talk to him, saw that he wasn't around, and left dejected. Obviously, at least to Billie, Fatima had been casing the joint.

"Could Fatima have been meeting up with Karl Sauer?" She moved the flashlight around, the beam locating darkened corners.

"I never saw her talk to him. Anyway, that guy was, like, on death's door."

Death's door? More like he was death's welcome mat.

"You happy?" Brian asked, shivering in his hoodie.

No, she wasn't. "Gimme a sec."

She walked the perimeter of the unit. Shining the light as if painting walls. There was nothing but concrete and – she bent down and called Brian over. "What does this look like to you?"

He squinted. "Paint? That Karl guy stored art here, maybe some of it–"

"Dry paint flecks; it doesn't form a puddle. This is oval shape and rust colored." She pointed along the floor. "Those dots that trail off into nothing."

"Blood, then," he said, looking pleased.

Question was, whose blood?

"Can we go back?" asked Brian. "I'm freezing my ass off."

"Yeah, yeah," she said. "I want to see any paperwork you have on Karl Sauer."

"What? No. You said storage unit. Fatima for storage unit."

"Running intermediary at Jenn Herman's swanky wedding is a far bigger deal than you unlocking a door you've been cleared to unlock. Wouldn't you agree?"

Brian groaned. "I swear, Billie, you're infuriating."

Maybe so, but she was on a mission now.

CHAPTER TWENTY

Billie flipped through a manila folder while Brian entered his password into an antiquated desktop computer in the cramped back office.

"Is this all the paperwork you have on Sauer?" The file was thin, containing a credit report, an application, and a lease agreement going back to the early eighties.

Brian roamed the cursor over the screen, hunting for the folder where his father kept the keycard logs. "He's been a long-time customer. Pays the monthly rent on time. That's all we really care about."

Billie paced around the small room. "Did the police make copies of this meager file?"

"Yup. And the keycard entries. They were pissed at my dad for not having security footage. He told them, 'This is not that kind of place. We're cheap. Services are cheap. Clients are made aware.'"

That was certainly the reason why Gramps stored his old cases files here. Sometimes it was good to have connections in low places.

Like now.

Smacking the file against her palm, she asked, "Did you ever talk to Sauer? Did he ever seem nervous to you? Did it ever look like he was being followed?"

By someone other than Fatima Mahmoud? But she said that part to herself.

Brian frowned. "I don't, like, stalk our customers, Billie."

"Is there anything, anything at all you can tell me about him?"

Brian sighed. "He was gruff. He had a slight accent. Mostly American-sounding but not quite."

"He was German," Billie said.

"Yeah, I know. But you said anything."

"Fair point."

"He was also kinda racist," Brian added unhelpfully. "One time, he snapped at Yusuf because he was speaking Turkish over the phone. 'Speak English, goddamnit!' Thought Yusuf was going to take him out, but I guess he's used to it."

Brian clicked on a folder and opened it. Then he pointed a finger at the screen. "This shows how often his keycard was used."

Billie scanned the list. Sauer mostly checked into his storage locker every few months, but there! "His keycard was used November 15th." That was the same day he hit the kid on his bike and abandoned his plans. Aaron had said Karl never made it to Paretsky's. The GPS tracker had shown him turning around. So someone else went in his stead.

Fatima?

Had Karl been dead by then?

"Is that all?" Brian asked.

Billie wasn't sure what else she was hoping to get out of this. Without camera footage, there was no way to see who stole the artwork from Karl's unit.

Could be Fatima. Could be Roza

All Billie needed to do was prove that it wasn't Aaron.

Sighing, she closed Karl's file and returned it to the old metal cabinet.

Brian swiveled in the desk chair. "Are we all done here? Can, you, like go now?"

"You know, Brian, you sure now how to make a girl feel welcomed."

"And you know how to make a guy feel used," he replied.

"Damn, soldier. Calm down." She leaned her elbows on the

desk and dropped her head. "This would be so much easier if you had security cameras."

"Well, they've been broken since 2010."

She scoffed, then rose from her stance, glancing briefly at the desktop screen. A folder was labeled *Hawks*.

She pointed. "You said *bird cams* earlier."

He looked confused. "What?"

"Bird cams; that's what you said before."

"Oh, yeah. I birdwatch."

"You birdwatch?" she repeated. "Brian, that's charming. You should lead with that more often." *Use this, Levine. Squeeze the life out of it.* "I would love to see footage from your bird cam. I imagine Fatima would also be smitten with such information." *Smitten? Ok, stop. You're going to blow it.*

"Um, ok." He danced the chair to the side to enlarge her view of the computer screen while he clicked open the folder. "There's a hawk's nest in the rafters, so weird as they're not known for doing that but it's safe up there, I guess."

"No shit," she said, impressed. "I didn't know Jersey was home to hawks."

"Oh, yeah. Lots of them. Northern harriers. Once I saw a Cooper's hawk, but this is a red-tailed nest. They hang out in winter. Once I spotted it, I knew I had to set up a camera."

Impatient, she twisted Brian's chair to face her but inadvertently spun it too fast and she wound up addressing his shoulder. Shoving him out of the way, she then thought better, and reeled him in. "While we're checking on the birds, does this camera have views of Karl's storage unit?"

"Maybe. It's on the far side of the first level, though." Brian got up from the chair and pointed to the poster-sized diagram tacked up on the wall. He tapped his finger at one corner. "This is Karl Sauer's unit." Then at the other. "This is where the nest is located."

"Brian, let's open the files. I mean, we might as well since we're here."

Disappointed, as he must've assumed Billie's angle by now, he sat back down. "You don't care about the bird cam, just your case."

"I care about birds, Brian, but I also care about my case. I wouldn't be asking if it wasn't important."

He double-clicked on the icon. "If my dad asks, I'm telling him you came to talk about hawks."

"Tell him I'm into pigeons. Or finches."

"Finches? Be real." Pointing to the screen, he said, "It's usually a live feed, but it's not running now. I do have footage of when the babies hatched."

"How many days, hours are we talking about?" she asked, hurriedly.

"A lot."

"Does it correspond to the dates and times that Karl's keycard was used?"

Brian shrugged. "I guess "

"Let's try the week he died," she said. "Roughly late-November."

Brian ran through the files' metadata until he clicked on a video. Talons came into view, along with dinosaur-sized eggs. In the background, storage units – none Karl's – and a long stretch of asphalt. "We're gonna have to fast-forward."

Brian dragged the cursor along the bottom and sped up the video.

"Stop!" she cried. "There!"

Sure enough, a U-Haul style truck came into view. "A plate!" She squealed, then frowned. "New York." Grabbing a pen from a mug on the desk, she jotted down the license plate number on her forearm.

The truck drove out of frame, and whatever excitement she had dissipated when she realized she couldn't see the driver's face. "The last time Karl was at his unit was," she checked the keycard login, "October tenth. Anything there?"

Brian sighed, exhausted from doing her bidding, no doubt.

His fingers flew over the keyboard, tossing open links one after another. He stopped. "Here."

A video loaded. Billie watched as Karl's Buick moved beneath the view of the hawk's nest. Then a figure, blotted out by shadow, followed at a distance.

That got Brian's attention. He peered at the screen. "Who's that?"

Billie squinted, trying to sharpen the outlines of the blurry figure. It definitely looked like a man, tall and wearing black. Not the hulking sight of one of Roza's crew nor the ashy brown mop of Aaron. Then it hit her.

She bumped Brian out of the way, to his annoyance, and signed into her Gmail account. She emailed the footage to herself, against Brian's protests of, "I don't want people to know about the nest; they could go after the birds."

"Seriously, Brian, what criminals do you think I'm dealing with that care about birds of prey?"

"That's my point. Criminals wouldn't care about conservation," he said, unconvinced. Then: "Do you know that guy in the video?"

"Yes," she said, annoyed, rubbing a hand across her face. But then she perked up. "Oh, this should be fun."

CHAPTER TWENTY-ONE

Gramps's text said: *met meat Ken hosue.*

Which Billie took to mean: *Meet me at Ken's house.* Gramps's sausage fingers were no match for his Samsung's tiny keyboard.

Billie pulled into a spot across the street from a neglected Cape Cod, the same parking spot she had occupied when she had watched Ken put a muzzle to his temple and pull the trigger. Billie decided to move up several yards, so she had a different vantage point, this one of the neighbor's house, outlined in twinkling Christmas lights. Then she rummaged in her glove box for ibuprofen which she chased with a gulp of seltzer.

Stifling a burp, she pinched the bridge of her nose as if the pain in her forehead was caused by sinus congestion and not the dizzying route she took to get home. Left turns and right turns and jug handles, just to shake off tailing phantoms. If she had been followed, she sure as shit was certain she had lost them, along with her equilibrium and appetite.

She really needed a new vehicle. And today she was going to get one.

She exhaled and prayed to the Advil gods to stop the throbbing in her brain. Hell, stop her brain from its rumination all together. She knew there were pills for that; she just didn't have them. Wasn't sure if she wanted them.

She got out of the car and knocked on the front door. Gramps called from inside, although it sounded more like a strained cry. She entered the foyer which was a swath of tile that led right into stained carpeting. The stairs were to the left of her. The living room was so tight, she could stretch out her hand and touch the opposite wall. It was also packed with piles of junk. An old tube television sat on a stand in the corner, coated in a thick layer of white dust. There was a couch, brown and threadbare, with piles of towels and blankets. And kitty corner from that was a recliner that looked like it had been abused by a cigar. Stacked on the seat were magazines. Billie lifted the first one from the pile. It was a *TV Guide* from 1995. *TV Guide!*

There was suddenly a grunt, followed by a yelp, and the clatter of items falling from a great height, and then Gramps's expected, "God dammit."

Billie walked the five steps to the kitchen and peered in. The cabinets were all opened and the kitchen table was covered in dishes, pots, pans and cloudy glassware. Gramps huffed as he gingerly made his way off the stepstool and crouched to pick up a black contractor bag from the floor, which he held open to accept white shards.

"Broke a mug," he said.

"When I suggested you took the Safe Horizons case to avoid this work, I didn't mean for you to labor over here. I meant for you to make some phone calls." She felt terrible for shirking responsibility, but there was no way she could muster up the time or energy to pitch in. Not with her current workload, sanctioned and otherwise.

Gramps frowned, taking in the scene. "Too expensive. Also, I don't want strangers sorting and tossing Ken's things. Judging him."

"They've seen worse." *She* had seen worse, just a few days ago.

Billie thought about the clutter that always congregated around their toaster at home. The papers. Bills. Medical tests. Doctor cards with appointment times scribbled on the back, dates that had come and gone. Her report cards from all four years of high school that her mother insisted she keep. As Shari got sicker, her desire to hold onto things grew stronger. Used stamps from holiday cards. An old paycheck. An employee ID from one of the hospitals she used to work at. "I need that," she had told Billie once, the badge poised over the trash can.

"For what?" Billie had asked.

"In case I go back," Shari said.

All this crap, mundane pieces of a life, evidence really; they added up over time. "Would you have described Ken as a hoarder?"

"You mean like those weirdos on that creepy reality show?"

"It's a mental illness."

Gramps dismissed the idea. "Get out of here with that." He gestured around the kitchen. "He just accumulated some stuff over the years."

"You need a dumpster and a match to clean out the place," she shot back. "That's not *some stuff*. You're clearly overwhelmed."

"Cuz I'm old. You could help."

There it was.

"I have a new investigation in my lap at the moment. So do you, apparently."

That stoked some interest on his part. "What's your case? Cheater? Insurance?"

Oh man, she wished.

Billie leaned against the part of the counter that had been cleared. "The daughter of the dead guy I found needs me to locate the owner of missing art, to assuage her guilt. It's complicated."

"Clearly," he said, then caught her eye. "So does this mean you're giving up on Levine Investigations? Gonna work for Esha Patel full-time?"

She couldn't tell him that it might be nice for someone else to be the boss for a change. If she could get assigned the cheaters and fraudsters, she could come home after a day of work, kick off her Docs, and stream Netflix like other women her age, instead of googling art heists for hours and confronting smug teaching assistants who thought they were better than everyone else.

"It's one case, Gramps." She yawned and stretched her arms above her head. "If you're not hiring a company, how are you going to balance this clean-out with the Safe Horizons work you took on?"

He sighed. "Didn't really give it much thought." He picked up a mug with a brown stain inside. "You think this can be cleaned?"

"Throw it away." A beat and an idea. "There's a solution to all this."

"Yeah?"

"Have David and Matty do it."

He made a face. "I know where you're going with this, and no."

"Come on, they're young. They have the stamina. They clean out the house, fix it up, and move in."

"No," he said again.

"You can charge them rent, be a slumlord."

There was a split second where he considered it. Then, "No. I'm not sanctioning any Goff relationship. Goes for you too, but I'm much more optimistic that you and Aaron won't make it."

"Ouch," said Billie. "By the way, when was the fridge last cleaned out? I guarantee there is a mayo jar in there from 2005."

Gramps bristled. "No." He was emphatic; she had to hand it to him.

"Suit yourself." Billie decided to leave Gramps to his tasks. His punishment really. Because despite their decades-long friendship, Gramps felt responsible for Ken's death. And if tossing old broccoli and mildewy shower curtains and gray towels that had once been white meant he could make amends, well then Gramps would sleep on a bed of unwashed sheets to get redemption.

Truth was, Ken really owed Billie. He did almost kill her. And as she passed by the little catch-all bowl on the side table next to the couch, she knew how Ken should make it up to her, even in the afterlife.

"Can I borrow Ken's car?" she called to Gramps.

He poked his head into the living room and cocked a brow. "The Oldsmobile? Why?"

She had to lie. If he knew she was being tailed, he'd freak out. "The Hyundai doesn't do well in the snow."

Gramps moved past her and pushed aside the curtain, his eyes darting at a snowless street.

"It's December. Weather can change in an instant here," she argued. "That Oldsmobile is a boat."

"The tires are new," he acquiesced. He went over to the bowl and grabbed the key attached to a small, black leather fob with the Oldsmobile insignia. "It's in his garage. Be mindful: it's a gas guzzler." He handed the keys out to her, then took them back. "You sure you want to drive it? It's a real – how do I say this – old man's car? Fit for an alte kaker, not a young person."

Exactly what she needed. A car that was untraceable and unexpected.

She grabbed the keys from his outstretched hand. "It's perfect."

CHAPTER TWENTY-TWO

The following morning Billie came down the stairs in her pajamas, arms raised above her head, trying to stretch out yesterday's burnout. She heard David and Shari in the living room. David was dressed in his mauve scrubs, ready for work, but he was sitting next to their mom, with his cell phone out in front.

"And what is this again?" asked Shari.

"Pinterest," he replied.

Billie waited for the inevitable follow-up question. Even before Shari had been diagnosed, she wasn't familiar with any social media platforms that weren't Facebook.

"What is the – what you just said?" Shari asked.

"Pinterest?"

"That word," she said.

"Uh, it's just a website where I can save pictures of things I like," he explained.

"Why are you doing that?"

David settled into the couch cushions. "To furnish my apartment. I'm going to move in with my boyfriend."

"Matthew," Shari said.

David beamed. "That's right."

But Shari remembering Matty's name had less to do with a sudden jolt of awareness, and more to do with the fact that he was cemented in her long-time memory. Because for as long as there had been a David, there had been a Matthew Goff alongside him.

The Pinterest board, however, was a concern.

In Billie's estimation, Pinterest was nothing more than a collection of dreams and wishes. Nicole liked to pin images of high-end designer clothing she couldn't afford or stone patios she could never install in her second-story condominium. "You trying to manifest a house?" Billie had asked her. And Nic had responded, "Can't get what you don't ask for."

Billie went over and held out her hand for David's phone. "Show me," she said.

David made a face, but obliged.

Billie scrolled through. Just as she thought. Pottery Barn style in a French country house. She turned the phone around. "Are you planning to move to a chateau in Marseille?"

"Give me that," he said as he snatched back the phone.

This wasn't realistic. This was a fantasy. As unlikely to happen as Shari getting her memory back, or Billie finding herself with disposable income.

If David was pining for reclaimed wood trestle tables, then he wasn't being serious about looking for an actual sofa that he would need to outfit the apartment. The kind one purchased from Bob's Discount Furniture.

Billie wasn't sure whether to be worried or relieved. David moving out could blow up her ability to handle casework and her mom's care, but if he didn't, then he was likely to detonate his relationship with Matty. Which bomb radius would be worse?

David rose from the couch. "We're looking at another apartment today."

"How many does that make now?" Billie asked. "Three, four?"

"Haven't found the one that's right," he said. "I sense a lot of homophobia from these landlords and management companies."

"Uh huh," she replied. Then to her mother, she said, "I'll bring you a cup of coffee. We have a doctor's appointment today, so I'll drive you to Safe Horizons afterward."

"Ok," said Shari blankly, but then a realization. "I don't want to forget my purse."

"We won't," said Billie.

"I'll need my purse," she repeated.

"I know," said Billie. "We'll bring it."

David caught her eye. "Neurologist?"

"GP," she replied.

Satisfied with that, he tucked his cell phone into his pocket and scooped his backpack off the recliner. He kissed Shari goodbye and headed out.

Billie put on the morning news and draped an afghan over her mother's lap. "I'll return in a few minutes."

Gramps was in the kitchen, rummaging in the fridge for breakfast when she entered, making a beeline for the coffee pot.

"Busy day ahead?" he asked while peeling off the top of a plastic soup container and sticking it in the microwave.

Pouring a cup, she replied, "Mom has a doctor's appointment, then I have to get to work." Looking for Roza, clearing Aaron's name.

He watched as the soup container spun inside the microwave.

"You gonna go to Ken's house again today?" she asked in between sips.

That caused Gramps to snort. He grabbed a dishtowel and gingerly removed the soup from the microwave. Steamed billowed from the top like a funnel on the Titanic. He set it on the table and went for a spoon. "No. I still feel grimy from yesterday. Plus, I wanna work that Safe Horizons case."

"Right," she said.

Gramps paused, his spoon held in mid-air. "You don't think I can do it?"

"When did I say that?" she asked as she retrieved another mug from the cupboard for her mother.

Gramps hiked a brow. "There's an implication in how you said 'right.'"

"There was no implication. You're being ridiculous."

Gramps harrumphed before he pulled out the kitchen chair and sat down. He blew across the broth. He slurped, winced, and set down the spoon. "It's a small theft. Probably a disgruntled employee or some drug addict who slipped past security, looking for easy things to pawn."

She held back from rolling her eyes at her grandfather's insecurity. "I didn't say anything. I have total faith in you."

He didn't look satisfied at her response, but he changed subjects, "So this dead guy's daughter? Your case for Esha?"

"Yeah?"

"She isn't concerned that you found her father? You know, dead?"

"What difference does it make? I'm looking for an artist. Who cares that I'm the one who discovered his body?"

"Clouds your judgement," he said, but Billie realized he didn't mean Karl Sauer. He meant Aaron's connection to this case could impede her decision-making; he was just too chickenshit to say it aloud. Probably feared her reaction, as he should.

In the interest of harmony and both of their blood pressures, she sidestepped the landmine. "All I'm doing is locating an artist. That's it. Anyway, her father was literally the son of a high Nazi official. I don't think my judgement will be the issue."

"And this woman married a Jew?"

"Yes and converted."

"We can always use more people," he said with a smirk.

"She has a painting her father left her, and she wants it returned to the descendants. I'm righting a moral wrong."

"How noble of you," said Gramps as he slurped down a matzoh ball.

"Now, who's implying something?"

"You gonna talk to Rabbi Schechter?"

"What for?"

"He's knowledgeable. He could help."

"I haven't spoken to him since my Bat Mitzvah. I'm going to feel like such an asshole hitting him up for information when I have completely bailed on temple."

"Eh, he's used to it. You kids jump ship the minute you finish your Haftarah portion. You think he hasn't dealt with this before? Anyway, he's incredibly connected. If he doesn't know the answer, I guarantee he knows someone who can help you. Might as well try."

The house line rang.

"Probably spam," said Billie as she rose to silence the cordless phone sitting on the counter.

It wasn't spam.

"Who is it?" Gramps asked.

"Dad." The phone continued to ring.

"For Pete's sake," said Gramps as he grabbed the phone from her. "Hello," he barked.

The last thing Billie heard as she went to the living room with Shari's coffee cup was Gramps beleaguered sigh, followed by a sharp, "Craig, the kids are not interested in attending your wedding."

CHAPTER TWENTY-THREE

Billie was reading the immunizations chart for the seventh time when Dr Kulkarni came into the room, her white lab coat floating around her like angel wings.

She was in her fifties with soft brown skin and long dark hair, and Billie was tempted, on more than one occasion, to inquire about her makeup routine.

As the doctor scrubbed her hands in the sink, she asked, "How's everything going?"

"I can't find my purse," said Shari from her perch on the exam table.

Billie raised her mom's knockoff leather bag and responded, "As well as to be expected."

"Hm." Dr Kulkarni tugged on several paper towels and dried her hands. She scrolled through Shari's chart on an open laptop. "Blood pressure looks good. Weight's good. Bloodwork?"

"Next week," said Billie. "David will bring her in for that."

"I imagine that'll be fine too," said the doctor. "Her body is still strong." Setting aside the computer, she unwound her stethoscope and addressed Shari, "Just going to listen to your heart."

Shari nodded. "I was a nurse for ten years."

Thirty, thought Billie, but who was counting?

"That's right," said Dr Kulkarni, softly. "ICU, was it?"

"I think so," said Shari hesitantly, then she grew more assertive. "Yes, intensive care."

The doctor stepped back. "Aside from the memory issues, is there anything else you want to discuss?" For this, she addressed Billie.

"Well–"

"Where's my purse?" said Shari, looking around frantically. Again Billie hefted up her mother's handbag. "Right here." Shari visibly relaxed.

"As you can see," said Billie, "my mom's anxiety has been a little high."

The doctor quirked a brow. "Her bag?"

"Yeah." Billie shot a glance at her mom. She always felt uncomfortable discussing Shari's issues so openly in front of her, like she was betraying her mother's confidence, but they were long past innocuous secrets. "She panics that she's forgotten her purse or her nursing ID, and she doesn't need any of those things. We bring them with us, but we have to constantly remind her that we haven't lost them."

"I imagine that her handbag is something she always had with her."

"Yes," said Billie, thinking back to when she and David were kids. Shari's purse had been a cornucopia of snacks, mints, school forms, coupons, credit cards, house keys, car keys, a copy of David's gym locker key, Billie's glasses and contact lenses. Her purse had been luggage.

"It's a tangible memory, an anchor to an old life, so when she can't feel her bag, she panics," said Dr Kulkarni. "As the disease progresses, so might her anxiety over these things. It's normal, if not reassuring." The doctor placed a gentle hand on Shari's shoulder. "Why don't I prescribe her an SSRI? Ten milligrams, nothing too potent. It will take the edge off a bit. Might help."

Great, another drug, thought Billie. But she smiled and nodded.

"And what about you?" said Dr Kulkarni

That startled her. "What about me?"

"Your shoulders are practically hunched to your earlobes. Perhaps you should schedule an appointment. I'd be curious as to your blood pressure."

"Oh, that's ok," Billie said quickly. "Work's a little stressful, but it'll pass."

The doctor pursed her lips. "Stomach upset?"

"Huh?" Billie asked.

"Do you get an upset stomach? The runs? What about tingly hands?"

"I'm fine," said Billie, flushing. "Truly. My mom?"

Dr Kulkarni nodded. "I'd like Shari to return in a month to see how the medication is performing." She leaned into Billie and whispered, "Perhaps I'll see you too." She slid her laptop off the counter and opened the door. "Always a pleasure, Shari. Give my best to your father-in-law."

Dr Kulkarni gracefully swept herself into the hallway. Meanwhile, Billie felt as if she'd been bulldozed.

As she ushered her mom out of the exam room, Shari said, "Where's–"

"I have it, Ma!" Billie stopped, leaned against the wall, and closed her eyes for the briefest of moments. She wondered if Kulkarni was watching her with the shrewdness she was known for. Billie exhaled and hefted up her mom's bag. Then she wrapped the strap around Shari's shoulder. "You keep an eye on it."

Shari nodded and followed Billie out to the car

CHAPTER TWENTY-FOUR

Esha had asked Billie to stop by the office, so she headed to Paramus in Ken's Oldsmobile.

But rather than drive into the building lot, she left the car next to the Dunkin'. She considered grabbing a coffee, but stopped at the entrance and did an about-face. Advice to lay off caffeine swirled around her brain. She couldn't give it up entirely, not unless she wanted a hapless and miserable existence, but maybe she should ease off a little, order tea once in a while.

But what was iced coffee really if not mostly water?

She then went back and ordered a medium dark roast iced with cream. Sure, it was *freeze one's tits off cold*, but this was hydration.

Crossing a cement median, Billie pulled up her hood and sipped her frosty brew. She didn't sense the phantoms, but there was no reason to think they weren't close behind.

When she arrived, Esha was standing by the water cooler, filling up a Nalgene. "You look furtive," said Esha as she screwed the cap on her bottle.

Billie followed Esha to her office in the back. "In our business, that's a compliment."

Derek Campbell had emerged from the men's restroom, still tucking in his shirt, this one crisp, white, and new. He eyed Billie as she went past. Then he said, casually, "How's the investigation?"

Derek, so desperate for overtime, he'd get petty over Billie

KIMBERLY G. GIARRATANO 131

snagging one case out from under him. She responded by shutting the door in his face.

Esha sat down and slid her reading glasses over her eyes. She opened a folder, and then noticing Billie still hovering like a hummingbird, pointed to the chair across from her until Billie sat. Which she did, removing her cell phone from her pocket and setting it on the desk next to her iced coffee.

"Where are you on the Cantor case?" Esha asked.

"Since yesterday?" said Billie.

Esha nodded, wordlessly.

Nothing. She was nowhere.

Billie wondered what kind of pace Esha was trying to set. "I met with an expert at Mahmoud's Auction House. She's going to offer guidance."

Billie would just have to make Fatima help whether she wanted to or not.

"We've done business with Mahmoud's in the past. They should be a resource."

Billie assumed the *they* in that sentence was not Fatima.

Esha removed a few sheets of paper from the folder and presented them to Billie like a last will and testament. "The copy of the inventory list. Extensive. Meticulous." Then under her breath, she mumbled, "Very on brand."

Billie snorted and ran a finger down the paper, noting the names and dates, and presumably, based on the dollar figures listed, how much Karl sold the pieces for. She flipped over the two sheets, saw a few had faint pencil marks encircling them. But there was no map key to decipher Karl's meaning.

"Supposedly," Esha began, "the detectives and restitution people are working to track this all down." She frowned and Billie twisted around to see Derek, skulking outside the glass windows. He at least had the decency to pretend he was reading an OSHA poster.

Billie turned and shifted in her chair. "What's his deal?"

"Fights with the ex," said Esha, sighing. "I know I should be spreading the cases around, but Derek's good at what he does. He's also the only one," she whispered, "without a life."

"Hence, fights with the ex-wife." Billie was perpetually busy; that didn't mean she had a life either. But all she said was, "Hopefully, this Cantor case will show you that I can be your number two investigator."

Esha raised a brow. "I thought this gig was just a side-hustle. You run your own firm, don't you?"

Billie shrugged. "It's nice not always being the boss."

That got a laugh. "Don't I know it!" She pointed to the paperwork, returning their focus to the task. "If you look at the list of artwork, some names are written clearly, others have initials. Some art is listed by title, but some don't even have titles. Christina thinks her father maybe didn't have that info so instead he–"

"Described the work the way he saw it," finished Billie, then realizing she interrupted, said, "Sorry."

Esha shrugged it off. "You understand. It's possible that something from this list fits the painting description and maybe Christina missed it."

Esha set the papers back inside the folder, now much thicker than Billie had initially realized, and pushed it toward her.

Billie's phone buzzed with an incoming call. DAD flashed across the screen. "That can just go to voicemail."

"Absolutely not," said Esha. "Family comes first. Answer it."

Billie did not want to answer it, not for all the full-time jobs and health insurance in the world. But Esha was looking so expectant, Billie felt like she had to receive the call, so as not to be rude – to Esha.

"Hello," said Billie, forcing a smile so Esha wouldn't see just how agonizing this was going to be.

"Hey, kiddo. Long time no talk." Her father sounded no different to her than when he called from the road to say he was never coming home. Billie wasn't sure what she had been expecting from him. Perhaps dejection and regret.

Esha shooed her out of the office, and Billie walked to an empty cubicle and fell into a chair, the momentum thrusting her back into the computer monitor. "Dad, I can't talk long; I'm at work." Technically true.

"What? No time for your old man?"

She could feel the conversation slipping sideways already. "I'm at work," she said again.

"Well, if you had answered my calls at the house, then I wouldn't have had to call you at work. I thought you were doing Pop's PI business."

"You know about that?" But what she really wanted to say was 'who told you?'

"I still read nj.com."

Everything that went down with the Torn Crosses. That had made headlines.

"Right," she said, feeling stupid, and oddly paranoid. Then she wondered if she was being paranoid about feeling paranoid And to think her brother offered her weed once.

She exhaled slowly, trying that stupid YouTube breathing technique again. In. Out. In. Out.

"You still there?" he asked.

"Yeah. Uh, how is Ms Casey?"

"Emily. She hasn't been your art teacher in a long time."

Six years, which was only long to fruit flies and goldfish.

"Right. Emily. How is she?"

"Real well. Excited for the wedding. Which is why I'm calling. We really want you and your brother to come–"

"And mom's doing well," she cut in.

Her mother was not doing well, but she was grasping at spider webs. She didn't want to be invited to his wedding, and by extension, then have to decline. "Her blood pressure is excellent."

"But not her memory."

Fuck you, Dad.

A long beat. "Did you put her in a facility?"

"No," she said, aghast.

"Just asking. No one would blame you if you did. You're young; you should be living your life. Hell, I'm still young."

"You're sixty."

"That's young nowadays. I eat right, exercise regularly. No reason I shouldn't live until I'm ninety. I know you kids are mad at me, but how fair would it have been for me to be there taking care of her when I have decades left to live? Aren't I entitled to happiness too? I worked hard my whole life. Don't I deserve a break? She was getting bad before you graduated college, but you wouldn't have known that because you weren't there."

"Because I was a student," she said.

"Ok, so? I did my part for almost thirty years, and now, you have to do yours."

Billie realized that the whole purpose of this call wasn't solely to invite her to his nuptials in Sedona; it was a grievance call. He had been saving this for her, squirreling away his gripes into a pile, just waiting for winter so he could gorge himself on his self-righteous narcissism.

Billie was stewing in her own fury so much that she didn't hear the rest of what he had to say. Instead, she gritted her teeth. "You're a selfish prick." And she hung up.

She found herself panting and sweating. She stripped off her coat, slung it over her arm, and made for the door.

Derek caught her. "My father was a son of a bitch too." He leaned back in his desk chair, his weight causing it to bounce under him. "Couldn't help but overhear. I think all calls with shitty dads sound the same."

"Yeah, I guess."

"My father was the three As." He counted off his fingers. "Alcoholic. Abusive. Asshole. Told me that I wouldn't amount to much more than a schlub." His eyes took in his wrinkled, albeit new, dress shirt. "Our folks don't know everything."

Billie shook her head, as if she needed to clear the air. "He wasn't always like that. He used to be, not kinder, but more fatherly. He took care of us. Now it seems, like, he wants credit for that. He wants recognition that he had been a decent dad most of the time."

Derek shrugged. "My dad was always a prick. I'm not sure what's worse. The scumbag who never changes, or the nice guy who turns into a scumbag."

Billie had never thought of her father as a scumbag. She wasn't sure she could. His phone calls did set off pangs of nausea, though. That shouldn't be her body's natural response to hearing from him.

Derek tipped the chair upright and went back to typing up his reports. "One day, Nancy Drew, he won't be there anymore, and you'll feel relief."

"Yeah," she said absently, but that didn't make her feel better at all.

CHAPTER TWENTY-FIVE

Billie stopped at Nagel's for a cup of matzoh ball soup because it was the cheapest thing on the menu, and also because Bernice would throw in an order of coleslaw, half-sours, and yesterday's challah without Billie having to beg. Bernice was skilled at preserving Billie's dignity. This was one reason that it was good to be William Levine's granddaughter.

She entered the deli and greeted Bernice's reflection in the wall-size mirror behind the glass counter. Packing up several Styrofoam containers and two quarts of soup, Bernice turned around and smiled. "The usual, dearie?"

"Please," said Billie.

"You're not sick of it?" Bernice's accent was heavy Jersey City, so heavy Billie imagined her voice had been dipped in a silver bath and hung to dry. "I figured with Hanukkah, you'd be over the matzoh ball by now."

"Do Italians get sick of pasta?"

Bernice gave that more thought than was necessary and shrugged. "Guess not." She scribbled Billie's order on a notepad – "give me a sec" – and headed toward the back.

Leaning toward the glass case, Billie peered at the row of desserts. Layer cakes, cream pies, hamantaschen with apricot filling, chocolate chip cookies the size of dinner plates. And her favorite, black-and-white cookies: half chocolate icing, half vanilla, all delicious.

"I'll put one on my tab if you come and sit with me," Doug Malley said from a nearby table.

"I can afford my own pastries, thank you very much. Besides, I sent you something and you didn't text me back." She sounded juvenile, despite the seriousness of her request. Thanks to Brian's bird cam, Billie had snagged the truck's license plate number, and she had sent that sensitive info over to Malley who promptly ignored it.

He waved her over, as if coaxing a stray dog into the open. "Come on. Let's talk."

Sighing, and with no Bernice in sight, Billie made her way over.

Malley pushed a chair out with the toe of his loafer. She dropped into the seat, giving Malley the specter of a disenchanted teenager who was being dragged out to dinner with her dad against her will.

If Malley had been Craig Levine, that's exactly what it would have been. But Malley was Malley, and he largely just wanted to keep her from veering off the hamster wheel, which was thoughtful if not infuriating.

Granted, she remained pouty. "The truck?"

"Stolen off the street in Brooklyn. No leads. No witnesses."

"No nothing," said Billie, sounding frustrated as she twisted in her chair, wondering where the hell Bernice had gone off to – the kitchen or the 1920s Lower East Side – for her soup.

Finally, Bernice came into view, carrying a large paper bag, but Malley held up his hand to stave her off.

For a moment, Billie's palms tingled with pins and needles. She shook them out.

"You ok?" asked Malley.

"Fine."

Malley leaned in and lowered his voice. "Aaron isn't clean in all this. You need to convince him to do the right thing. Give up his partners."

"His partners?" She found herself skirting the edge between anger and hysteria as she gritted her teeth. "He didn't steal the art. You – the BCDB – are looking at the wrong guy. You, them, everyone should be looking at a woman."

Billie thought of Fatima. "Women," she corrected.

But Malley could not be persuaded as he threw down a napkin. "We know that he's messed up in this and likely to go down. Maybe you can convince him to give up information. We can be reasonable."

Aaron didn't trust the BCDB, and he had good reason not to.

Malley rose from the table, excused himself, and made his way toward the men's room.

Billie went to the counter where Bernice was holding her to-go order. "It's $12.50."

"Can you throw in a black-and-white?" said Billie. "Malley said he'd covered it."

"The cookie or the whole order?"

"The whole order." He could swing it with his future copper's pension.

Bernice shrugged, mainly because they both knew there would be little pushback from the detective. He was good for it, and as long as the bill was paid and her tip inflated, Bernice didn't care by whom.

Billie reached for the paper bag and made her way to the door just as a woman in a long fur coat reached the same spot. She and Billie did that awkward dance people do when confused by door etiquette. *You go first. No, you.* Finally, Billie pressed her back against the glass and pushed it open with her tush, letting in a blast of frigid wind. The lady smiled.

"Thank you, honey," she said in accented English. "I love Jewish food, but don't get to have it much where I'm from. Anything you can recommend?"

Billie impatiently hefted her brown paper bag in the air, her matzoh ball soup growing colder by the second. "It's all good, but their pastrami is the best."

"What about pierogis?" she asked.

"Uh, that's not really something they do here. Try the knishes or latkes."

"Shame," said the woman, still lingering on the sidewalk. Billie hovered there cold and uncomfortable, before finally letting the door close.

Fur coats were so taboo; she never saw them anymore. But this woman didn't strike her as someone who cared what others thought. She carried herself like she owned the deli or the street, like she could buy and sell New Jersey if she wanted to.

Billie and the woman stood outside Nagel's, staring at each other as if their gazes were tethered.

"Did you like the poppies?" the woman asked.

For a moment, Billie forgot about the customers inside, or Bernice refilling cups of decaf, or that Malley was hunched over a plate of kishka, completely unaware that Billie was examining a woman with hair like a black sapphire and a mole above her lip a la Madonna.

"What do you want?" Billie asked Roza Filipek.

A gruff sentry leaned against the towncar parked at a meter, his jacket opened enough to subtlety reveal a holstered gun.

Another bodyguard, this one bald, got out of the car just as Roza threaded her arm through Billie's elbow. She leaned her head in slightly, as if they were old friends. "Let's walk."

The street was busy as cars drove past, but the sidewalk was empty, aside from a few pedestrians, huddled in thick coats, their eyes cast downward, backs hunched, making themselves small enough to hide from the chill. Or perhaps they sensed the danger from Roza's death squad, a group of men built like redwoods, whose mitts could crush windpipes with little effort.

Billie should scream. Malley would hear her. But a bullet was faster than his reflexes.

"Dangerous for you to come here," Billie said.

Roza laughed, a playful sound. "Oh, honey, the police are no threat."

Several storefronts over, Billie halted abruptly in front of the CVS. "Oh, I didn't mean cops."

Roza cocked her head slightly to the side, "Your lack of fear is quite refreshing. Stupid, but refreshing. That's why I've been keeping an eye on you. You're a valuable asset."

"For what?" Billie snapped.

"You confuse the police, annoy them. They don't know which way they're going. The handsome one in particular. His anger gets in the way, makes him sloppy."

"I don't think I'm to blame for that," said Billie, feeling like her dignity had somehow slithered from her body and into the sewer.

"No, you're right. I shouldn't credit you for the mistakes men make. That is on them. Look at your boyfriend, Aaron. He messes up a lot. And the consequences will be deadly."

"Leave him the fuck alone," Billie snapped.

Roza's eyes darkened. Her man stepped forward, but Roza signaled, and he quickly stood down. "You will be thanking me."

Billie's voice hitched. "No, bitch, I won't. You won't get away with threatening the people I love. For taking photos of me in my car."

"You give me too much credit. You're not that interesting of a person, but Aaron is an albatross around your neck. You're meant for bigger things." Roza traced a gloved finger along Billie's trachea. "He goes to prison, and you're free. Free to grow. To be more."

Billie flinched away from her grasp. "I don't need your brand of toxic feminism, thank you very much."

"You called me a bitch, and I called you an asset. Who is being toxic?" Roza sighed. "Men should be doing your bidding. Instead, you're chasing them around, trying to save them from themselves."

"I'm only trying to save one, from you. You stole Karl's art, but Aaron's going to take the fall."

"Oh," said Roza, almost gleefully. "He's going to go down for more than that." She leaned in close, her breath hot on Billie's cheek. "Wait until you hear how Karl died. Hint: it wasn't from natural causes."

Billie's gasp was smothered by the sound of Roza clapping her hands in rapid succession. The black towncar appeared as if incanted by a spell. The bald minion opened the back passenger's-side door for Roza who gracefully climbed inside. "You should work for me. I could use a woman like you."

Stunned into silence, Billie watched the towncar pull away, crest the hill, and disappear from view.

CHAPTER TWENTY-SIX

A figure ran toward her, halted, bent forward with hands on hips, and panted like a German shepherd in heat.

"Was that her?" said Jeremy Yang as he righted himself, his breath churning out moisture like a fog machine. He inhaled and gulped air. "It was her, wasn't it? Holy hell."

Billie nodded, slightly dumbfounded.

He slapped his knees. "Dammit. Fuck! How could you let her get away?!"

There was satisfaction to be had here, only because Jeremy was so miserable. There was also audacity. "Me?" she cried. "How did I let her get away? An international art thief who uses a literal Eastern Bloc for protection? Are you out of your mind? Did you think I'd make a citizen's arrest? With what?" She raised her Nagel's to-go order bag. "I'd take out her guys with a matzoh ball?" And then came the accusations: "Where the hell did you come from? Why are you even here? How far did you sprint?"

He exhaled and pointed in the far distance. "I was at the Walgreens, and then I saw the town car, and then the big guy and then the fur coat, and something clicked, and—"

A car honked in the intersection, and both Billie and Jeremy jumped.

"The mole!" He drew an imaginary circle around his face. "I saw it."

She shifted her Nagel's order to her other arm and cradled it as if holding an infant. The bag grew heavy and uncomfortable. "Impossible. You couldn't have from that distance."

"Well, then, I sensed it."

"You're being ridiculous, not to mention unsettling. This is bordering on obsession."

He retreated a step, the result of Billie's verbal smackdown or the weird look he'd received from an old lady standing beneath the green roof of the bus stop.

A thought needled her. "You don't live around here, do you?"

"That's what you're worried about?" he asked incredulously. "That we might be neighbors."

Yes.

"No, of course not." Then, tugging him by the sleeve of his North Face puffer coat, Billie walked him back toward Nagel's.

"You're going to tell Detective Malley that you saw Roza Filipek. I need corroboration."

"Sure." said Jeremy.

"And that you were also tailing Karl Sauer to his storage locker at Paretsky's," she added.

He stopped short and she almost dropped the takeout bag.

"Not gonna happen."

"It needs to happen. He likes my boyfriend for this insane scheme, and I need someone not related to me to set him straight. Tell Malley that other people, namely you, had access to him."

"No."

"Yes."

He stood there defiantly as he challenged her with a stare.

She laughed, swelling with victory as she combated smugness with smugness. "There's video, you dummy."

Jeremy shook his head, disbelieving.

"Of a hawk's nest," she said, and then quickly added, "There was footage of a bird's nest, but you're in the shot. Sauer's keycard and the video's metadata prove when you were there."

"I didn't do anything," he said.

"I'm not suggesting that you did something to him, but you're a witness." She let that sink in for a moment. "A witness who casually left out that you were stalking the old man to his Aladdin's cave."

Jeremy tilted his head toward the doorway of a closed Indian grocery. The tiny alcove provided some protection from the chilly wind sliding through the street like a cobra.

Remembering what Aaron had told her about the GPS tracker, Billie surmised Jeremy must've done something similar. How many people were tailing Karl Sauer? His car was probably covered in trackers like a child's sticker book.

Jeremy raised his hands in surrender. "I was following him."

"Yeah, I know."

"I'm writing my dissertation on the art underworld in Europe and this was too big an opportunity to pass up," he explained.

Translation: *this could make my career.*

"Back in your office you mentioned chatter," she said, opening and closing her fingers as if she was conducting a very lame puppet show. "You're the chatter."

"Last year when I was doing research in Milan, there was a footnote in an obscure text that one of Hitler's art collectors had an assistant who disappeared with a bounty. So I dug around a bit, built a family tree, traced movements and name changes, and eventually I funneled it down to three people: an old guy in Heidelberg who died ten years ago, a German bank teller in Buenos Aires, and Karl Sauer."

Narrowing her brows, she said, "How do I know that you didn't clean out Karl's storage unit for your own gain?"

This caused Jeremy such great offense that he spewed saliva at her as he sputtered, "Are y-you serious right now?"

"Take it easy," she grumbled, wiping her cheek.

Billie could make one last attempt. An appeal to reason. She softened her tone, took it down a decibel, the way a parent might when trying to subdue an irate toddler. "I *need* you to come clean about what you saw when tailing Karl. It could mean my boyfriend's freedom."

"You mean his life once Roza gets to him," he said, cutting an imaginary line across his Adam's apple.

Billie couldn't stop herself; she shoved him against the storefront window. The attack caught him off guard as the force of her anger made such a loud cracking noise, she thought she broke the glass. "You're impossible to like. Also you're selfish and a dick."

She stalked away and called over her shoulder, "I don't need your cooperation; again, I have video!"

Billie was a few feet from Nagel's door when his hurried footsteps caught up to her, and she spied Jeremy's reflection in the deli window.

Dusting off the grime, he hissed, "You win."

She stopped, turned around, and waited. Billie didn't see the need to point out that Malley had already left, his favorite table now occupied by a couple and their baby.

"I followed Karl once," said Jeremy, holding up his pointer finger. "One time. I snapped a few photos, trying to see inside the unit, but I didn't get to stick around long enough to get closer."

"Why not?" she asked.

"Because he got into it with a guy. There was pushing and shoving, and 'fuck you' in English, maybe a few in German."

"He got into an argument at Paretsky's?"

"More like an altercation if you ask me," said Jeremy. "It got physical."

"Don't keep me in suspense, did you recognize the guy or not?"

"Yeah," said Jeremy, bobbing his head up and down, the adrenaline fueling his confession.

"I swear to God, if you don't tell me."

"You cannot mention that I was tailing Karl to his storage unit. One, I'll deny it; I'll say that I was checking out the place."

"Let me guess number two. Two, Karl Sauer lodged a complaint against you with the college. Said an Asian man - or something much worse - was harassing him about an art collection he knew nothing about. Your TA position is on the line, hence you being Finkel's lapdog."

Jeremy's eyes grew to the size of Nagel's dinner plates. "How did—"

"I'm a really good detective. You think I haven't looked you up?"

"Nicole Mercier told you," he said flatly.

"She might've."

Eyes narrowing, he replied, "It was the neighbor."

"Huh?"

"It was Karl's neighbor. The altercation at the unit. He's the guy. Whatever video you have should show his car too – an older model Explorer."

"Gary Amato?"

Jeremy nodded. "And I'll tell you something else, something entirely free."

"What?"

"He was cheating on his wife." And with that, Jeremy shoved his hands in his pockets and sauntered off toward the intersection.

"With who?" she called after him. "With who?!" But he wouldn't answer.

It didn't matter; she could guess.

She now had a lead.

Billie called Brian. "Gonna need your help again...don't be like that. You only have to send me an email."

CHAPTER TWENTY-SEVEN

Billie leaned against the outside of the building and burrowed into her scarf. Turning to Aaron, whose cheeks now matched the brick exterior, she said, "What time did he tell you again?"

"Eleven." He kicked a rock and sent it flying across the empty parking lot. It skidded to a stop inches from the only remaining vehicle, a souped-up blue Civic, that Billie imagined was the result of this guy's side hustle. There was good money to be made in selling secrets.

"A hundo, right?" she asked, still staring at the car's shiny rims and the stupid set of reindeer antlers on the roof.

"One crisp Benjamin. Do you want me to cover—"

"No!" Then softer: "No. I got it." Billie felt around her pocket and withdrew a crumbled wad of bills. She slapped them into Aaron's hand. "He'll have to settle for wrinkly Jacksons and a couple of ripped Hamiltons."

"Accurate description of our nation's forefathers," he noted before shoving the cash into his pocket.

"Better be worth it," she said, sighing. "If I consider what I'm doing is like bestowing a holiday bonus, you know, how people tip their hairdresser during the Christmas season, then maybe I won't feel like I'm being taken for a ride. I wonder if I can write this off on my income taxes."

"Bribing a county worker? Don't think so, although if you use my dad's accountant, you can deduct anything. Even a crime scene cleaning."

Billie held up her gloved hand. "We should stop right there."

"What are you hoping to get out of this?"

"I want to know how Karl died. If this whole ordeal is about theft or murder–"

"Or both?"

"Or both," she finished with an exasperated sigh.

"Let's be real. You just want to know if I'm facing twenty-five to life."

"Don't you?"

"They don't have anything," he said. "And what they do have is circumstantial."

"I'd rather we weren't surprised. Hopefully this clown can clue us in."

Billie did not confide in Aaron that Roza had paid her a visit earlier that evening, that Billie's hunch had been fed to her by a scary Gen-Xer with a penchant for sadism. Were those fur coats made out of ferrets or the hairy men who had wronged her? Who was to say? Besides, a good gumshoe rule was never to offer up information that might cause a migraine down the line. And squealing to her high school sweetheart that she had been, not just approached by Roza and her Slavic muscle, but offered a position on her crew would've given Aaron an aneurysm.

She insisted on his transparency, but her business was best left opaque.

Aaron checked his phone. "Dude's on his way, and I'd suggest you not calling him a clown to his face. His name's Kevin."

Billie heard the machinations of the door opening before she saw a scruffy man come out with a cigarette half-way to his mouth.

The med tech. More accurately, the body janitor – cleaning up blood and viscera – had to have a steel gut for that line of work.

Billie supposed the hundred bucks wasn't enough, but it would have to do as she wasn't an ATM.

Kevin had a ginger beard and stocky build and wore blue scrubs with indeterminate stains on them. Headphones encircled a pink neck, and he reeked of bleach, smelling like a community pool locker room. His cheeks were flushed, either a result of the cold, his Irish heritage, or a painkiller addiction. Jury was still out.

Grabbing a lighter from under a shrub, Kevin lit a cigarette and spoke around the filter. "You got the cash?"

Aaron handed him the money.

He exhaled a trail of nicotine and said, "Five minutes."

Billie held her breath as she tried to skirt around the cigarette smoke. "Karl Sauer: has his cause of death been determined?"

The guy flicked ash on the ground, narrowly missing Billie's boot, before tapping the back of his skull. "Preliminary examinations show blunt force trauma. Your mummy took a hit."

"Was he attacked with something or did he die from the impact of the fall? Did they recover a murder weapon?"

"My guess is he was clobbered when his back was turned," said Kevin. "And as far as I know, the BCDB haven't recovered any weapon, but the ME thinks it was heavy and made of concrete. He's taking a bunch of half days this week. Typically, not much gets done during the holiday season."

Detective Morales was wrong: death must wait like everyone else.

He sprinkled more ash. "We got another ME on loaner, but she's not in any rush to draw conclusions."

This brightened Billie's mood considerably. Real police work took time – weeks, months – that stretched like gum, so long and stringy it no longer tasted of fresh mint. That could only save Aaron's bacon.

But just to be clear, Billie asked, "So he didn't die of natural causes?"

The guy shook his head. "They'll rule it a homicide." He blew a gray circle. "Eventually."

"Shit," she said and fell back against the wall, even though this news felt inevitable.

However, there would be time to figure it out.

"Your mummy also had a faded bruise under his eye." Kevin stubbed out the cigarette on the brick and dropped it to the ground. "A bruise that isn't consistent with the time of death."

That perked her up. "What are you saying?"

"That someone clocked him way before he died."

"Could've been the car accident," Aaron pointed out.

"He has bruised ribs," Kevin said. "But the shiner was newer than that."

"But older than his time of death?" Billie asked.

That corroborated Yang's account of Gary Amato getting the jump on Karl Sauer.

Kevin nodded and adjusted his headphones, revealing a name written in Sharpie marker, a name that was not Kevin. "You get your hundred bucks worth?"

She waggled her hand. "I feel like we're only at the seventy-five dollars level. What else you got?"

Kevin twitched his nose, reminding Billie of a field mouse. "They found blood at the scene."

"Vic's?" asked Billie.

He shook his head. "My guess, killer's blood. They're gonna test a carpet remnant."

"All right." But inside she was thinking, this is good. It won't be Aaron's.

"Now you satisfied?"

"Yeah," she whispered.

Kevin leaned his nicotine-scented body toward Aaron and they did that bro hug where they clasped hands and brought each other in close, ending with pats on the back. Kevin placed his expensive headphones onto his head and headed inside.

Aaron and Billie made their way back to the Oldsmobile. It took her a moment to compose herself before she could start the car.

"Are you all right?" Aaron asked.

Billie nodded. "I think we just received good news. Blood was found at the scene. Killer's blood. It's obviously not your blood."

"Billie–"

"So once they test that, get the DNA, they'll rule you out."

"Billie–"

"Wonder if they can put a rush on that–"

"Billie!" Aaron sat back, tilted his head toward her, and sighed. "It'll be my blood."

She laughed, waiting for the inevitable punchline. Aaron only shook his head.

"That can't be possible," she said, the humor dying a slow death. "You aren't injured, so where would the blood come from?"

"It's hard to explain–"

She then grabbed at his jacket, his shirt, pushing down his collar to see where he'd been cut, where he could be hiding a bandage, but he gripped her hand. "It's from before." With his other hand, he pointed to the scar along his neck. "I'm being set up."

Billie shook out her fingers before pressing her forehead to the steering wheel. "How could Roza and her crew have gotten your blood to set you up?"

"I'd imagine from the hospital when I was in Poland. They took my blood for tests. Not hard to bribe a nurse. Why do you think Tomer had me transported to Tel Aviv?"

Billie whipped up her head, causing a bolt of discomfort in her neck. She rubbed at the tension. "Is that a thing villains do now? Keep someone's blood lying around in hopes they can use it later?" She grew flustered. "Don't they need some type of storage situation? You can't just walk around with vials of blood like some goth weirdo or a fucking vampire. Does she have a phlebotomist on retainer or some shit?"

"I don't know," he said again, resigned.

But Billie wasn't. "You know what? Screw that. I can fight fire with fire. Roza makes mistakes."

"How?" asked Aaron.

"For starters, she screws over the wrong people. Russian oligarchs and me." She glanced at the near empty gas tank and cursed. "And I will formulate a plan after I fuel up."

Aaron shoved his hand inside his jacket and tossed her a bunch of bills.

"I don't need your money," she said.

"Not mine. Yours."

The bro hug. "Did you steal back the bribe money?"

He shrugged.

"Didn't you just burn your bridge there?"

Again, he shrugged. "I have it on good authority that the dude's gonna get fired. I'll just make friends with the new hire. Plenty of lowlives to bribe."

She put the key in the ignition and crawled out of the parking lot. "Has this whole ordeal taught you nothing? Make friends with better people."

Aaron said, "And what fun would that be?"

Billie eased the car in front of Matty's apartment building, glanced up at the third story window flickering with light from the large flatscreen television, and drove past.

Aaron pointed at the lobby door, now far from view. "You missed my stop."

"Last time I checked, I wasn't a bus driver." She turned a corner and pulled the Oldsmobile into a nearby commuter lot.

Swiveling his head side to side, Aaron smiled with realization and said, "We're so going to get busted again."

"Not here we won't." The issue they had before was they kept getting caught fooling around near schools, parks, and in one case, a defunct bakery. Places that were closed after hours, places with parking lots that should be empty. So when a lone

Acura or Hyundai suddenly showed up, cops and security guards got curious, then suspicious. They saw the car rocking and they came knocking.

But now...

"We're camouflaged," said Billie as she cut the engine. "We won't look out of place here." She opened the driver's-side door, shrugged off her coat, and hopped into the back.

Aaron took a beat, a bemused smile spreading across his face. He ran his thumb along his bottom lip, and then did the same.

The moment he joined her, she climbed over him and straddled his waist, her knees pressing into the upholstery. Leaning over him, her hair fell across her cheek like a shadow.

Aaron's kiss tasted like whiskey, a bourbon he had sipped while waiting for Billie to wrap up at Paretsky's. Top-shelf, most likely. A limited run, aged in wine barrels. Special. Daring.

Billie never touched booze, but Aaron's mouth made her want to drown herself in that whiskey.

Pushing the hem of her sweater off her skin, Aaron's fingers moved up along her back and tugged down the straps of her bra. He released her lips and buried his face in her stomach. Billie gasped. Grabbing Aaron by the front of his shirt, she shifted positions and eased him on top of her.

Hands began clawing at buttons.

It was cold outside, but the car interior was hot and sticky and dark. As vehicles skated past, shadows shifting and coasting along their bare skin, the headlamps moved in rhythm to their heavy breathing.

The outside world wanted so much from Billie. But inside the car, her back pressed into the upholstery, her mind scrambled from pleasure, Billie thought only of her own wanting. There was no greater urgency waiting for her.

CHAPTER TWENTY-EIGHT

The following morning, Billie made a surprise stop at one French-press drinking detective's home.

Doug Malley lived in a weathered split-style home in Ridgewood, which made sense based on his many divorces and cop salary. Unlike the Dereks and Craigs of the world, Malley never had kids. He did have a stepson he took out to dinner a few times a month, whose speeding tickets he disappeared like vapor. Malley was a good parental figure; Billie could attest to that.

He was also super fucking wrong about Aaron.

She parked Ken's Oldsmobile across the street and waited a few beats while a curvy brunette stood inside the foyer. Billie watched as she stood on tiptoes to give Malley a kiss on the lips.

Malley still smoked, definitely still drank, but man could he get it. She'd be impressed with such sexual prowess if she hadn't just been waxing poetic about him being a stand-in dad. And if she wasn't still relishing in her own afterglow.

Once the woman – who Billie recognized as a BCDB precinct secretary – left and drove away, Billie got out of the car with her cell tucked in a pocket. She knocked on Malley's door, genteel-like to make him think his paramour had returned for a forgotten hair tie or house keys. That must've worked because he didn't look through the window to actually see who stood on his front stoop. For if he had, there would be no smile.

In fact, he dropped his grin the minute Billie opened her mouth.

He went to close the door on her. She shouldered her way in and he immediately gave up. Billie could drain the fight out of anyone.

"Come, look at this," she said as he advanced into his home, his dress shirt unbuttoned, his tie nowhere to be seen.

He went for an orange juice in the fridge. "Billie, this is highly improper."

"What? Me showing up with evidence or you shagging your secretary?"

He had to hand it to her there.

"She's not a secretary. She's a court stenographer," he said.

Billie hovered around him in the kitchen.

"What do you want?" He sounded exhausted, but it all looked for show. His cheeks were pink and his lips were raw, sustained by radiance and oxytocin.

"Gary Amato attacked Karl Sauer."

He took a swig of his juice, considered that bit of news. "Evidence?"

"Eyewitness account," she said, wondering if Jeremy Yang would testify to this. He could be convinced if she used blackmail.

Table that for now.

He sighed, took another sip. "That's not gonna cut it. Besides, ME hasn't ruled cause of death yet."

"Let's be real; when everyone gets back from their Christmas vacation in Boca and Ft Lauderdale, they'll rule it a homicide."

"What's Amato's motive?"

"It's possible that he was having an affair," she said.

"Possible?"

"Probable?"

Malley rummaged in his fridge for a snack, before slapping a few waxed parcels of cold cuts onto his countertop. "You want?"

"Not at 9am."

He gestured at her with a piece of baloney. "I can't be discussing this case with you. You're too close to it."

"So let's not discuss the case, but Gary Amato instead. What do we really know about him? He's lived next door to Karl Sauer for a long time. Sauer is a hoarder, a racist, the worst of the worst. He drives the property values down all around him. The Amatos wanted to sell their house but couldn't because of Karl. And if Gary is having an affair, and Karl knew about it, there's motive right there."

"So you surmise. There's no evidence to suggest anything you're saying is true."

She opened her mouth, but he was right. Jeremy had nothing but a hunch. She shut her trap.

"No evidence that we have anyway," he said pointedly. "Besides, I thought you said Roza Filipek cleaned him out."

"She did."

"You just said Gary killed Karl."

"He could've."

"Let me get this straight. Mr Amato murdered Karl Sauer, but Roza stole all his art. Doesn't make sense."

Billie smiled. "Doesn't have to make sense; it just doesn't make Aaron guilty. Reasonable doubt. A Hanukkah miracle."

He shoved a whole piece of Swiss cheese into his mouth and spoke around it. "This is just like before. You want us to look at other people to take the heat off the Goffs."

"I was right about that! I was right about everything."

"You got lucky," he replied before chasing his breakfast with the last dredges of Tropicana. He wrapped up the deli meats and tossed them in the fridge, then slammed the door with such force, she was surprised the entire thing didn't implode. "You almost died."

She felt herself grow indignant. "What's your point?"

"My point is you're an investigator. Your job is to tail adulterers and insurance fraudsters and run background checks and serve court papers. It's our job," he pointed a thick finger at his chest, "*our* job to go after bad guys."

"You're after the wrong bag guys. You think Aaron stole millions of dollars' worth of art, but he didn't. That blood at the scene and in the storage locker, that was Roza's doing. A set-up."

Malley glared at her. "Who've you been talking to?"

"Not important."

Malley went to the couch and grabbed Billie's bag and slung the strap over her shoulder. "Out. Time to go. I gotta get to work."

"Just last night you couldn't wait to talk to me, now you're demanding I leave."

"That's right," he said. "Cuz I'm the adult here."

"I'm an adult."

"I often forget that." He pushed her into the foyer, firmly gripping her shoulder while he twisted the doorknob. Then he lightly shoved her outside into the cold like some Dickensian orphan.

The door closed firmly behind her.

CHAPTER TWENTY-NINE

Later that hour, Billie drove to Karl Sauer's house at Christina's insistence.

"I found something weird in the basement," she had told Billie over the phone.

Billie's initial hesitancy at returning to the chamber of horrors was momentarily alleviated by the giant dumpster that was now parked in the driveway, and the mountains of garbage bags sitting inside the green metal bin. Christina had been busy.

If only Gramps could've made half that progress on Ken's house, he might actually have a chance of finishing before his next birthday...in August.

Front door's unlocked, Christina texted. Then: *Duh, lock is broken.*

Billie plugged her nostrils as she descended the basement stairs, only calling out when she reached the bottom. She inhaled tentatively, but the stench of mildew was overwhelming. Christina met her in the middle of the cellar, a pile of bins on one side of her, holding an KN95 mask which Billie gratefully strapped over her nose and mouth. She'd rather breathe in her onion bagel breath than whatever was rotting beneath the boxes.

"He kept so much stuff," Christina said, her voice slightly muffled. "Stating the obvious, but look." She held up a Santa Claus, built from faded construction paper and brass fasteners. "I made this in third grade. He never threw it away."

"Art," said Billie by way of an explanation.

"Yeah, I guess. There's so much of it. I thought about asking my sons to help, but I don't want to traumatize them. 'Help your mom clean out your Nazi-affiliated Grandpa's landfill house.' It's not their burden to bear."

One could argue that it wasn't Christina's either, but if there was anything Billie could relate to, it was a daughter's complicated obligation to her parents.

"What is it that's so weird you needed to show me?" Billie asked, hoping to hurry this along.

Christina pointed to the concrete floor. "That."

Billie glanced down at what looked, if Billie was being honest, to be a fairly standard concrete floor. "Let me define weird for you."

"Look closer," said Christina as she crouched down and pointed with a gloved finger. "See how the cement doesn't look the same."

Billie peered down, then crouched low. She grazed her bare fingertips along the uneven and unmatched surface. "Patch job."

"Yeah. But only there."

How can you tell? Billie wondered.

Something was needling Christina.

"Something is under there?"

Christina stared at Billie with round eyes. "My mom said my father might've been too paranoid to trust banks." She stood up, brushed dust from her hands. Pointing upstairs, she said, "He hoarded everything. Why wouldn't he hoard money?"

"I don't know," said Billie. "Why hide cash like that, where he couldn't access it? And then why not tell you?"

Her voice became excited. "He always spoke of inheritance. What if that's my inheritance? What if it's treasure?"

"Treasure means it's stolen," Billie chastened.

"Then it will go back, if that's what's down there."

Any money Karl had accumulated over the years would've belonged to someone else, but with Billie's curiosity now piqued, she bit the inside of her cheek. "You wanna call the BCDB or tear up the floor ourselves?"

Christina answered by darting to a corner, hidden by boxes, and re-emerging with a shovel in one hand and a pickax in another. "Will this do?"

Billie wasn't sure of her strength, but she was willing to convert her anxious energy into raw power if it meant destroying something with permission.

Christina handed over the pickax and a pair of safety goggles, which to Billie's shame, she hesitated to take. "They're new," explained Christina. "Bought them at Home Depot a few days ago."

Billie opened her mouth to apologize, but Christina dismissed that at once. "Don't feel weird."

Nodding, Billie asked Christina to stand back before she choked up on the handle and clawed at the cement.

"Interesting technique," said Christina.

Billie didn't want to go into detail about how her father had told her that the best way to use a pickax was to paw at the ground rather than raise it above one's head. So she simply said, "Yep."

As she broke up the concrete in jerky movements, her arms ached. "I'm a runner," she said as she pulled down the mask to suck in air. "Good for the cardio, less so for upper-body strength. This could take a while."

"I'll call my husband," said Christina. "I'm not sure he'll come. We're not doing well right now."

"Your decision," said Billie with a long exhale. "I'll keep at it, see if I make headway."

Christina shook her phone and pointed toward the ceiling. "No cell service here. Be right back." Then she shuttled up the stairs, and Billie once again chipped away at the floor. A larger chunk came away this time. Maybe she would be able to do this by herself, no man necessary. She could pretend the floor was Jeremy Yang's face. She carved into his nose, and a hunk of concrete came away. "There better be a bazillion dollars buried under here," she grumbled to herself, already sweating in the cold, dry basement.

She heard heavy footfalls on the steps. Mr Cantor must've been close to arrive so quickly, but then Christina said, "I'm so glad you were home."

And another voice, familiar: "Not a problem. Happy to help."

Gary Amato stepped into view, only to halt at the sight of Billie with a pickax. Good, she thought. We've established dominance.

"Billie, this is Gary," said Christina handing Gary a mask.

"We've met," she said just as Gary refused the mask and muttered, "Smelled worse on some job sites."

Where? The morgue?

Gary reached for the pickax, but Billie held it back.

"Billie," Christina said kindly, as if Billie's reluctance to turn over a pickax was because of her staunch feminism and can-do spirit, and not because he and his homewrecker girlfriend were potential murderers.

"Let him help," said Christina.

"Yeah, Billie. Allow me," said Gary.

Billie turned over the pickax, but she immediately grabbed the shovel, swapping one weapon for another. Gary eyed her suspiciously before raising the handle above his head and slamming it down with such force that Billie winced.

For ten minutes, Billie and Christina watched as Gary continually hacked at the floor, removing his company fleece and sweatshirt in the process, leaving him in a white T-shirt with yellow pit stains. But as Gary continued to beat up the floor, Billie became increasingly antsy, struggling to contain the fluttering going on inside her head and stomach. She wanted to scream, "Just finish already!" Billie didn't care if there were gold doubloons down there (which she wouldn't put past Karl to have stolen) or a shoebox of cat bones from a pet he forgot he had. She just wanted to flee. Aaron was in trouble, and Christina's case might be admirable, but it was a waste of Billie's time.

She was two seconds from darting to her car and peeling out when Gary said breathlessly, "I think I hit something."

He effortlessly took the shovel from Billie's grasp, because she was no longer thinking straight, and scooped up the debris. So much for weaponry. She and Christina then leaned over the little pit and peered in.

Billie crouched down and wiped away gray dust to reveal a tarp made of thick canvas. For a moment, she imagined herself as Indiana Jones on a dig in Jordan, but reality was far too bleak. Poking out between the tarp and dirt was a heavy ceramic object. She poked at the tarp, then grabbing the shovel, she used the tip to dislodge the tightly wound fabric. White bone gleamed, its exposure so startling, Billie immediately scrambled backward and landed hard on her ass.

Christina's eyes widened. "What is it?"

"Not what," said Billie, her voice so commanding she could have mistaken it for someone else's. "We need to call the Bergen County Detectives Bureau."

Christina and Gary leaned over the little hole, glancing from its discovery to Billie.

Billie pointed to the floor. "There's a body in there."

Christina gasped, but Gary just dropped the pickax and grumbled, "What is it with this family?" He grabbed his shirt and fleece and padded up the steps while Billie watched his retreating back.

Christina fumbled for her cell phone. "I gotta-gotta go upstairs, no outside. Outside to call the police." She ran up the steps, leaving Billie alone with the corpse.

She wasn't stupid enough to touch the body, but the ceramic object could potentially be the murder weapon, depending on its weight and heft. She put on Christina's gardening gloves and began shifting the object ever so slightly. Definite heft. It seemed to be made out of the same material as the floor. Concrete.

Yet, like the rest of the stuff in Karl's house, this object was very much a piece of art. And art was often signed.

She fumbled for her phone. Tilting her head slightly, she aimed the lens toward the bottom where initials and a date were etched in white paint.

AS

'77

Well, she thought. I've found the original owner of the painting. Esha should be thrilled.

CHAPTER THIRTY

For a second time in a week, Billie stood outside Karl Sauer's house ready to give a statement regarding a dead body.

This time, she stood beside a near catatonic Christina Cantor, who did nothing but stare across the lawn at the opposite house and shiver in her down jacket.

Billie wanted to comfort her, but she found she wasn't good at relating to people without making it about herself. The only comfort Billie could provide as they watched the guys in white suits carry out the canvas-wrapped skeleton was to put her arm around her. Being present was going to have to be enough.

Detective Morales came out of the house first, his breath white in the cold. "Mrs Cantor, I'm going to drive you to the station. We can talk there." Then to Billie, "Malley'll take your statement, and you can go home." He sounded docile compared to his combative self just days ago, and Billie wondered if she should be worried. Or maybe Morales was just drained by this case.

Nodding, Billie watched as Morales escorted Christina to an unmarked police cruiser. Malley arrived a moment later with a disapproving look on his face. Not sure what was with all the judgement. Billie didn't ask to be here.

"So things just took a turn, huh?" she said.

He cocked a brow as if Billie had just asked him a Final Jeopardy question on Shakespeare. That was not the reaction she was expecting, and she grew belligerent. "Come on, Malley. A dead body was just found in the cellar. Maybe it's all connected. Karl's murder. The skeleton. The art."

"Oh, really?" Malley asked innocently. "We don't know when the body was placed there. We don't know if Karl Sauer was living here when she was buried. We know nothing."

Billie smirked. "We know it's a *she* apparently."

Malley swore under his breath. "The eggheads took a guess based on the pelvis. It's not definitive."

"The thing she was buried with had a year painted on it: 1977. So Karl was definitely living here at the time."

"You handled evidence?"

She thought if a person could literally blow their top, Malley was coming awfully close to doing it. "I wore gloves," she said.

He leaned in close and hissed, "This isn't your rodeo." He sighed and rubbed a meaty paw over his scruff, before offering up a look of pity. She'd rather face wrath than someone who felt sorry for her. "Listen, no matter what you think, this revelation isn't going to change the fact that your boyfriend is in serious trouble and there's nothing you can do to get him out of it."

"Wanna bet?"

Malley pointed a finger at her. "Don't."

"Or what? You're gonna tell on me? Ground me?"

"Evidence points you in the direction. Not your gut or misguided wishes." Malley walked off, ending Billie's interview.

As she made her way down the street to where she had left Ken's Oldsmobile parked under a naked maple, she considered Malley's advice to follow the evidence, not her sour stomach. A sound suggestion, but Malley was wrong if he thought the evidence led to Aaron. Evidence, like people, could mislead.

Roza Filipek was responsible for the theft of art from Karl Sauer's storage unit. There was no question. But Karl Sauer's death? That might have to do with the newly-discovered body in his basement. Or might not. Depended on when she died.

Gramps always said, too many coincidences are not a coincidence. Perhaps Malley should take instruction from the PI School of William Levine. There were plenty of solid lessons to learn, even for the old-timers like Doug Malley.

CHAPTER THIRTY-ONE

Jenn Herman's wedding was held at a swanky catering hall in Belleville that rivaled a villa in Tuscany but was out of place in North Jersey. Terracotta tiles, Italianate columns, and a Roman-style fountain in front of a circular drive seemed to actively fight the tin-colored sky and garland strands draped across its facade.

Christmas decorations at a Jewish wedding. Par for the tribe, Billie could argue.

Young men in black slacks and coats hovered around to park cars, but Aaron always refused to leave his keys with strangers. Billie wondered if it had anything to do with making a quick getaway. Equally likely Aaron was remembering a high school scam where he had posed as a valet to steal a 2005 Ferrari. A crime she had wisely stopped before he spent his birthday in juvenile detention.

Wrapped in her grandma's vintage stole, Billie met David at the lobby. He was dressed in a sharp blue suit that she wasn't aware he owned.

David awkwardly adjusted the white handkerchief in his pocket. "You like? Matty picked it out."

Matty also purchased it. Neither Levine was proud of having someone else pay their bills, particularly if that money was acquired through ill-gotten means, but also neither Levine was flush enough to buy decent attire. Or write a check for three hundred dollars as a wedding gift to a girl who was a royal bitch to them in high school.

Billie shuddered against the cold and eyed several guests as they exited Beemers and Audis. Once Aaron and Matty joined up, they made their way to a large room with rows of tulle-covered chairs. Billie spotted a man in a priest's collar roaming around, but she supposed he was a pastor or reverend or something.

Aaron spotted him too. "Guess she's not marrying a Jew."

"You're realizing that now?" she said. "Not the O'Connell name on the framed invitation out front?"

"Very funny," he said as he received a glass of champagne from a server in a black vest and white top. Party penguins, Gramps called them.

Billie skipped the booze and opted for what looked like a menu card, made of baby pink stationery and tied with a white ribbon, handed out by a short gentleman in a tuxedo. Matty peeked over her shoulder as they sat down in one of the last rows. "Is that a program?" he asked.

"Yup," she said. "Just in case you've never been to a wedding, or seen one on TV, or read about one in a book. In case you're an alien from space and wondered the order of events. Did you know the vows come before the kiss? News to me."

A middle-aged woman flitted by and Billie heard her say, "Peter claims he has COVID, but really I think he just didn't want to drive in from Massachusetts."

Peter had the right idea.

The room began to fill up with bodies. Billie recognized a few girls from high school, and then David's phone buzzed. He checked the number and said, "Dad."

Billie growled, "Are you freaking kidding me?"

"I'm ignoring him. Don't worry. Now isn't the time anyway."

She faced him. "When would be the time?"

David shrugged.

Billie leaned into Aaron and whispered, "I remember Jenn Herman telling me in tenth grade that I was going to Hell for eating bread during Passover."

Matty whispered, "We don't do Hell."

That wasn't the point. What was the point? Nothing, except apparently Billie harbored resentment in her bones like marrow.

She sensed hurried movement behind her. People began filing in quickly, like ants swarming a cookie crumb at a picnic. A woman in a full-length black gown sat down at a cello and began playing while another woman stood tall and began singing in operatic style.

Billie knew if she ever decided to get married, it would not look like this. Maybe she'd just elope, or stand before a justice of the peace. Although, why bother with any of it if she wasn't planning on having kids? She doubted Aaron wanted children either, although they had never really discussed it, nor would they soon. Talking about potential offspring seemed as practical as making vacation plans on the moon.

The doors opened and Billie watched as the mothers were escorted down the aisle by men in tuxes. A flower girl came next, dumping petals to the rug below, while revelers good-naturedly cooed and chuckled. Then came the first bridesmaid, a teenager dressed in champagne pink. A cousin, probably. Then another bridesmaid, her makeup so bright, she'd give Mama Ree a run for her drag money.

Then, eventually, Fatima Mahmoud.

Billie wondered if a wedding was the appropriate occasion to interrogate a suspect.

Several more girls came down the aisle and finally Jenn Herman. Billie had to admit, she sure looked like a million bucks. She probably spent that much on this ridiculous affair.

She was surprised when two officiants gathered under a small, latticed pergola (was that supposed to be a chuppah?): a woman in a yarmulke – the rabbi – and the reverend (minister?) she had spotted earlier.

Billie imagined the joke: a priest and a rabbi officiate a wedding. But what was the punchline: the marriage was interfaith, but the divorce was interesting?

Needed work.

There were sips of wine, a joke or two courtesy of the rabbi and then the groom, whose name Billie had yet to remember, stepped on the glass. There was a cry from the room and several Mazel Tovs lobbed over the couple before they clutched hands and went down the aisle to a symphonic rendition of U2's *Beautiful Day*.

Billie and Aaron waited for the rows to empty before they slithered out. "I could use a drink," said Matty.

Billie rested her head on Aaron's shoulder.

"That wasn't so terrible. Was it?" he said.

Billie's reply was cleaved by the sight of a couple still seated in the back.

Jeremy Yang and his date.

"The night is young," she said to Aaron. "The night is young."

CHAPTER THIRTY-TWO

If there ever was a cause to drink, Billie felt weddings would give her the excuse. The torturous small talk, the uncomfortable glances from high school chums, the pressure to dance, the lack of adequate seating at the cocktail hour, the tiny plates she couldn't hold alongside her beverage and phone.

Well, she could solve one problem. Shoving her cell at her brother, she said, "put this in your pocket," before making her way to the sushi bar. If she was going to be stuck at this wedding, she might as well enjoy the mediocre, albeit costly, raw fish she would otherwise not buy herself.

With the small tongs, she plucked several rolls and dropped them onto a plate not much bigger than a coaster. Then she swiveled in time to see Jeremy Yang and his date, a gorgeous South Asian woman in a slinky, silver dress, standing at a table only a few yards away. Billie ducked her chin and darted toward an alcove while her mind churned questions. What was he doing here? Did he know Jenn or the groom? Was that his girlfriend or a student? Did he date students? And the biggest: why did she care?

The irrational part of her thought that Jeremy was here to spite her because she wouldn't put it past that smug son-of-a-bitch to somehow get invited to a wedding she herself didn't want to attend just to make her life infinitely worse.

David found her and dipped his voice. "Don't look but remember that guy, Vlad, no Varun, no–"

"Victor," she finished for him.

"Victor!" he cried in triumph. Then a whispered *shit* and the duck of his head. "Anyway, he's here as Fatima's date."

Billie turned around to look, which got a rise out of David. "Don't be so obvious," he hissed.

She gave up and picked at the sushi roll. "What's the deal? Did you ghost him?"

"Yes," said David.

"Oh." Then she asked, "Fatima brought him?"

David shrugged. "Guess so."

Billie subtly glanced around until her eyes landed on Fatima and a gentleman with a similar complexion. "Are they related?"

"How should I know?" David snapped, but uttering a casual, "sorry."

"Are you worried about it being awkward, or about Matty getting jealous?"

"The first part," he replied quickly. Then, brighter, he said, "Why? You think Matty would get jealous?"

"You know what? This is a *you* problem." She waved her hand around his face. "All you." She took off for the display outside the reception room. She had already plucked her and Aaron's table assignment from the little folded cards, as had most people. She shuffled into the lobby where she found a squirmy Brian Paretsky milling about.

"You see Fatima?" he asked, pulling his collar off his neck, clearly itchy in his ill-fitted suit.

"I saw her walk down the aisle," she said. "And I'm nearly certain she brought her gay cousin as her date, so you have a decent shot."

Brian nodded several times, likely trying to convince himself that this stupid idea had, in fact, been smart, and that of course Fatima Mahmoud might be interested in him. Billie just had to work her magic.

"Anyway," she continued, "I'd hit up the sushi bar if I were you." She left her empty plate on the lip of a fake potted plant, before sauntering away in search of the restroom.

Which she found up a set of carpeted stairs and down a yellow-lit hallway. She'd hand it to swanky catering halls – they had decent bathrooms. On her way out, she bumped into Fatima's date or David's short-term ex, neither delineation mattered much. He was shaking off water droplets, which got on Billie's dress.

He smiled apologetically and in a British accent to rival Prince Harry said, "No hand towels in there and the dryers are nothing more than a catalyst for disease."

She smiled back, wondering if he might recognize her. He did. "Oh, Billie! If you're here, Aaron must be here too. I'm pretty certain I spied David, but I believe he's avoiding me."

Oh, he is. And Aaron was here somewhere. Last she saw, he was at the carving station, talking to an old classmate, who if rumors were correct, was also an ex-con.

"How's it going, Victor? I didn't know you were friends with Jenn Herman…or," she mumbled, "Whatshisface."

"Oh, I'm not." They talked as they descended the stairs. "Fatima's my cousin, not sure if you knew that–"

Aha!

"And she didn't want to come alone."

"It's tough to be single at weddings." Or secretly banging a married man?

"Well, her girlfriend is in London," he said.

Down goes that theory.

"Girlfriend?" Billie said.

"Ah," said Victor, with a hint of mischief. "You didn't know?"

"Guess not," said Billie. "In high school, I seem to remember quite a few boyfriends."

"Fatima swings whichever way the wind blows, and in this case, it was blowing up the skirts of a university librarian."

"That's some metaphor," she said, smiling, but then she remembered Fatima's puffy face in her office. "And they're happy?"

"Fatima just put a down payment on a gorgeous flat in Knightsbridge for them both."

"Really?" Papa Mahmoud could not pay that well. Like New Jersey real estate, London apartments didn't come cheap. "She's going to relocate to London?"

"That's the plan," said Victor.

"What about the auction house?"

"Unfortunately, my uncle has high expectations and low patience. She was going to wait for him to retire, but then she'd have to buy out her brothers first."

"They own a piece of the business?" asked Billie. "The sign says Mahmoud's, with the apostrophe before the *s*. Makes it seem like it belongs only to Mr Mahmoud."

Victor said, "He founded it before he had children."

"Also I just met with her recently for work, and I didn't see any brothers there."

"You wouldn't," he said with a conspiratorial wink.

A woman compensating for the laziness of men. Tale as old as time.

"Fatima does everything," said Victor. "Automating their system, consulting, acquisitions, scheduling, deliveries."

"That's a lot," said Billie. The sign *should* read Mahmouds' Auction House. Plural.

"She works like a dog and is paid like a daughter," he noted.

Well put. "You in public relations?"

"I am! Why?"

"No reason."

"I'm hoping to work for Fatima's new company once she gets it off the ground," said Victor.

Billie took a stab. "In the UK?"

Victor nodded. "Hopefully. She said there's been a wrinkle in the plans, but she intends to move forward soon. I love the States, but I miss home more."

Billie nodded, as if she could relate, but it was hard to miss a place you never left.

As Victor bade her goodbye, Billie watched him go, and wondered what kind of wrinkle Fatima had to iron in order to make her dreams come true. What if smoothing out said wrinkle had led to murder?

CHAPTER THIRTY-THREE

Billie made her way into the reception area, only to see that the best man was giving his toast. Hoping to avoid the cringe that accompanied such speeches, she slipped out to the bar and ordered a seltzer. "But add a lime for flourish," she told the bartender.

"I guess someone is trusting you to drive them home in one piece," said a voice to her left.

Jeremy Yang stood beside her, sipping from a martini glass, looking like Henry Golding, but acting more like a pompous ass.

"Oh, if it isn't everyone's least favorite teacher, Professor Gilderoy Lockhart," she said.

"A Harry Potter joke?"

"Yeah, well, I didn't know you'd be here, so there was little time to perfect my act." She exhaled. They said nothing. Then: "Why are you here?"

"My date is friends with the groom." He tipped his glass toward the gentleman up front being roasted by his supposed best friend. "They went to undergrad together." He picked up the toothpick and removed an olive with his teeth. "And you?"

"Oh, I wasn't invited," she said. "I'm here against my will."

He toasted that sentiment.

She pressed her back against the bar and propped her elbows up, taking in the scene.

He gulped, winced, and gestured toward Fatima who was doing a line of shots with a bunch of other bridesmaids. "That's the girl who's fucking Karl's neighbor."

"You're wrong about that," she said. "Fatima Mahmoud is dating a woman."

"Doesn't mean anything," he said.

"It means you're wrong, something you often struggle to admit. It also means that their partnership isn't romantic."

"Then what is it?"

"Business."

"How so?" He set down his now empty martini glass.

"Gary Amato runs an international moving company," she said. "Fatima works for an auction house. You do the math."

"She uses him to smuggle black market goods into other countries."

Billie tapped the side of her nose. "Ding, ding, ding. And everyone gets a cut."

Might explain how Fatima could afford a bachelorette pad in a ritzy London neighborhood.

Jeremy nodded appreciatively. She liked it when she impressed him.

He signaled to the bartender, then asked her, "You want anything?"

She held up her club soda as proof that she didn't.

"Teetotaler?" he said.

"That's a word one doesn't hear outside of the 1930s. I don't drink."

"Is there a reason?"

"Not one you have to concern yourself with."

"Fine." Jeremy lifted his fresh martini and sipped.

Billie watched Fatima on the dance floor. She thought about the body in Karl's basement.

"How much do you know about Karl Sauer?" she asked Jeremy. "You said you traced a family tree? Anyone hiding in those branches with the initials AS?"

Jeremy set down his drink and gave that some thought. "His mother's name was Anna, maiden name was Haas, though. She was an Austrian national, that part was true, but her being friends with Picasso was obviously a total fabrication. Just a cover for Karl to sell the sketch without having to explain where he got it from, not that anyone would've checked. Even back then, researching provenance cost a fortune. Anyway, his mother died in the late sixties from heart failure and his father, Heinrich, fell off the face of the earth. Literally, dropped off a cliff in the British Isles."

"Pushed?"

Jeremy looked at her funny. "Why does your brain immediately go there?"

"So Heinrich Sauer…"

"Sauer wasn't their original last name either. Heinrich changed it from Braun after the war because Heinrich had worked alongside Hildebrand Gurlitt. Gurlitt loved modern art, all the stuff Hitler called degenerate, and tried to save it from the bonfires. He also had a Jewish grandmother. After the war, Gurlitt convinced authorities that he was a victim, but he hid over a thousand pieces of stolen works."

"Gurlitt had a Jewish grandma, but somehow became Hitler's art broker?"

"Hitler saw that Gurlitt knew his shit. He'd owned a gallery before the war. Anyway, Gurlitt employed Heinrich to help him pilfer artwork. Funny story, Hildebrand's son Cornelius inherited his father's collection just like Karl, but he got busted for it in 2010."

She chewed on the paper straw, giving thought to how history never stayed dead. "But now Karl's treasure trove is missing."

"Roza," said Jeremy.

"Yeah," said Billie.

Jeremy tossed back the rest of his martini. "It's as good as gone."

Billie watched Fatima slow dance with her cousin. Fatima who had put a hefty down payment on a flat. Who was hoping to start her own lucrative auction house, albeit less upstanding than her father's. To do either of those things one needed money. More money that smuggling antiquities in moving boxes could provide.

"Maybe," she said to Jeremy. "But maybe not."

"Can I borrow her for a minute?" Aaron appeared with a drink which he set down on the bar. He seemed to be addressing Jeremy who responded, "Only if you promise not to bring her back."

That got an eyebrow raise from Aaron, but Billie tugged his outstretched hand toward the dance floor. He pressed his palm to her back. A Sinatra tune played, something Gramps would appreciate. "You smell like whiskey," she said.

Aaron leaned down and kissed her on the mouth. "Taste like whiskey, too," she added. He gently spun her around, nearly causing her to bump into an elderly couple. When he brought her back, he jerked his chin toward Jeremy and said, "Who's that?"

Billie rolled her eyes. "Professor from Kentwell." That didn't seem to satisfy him, so she added, "He's helping on a case."

"Bit of a dick," he said.

"Yes." Billie brushed her lips against his ear and whispered, "He's an expert on Polish art thieves, so I gotta put up with him for a little while."

Aaron slightly leaned back. "Billie…"

"He can help."

"At what price?" he said.

"My pride, for one. He's very smug. However, he knows his shit."

Aaron stopped dancing and tucked a strand of hair behind her ear. "One could argue that I too know my shit about a Polish art thief."

"How well?" she asked.

By way of answering, Aaron tugged her close as the song was not over yet. It was, of course, not an answer to her question.

CHAPTER THIRTY-FOUR

The wedding dragged on. At one point, Billie was served an overcooked piece of salmon, which she choked down for the omega-3s.

Restless and tired of Jenn Herman casting her odd side-glances, Billie grabbed her vintage stole and went outside to find Fatima.

She'd been trying the whole night to get that girl alone, but every time she grew close, Fatima would be whisked away for photos or an awkward dance with a groomsman. Billie had managed to corner her during the Viennese hour, only for Fatima to announce suddenly that she was gluten intolerant and disappear.

Mr Mahmoud might've disavowed Karl Sauer, but Fatima likely glimpsed his haul – Matisse, Chagall, Klimt – and used it as a way to tunnel into Roza's inner sanctum. But if Fatima was working with Roza, did that mean Aaron was too, and lying about it?

Moving past a cloud of cigarette smoke and the valet, Billie meandered until she came to a park-like area with a dry waterfall feature and a little white bridge over a still koi pond. The koi, like much of New Jersey, had hunkered down; their mood only to be brightened by a burgeoning spring and trips to the Shore.

Billie couldn't be the only one who saw time pass as increments of future joy.

She sat down on a cold stone bench, tipped back her chin,

and stared up at a dark sky tinged with light pollution. She wondered what real stars looked like, those far removed from the Manhattan skyline. They must dazzle out there. Would she dazzle if she was somewhere far away? Wouldn't it be extraordinary to live so ordinary?

She'd love to try.

A murmuring of voices disturbed her reverie and she turned toward the sound. Behind a tall naked shrub, on the far side of an unused fire pit, she spied Aaron and Fatima. Their faces were several inches apart, but Fatima's body language was closed off, her arms wrapped around her middle even in her puffy coat. Aaron was pointing to her, his lips unreadable at this distance, but the context was clear. He was angry.

Billie could guess why.

Either Aaron brought Roza and her army to Fatima's front door, or Fatima stumbled upon the skirmish. Regardless, they were all in it now. Nothing to be done but fight, retreat, or use each other as shields.

Aaron stormed off. Billie was tempted to call for him, but that would taint the mission.

She retraced her steps to make it appear like she was simply out for a late-night stroll along the garden path. Fatima saw her coming and fished out a cigarette from her coat pocket and lit up, her hands shaking. She scattered ash to the cement beneath her and pointed with the lit end of her cigarette. "Aaron went that way."

"I wasn't looking for him."

Fatima remained unconvinced. "I imagine you two are the kind of people who reach for each other in your sleep."

Once Billie wanted to say, but not lately. Really hard to make romantic overtures in bed when you were trying to shake off nightmares. Also when was the last time Billie and Aaron had slept together in a bed?

More softly, Fatima asked, "Do you mind if I smoke?"

"Go right ahead," Billie said, which earned a scoff.

"When people say *go right ahead*, they're really saying, 'what do I care if you give yourself cancer?'"

"You got me. That's exactly what I was thinking."

It was.

They stood next to each other, the nighttime stillness struggling to dissipate the tension, tension that had existed even during high school. Because while there had been no Venn diagram when it came to Billie and Fatima's social circles, they had crossed into each other's domains. Fatima had played rugby for God's sakes, something Billie had discovered when, on Jenn Herman's insistence, Fatima demonstrated how to do a proper tackle...on Billie.

Now was different.

Billie said, "I met your cousin."

Fatima cringed. "He's my designated driver."

"I wasn't judging."

"Sure you weren't." More silence. "Did you ever find the artist you were looking for?"

Billie shook her head. "No, and don't think I didn't notice you ignoring my texts."

"Sorry, I've been preoccupied," she said. "And no offense, but it's a stupid assignment."

"None taken, but I'm getting paid, so..."

"Right. I always forget this is how you make your money."

"Family business. No weirder than working for your father at his auction house."

"I went to Rutgers for this, and it's *our* auction house. I handle everything."

"Good on you," said Billie, which came out a lot bitchier than she intended.

Fatima flicked ash, took a long drag, and then stubbed the cigarette under her blush-colored pump. "Yeah, well, it means nothing to my dad. I'm his daughter, so I should be doing all this, right? Can't fuck off to Alexandria like my older brother or rent a Shore house for a week like Ali."

"I can't do those things, either," said Billie.

"I bring in the most money, but I'm salaried," said Fatima, not even bothering to hide her disgust. "Even your boyfriend qualifies for overtime pay."

Salaried employees didn't buy swanky London apartments. How much more could Fatima lie to her?

Let's find out.

"Is that why you and Aaron were arguing? I couldn't help but see there was some tension. Is everything cool at work?"

Fatima laughed. "Yeah, everything's cool. Aaron just likes to tell people how to do their jobs." She cast Billie a side-glance and when Billie didn't look convinced, added, "And he got into it with Marcus."

"Right."

"Marcus is very protective of our business and gave Aaron shit for how he was handling some artifacts. Honestly, it was dumb."

One thing Billie had learned through the years was that when someone said *honestly*, anything that followed was a big fat lie.

"Sure. That sounds super plausible. Or maybe you had a disagreement because you're in business with Gary Amato, using his international moving company to smuggle black market antiquities. Of course, now I wonder if you're also smuggling Nazi-looted art. Let me know if I'm warm."

"Fuck you," said Fatima before charging off toward the reception hall.

"We need to talk," Billie said, racing after her.

"No, we don't," Fatima cried, only stopping when she nearly collided with a group of guys from high school. She reversed course and cut across the parking lot.

That's when Billie heard it – the roar of an engine and the sound of squealing tires. Billie hollered Fatima's name, which only caused the girl to turn and look back. "For fuck's sake, what?"

"Look out!" Billie screamed as she sprinted to push Fatima out of the way, but she wouldn't make it in time.

A body leaped from the darkness and tackled Fatima onto a patch of grass while a black SUV sped off, its taillights swiveling in the night like devil's eyes. The screech of rubber grew fainter as it disappeared.

Brian Paretsky lay straddled on top of Fatima. "Are you ok?"

Billie ran over and grabbed Brian's hand to ease him off Fatima's petite body. She looked like she had been splatted by an anvil. "Did anyone get a plate number? See a face?"

Several onlookers shook their head.

Billie helped Fatima upright. She had a scratch on her brow but was otherwise unhurt. Fatima stared up at Brian with swirling irises. She opened her mouth to utter something, but instead puked all over his shoes.

And then she started to sob.

Billie suddenly felt protective of the girl. She shooed Brian away, asked him to get Fatima water, and told him to take the high school football team with him, which seemed to cause him more fear than the SUV that had nearly flattened him into nothingness.

"Now!" Billie barked.

As Brian took off, Billie crouched down to a weepy Fatima and said, "It's going to be fine."

"No, it won't," said Fatima through sniffles. Then a whisper, "I did a bad thing, and now I'm going to pay for it."

"Is it Roza or Gary?" Billie said, pressing her ear to Fatima's mouth. "Is it Gary? Did he do this?" She implored, "Let me help you. I can help you."

"You can't," Fatima said as she wiped at her mouth. "No one can."

CHAPTER THIRTY-FIVE

Since Aaron had driven Billie to the reception, and Fatima had presumably hitched a ride in the bridal limo, Billie borrowed Brian Paretsky's Prius to drive her home.

They drove with the passenger's window down, Fatima shakily dropping cigarette ash outside, the December chill no match for her nerves. Once the butt followed, Billie attempted to close the window but Fatima protested. She dug around her purse and withdrew a little bottle of mouthwash. "Swiped it from the ladies' room," she explained as she unscrewed the cap, swished it around her gums and spit a green stream out the car window.

"Between puking on that guy's shoes and the Marlboros, my mouth tastes like the inside of Karl's house," she said.

Billie shivered. "Can I close the window now?"

Fatima gestured her complaisance, so Billie pressed the button to seal off the car.

Fatima pointed and said, "Make the jughandle here. It's faster than taking the exit further down."

Billie did as she was told, drove on the ramp and crossed the highway. "Are we going to talk about what happened?"

"No," said Fatima.

"You nearly were killed," Billie pointed out.

"I'm well aware."

"Tell me who did it."

"I don't know who did it," she said.

"Tell me who you think did it."

Fatima shrugged.

"You need to call the police," said Billie.

Fatima laughed without mirth. "That's not going to happen."

"Why?"

"Doesn't matter." She shook her head. "Just, no."

"By the way, the guy who saved your life, whose shoes you puked on is Brian Paretsky," said Billie. "We're driving his Toyota."

"Ok," said Fatima.

"You've met him before."

"I have?"

"His father owns the storage place. You flirted him up when you were staking out Karl's unit."

"Oh."

"The night he was found dead."

Fatima had no retort, she simply sank further into the seat. Billie took that as her cue to lay it all out there. "You wanted to get a jump. With the old man dead, his storage unit was there for the taking, so you ditched me and headed straight there, except you found it empty. And panicked. Am I close?"

"A little," she grumbled.

"How long were you and Karl in business together?"

Fatima burped. "When my father declined the opportunity, I met with Karl and lied, said we had changed our minds. I sold a Charlotte Salomon piece for him, and he was delighted. That Picasso money lasted him decades, but was running out and taxes were due. He only wanted to sell a sketch, practically a doodle, that wouldn't bring in more than fifty grand. He said he could survive on that for a year."

"But not you."

"At best, I could skim ten Gs off it, but not more."

"Not enough for a place in London," Billie finished.

Fatima opened the window again. "I might throw up."

Billie remembered the circles drawn in faint pencil around various art works on the inventory sheet. Karl knew exactly what was missing because he knew the exact placement of his collection in that storage unit. "Let me guess: Gary follows Karl to Paretsky's and attacks him, grabs what he can in the moment, like a twenty-second supermarket sweep. Total surprise what he gets, but enough for Roza Filipek to broker big deals to those billionaire clients of hers. He smuggles it through shipments, and you both earn a cut."

Fatima swallowed and pressed her hand against her torso. "My whole chest feels on fire."

"Guilt will cause that."

"Please stop the car."

But Billie kept going. "Karl's storage locker was an Aladdin's cave. You just needed him out of the way to access it. Once he was out of the picture – pun intended – you could have all the Knightsbridge apartments you want. You and your librarian lady could live it up."

"Leave her out of this."

"Was it you or Gary who bashed the old man over the head?"

"The way Karl lived, death was a mercy." Fatima swallowed and pursed her lips, conceivably trying to rid herself of the bitterness coating her tongue.

"You didn't answer my question. Was it you or Gary who killed him? Or Roza, but she doesn't seem like the kind of woman who does her own dirty work. So either she paid one of you to do it for her, or sent a goon."

Fatima leaned back on the headrest and looked over to Billie. "You're really self-righteous, aren't you?"

"When it comes to murder, I feel I have the moral upper hand," said Billie.

"Drop me off at the auction building. I'm safer there than at home. We're alarmed to the hilt."

Billie pulled to a stop outside the awning.

Fatima burped a foul odor and reached for the door handle. "Thanks for the lift." She paused a second, and then added, "Tell that Brian guy, thanks."

Before Fatima could head inside, Billie grabbed her wrist. "Aaron is fucked if you don't come clean to BCDB."

Fatima yanked her arm back, but Billie was stronger. "I could lose him."

"Hate to break it to you, but you're going to lose him anyway." Fatima snatched back her wrist, breaking Billie's grip. "You got nothing, Billie Levine."

Billie watched as Fatima keyed in the alarm code, opened the door, and disappeared inside.

CHAPTER THIRTY-SIX

Billie could not quit the Karl Sauer case, and so, the next morning, she groggily drove down Karl's block. She was surprised to see the cops still milling about his front lawn, keeping an eye out for busybodies (Billie assumed she was on that list somewhere in the BCDB's database of troublemakers) while the crime scene techs took care of finishing up business inside the basement.

She idled the Oldsmobile in the cul-de-sac and watched an elderly woman in a pink sweatsuit and thick winter coat pace the sidewalk outside the Sauer home. She was pantomiming with an unlit cigarette. Every so often, she would bring it to her lips and tap invisible ash to the cement below.

Busybodies unite.

Billie got out of the car – nosey neighbors tended to be excellent resources – and approached the woman, wondering how she should play this.

The woman immediately sized her up. "You selling something?"

"No," said Billie, caught off guard for once.

"You from a real estate agency?"

"No."

"The police?"

"Nope."

"Who are you then?"

Billie supposed she would just have to play it straight. "Billie Levine. I'm an investigator."

"What are you doing around here then?"

"Same as you, I suppose. I found Karl Sauer's body, and the other body come to think of it."

"In the basement?"

Billie nodded.

The woman's eyes lit up, and she ushered Billie toward Gary Amato's house. "Come in. I have an Entenmann's."

Billie pointed. "There?"

The old lady looked at her. "It's where I live."

The mother-in-law.

At that moment, Billie felt like Moses as the Dead Sea parted for her. She followed the old lady into the home, walked into a small foyer and toed off her dirty boots, leaving them on a black mat under a table by the staircase.

Framed photos hung on the wall above. She spotted a teenage Gary in one, standing center among a group of boys in track uniforms. Billie scanned their faces, squinting harder at one boy in particular. She stood back and read the text printed on the photo.

Hackensack High School, 1994

"That's my good-for-nothing son-in-law," said the old woman as she tucked the unlit cigarette in a junk drawer. A prop to be used for another day.

"Is he home?" Billie asked innocently.

"Work," she said. "Come. I'll make tea."

Billie headed into the kitchen, pulled out a chair, and plunked down. She then removed a small notebook from her messenger bag. "Mind if I take notes, Mrs Am–?" She caught herself. Gary was the good-for-nothing son-in-law, so–

"Palumbo," she said, not registering Billie's slip. She busied herself with an electric kettle. "But call me Gladys."

"All right, Gladys," said Billie, mentally building her story. "I'm working on behalf of Karl Sauer's daughter for a separate matter, so I'm hoping you can answer questions for me."

"As long as it's a fair trade, I don't mind," she said, dropping a Lipton tea bag into a cup.

"I'll be as equitable as I can. How long have you lived here?"

"Oh, since the late sixties. This was the first house Joe and I bought after we were married."

Billie jotted that down. "Did Karl Sauer live next door at that point?"

Gladys brought over the cups of tea. As she settled into the chair, she cut a slice of coffee cake and arranged it on a paper plate, scattering crumbs on the tablecloth. "Karl moved next door in the seventies sometime. Paid cash for the place, which not everyone could do back then. He got married at some point, and the little girl, Christina, came later, but she and her mother weren't around for long."

Billie wrote that down.

"Now you," said Gladys. "What did you find in the basement?"

"A skeleton wrapped in an old tarp."

Gladys squealed and rocked back in her chair. She presented Billie with a little bowl of sugar cubes.

Billie plucked a white square and dropped it into her tea. Taking a sip, she opted for another cube.

"Back then, Karl never left the house much. Joe thought that was so odd. 'What's his job?' Joe would ask all the time. 'How does he support that family of his?' Karl would go out sometimes, but once the wife left, that was it. He'd even get his groceries delivered like an invalid. That wasn't a thing we did back then. Such a shame."

Billie sipped her tea and took a bite of cake. "Why?"

"He was handsome in his younger days, believe it or not. Reminded me of Steve McQueen."

Billie's brows shot up.

"Yes." Gladys chuckled. "Thought Joe was jealous at first, but then—" Her voice grew soft and contemplative. "Well, then Karl just stopped coming outside, and that became pretty sad after a while, especially since his little girl never visited either. And then his house started to look equally sad." She shrugged. "You just never know what's going on with folks."

Billie nodded. "Did the police interview you yet? About Karl?"

Gladys dismissively flicked her wrist. "They spoke to Gary, but he just told them that Karl was an old recluse. Sure, that's true, but he was more than that once. We all were." She slowly got up from the table and limped to the fridge. "Forgot the milk. That's how the British drink it."

"Oh, I'm fine," said Billie.

"Not you, young lady. It's for me."

Not everything is about you, Billie.

Gladys came back to the table with a half-gallon of skim from Lidl. "My daughter and son-in-law are selling the house. He says the house is too small for me, them, and the kids. Of course, this house was once mine. But that's what it means to get older. We're not pharaohs. We can't be buried with our belongings."

Karl didn't get that memo.

"But I can't complain," continued Gladys. "I call him a good-for-nothing, but my son-in-law put a down payment on a beautiful home, five bedrooms, in Glen Rock, and I'm going to a retirement community not far from them."

"Guess business is going well for him," said Billie because she couldn't help herself.

That earned her a weird look from Gladys. "It was hard during COVID. My son-in-law owns an international moving company, and no one was going anywhere during lockdown so they were hurting for a while, but now he's actively hiring, so things must be good."

Billie assumed how Gary made up the deficit. She wondered if his wife knew.

Gladys smiled. "I hate to say it, but with Karl gone, we will finally sell the house. Before it was a struggle. No one wanted to live next door to a mess like that. But Gary said, 'wait until after Thanksgiving. You'll see.'"

Wait until after Thanksgiving? Did he know Karl was already dead?

Gladys turned to Billie. "So the skeleton...man? Woman?" Her eyes grew in horror. "Was it a child?"

"I don't think so," said Billie, suddenly hoping it wasn't. "The body was female, though, but keep that between us."

Gladys chewed on that, and the Entenmann's, for a moment.

Billie asked, "Did you ever see Karl with a woman who wasn't his ex-wife? Anyone ever come to visit him?"

Gladys gave that some thought and shook her head. "Not back then. He was always alone. No visitors that I can recall."

"Just his grocery deliveries," said Billie.

"Yes. Joe used to offer to pick up his produce, but Karl never took him up on it."

"Joe sounds like he was a good man," said Billie.

Gladys smiled. "Oh, he was, he was. I was lucky. Some women get stuck with real losers." Her eyes shot to the window that looked out on Karl's backyard. "But Joe was like a father to everyone. Even Gary, whose dad was a real piece of work."

Billie supposed Detective Malley was like Joe. As for Gramps, well, Billie could only ever see him as her grandfather, curmudgeonly with creaks in his bones, slipping her candy before dinner. He'd taken over the parenting role once Craig had left, but he'd always be Gramps to Billie.

Gladys got up from the table and cleared the plates. "Gary didn't have it easy growing up. I'm glad things are turning around for him now."

Billie rose too. Gary might be a decent family man, but his shady dealings might not just cost him a gorgeous house in Glen Rock. If he wasn't careful, it was going to cost him his life.

CHAPTER THIRTY-SEVEN

After saying goodbye to Gladys, Billie drove to Amato's International Moving and Storage offices in Carlstadt.

The offices took up a corner of a giant industrial warehouse where a fleet of hefty trucks sat parked, looking like a pod of whales taking a nap. Each truck had the Amato logo emblazoned on its dingy, gray exterior.

Billie wasn't quite sure what she was doing here. She certainly didn't expect Gary to welcome her inside with coffee cake like his mother-in-law. And if Fatima had a lick of self-preservation, she would've informed Gary of Billie's suspicions by now. Perhaps, though, because Gary was a beefy dude, he'd be as frightened of Billie as a bear was of a fawn.

Now if Fatima was smart, she'd be on a plane to Heathrow, not – Billie squinted through the windshield – walking out of the offices at this exact moment. And – she squinted again (did she need glasses?) – meeting Gary and getting into his truck.

Billie slunk in her seat as they drove by. She glanced in the rearview mirror and watched as Gary's Explorer crested a slight hill and disappeared.

She wondered if she should have followed them, but thought better of it. If Gary was using his business to smuggle art, it was possible one of Roza's minions could make an appearance. Billie glanced at her camera on the passenger's seat. She longed to play paparazzi.

Resting her head against the steering wheel, she opened the

YouTube app and scrolled for a Graham Norton compilation – the Chris Pratt one always delivered – to kill time.

She once read that a few minutes of laughter could alleviate stress, reduce inflammation, and provide relaxation, which seemed like a lot of pressure for a late-night talk show.

Oh, good. Chris Pratt doing his British accent. She shook out her tingling hands. And suddenly her stomach was out of sorts.

Shit.

She had to shit.

She was going to have to go inside the Amato offices, unless she wanted to take her chances trying for a gas station bathroom. The thought made her shudder.

What was it Gladys had said? "He's actively hiring, so things must be good."

Billie would have to mine that as she got out of the car and headed inside, ignoring the *no public restrooms* sign taped to the glass.

Upon entering the offices, the first thing Billie noted was a water cooler, gurgling like her stomach, next to a desk occupied by a white woman with long dark hair and even longer eyelash extensions. She was slim, tall, and curvy in places that most women appreciated the extra padding. She wore black leggings covered in cat hair and a striped sweater.

"Can I help you?" she asked in a distinctly New York accent. Long Island?

Billie's eyes darted to the hallway behind the woman's head where she spotted a door with the unisex bathroom sign on the front.

"Yeah," said Billie. "Could I get a job application?" Then for good measure, "I heard you were hiring."

"Uh, sure." The woman rolled her chair over to a short metal cabinet and removed a single piece of paper. "We have several positions available. Movers," she eyed Billie's short stature, "Logistics, customs…"

"Customs," said Billie. "I have several years of Spanish."

"That would help us more with our local workers than anything abroad." She attached the application to the clipboard and stuck a pen at the top, then used it to gesture to a bank of chairs by the photocopier.

Whatever Billie had eaten that morning felt like it was sliding toward her socks. "Can I use your restroom?"

The woman's face expressed reluctant agreement. Maybe in her line of work, when people asked to use the bathroom, they needed a hit of something to get them through the moment. Billie just needed to go to the fucking bathroom.

"Of course." With a tight smile, the woman rummaged in a drawer and located a key which she handed off to Billie. Pointing behind her, she said, "That bathroom is mostly used by the guys. If you round the corner, there's a nicer ladies' room."

Billie could've kissed her. She grabbed the key and made a beeline for the safe haven that was a clean toilet.

Five minutes later, she emerged from the bathroom feeling quite undignified. As she made her way back to the front, she collided with a man's thick, yet soft, chest.

"Sorry, so sorry," she said rapidly as she glanced up to find Marcus, the hired muscle from Mahmoud's Auction House, staring down at her.

"This is your second job?" she said at the same time he asked, "What are you doing here?"

Billie grabbed the clipboard and job application off the woman's desk and held it like a shield. She then backed up into the watercooler and fell into a chair. "Looking for extra work. You're not the only one who needs a *second job.*"

The woman glanced from Billie to Marcus. "You two know each other?"

Billie stared at Marcus so hard, her eyeballs froze in that *I dare you to rat me out* position.

Marcus said, "She's an investigator."

Damn him.

Now it was the woman's turn to look suspicious. "For Esha Patel?"

Billie shook off Marcus's intimidation and turned her attention toward the woman. "How do you know her?"

But the woman was already on her feet. Grabbing the clipboard from Billie's grasp, she stabbed a finger at the door. "Did you even need the bathroom? Are you really applying for a job? Did my ex send you?"

Billie was stunned by the rapid-fire questions. "Your ex?"

"That son of a bitch! Are you spying on me?"

"No," she said. "Who's your ex?"

"Don't play dumb with me, bitch." Billie tried to get up from the chair, but the woman pushed her down and then placed her arms on either side of the wall, boxing Billie in. "Tell Derek he can spy on me all he likes, but he is *not* getting custody. I don't care if he moved into a new condo."

Billie squirmed out from under the woman's cage, making her apologies as she did so. "He didn't send me."

Grumbling, the woman returned to her desk chair and reached for a phone. "I'm calling security." Then turning to Marcus, "Actually, you get rid of her."

Billie held up her hands. "I'm leaving. I'm leaving."

"Asshole can't even show up to his son's basketball game, but he has the nerve to demand full custody." As she crumbled Billie's empty application in her fist, probably imagining it to be Derek Campbell's head, Billie shrugged off Marcus's grasp and left.

Her dignity had been zapped in more ways than one.

CHAPTER THIRTY-EIGHT

"You're off the Cantor case." Esha's voice over the phone was firm, but kind. Nearly maternal, which made Billie's outrage all the more excruciating.

"Why?" Billie paced around her kitchen with the fridge door open. She stopped abruptly, remembering the half-and-half which she located behind a jar of pickles that hadn't been touched since the summer of last year. Billie abandoned the creamer and slammed the door shut, her anger radiating from her fingertips to the poor fridge, the door now misaligned. "Dammit," she hissed. Then to Esha, "That wasn't meant for you."

There was a loud sigh on the line. "This isn't a punishment, although I'm sorely disappointed that you didn't reveal how close you are to this case. I can't have you digging around Karl Sauer's past when your boyfriend–" she stopped. *Is a suspect. Is involved. Come on, Esha, say what you want to say.* "You also showed up at Amato's International Moving and Storage. Claimed you were looking for a position? Andrea Campbell is furious. She thinks you were sent there to spy on her. Derek said you messed things up for him with his ex-wife and son. I had to calm them both down."

"I'm sorry, but that was entirely a coincidence. I didn't know she worked there."

"You can see my dilemma. This is a major conflict of interest. You're clearly not working on behalf of Christina, are you? More likely you're gallivanting all over North Jersey trying to clear Aaron's involvement." There was a long breath. "I'm tempted to fire you all together."

Billie fell into the kitchen chair. The problem with anger was that it quickly depleted its host, transforming it into a shell of a thing. She rested her cheek against the cool table and whispered, "So now what?"

"You can still do the process serving. And Derek will handle the investigation."

She bolted upright. "Derek has the case now?"

Again, that sigh. Couldn't Billie be reasonable? Couldn't she see this was a problem? That Billie was a problem?

"He's my best investigator," said Esha.

"Christina wanted a woman. She specifically requested me."

"We all want things, Billie – doesn't mean we get them. I'll explain it to her."

Another long pause. Billie imagined Esha removing her reading glasses, rubbing the tension from her brow. Billie was stressing her out; she stressed out a lot of people. "This is a good thing. It's a break. I mean, isn't that why you came to me in the first place? You were burnt out?"

Had that been why she went to Esha? Took Malley up on his offer to work under someone else? She had simply wanted someone, other than herself, to be in control for a little while.

"This will give you time to focus on your family," added Esha.

Focus on family was all Billie ever did. Her mother. Gramps. David. Aaron.

"Yeah, sure." She attempted to regulate her breathing, blowing in and out, long and slow, but her heartbeat pummeled away in her chest like she was running a marathon, not simply sitting at her kitchen table drenched in pity. Then again, she supposed carrying around the weight of self-loathing would labor anyone.

"Check in with me next week," said Esha. "I've got a few things coming in from the Hennrikus Firm."

Billie nodded, and then before she could murmur a *yes* Esha had disconnected the call.

Rising from the table, Billie stared at her cell phone. She could feel the ire rising, climbing through her body like mercury in a thermometer, poisonous to touch but a fairly good indicator of temperature. Billie's was about to reach a nuclear meltdown.

She dialed Detective Morales's personal number. She didn't expect him to pick up. She could yell what she wanted to yell into his voicemail. The target remained the same.

Except he answered. "Billie, I'm busy."

"You spoke to Esha Patel." She didn't phrase it like a question because it wasn't.

"I sense that you're mad," he said.

Her voice rose. "About what? You targeting Aaron for a crime he didn't commit or you interfering in my ability to make a living?"

"You're taking that last part a bit far."

"I'm not!" She tempered herself and inhaled deeply. "If anyone should be removed from this investigation, it's you. You and your jealous vendetta against Aaron Goff. A defense attorney will eat you alive on a stand."

"You don't know anything about legal proceedings."

She scoffed, then imitated a lawyer. "Tell me, Detective, did you have sexual relations with the defendant's girlfriend?"

Morales's response: nothing.

"Yeah, I thought so." She growled into the phone, "Stay out of my way." Then she hung up.

Unfortunately, her feeling of triumph lasted mere seconds. In the war for Aaron's freedom, this win felt far from glory.

This is an opportunity, she thought. Without the Cantor case weighing her down, she could get ahead of Roza Filipek. She could take her on and save Aaron. She didn't need Morales, but she did need help. And it was going to hurt her to ask.

CHAPTER THIRTY-NINE

Jeremy Yang opened the door with a scowl. "How did you find me?"

Billie pushed past him into the apartment. "Wasn't hard. You said you lived in this building. I just checked the directory for your name."

"When did I say I lived in this building?"

Billie whirled around. "Last week when Roza showed up. You said you lived in Teaneck, and I doubted it was in a house because you're a student with debt, even though you dress kinda expensive. Anyway, there are only so many apartment buildings. I ruled out those with exorbitant rent. Another building was a possibility, so I asked around, and a woman said, "'No Orientals lived there'– so glad we've made headway as a society on that front – and now I'm here."

"Christ, I regret asking, but also nothing you said makes sense, so I'm going to assume Nicole Mercier had that boyfriend of hers look up my address in the HR database."

"I'm not saying that's not a possibility. I'm also not saying that your downstairs neighbor called you an Oriental when I knocked on her door by mistake."

Billie took in her surroundings. It was a small space, cozy but warm, and surprisingly neat for an XY chromosome pairing. A leather brown sofa sat opposite a large flat-screen television. And next to the sofa was a bookcase with a slew of true crime tomes, reminding Billie of the Jasmine Flores case. She never thought to ask Jeremy if he had taught her – guess it didn't really matter now. Game controllers littered a coffee table. A galley kitchen, off to the side, had little countertop space and what was available was crowded with appliances – an air fryer, a toaster oven, and a coffee pot. And on the wall were framed art prints and posters of basketball players. What a weird mash-up.

"You're really into the NBA, huh?"

"I'm into you leaving my place," Jeremy said, tugging on her coat as he tried to coax her back out.

"I got wind that Roza's still local," she said.

That stopped him. "Who told you that?"

"More like, I figured it out from the absence of information."

"That's gibberish." Jeremy flopped onto his couch.

Billie paced around the room, her brain spitting out questions as if her thoughts were paint-gun pellets. "So, I think she moves the art through Amato's International Moving and Storage. Gary Amato, owner and operator, would typically smuggle pieces of art into his clients' belongings. You know? A family relocates to the UK, so he tucks a painting or two into their personal stuff, fails to inform customs, and then once it arrives across the pond, his team unpacks it, sends it on its way. But Karl's stash is too big to move like that. So where do you think it would be? Ideally, you want something climate controlled. Also BCDB can't monitor all ports, can they? Karl's storage unit was emptied at least two weeks ago. What's the hold up?"

"I swear if I wasn't already in on this, I'd think you're schizophrenic. That was a lot to process. Anyway, it's the holidays."

"The holidays, right." Billie stopped and looked at him. Then she glanced around the apartment. Not a spec of garland to be found, although there were plenty of cards scattered on his fridge. "Pardon my ignorance: do you do Christmas?"

"Do I *do* Christmas?"

"Celebrate it?"

"Yeah, I got what you meant, and you're not pardoned. Like commercially speaking, yeah; my folks in Metuchen go to their friends' houses and exchange gifts." Then chastising himself, he added, "Wish I didn't tell you that."

"Not gonna show up on their doorstep."

"So you say."

In her pacing, Billie picked up items from shelves, then set them back down. Pick up a geography bee trophy from ten years ago. Set it back down. Pick up a basketball card in a plastic case. Set it back down.

"Seriously, what are you–"

Billie cut in, "Could Roza have family in New Jersey? Is that why she's still here? Or a lover, perhaps?"

Jeremy leaned forward, then bolted upright. He said nothing for a moment; his eyes just flitting back and forth, combing through information like an old-school word processor. "No," he said finally. "But I think she has a nephew."

"A child?"

"An adult, I think."

"You think?"

He rose from the couch and grabbed his cell phone off the kitchen dinette. "I got a contact in the State Department. She might know. I'll reach out."

Billie fell back on the loveseat. "Great. I'll wait."

"No, no, no," he said. "You've infiltrated my domicile more than enough. You go home, and I'll tell you what I find out." Jeremy pointed to the exit. "Go."

Billie exhaled. "Are you sure you don't want company?"

"Yours? Never." He waited for Billie to hoist herself off the couch and head toward the door.

As he escorted her out, she leaned into him and whispered, "If you freeze me out, I'll make your life a living hell, and I have the power to do that."

He whispered back, "I don't doubt you." Then he put his hand on her back and pushed. She tripped over the saddle. He immediately closed the door, and Billie heard the sharp sound of a deadbolt turning.

She yelled to the door, "Obviously, I know where you live!" before trudging away and into the stairwell.

CHAPTER FORTY

The problem with other people's crap, Billie surmised, was that it became your problem when they died. And crap, like lice, wasn't easy to get rid of. It required renting dumpsters or making multiple trips to the landfill or grouping contractor bags along the street for township clean-out day. It required time and energy and able bodies, a sheepish trip to Goodwill, hoping other people might pony up a few bucks for the junk you once paid top dollar for.

And after a shitty night's sleep, made worse by an overactive brain, it seemingly also required Billie.

David had texted her before she had even woken up, asking – no begging – for her to help clean out Ken's house.

For Gramps, he had written.

For Gramps, she had conceded.

When Billie rose this morning, groggy, feeling kinda hungover for a girl who didn't drink, Gramps had already left for Home Depot, and Billie had ended up in Ken's kitchen. David, meanwhile, was perched atop a rickety chair, examining dishes and mugs – which to donate, which to toss. He found a German-style beer stein. "Should I keep this?"

"For Oktoberfest?" Billie's quip was cut off by a yawn. She snatched the mug from him and placed it in a cardboard box. Efficiency went out the window when one stopped to examine every item's potential use. Could this chipped serving bowl be repurposed into a birdbath? *No. You're never going to do that, Janet.*

"Let's keep this moving," she said.

"What's your deal?"

"Nothing. Just got stuff to do."

"Don't we all?"

While David scrubbed greasy gunk off cabinet shelves, Billie checked her phone for the millionth time.

"Aaron?" asked David.

"What?" Then: "No." She shoved her cell into her back pocket. "Work thing."

More like Jeremy thing. Billie had been hoping that Jeremy would text her to say his contact in the State Department had gotten in touch. Also: *I was wrong to kick you out of my apartment, Billie. You're not the problem; I am.* Ha! If only.

"All this effort," she said, "and for what? You think Gramps will sell the house?"

David sprayed Windex along the cupboard's surface. "Probably."

"You could live here," Billie said, a suggestion Gramps had swatted out of her hand like a live grenade.

"No," said David. "This place is a mess."

"Yeah, now. But we're cleaning it out." She glanced around. "Paint the walls. Replace the carpet."

"That costs money," said David.

"No more than a security deposit and one and a half month's rent, which is what you'd have to pay a landlord. Gramps won't ask you to do that."

David cackled.

"We can put him off."

David paused in his cleaning and squinted into the living room. "Matty won't like it."

"Why not?"

"Cause it's like taking charity from William Levine."

Billie waved her arms around the scene of garbage bags and cleaning products and boxes of grimy junk. "Charity?! Are you kidding. You're going to earn this."

David went back to scrubbing. "I don't know."

Billie sighed, trying desperately not to appear like she was itching for a battle. Keeping David close was selfish but necessary. It wasn't just their mom's care that she needed him for, but the buffer he provided between her and their grandfather. David was the rubber that grounded their volatile bolts of electricity.

A voice called out from the front door. Matty entered, dressed in a black puffer coat and Adidas sweats. He had three-day-old scruff and bloodshot eyes. Apparently, Billie wasn't the only one who didn't sleep. "Have you spoken to Aaron this morning?"

She greeted him at the door and kicked bags out of the way so he could get through. "I texted him last night, but he didn't write back. I fell asleep."

"He's not returning my calls. He hasn't been to the apartment." He lowered his voice. "And the BCDB issued a warrant for his arrest."

"I'm sorry. What?"

David jumped down off the stool and took four giant steps toward them. "What's happening?"

"I can't get in touch with Aaron," said Matty.

"He's under arrest," Billie said. "The BCDB have him in custody?"

"No," Matty said, shaking his head because of course Billie was jumping ahead of facts. "They don't. He's gone."

"Shit," said Billie, not sure if that was worse.

Matty went over to David. "We have contingency plans in place for this. I haven't heard from him since yesterday afternoon."

"Are you sure he isn't just laying low?" Billie asked.

"No," Matty answered emphatically. "If we don't hear from each other, we can only assume–" He stopped speaking, but Billie understood the implication.

"You only assume the worst," she finished.

Matty nodded.

"Ok, let's not get nuts," she said, but panic was rising inside her like high tide. "The BCDB must've gotten something big," she said. "Something we didn't see coming."

"Murder weapon," said Matty. "Found in his car."

David asked, "The old man's death wasn't from being an old man?"

"No," said Billie. "How timely to find the murder weapon *now*."

Matty said, "My dad called in a favor, found out that some anonymous shitbag had phoned the tip line. Next thing, there's a warrant for the Acura. It's been impounded."

"It's happening too fast," she said. "There was supposed to be more time." Focus, Levine, focus. She attempted to pace the living room, but found there was little space to move. She kicked at a garbage bag, her toe colliding with something painfully solid. "Fuck!"

David jumped in. "Calm down, both of you."

There was a loud bang, and Billie and Matty ducked.

Matty reached behind his waistband and grabbed his Glock.

"It's the garbage truck," David cried from the window, but as soon as he caught a glimpse of Matty's gun, he lost it. "Are you insane?"

Matty ignored him and went straight for the curtain, pushing it aside with the muzzle. "We know it's gotta be a set-up, but Dad's put in calls to the Calabrese crew in South Jersey; the O'Learys in Sussex; the Ramirez racket in Newark. No one knows anything."

"Roza Filipek."

Matty stared at her.

"Polish Queenpin. Nothing your old man or his cronies would have their radar tuned to," she explained. "I'll go to Fatima. Shake her down."

Matty said, "I'll check with our bouncer. He has connections to the Eastern European outlets."

David hollered, "Would you two listen to yourselves? Shakedowns and mobs!" He turned to Matty. "We're not gun people. I'm not a gun person."

"David–"

"No! I'm not moving in with you if you have guns around," he said emphatically before turning to Billie. "Stop bringing this shit here. To our house. To our family. I've had enough...of both of you." David grabbed his coat off the couch and stormed outside. Matty called to him but made no effort to follow.

David wasn't wrong. She did bring this shit to their home because people like Roza had no boundaries, no respect for anyone she couldn't use. And it was up to people like Billie to stop her.

CHAPTER FORTY-ONE

Billie pounded on the door of the auction house. "Fatima! Open up! Now!"

Marcus appeared in the entranceway, irritation spreading along his features like a bloodstain. "She's not here," he barked.

Billie tried to push past him but he blocked her way. "Fatima! You have to talk to me!"

"She's not here," he said again, this time more roughly.

"I don't have time for your bullshit," said Billie. "Aaron is missing."

Marcus crossed his arms and shook his head. "Not my problem."

"Well, make it your problem." Billie heard her voice then – phlegmy and brittle – one wrong thing and she would crumble under the weight of it all. "Did they take him to Amato's? Is that where they're holding him?" She held up her phone, waved it around. "I make one call to BCDB and–"

"Stop," said Marcus. Suddenly his agitation subsided, and in its place: pity. That was worse. Marcus leaned out of the doorframe and gazed into the empty parking lot, as if trying to pinpoint an invisible trouble. "Your boy isn't there."

"Well, then, where is he?" Billie dug her fingers into her eyes, hoping the discomfort would distract her from the feeling that she could be blown to bits like a dandelion. She pointed accusingly at Marcus. "You did this, you know? You set off the chain reaction."

He scoffed. "How?"

"You're the bridge that connected Fatima and Gary. She was doing fine before you, but you," she jabbed her finger into his chest, "set her up with Gary's company, showed her how easy it would be to move art out of the country. I assume you got quite the cut from that. Now, Fatima is scared shitless of being murdered. Want me to go on?"

Marcus shook his head, but another voice said, "Continue."

Mr Mahmoud appeared behind Marcus's shoulder. He looked shorter than he had a few days ago, his back curved like a scythe with shoulders tipped forward. "What's going on with my daughter? Is she in trouble?"

"She's fine, Mr Mahmoud," Marcus cut in.

"She's not fine. She screwed with the wrong people."

"Well, then," said Mr Mahmoud. "I'll have a talk with her when she returns."

"You don't get it. She may not return," Billie said harshly.

Marcus said, "Billie's just worried about Aaron."

Mr Mahmoud's dark eyebrows rose in unison. "Aaron? I saw him yesterday morning. He got into a black SUV and didn't return. My guess is that he did not go willingly."

"Black SUV?" said Billie, but her guts were coiling into new shapes. She leaned over the stair railing, wondering if she might throw up. Hold it together. "And you didn't think to call the police?"

Mr Mahmoud shook his head. "In the past, law enforcement has ignored my pleas for help." He patted Marcus's shoulder. "Why do you think I employ this gentleman?" He turned to head back inside the auction house. "Fatima will return and when she does, I'll let her know you stopped by."

As she headed back to the Oldsmobile, Billie's cell phone rang. Fatima's name glowed across the screen.

"How serendipitous. I'm leaving your business now. Where's Aaron, Fatima?"

"I don't know."

"I don't believe you."

"You don't have to, Billie. It's the truth. Did you talk to my dad?"

"I did, and I spilled all your secrets. Next on my list: Detective Malley."

"Fuck you," Fatima spat.

"Are you with Roza? Did you set Aaron up? A murder weapon was found in his car. Was that your doing on her orders?"

Fatima laughed. "Oh, Billie, you have everything so wrong."

Billie unlocked the car. "Well, then, tell me how to get it right."

"Roza does have Aaron," she said. "But she's not the biggest boogie man under the bed right now."

"What does that mean?"

The line went silent.

"Fatima, what does that mean?"

"Nothing," she said, suddenly sounding exhausted. "I hope the cut was worth it."

"What cut?"

"The money you made from Karl's haul. You brokered the deal with Roza, so I assume with all that art, worth millions, hell, maybe nearly a billion, you can own countless London flats."

There was a choking sound on the other end of the phone, and then sobbing.

"Fatima?" said Billie.

"I didn't get a cut of any haul."

"How's that possible?"

"Someone beat us to it. Got to Roza and told her about Karl's storage unit. That was our only leverage; we would never have given it up to her without guarantees."

"Gary?"

"Gary's not moving out of his cramped house anytime soon. I'm gonna lose my London apartment."

"Well, then, who knew about the unit other than you and Gary?"

"I can't tell you," said Fatima.

"Can't or won't?"

Silence.

"Can't or won't?"

"I tell you, and I die."

"Fatima, so help *you* God, you don't tell me and I will personally kill you myself."

But at that point, Fatima had disconnected the call.

CHAPTER FORTY-TWO

Billie phoned Jeremy Yang from the road.

"I told you I would call you if my State Department contact got info," he said. "So far, she hasn't."

"Aaron's been abducted. Call her again. Tell her it's urgent." A truck cut her off. She slammed on her breaks and leaned on the horn.

"Jesus Christ," he said. "Don't die. At least wait for me to hang up first."

She swerved around a slow-moving minivan. "Roza and her crew took him. There's no fucking time. Do you have other contacts?"

"Maybe. Listen–"

"Call them!" She checked her rearview mirror and spotted a tail, or at least, she suspected it could be. Another black Suburban. But this was North Jersey, and oftentimes, every third truck was a goddamn black Suburban. "Shit."

"What now?"

"I might have a shadow."

"Might?"

"I don't know!"

"Calm down." Jeremy sighed. There was a beat, a moment of agonizing silence, and she wondered if he had hung up on her.

"Yang?"

Another exhalation of breath. "I'm here. Despite not wanting to be. Pull over somewhere."

"I can't. I'm in a residential area." She glanced back, spotted the same black SUV, trailing three car lengths behind.

"Are you near campus?"

"No."

"Ok. Can you get to campus?"

"No."

"What do you want me to do, Levine?"

"Call your source," she said through gritted teeth as she turned left down a service road that ran alongside the highway. A glance in the rearview mirror revealed a swath of space. "Wait, I think I lost them."

"Great. So I can go now."

"Explain the urgency." A gray sedan pulled out of nowhere, fishtailing directly in front of her. She slammed on her breaks. The Oldsmobile skidded to a halt. For a moment, Billie thought she tasted burning rubber in her throat.

Her cell phone flew off the passenger's seat. She could hear Jeremy's muffled voice from beneath the floor mats.

She put the car in park, unclasped her seatbelt, and slapped her hand around for the phone.

She heard the crash before she felt it, but by then it was too late. The Oldsmobile lurched forward. The airbags deployed, and Billie screamed from the surprise.

There was the retreating sound of spinning rubber. Then the growl of an engine revving, and squealing tires.

"Fuck. Fuck. Fuck." Billie pushed her body upright and shifted the car into drive. She slammed her foot onto the gas pedal and turned the wheel, driving the Oldsmobile into an intersection. A bus honked just as the gray sedan flew past.

Several more drivers pressed on their horns until the air was thick with noise. Billie couldn't process what was happening.

A man got out of a car, and she freaked. She drove down the road at a clip, amazed the engine still ran; the sound of a tailpipe scratching the asphalt carried her until she pulled into a small shopping plaza.

Billie found her phone under the driver's-side seat, opened the door, and slid out of the car like ooze. While several onlookers gathered round, a beefy dude with tattoo sleeves whistled at the damage. "You need a tow?"

Billie couldn't respond; she could barely catch her breath. She slithered around the car, trying to evade the onlookers. Her coat picked up the dirt that clung to the scratched paint, and she pressed a hand to her chest.

He followed her – "Yoo-hoo" – and snapped his fingers in front of her. "You all right?"

She fell to her ass. Legs splayed out in front of her, her vision grew blurry until it tunneled into pinpricks. All the while she could still hear the man's voice.

"Should I call an ambulance?"

She had the wherewithal to shake her head and hold out her cell phone. "Detective Doug Malley," she whispered. "Bergen." Wheeze. "County." Wheeze. "Detectives…"

At some point, she got on all fours and tried sucking in air.

A voice said, "I got a girl here. She's either on drugs or dying or something. She didn't want an ambulance."

Billie didn't hear the rest.

CHAPTER FORTY-THREE

Billie lay still on a sofa, her cheek pressed so firmly into the leather, she wondered if Malley had glued her in place. Wouldn't put it past someone to shackle Billie down so she couldn't flee and cause further damage. No different than if she was an escaped rhino from the Bronx Zoo.

She pulled herself up and rubbed gingerly at her skin.

The light cast stripes along the living room floor. Her shoes had been removed, less to make her comfortable and more to keep Malley's furniture in pristine condition, but she appreciated the gesture nonetheless. Her bag lay next to her Doc Martens. Her coat was likely hung up in the closet. A furry tail flitted into view, followed by the backside of the cat it belonged to. So the feline wasn't dead after all. Maybe the cat had never been the excuse; maybe Malley just needed to come around to wanting a new couch.

Billie then wished that she was a cat. Cats lived their lives with obligations only to themselves. That sounded like a pleasant way to exist.

Malley trudged up the steps, emerging from a lower level Billie had never seen. The house was a split style so she had assumed he had been in the living room watching television, but the towel draped around his neck and his gray sweats suggested he had been in a basement gym. The idea of Malley exercising caused Billie to question if she was dreaming.

"You're up," he said.

"Had I been sleeping?" she asked.

"Well, you weren't exactly present."

Her head ached. It hurt to even blink.

"You had a panic attack."

"I was in a car accident," she pointed out.

"Because you were having a panic attack."

"Because I was being followed."

The doorbell rang. Billie glanced over and saw a feminine outline behind the cloudy glass. "You're expecting company. Now?"

"It's not what you're thinking," he said as he opened the door.

Dr Kulkarni entered the foyer, dressed in a gray wool coat and heels. White fabric peeked from beneath her outerwear.

"You called my doctor?" Billie said.

"I called a friend," Malley said.

Billie wanted to roll her eyes, but imagined the pain wasn't worth the judgement. Of course Malley knew Kulkarni. What hot middle-aged woman had he not bedded at this point?

"I don't typically make house calls," she said, dropping a medical bag at her feet. "Then again, who makes house calls in this day-and-age? But I'll make an exception for Billie, especially because it gives me the opportunity to say I was right."

That evoked an impressive eyebrow raise from Malley.

"I was in an accident," said Billie emphatically.

"You then had a panic attack," said Malley.

"Because someone tried to kill me." She massaged her forehead. "How many times do I have to say this?"

Kulkarni sat next to her on the couch and took out a blood pressure cuff. Billie pushed up her sleeve, exposing bare arm.

"Bruising?" asked the doctor.

"My head hurts," said Billie. "The airbags weren't exactly gentle when," she cast Malley a look, "the other car slammed into me."

"Get a look at the driver?" he asked.

She shook her head and then regretted it. Wincing, she pressed a palm to her scalp. "Gray sedan."

From somewhere, Malley found his cell phone and began tapping fervently at the screen. "I'll have a lackey call local mechanics, see if any gray cars come in for body work. I'll also call a guy in transportation, see if we can pull footage from the traffic cams."

Dr Kulkarni pressed a stethoscope to Billie's chest and listened while Billie attempted to take big inhalations without breaking down.

"Gonna write you a script for Lexapro."

"I don't need meds–" Billie began, but Malley interrupted. "I'll pick it up."

Billie shot him a look, and he aimed one right back at her. "You need something to take the edge off."

"Then," said Kulkarni as she unwound her stethoscope, "you'll make an appointment with my office so we can see how it's working. Might have to play around with different brands and doses."

Billie sighed.

"We'll start you on a low dose. But you need to get into therapy. I can handle the pharmaceuticals; find someone who can handle…" She waved her hands around Billie's body like a magician unveiling an illusion, "…you."

Billie's voice took on a mocking tone. "Another Jew with an anxiety disorder." She sulked. "I'm a goddamn stereotype."

"We live in a modern society with stimulation coming at us all from all ends. Frankly, I'm shocked at the people who don't have an anxiety disorder." Kulkarni rose from the couch with her bag. Billie watched as the doctor skated a hand across Malley's stomach. "Saturday?"

Malley nodded, and Billie wondered if there was a script for an anti-nausea medication in that bag of tricks as well.

Kulkarni handed Malley a piece of paper. "Any pharmacy will fill it." Then she turned to Billie. "Call my office. I mean it."

Billie nodded and fell back onto the couch while Malley walked the pretty doctor to her car.

When he came back, he said, "I need to monitor you for concussion."

"I don't have a concussion," she said.

"Sure, let me take your word for it because you have a medical degree and everything. Forgot about that, Dr Levine."

A buzzing sound emanated from the bag at her feet. She scooped up her cell phone and noted the number on the screen. Suddenly, the phone's vibrations matched the fluttering in her chest. She tipped over and stuck her head between her legs.

Malley grabbed the phone from her and answered before she could stop him.

"This is Detective Malley. Who's this?"

"My dad," said Billie as the blood rushed to her head. She flipped back up and fell against the couch cushion.

"Mr Levine," said Malley. "Now's not a good time...This is Detective Doug Malley speaking...I'm helping her out... She's not feeling well...A family friend of your father's? Yeah, sure."

Billie held out her hand and beckoned for the phone. If she didn't deal with this now, she'd never get past it. Avoiding her father's communications would become a full-time gig. Her stomach would never unfurl itself every time her phone rang.

Malley obliged and Billie sighed. "Dad?"

"What's going on over there? You ok?"

"I've been better. Had a little car accident" – and panic attack – "so I'm resting."

"I'm sorry about that kiddo. I just need to know if you're coming to Sedona next month. Emily keeps asking. She needs a headcount."

"Next month?"

"Yeah. January 7th."

"Dad, that's like only a few weeks away."

"So? You freelance. You don't need to ask a boss to take time off."

"Ok, well, David would need to give more notice."

There was a scoff on the line, which to Billie's credit, she ignored. "When did you get engaged?" In the grand scheme of things, this wasn't an important point, but it brought to mind something that had been needling Billie for a while. Sure, some weddings could be planned within a week if one wanted, but most times venues had to be secured, dresses tried on, suits rented. Friends notified.

"Over the summer. What difference does it make?"

"You don't actually want us there," she said to him. "If you did, you would've called us in August. Instead, you've been hassling me to come to a wedding scheduled in three weeks."

"Need I remind you that you've been dodging my calls."

"Ok, so say I answered when you first rang. That would only put you one month out. You don't really want us there. Emily insisted you call us. You're trying to make her happy."

He said nothing, but Billie knew she was right.

"I can't come to your wedding."

"If it's about the money, I'll pay for the airfare."

Malley stared at her, probably wondering if she was capable of crushing a cell phone in her fist. She wondered too. "David messaged you last spring asking if you would help us get the roof repaired, and you said, and I quote, 'Not my problem.' Remember that? So no, I don't want you to pay for the airfare. I don't want to go. And I don't want you to call me anymore. You left. You wanted to enjoy the rest of your life, well you can do that, but you don't get to do it with my blessing. Understand?"

"Listen, kiddo–"

She hung up.

CHAPTER FORTY-FOUR

Malley left her with a blanket on her lap and a television remote in her hand. He had started to explain which buttons to press for cable, which controlled the TV, but she interrupted him with the wag of her phone. "Gonna watch Graham Norton on YouTube."

"Who?" Then a shake of his head. "Doesn't matter. I'm gonna get the script filled and then pick up dinner. We'll eat, and I'll drive you home."

"Where's the Oldsmobile?" she asked.

"Your Gramps gave me the name of a mechanic in Leonia, someone who owed him a favor, so I had it towed there."

Gramps was probably super pissed that she had smashed up Ken's car. Just another one of Ken's possessions that was now trashed.

"You want Chinese? Pizza?" he asked.

She shrugged. "I literally have no opinion."

"That apathy is a direct result of your brain shutting down to protect itself. I shouldn't have even asked."

He left, and she waited until she heard him pull away before she bolted from the couch (her skull instantly regretted that motion). She glanced around the living room. "If I were case files, where would I be?"

Detectives weren't CIA. They could, and often did, take documents home with them. There would be no Feds assigned to investigate Malley's basement.

There's an idea. Let's head to the basement.

Billie eased down two small flights of stairs, so short she could leap them if she wasn't concerned about twisting an ankle or causing more brain damage. She hoped that what she wanted was in Malley's home gym so she wasn't forced to rifle through his bedroom nightstand.

Malley's basement was nothing more than a man cave, which seemed superfluous since his entire house was free rein. Then again, for Malley to score with the ladies as much as he did, his home had to give the appearance of respectability, hence the new couch and lack of dirty underwear strewn about.

She noted a box, the kind people packed up when they got sacked from a company, next to the elliptical machine. She checked her watch. Malley had been gone merely minutes. This all felt too easy and she wondered if he had cameras set up for this very purpose.

"Get a grip, Levine. Malley is not using a nanny-cam to catch you snooping through his files." If she said it aloud, then it must be true.

She dropped to her knees and knocked the lid off the top. Sure enough, inside were piles of manila folders. She picked up the first one, but it contained nothing more than newspaper clippings of Malley's solved cases. She selected the next folder – mortgage documents.

"Dammit!" She felt like she was being set up.

Billie returned to the living room, her gaze moving upward toward the open doors in the hallway.

"Bathroom break," she said to no one because no one was there.

Obviously she bypassed the bathroom, and then proceeded down a hallway decorated with photos of Malley from his police academy days, before heading into the master bedroom, feeling squeamish as she did so. This was treasonous, but Aaron was in danger. God, for all she knew, he was–

Focus, Levine.

She opened Malley's closet door, checking the top shelves for boxes. There were none. He did have several suits, dress shirts, and slacks. A row of shiny Oxfords sat next to a pair of worn, black, military-style boots. They were dusty from disuse.

Turning her attention to the nightstand, Billie spotted an alarm clock – who had those anymore? – and a little notebook.

She felt ill at-ease, even though she wasn't combing through his porn collection – gag, gross, why did her brain go there? – but a little pad of paper.

She stopped herself and stared at the nightstand, noted how the notepad was tilted at a 45-, no 35-degree angle, its metal spirals facing the closet door. Its bottom edge lined up perfectly with the hexagonal design in the wood.

Then she picked it up and flipped through. Notes on Fatima. The neighbor. Mrs Amato supplying an alibi for her husband that Malley marked as questionable. Hmmm…

Then she saw a scrawled statement: *murder weapon – concrete statuette, origin unknown, Restitution people notified. Description not found on inventory list.*

The murder weapon was not on the inventory list? Is that what Malley was getting at? Maybe it wasn't from Karl's collection. Maybe it was some random object he acquired over time, that had not been confiscated by Nazis.

A car door slammed and Billie froze. Then a key in the lock. And the distinct smell of pork fried rice.

Shit!

She put the notebook back – 35-degree angle, facing the closet door – and darted into the bathroom.

"Billie?"

She flushed the toilet and washed her hands for good measure, making sure he could hear the water running.

She emerged from the hallway bathroom and said "better" even though Malley hadn't asked.

He eyed her oddly as he hefted up the takeout bag. "Wonton soup?"

She nodded and grinned, but felt it was too much and dropped the smile. "That sounds good."

When she came down the stairs, Malley had set out the food on the dining room table. A pill bottle sat next to a water glass.

"There's only a month's supply. Ten milligrams. Meant to tide you over until you can get into Kulkarni's office," he said.

She rattled the plastic. For some reason, the small amount made it seem worse. Like she had to ration her sanity.

"Take it with food. Your stomach isn't made of iron," he said.

"More like cotton candy, but sure." She popped a pill, swallowed, and stuck out her tongue.

"Cute," he said, gesturing to her with a spoon, "but you're not in an asylum."

"Yet."

Malley laughed and tossed her packets of duck sauce. For the remainder of the meal, they said little, but Billie had to admit: this felt nice.

She may not have Craig Levine as a father anymore, but she wasn't without decent men in her life.

CHAPTER FORTY-FIVE

Billie awoke the next morning from a Lexapro-induced slumber that left her with emotional apathy and terrible breath.

Malley had driven her home last night, but she didn't remember the climb into bed, which would also explain why she was still dressed in yesterday's jeans and heavy socks.

She recoiled at her own odor and tossed the covers off. Glancing back at her pillow, she wondered if she could just go back to sleep for the next year – Rip Van Winkle her life away – but alas, her bladder won the round.

She got up to pee and passed David in the hallway.

"You look like shit," he said.

"Thank you, Captain Obvious," she replied as she pushed past him into the bathroom. Outside the closed door, David said, "You need to see someone about this."

"Can't hear you!" she cried over the running water, even though she heard him perfectly well.

"You need help!" he yelled. "Why not see Dr Arvita? She's my shrink, and she's great."

She finished brushing her teeth and flung open the door, a towel pressed to her chin and neck. "I don't have health insurance, David. Therapy might be a ways off."

"What about seeing the rabbi?"

"Are you out of your mind?"

"No, you're right. Also the rabbi can't prescribe meds, and I don't think talk therapy is going to do you any good."

"Kulkarni prescribed me Lexapro. My tongue is all gross and I'm groggy. How can I work like this? I can barely think."

"There will be side effects, but they go away after a while." He leaned against the wall, arms crossed, his posture thoughtful. He snapped his fingers. "Kentwell offers counseling."

She went back upstairs to her attic bedroom, David on her heels, not taking the hint. "I can't think about therapy right now. I have more immediate concerns." She rummaged through dirty laundry and unearthed a pair of jeans. Billie smelled the crotch. Clean enough. "I first need to find Aaron, then I need the BCDB to drop the charges against Aaron. And after all that, as an added bonus, I need you to figure your shit out with Matty. And once that's all done, I need people to give me space."

If David was upset, his laughter belied any offense. "None of that's ever going to happen. You need to learn how to cope." He wiggled his fingers around his head, making it look like fireworks were going off. "Your brain is on the fritz. Taking meds will sort it out."

"News alert: my brain is always going to be on the fritz. That's my future." She opened up her dresser, found her last clean pair of underwear, and slammed closed the drawer. There wasn't even time to do a load of laundry.

"You're irritable."

"Yeah, no shit."

"All that anxiety leads to brain shrinkage," he said.

She stopped, turned around slowly. "What do you mean?"

"Anxiety and depression, if gone untreated, can shrink your brain." He blinked at her, waiting for the realization to register. His voice softened as if he just realized what he said, "Or so I've heard."

Dr Kulkarni made no mention of that yesterday.

"My brain is already going to shrink," she hissed.

"You don't know that."

They both stared at each other for a minute, and then Billie collapsed onto her bed and began to cry.

David sat down beside her and rubbed her arm. "You cannot do this alone. I've been saying it forever. You can't solve everyone's problems yourself. Aaron gets into trouble, let him find a way out. Me and Matty? We'll work out our issues together. We don't need you for that. And Esha? Well, you're the proprietor of Levine Investigations. You don't need her employment. Unless you don't want to do this anymore, which is fine. There are plenty of other places to work."

While that might be true, no other job could ever make her feel this much alive. She sat up and wiped her snotty face with her Bubble Guppies pillowcase. "I have a headache."

David rose from the bed. "I'll make a pot of coffee and set out ibuprofen for you on the kitchen counter. I do think you need to rein in your caffeine intake."

"Baby steps," she mumbled into her pillow.

After David left, Billie fell back onto her pillow. Paralyzed by inertia, she felt around her nightstand until her hand encountered her cell phone.

Billie dialed Nicole.

She picked up and said, "I sense something is wrong."

"Everything," said Billie.

She heard Nicole rustle around a bit. An object was being handled and set back down. There was a gulp of liquid and suddenly, as if flicking a light switch, the noises settled. "Ok," said Nicole. "I'm all ears. Spill it."

So Billie did, talking Nicole's ear off for twenty minutes, only taking a breath every so often to sob.

After what seemed like an eternal pause, Nicole finally said, "Aw, honey. I'd be having a mental breakdown too."

"I miss the days where our biggest problems were finding vintage shops that stayed opened after 4pm," said Billie in between shaky breaths. "Or trying to write a history paper with three hours to spare before deadline."

"Me too."

"Who would've guessed that those days would be the easy ones?"

"Not me," said Nicole.

"Worst part is the only person who can help me track down Roza is freaking Jeremy Yang," said Billie.

"I don't think that's the worst part," said Nicole.

"Feels like it. He's not exactly forthcoming."

Nicole took another sip of whatever liquid she was drinking. At this hour, espresso. "If you need his help, demand his help. You're a tough broad; you can get people to listen to you. He has office hours. Go to his office."

Billie exhaled a shaky breath. "You're right. I will."

"And when this is all done," said Nicole, "we're going to dinner at a nice place where they give you warm bread on the table, and we're *not* going to talk about work or men or stress or crazy European women with revenge schemes."

"That sounds great," said Billie. Then after a beat, "Only what would we talk about?"

CHAPTER FORTY-SIX

Billie waited for Jeremy outside his office. Leaning against a bulletin board, she watched as several students popped in and out of the room, one fleeing with wet eyes. She wanted to offer a sympathetic pat and say no man was worth crying over, but that was patronizing at best and hypocritical at worst. Billie found herself constantly skirting a knife's edge of tears, and Aaron was at the center of it. Last night, she bawled over a YouTube ad for a pharmaceutical company because the actor suffering from psoriasis was wearing a leather bomber jacket.

Finally, the office door opened and Jeremy emerged. He took one look at Billie, and rather than sprint off in the opposite direction like she had expected, he grumbled into his cell and spun his wrist in a hurried crisis-alert pattern. He hissed at her, "Get over here."

She found herself getting weepy again, overwhelmed by relief, and then pissed at his demanding tone.

"What the hell?" she started, until Jeremy ushered her into his office. He mouthed 'State Department source' and pressed a button on his phone. "You're on speaker. Can you repeat that for Billie?"

"Uh, sure," said a woman. "Roza doesn't have a nephew–"

Billie cut Jeremy with a confused look just as his gaze narrowed.

"She has a son, and he attends college in New Jersey."

Jeremy grinned. However, for a nanosecond, Billie felt dirty.

It was real sleazy using someone's kid to get to them. But she got over it quick. This was how they would save Aaron.

"Hope he's close," said Billie. "Just our luck, we'll have to drive to freaking Rowan or something."

Jeremy shushed her.

"No, it's Kentwell," said the woman. "Much closer."

Man, when stars aligned, they really freaking aligned.

"What's his name?" Jeremy asked. "I doubt he's registered under Filipek. I mean, would you register for college under a World's Most Wanted name?"

Billie wasn't sure. Aaron only went through life as Aaron Goff, which both opened doors and slammed them in his face in equal measure.

The woman said, "Tytus Nowak."

Jeremy uttered a thanks before disconnecting the call.

"Tytus?" asked Billie, frowning. "Isn't he your–"

"Student," Jeremy said before frowning himself. "Wait, has he been playing me? You know the amount of work I've assigned him in regards to Roza Filipek?"

"Someone's not a good judge of character," Billie said in a singsong voice.

He cast her a side-glance. "Yeah, I'm seeing that."

"Do you know where he lives?"

"Fellman, I think. Not sure of the room number. I could check my Google docs, I think I ask for that information at the start of term."

But Billie was already on the phone, texting Nicole an S.O.S. "How do you spell his name?" Billie asked Jeremy, who was still frowning. She knew how he felt at that moment, that emotional implosion when people turn out to be liars. She snapped her fingers at him to get his attention.

"Uh," he said. "N-O-W-A-K. Tytus is spelled with a Y."

She tapped anxiously on her phone, then waited several seconds before she received an incoming message. "Fellman 207."

Billie thanked Nicole, feeling proud and in control. For once she was steering the ship and not merely being tossed about by stormy waves. When she turned around, Jeremy had already taken off.

After this was all over, Billie resolved that she would forget about Jeremy Yang. Sure, she needed his help now. But there was no way their lives would intersect again.

She would make sure of it.

CHAPTER FORTY-SEVEN

Last month, Billie had spent a lot of time in Fellman Hall when she was chasing down a missing college girl. Now Billie was on the hunt for an international art thief's son. For a girl who graduated from college two years ago, she sure as shit focused too much energy on a school that gave her nothing more than a diploma and debt. She also questioned Kentwell's admission standards – perhaps they should vet their students more closely. They could've started with her.

Billie pressed her ear to the dorm room door, listening for sound, only for Jeremy to edge her out of the way and rap his knuckles. "Knock like a normal person."

She then pushed him aside as she banged the door with the edge of her fist. "Like you mean it."

"Just a sec," said a voice.

Billie raised her brows. "See?"

Tytus Nowak appeared in a holey black T-shirt and sweatpants. Billie noted his tattooed arms and myriad of facial piercings. His hair had been recently bleached, the roots nearly green from the chemicals.

"Prof Yang?"

Jeremy pushed past Billie and into the boy's room. "We need to talk."

"About the final exam? Or the conference paper because I have some ideas."

There it was: that Polish accent. So subtle that Billie could've missed it had she not been hours-deep in YouTube documentaries.

Billie followed Jeremy inside and smiled apologetically for the intrusion, because it wasn't Tytus's fault that his mother was a nightmare. Were toxic parents ever the fault of their kids? Of course not.

"No, not the final, although I'd like to hear your thoughts for the conference paper because the topic is due in January. No, wait." Jeremy shook his head as if clearing the cobwebs of deception. "You played me. Your mom is Roza Filipek."

"Oh."

Billie did her best impression of a witch and cackled. She took up residence on the bed. "You had to know this would come out eventually."

Jeremy grabbed a desk chair and sat on it backwards. "Has the FBI been here to see you?"

Tytus furrowed his brow. "The FBI?"

"You playing dumb?" said Billie, suddenly aiming for bad cop but sounding more like a bad person.

Tytus replied, "I'm not playing anything."

"How could you never mention that your mom is Roza Filipek?" said Jeremy.

Tytus's eyes darkened. "We're not close. I didn't think it mattered."

"That's a big fucking detail to let slide," said Jeremy. "Since she's been the center of my academic work for years."

Billie got up from the bed and roamed around the space, opening up desk drawers. She found a glass bong, some rolling papers, and condoms. She held up the box of lubricated Trojans and raised her brows. Tytus said nothing. She put them back. She wondered if this was how Malley felt every time he interrogated a potential suspect. Powerful. And kinda creepy.

"You can't come in here and look through my stuff. This is a violation."

"Where's your mom right now?" Jeremy asked.

"I don't know. St Barts? Virgin Islands? I haven't seen her in years."

"Except that isn't really true," said Jeremy.

"Not true at all," Billie repeated.

Tytus's Adam's apple bobbed.

Billie continued to case the room. She went over to the cork board above his desk and noted the class schedule.

"It's not what you think," said Tytus. "I'm not playing you. I don't like my mom. She's never been a parent; she's a stranger."

"So why hide it?" Jeremy asked.

"Because then you would assume ulterior motives. Like now."

Billie read off his classes. "Criminal Psychology. History of the Iron Curtain. Modern Art." She turned to Tytus and said, "What's this all about?"

Tytus shrugged. "The history class helps me understand who my family is – the grandparents I never met – and where they came from. The psych class teaches me my mom's motivations. The art class helps me grasp how much her business is worth." He turned to Jeremy. "The truth is: she didn't raise me. An uncle did. But she pays for college. I don't like her, but I owe her."

Billie softened. "No, you don't. We aren't asked to be brought into the world. They owe us everything; we owe them nothing."

Jeremy gave her a look just then. She wanted to scream at him to stop.

Then she said to Tytus, "But you do owe me. Roza's holding my boyfriend hostage. You enjoy being an American college student?" She went back for the big box of condoms and produced them as evidence. "You like banging whoever it is you're banging? You want that to continue? Then you need to tell me where she is."

Tytus glanced from Jeremy to Billie and then back to Jeremy, seemingly requesting help.

He said, "You say I don't owe her anything, but maybe I owe her loyalty."

"Listen," Billie said, trying to appeal to their shared trauma. "I'm struggling with my own father. Despite how shitty he makes me feel, I still love him. Which is sorta worse, you know? It would be much easier if I didn't. There are times that I wish he was more of a son-of-a-bitch so that I could hate him and feel justified. Instead, I mostly feel sad. I can't tell you how many times I think I should be a better daughter. I should call him more often, see how he's doing. I should be more patient, more understanding. He's only human after all. Whenever I think of my dad, I think of the ways I could try and make things better, and it's not fair. I didn't do anything wrong, but I feel guilty for how things aren't."

Tytus said nothing.

"It's not a kid's job to fix their parent," she added, while waving her hand over his course schedule. "You can't take a psych class or a criminology class to better understand your mother and why she isn't the parent she should be. The only way you're going to do that is if you talk to her, and that's only if you want to. She should be extending the olive branch here, not you. Except in this case, you're going to have to contact her because I need to get my boyfriend back."

Jeremy got up from the chair. He looked like he wanted to say something to Billie but she shot him a look – *do it and you're dead*.

Tytus fell onto his bed. "She wants to see me for Christmas."

"Nearby?" asked Jeremy.

"Poconos," he said. "A little estate in Dingmans Ferry. Secluded with a warehouse for her art collection. Your boyfriend is likely being held there."

"Why the Poconos?" Jeremy asked.

"No local law enforcement, just State Police that barely monitor the speed limit, let alone the comings and goings of a woman and her entourage on a piece of private property. Also, she likes it out there. It's pretty."

"We'll need GPS coordinates," said Billie.

Tytus grabbed a pen off his roommate's desk and jotted down an address which he passed off to her.

There was a knock at the door. Tytus closed his eyes, a brief moment of reprieve. Tonight had been a lot. "That's my girlfriend. Please don't mention any of this to her, ok? She thinks my mom died."

"Wouldn't that make everything easy?" Billie mumbled.

Jeremy nodded, glanced at Billie, who also nodded. Jeremy fixed the cuffs of his jacket and said, "We'll leave."

Tytus opened the door and then took several steps back, hitting the desk and rattling the monitor on top. It was as if he'd been thrust into the furniture by cannonball fire.

A behemoth of a man with a shiny bald head and a tattoo on his neck entered.

He spoke to Tytus in Polish, then jerked his chin at Billie.

"He wants us to come with him," said Tytus.

"Yeah, I gathered that. Tell him 'No thank you.'"

"I don't think it was a request," said Jeremy.

"Gathered that also," she hissed.

The man flashed his gun. Billie didn't need a translator to know what this meant. If the remaining students in the dorm were to be safe, Billie, Jeremy and Tytus needed to exit the building with little fuss.

She had been worried about locating Aaron. But she supposed that being led to him, even at gunpoint, was better.

As the goon forced the three of them into a black Suburban, all she could hope was that Aaron was still alive, and that somehow when this was all over, she would live to see another panic attack.

CHAPTER FORTY-EIGHT

Billie hadn't been this far north since her parents booked a camping trip in Stokes State Forest. It had rained the entire weekend; the local area lost power; and the grilled cheese she had ordered at a nearby diner caused her to vomit up her guts at 2am. Her father had been pretty cool back then – waking up with her, holding her hair back as she upchucked into a wet pile of leaves while David slept peacefully.

After they had been relieved of their cell phones, and by relieved, their phones had been purposefully crushed under the Suburban's tires, Jeremy had been forced to sit up front. Billie and Tytus sat together in the back with the understanding that if anyone tried anything, they would be tossed out of the car and into traffic on Route 80.

That was all said in Polish which Tytus translated.

"Tytus," she leaned in and whispered, "what are we headed into?"

He dipped his chin and brought his hands to his mouth as if scratching his stubble. He mumbled, "Several armed guards will be stationed in and around the compound. Your boyfriend'll be in one of two outbuildings. He'll either be in the red barn, or the climate-controlled warehouse in the back of the property."

The driver spoke harshly from the front, startling them all.

Tytus muttered something in Polish, which elicited a grunt from the driver. Billie decided it was too risky to ask more questions.

The Suburban exited off the interstate and merged onto Route 15; this highway was smaller and more provincial, the speed limit also highly enforced by local Jersey cops. The SUV began a deliberately lawful pace as they passed an army base, gas stations, a mega-church and more gas stations, including a Wawa and QuickChek on opposite corners.

Eventually they headed beyond the Sussex County Fairgrounds where the open fields were barren and desolate with only a light layer of gray snow to protect their dignity, and then on to the woods with naked trees. This stretch of road seemed more sad than festive.

"We're gonna cross into Pennsylvania," the driver grunted. "You say nothing. Understand?"

No one responded.

The driver took out his gun and suddenly everyone was like, "Understand!"

The Suburban rattled across an old, wooden bridge, so narrow it was like a balance beam. Billie waited for them to scratch the paint of an oncoming car – that would actually be a relief, they'd have to stop and address it – but the driver managed to cross like Simone Biles.

An old man in a safety vest and name tag collected the toll. "Drive safe," he said kindly.

Billie would've been charmed by it all if they weren't heading into a literal death trap.

They passed by more stretches of trees, a pizzeria, and a Dollar General until Tytus pointed to a turn in the road that if Billie sneezed, she'd have missed.

Roza's henchman eased onto a gravel driveway.

"There are security cameras everywhere," whispered Tytus as the SUV passed through an electronic gate with barbed wire. Ahead were a farmhouse and two buildings as well as three shipping containers, all labeled with the Amato's International Moving and Storage insignia, lined up like soldiers. Some were attached to trailers and others abandoned.

The driver stopped and several more thick-necked men approached the car, each waving guns. Doors were opened, and Billie was tugged out of the vehicle. Her elbow was grabbed roughly by a man with scars crisscrossing his cheeks.

As they were marched toward the compound, Tytus exhaled cold breath.

Another henchman grabbed Jeremy and pushed him in a different direction, toward a crop of outbuildings behind the house, just as Tytus had described: one blue, one red. "If I'm murdered," Jeremy hissed. "I'll haunt the living hell out of you."

"Fair," she said.

The goon said something in Polish and Tytus translated, "He's taking us to the house. We're going to see my mom."

CHAPTER FORTY-NINE

Billie and Tytus were escorted to an old farmhouse perched atop a hill that sat in front of the two modern outbuildings. The farmhouse was charming in the way old homes often were. White paint, green shutters, rickety steps. What ruined the house of its history, though, was the cameras bolted to corner eaves, and the mechanical buzzing sounds that followed Billie's movement. She couldn't blink without setting off an electronic lens.

When they entered the house, what would have been a parlor was clearly being used as an operations center. Large monitors covered one wall. Mechanical eyes grazed the compound, and one specifically pointed at a man tied to a chair, his mouth covered with duct tape, his head lobbed to the side.

Aaron.

Billie lunged, as if she could save him through the screen, only for another one of Roza's colossal men to block her path. He forcibly turned her around and shoved her toward the living room where Tytus was already waiting.

Roza Filipek sat in an upholstered chair, sipping from a floral teacup. She wore yoga pants and a slouchy top as if headed to the gym rather than running a criminal empire in the middle of nowhere. She gestured toward a spread of food on a nearby table and addressed her son in Polish, but Tytus responded in English, "Not hungry."

"Is Aaron alive?" Billie jerked her chin toward the monitor

in the other room. The amount of self-control she mustered to not run from the house and toward the building out back could tranquilize an elephant.

Roza made a face. "For now."

Billie stepped toward her only to be anchored into the couch by a meaty palm.

Roza turned to her son. "You will come home to Poland. The United States is not a safe place to do business anymore."

"No," said Tytus. "I like it here."

"I'm not asking."

"I'm not leaving."

It occurred to Billie, not for the first time, that stand-offs happened to all parents and children, regardless of culture, socio-economic status, or criminal inclinations.

Tytus implored, "Stay here and be my mother."

"And do what? Shop at Target? Complain about my wrinkles? Join a book club?"

"Yes. Those are normal mom things, and there's nothing wrong with them."

Roza set down her teacup and Billie noted the restraint in how she placed the saucer on the table, slow and deliberate, using two hands.

"I *am* a mother," said Roza. "I work so you can have your expensive high-tops and nice car. So you can take that dumb girlfriend of yours on Caribbean vacations. And what do you give me in return? You don't answer my calls or texts. You don't come home for the holidays. I have to sneak into this country to see you. I have to threaten a Jewish girl to see you."

"I don't owe you anything," said Tytus, not just echoing Billie's words to him earlier, but glancing at her as if seeking her approval. A look that didn't go unnoticed by his mother.

Billie sank into the couch.

Roza nearly growled when she said, "I'm selling off the art."

Tytus narrowed his eyes at her. "Really?"

"A Colombian delegation is coming to buy it."

Billie couldn't help herself. "Delegation?"

Roza waved her hand about. "I was being polite. Didn't want to come across as racist. You Americans and your racism." She followed that with an eyeroll. Then when Billie clearly wasn't picking up the hint, Roza clarified, "A cartel. Cartagena."

"Cartagena?" said Billie. "The Vargas cartel?"

Roza waved this away. "Yes. Vargas. Armando is coming."

"Armando Vargas is coming?" said Billie, still trying to process what she was hearing.

"Yes," said Roza impatiently. "Armando Vargas."

Billie couldn't help but be impressed. Vargas was notoriously elusive; rumors circulated that he frequently changed his appearance to thwart law enforcement. Morales once told her that Vargas had avoided capture by living most of his adult life on a yacht in international waters. Cocaine profits yielded a really big yacht.

"Nearly a billion dollars is at stake," Roza said to Tytus. "We'll be set."

Tytus leaned forward. "So why can't I stay in New Jersey? At Kentwell?"

"Why can't you come back to Poland? Don't you want to be with me?"

Tytus slumped back in the chair, and Billie noted the fight leaving him.

"I've given you everything," said Roza. "All I ask is that you return to Poland. There's more than enough money. You don't need school."

"I like school."

"Then you can like it in Poland."

"You don't even like Poland," said Tytus. "All those stories of you growing up without anything."

"You have everything because I provided! This isn't up for debate. You will go."

Roza snapped her fingers, and a man with dark hair emerged from the shadows and grabbed Tytus at the bicep. "Hey!"

"Put him in the bedroom," she said. "We leave tonight."

"What about Aaron?" Billie asked.

Roza ignored her and rattled off what Billie could only assume were instructions in Polish.

A set of hands grabbed her and she found herself being hauled to her feet. As she passed by the monitors, she noted several black SUVs on camera. Billie didn't need a translator to understand that the Colombians had arrived.

"Take her upstairs," said Roza.

CHAPTER FIFTY

Billie was dumped in a bedroom with peeling wallpaper and antique furniture. The room was dark, as was the sky. The only light that filtered in was from outside shadows caused by SUV headlamps.

She peeked through sheer curtains to see an army of men with beards and military-style weaponry. Roza's fair European crew was a direct contrast to the Colombians, like sides of the moon.

There was no point in screaming for help. The Vargas cartel was unlikely to hear her, and frankly, she didn't want their rescue.

Roza or Armando Vargas? There was no lesser of two evils here.

She was more worried about Aaron than herself. She, at least at this moment, was healthy with all body parts intact. Aaron was beaten up and bloodied. He'd be lucky to only have a few fractures. Who knew if there was internal bleeding? Jesus Christ, she needed to get him out of there.

She wondered if the room was being guarded from the outside. She pressed her ear to the door, trying to discern breathing of any kind. All she could hear were voices from the front yard, a mixture of Polish, Spanish, and English. A United Nations of bad guys.

She groaned in frustration.

A voice from outside the door said, "Are you hurt?"

"Tytus? How are you free?"

"This isn't the first time I've been locked inside a room. I know how to help myself. I'm going to kick down the door. Ok?"

Billie backed herself against the far corner. "Ready."

She heard a foot connect with solid wood, or maybe it was a shoulder. Then a grunt. "Wait a second."

Say what she wanted about Craig Levine – he never locked her in a room. Didn't make him any less a difficult dad, though, just made him *not* a criminal.

A minute or two passed before the door suddenly split like an egg, the edge of an ax protruding from the center. Like Lizzie Borden, Tytus took a few more whacks until he was able to cut a hole big enough for Billie to climb through.

She fell onto the hall carpet in a heap. She wanted to stay down there forever, mental exhaustion overwhelming any physical tiredness, but Tytus helped her to her feet. "The warehouse," she said.

"The Colombians."

Pressing herself up against the wall, Billie made her body as flat as possible. "Where are the bodyguards?"

"Everywhere," he said.

"Excellent."

Billie and Tytus slipped down the stairs, past the now empty monitoring room, and into the night. They ducked their heads and crept past a black vehicle, where a dark-haired man smoked a cigarette. Another held an automatic rifle at the ready.

As Billie scrambled around an Amato shipping container, Tytus ran in the opposite direction, swallowed up by inky swaths of woods. So much for banding together.

She placed her hands on the cold ground to situate herself. The farmhouse sat in front of a blue metal building where Tytus had said Aaron was most likely being held. The red barn was fifty yards from there. She had also spotted a hedge separating the backyard, or what would be a backyard if normal people resided here, from the two outbuildings.

Voices meandered her way, all in accented English, the shared language of those who would not hesitate to kill her.

She had to move.

She crawled along the hedges before darting to a darkened corner where the barn's pitched roof and wall created a shadowy alcove. She slunk around the side of the barn, her coat snagged by rusted nails and splintered panels, until she came to a darkened window.

It was nearly impossible to see past the grimy glass, but she managed to spy stalls and dried hay.

Billie wondered if Tytus had gotten it wrong. A bloodied man seemed like an unsettling prop for a business meeting. Perhaps Aaron was just on the other side of the wall. She inched around the building and found the double doors slightly ajar.

Billie sucked in her stomach so as not to disturb potential squeaky hinges and shimmied inside. She sank down to avoid grungy windows and glimpsed stalls that at one point housed horses. She only found decaying piles of hay.

No Aaron.

But she did, however, stumble upon Jeremy Yang, shackled to a chair with plastic zipties. A sizable piece of duct tape covered his mouth. His eyes widened, then narrowed. She couldn't see his mouth, but she could read his expression. And he wasn't exactly happy to see her.

Billie sighed. "Hold on," she whispered as she approached him, pinching the edge of the tape between her fingers. "This will probably hurt." She was not gentle as she ripped off the tape, but to Jeremy's credit, he did not scream. He did say, "I'll fucking get you back for that."

"Yeah, yeah. I gotta find something to cut those binds."

She began a quick tour of the barn, but aside from gray straw, it seemed empty.

A tap on her shoulder caused her to spin around and land a punch in soft tissue. Tytus bent over and wheezed.

She covered her mouth with a hand, then leaned over him as he gulped in air. She had gotten him right in the belly. While he tried to draw in breath, he reached into his pocket and handed her a small, folded knife.

Billie hesitated, her hand hovering around his shoulder, but he waved her off so she could cut Jeremy loose. Which she did to lackluster gratitude.

As Jeremy rubbed his wrists, he grumbled, "I'd let the motley crew of bodyguards outside kill you if I didn't think it would be so unsatisfying."

Tytus rounded the bend, looking as green as the roots of his hair. "This way."

They approached the barn doors just as the shadow of a man passed by, and they instinctively ducked.

Billie mouthed, "Aaron."

Jeremy rolled his eyes. Tytus nodded and pointed outside, presumably toward the blue building.

They waited several beats before sliding out of the barn doors. Billie spotted a tractor and signaled that she was moving toward it. The guys followed her, darting beside its large wheels.

The warehouse's garage door was open and inside was lit up like an atomic blast.

Roza was sitting across from a man – tall, fit, dark hair – with an obscured face. On one side were his Colombian worker bees – men in black jackets, fatigue pants fit for a private army – and on Roza's side, men thick as redwoods, with ashy hair and light eyes. Some that had seen an Iron Curtain fall and figured out how to use the rubble to their advantage.

And almost between them, propped up by two men, was Aaron.

Billie stifled a gasp. This close, he barely appeared to be breathing. Logic left her at that moment as she spied a tire iron near the tractor. She started to reach for it when an arm shot out and yanked her back hard.

Jeremy hissed in her ear, "You'll get us all killed." He vehemently shook his head, but Billie couldn't let Aaron suffer like this. She began struggling just as Roza barked an order and a man appeared with an easel. She snapped her fingers and another man lay a canvas on top. "Chagall," she said.

Then she pointed around her in a clockwise fashion, spouting off names Billie had only ever seen in museums. "Klimt. Manet. Renoir. Matisse."

"I assume you won't mind, but I brought a man to authenticate," said the Colombian cartel boss, who at that point, Billie assumed was Armando Vargas, except–

She stopped flailing because she recognized that voice, although the accent had been exaggerated.

He pointed to a man who cut the figure of a tree limb.

Ruiz.

Detective Ruiz.

Esteban Morales turned around and caught Billie's eye. So much for her hiding place. His expression nearly slipped, but he held on. He beckoned to Ruiz and whispered in Spanish. Ruiz nodded and approached the first painting – a Chagall – with a leather bag. He opened it, withdrew a tool, and leaned over to scrutinize the canvas.

Billie wanted to stay for the performance, but if Morales was here, she had to imagine that meant the FBI was lurking in darkened crevices. She had to get to Aaron before stray bullets got to him first.

This charade would only last so long before Roza got suspicious that the cartel men were nothing more than North Jersey coppers with Sherlock Holmes-style technology.

Morales grimaced at Aaron. "Can you get him out of here? He's diminishing the artwork."

Roza nodded and the two soldiers hoisting up Aaron's broken body dragged him away, his black boots leaving trails of rubber along the floor. He fell in a heap by a machine, a large-scale dehumidifier if Billie had to guess.

That was her moment, but to reach him would expose her to Roza, the fake cartel, and the FBI agents who may or may not be behind her.

Ruiz gave a curt nod, and Morales twirled his finger in the air. "We have a deal."

Roza's men gathered the artwork, rewrapping canvases in plastic wrap, burying frames in crates, the tips of gilded wood sinking beneath waves of insulation. They carried boxes outside, presumably toward the empty Amato trucks. The art would have to be secured before law enforcement made their move. No way would they endanger invaluable cultural artifacts that hadn't been seen in nearly a century. Billie was certain that her life wasn't worth one missing Chagall, at least not to the government.

She then heard muffled voices just off to the side. This felt like the moment. Whatever was about to go down was going down now.

She took her chance and ran toward Aaron.

Gathering her arms around his chest, she tried dragging Aaron toward the door, but he was too heavy. She briefly wondered if she could disguise him with a giant tarp. Toss a piece of plastic over him and hope no one noticed, then smuggle him out in the morning.

Detective Morales spied her again and began barking orders loudly in Spanish. He pointed aggressively toward the last crate as it was moved by Roza's men out of the building and into the night. He beckoned to his partner Ruiz with a snap of his fingers; a laptop was brought to a flimsy table where Roza waited as Morales typed a passcode. "Money is transferring," he said. An electronic payment to one of her many bank accounts, Billie assumed. Hope Roza liked her money cold as it was about to get frozen.

Once the status bar filled in, Roza held out her hand for a formal end to the transaction. Billie watched as Morales stared at the gesture, probably imagining slapping on a metal bracelet. But, alas, that fancy suit didn't hide handcuffs very well.

Instead, Morales bent down and kissed Roza's knuckles. Roza smiled and said, "You want the girl?" She jerked her chin toward Billie and Aaron, their hiding spot betraying them now that the building had emptied out. "The boy must die, but the girl is yours."

Billie halted.

So, unfortunately, did Morales. Vargas was known for trafficking in women, and Morales's brief hesitation – hell, the fact that he hadn't asked if he could take Billie – proved to be a mistake. He'd blown his cover.

Roza cried out in Polish. Men swarmed the area; guns discharged. Morales screamed Billie's name, but she was focusing too much on trying to drag Aaron to the building's side door, the best exit to make it to the surrounding woods.

"Aaron, you need to get up," she said tugging on his sleeve, but also fearing she was about to dislocate his arm. A bullet whizzed by her head and embedded itself into the aluminum wall. "Shit!" She dropped to the ground.

Men in Kevlar darted past a window. Aaron groaned. A voice said, "You take one arm; I'll take the other."

Jeremy wiggled under Aaron's frame and hoisted him up. Billie did the same. Another bullet barely missed her.

"Go! Go!" Jeremy cried.

Together they half-carried, half-dragged Aaron out of the building and toward the farmhouse, hoping to seek refuge among the trees. Morales's men – a mishmash of law enforcement from various agencies – yelled at them with guns aimed at their heads.

Morales ran from the blue building just as an explosion erupted, thrusting him into the line of shrubs that separated the yard from the rest of the compound. Billie moved toward him, but saw Ruiz, holding a walkie talkie, dart over and skid along ice, sliding into the dirt alongside Morales.

A hand grabbed her bicep, hauled her onto her feet, and threw her into the back of a van. Jeremy and Aaron quickly followed. Billie spotted the FBI insignia on a blanket that Jeremy was kind enough to drape over Aaron's shoulders. The pops of gunshots continued to pepper the night as a nameless driver took off down the driveway and toward, what Billie could only hope, was safety.

CHAPTER FIFTY-ONE

They were in a hospital because of course they were. Hackensack University Medical Center had sent out a chopper to life-flight Aaron to surgery. It wasn't just Aaron who needed medical attention; several FBI agents had gotten hurt, and some of Roza's people had been shot. A few were dead.

Roza was in the wind, and so initially had been Tytus, but he had shown up hours later in a Target parking lot in Rockaway, trying to flag down local law enforcement. They were the ones who contacted the Feds, and Tytus was probably being grilled like a steak on everything he ever knew about his mother.

She tried explaining all this to Aaron who was groggy from surgery. "They repaired your spleen," she told him. "Your insides bleed a lot. Did you know that?"

Aaron didn't bother opening up his eyes, just mumbled, "What's a spleen for again?"

"Dunno. I could google it, but I don't want to." She brushed back his hair, which was somehow both greasy and dry. He had shiners on both his eyes and a split lip. A tube was down his nose. He looked fragile underneath the blankets, hooked up to machines that monitored his vitals and dripped drugs into his system.

"Matty wants to come in, but I have to leave before they'll let him through," she said, getting up from the folding chair the nice nurse had set out for her.

Aaron reached out a hand. "Stay," he said, the word sounding like a breath.

She sat back down and took his palm. Hospitals made her antsy. She'd never relax in one, so having to feign calm took as much effort as trying to coax an elephant through a tunnel. "Were you working with the FBI this whole time?" she asked.

His moved his head side to side. A barely perceptible *no*.

Relief swelled inside her. Sure, it would've been comforting to know that Aaron had been on the right side of the law for a change, but to think that he could've been conspiring with the Feds to take down Roza Filipek, while Billie nearly combusted trying to save him from dying in the slammer, would've pushed her off a cliff.

Another thought needled her. "Do you think Malley knew about this?"

Aaron attempted a shrug.

Detective Esteban Morales opened the curtain that divided Aaron from other patients in the recovery room. He was still wearing that expensive suit – his cartel costume – but his arm was in a sling.

Billie jumped to her feet. "You can't question him."

"Relax, I'm not going to." Morales could only placate her with one hand. "He's untouchable. You can thank the FBI, CIA, Mossad, Interpol – I'm sure I'm missing some groups." It was great news but the way Morales had delivered it, Billie would've thought he had just said trucks with puppies had crashed on the Turnpike.

Morales ignored Aaron and spoke directly to Billie. "Roza's gone, and I blame you. This is your fault."

That metaphorical slap caused her to retreat a step. "I didn't help her."

Morales leaned in close. She smelled his cologne, felt his breath on her cheek. "My judgement has not been off because of Aaron; it was off because of you. I held back at the compound. I saw you, and I held back. And now's she gone."

"Seriously…" but she couldn't think of what else to say.

Morales grabbed Aaron's ankle and shook it with little tenderness. "Get well, Goff. And stay out of my sight." Morales saw himself out.

Billie glanced at Aaron's prone body and exhaled. "Let Matty come in. He's worried himself into an anxious mess, and he's making David nuts."

But Aaron had fallen asleep.

CHAPTER FIFTY-TWO

The next afternoon, Billie had arrived at Nicole's cubicle with the remnants of a headache that refused to relinquish its grip. She had been tempted to cancel lunch plans, but she was reminded of Nicole's past ire, how their friendship often hung on by delicate strands. How Billie frequently ran to Nicole for information – Jeremy's office hours for example – rather than ask her about her day. Billie often suspected that Nicole felt as used as Kleenex, and Billie wouldn't blame her if she did. So Billie had driven to Kentwell in a fog, her brain far too defeated to even fight.

Billie headed toward Nicole, who was dangling a black pump off her toe at a table in the faculty-only restaurant, and dropped into the opposite chair. A bubbling glass of seltzer waited for her.

"I'd hug you," said Nicole, "but I worry you'd disintegrate in my arms."

That got a much needed laugh out of Billie.

"I'm all right," said Billie. "Really. I think my brain is broken, but I'm holding it together. I'm taking Lexapro."

"How's that working for you?" Nicole asked.

"Too soon to tell, but I did watch a TikTok about a dog adoption and didn't cry, so it must be doing something."

Nicole flagged down a server. They ordered, Billie opting for whatever special was written on the chalkboard by the host stand. Nicole waited for the guy to leave before asking, "Aaron ok?"

"He'll live," said Billie, bobbing her chin several times as if the constant movement would stave off her emotions.

"It's ok to be overwhelmed," said Nicole. "Billie, in the past few months, you've been through a lot. I feel like I've lost count with how many times you've nearly been killed. You need to talk to someone." Nicole crossed her leg. "Hell, I should talk to someone about how many times you've nearly been killed."

"Funny." Billie sipped the seltzer and suppressed a growing burp. She ran her hand across her mouth.

"Seriously, Billie, Kentwell has counseling–"

Billie cut in, "Our food is here."

Nicole frowned. Then seeing what Billie ordered – meatloaf – her frown deepened and she gestured to the server. "Can you send this back for a turkey club?"

Billie sighed. "What did you do that for?"

Nicole stared at her for so long, Billie shifted uncomfortably in the chair.

Nicole said, "You ordered your least favorite food in the entire universe. Did you not realize that?"

Billie's reply was a quiet, "Oh." She should've read the specials board more closely.

Nicole picked up a knife and stabbed her chicken with a fork. "We're getting you some help."

At Nicole's insistence, Billie followed her back to her cubicle in the administration building. "You can say hi to Calvin," said Nicole as she shucked off her coat and draped it over a rack by her desk chair. A chair that was strangely inhabited by a man – a vainglorious teaching assistant who was super fortunate that Billie didn't carry a taser as a matter of habit. Granted, he had been kidnapped and tied up as a result of his connection to her, so she should be nice to him for the time being. A short time, but still.

"Oh, Professor Yang," said Nicole in mock surprise.

"Jeremy," said Billie.

"Levine," he replied.

Nicole made a performance of checking her cell phone screen. "Calvin ran out for a bit, so I'm afraid you'll have to see him another time. Jeremy, you wanna walk Billie out to her car?"

"That's not necessary," said Billie.

Jeremy steepled his fingers together as if he was going to reveal an evil plan. Billie began to fret that that was exactly what he was going to do. "Sure," he said, rising from the chair. "Follow me."

He brushed right past her and out of the office.

She debated on just standing there, but a shove from Nicole pushed her toward the exit.

"What are you doing?" she hissed to Nicole.

Nicole shoved her again. "Trust me."

"Traitor," Billie said to her before running after Jeremy. "We're not going to my car, are we?"

"Psych building," he said, zipping up his jacket as he pressed the elevator button.

Billie went straight for the stairwell door and scuttled down the steps. "No."

"Yes," Jeremy said, fast on her heels. "God, you're a stubborn child. You'd never make it in a Chinese household."

"I can't believe Nicole sold me out like this," she said, moving faster. "And why rope you into it?"

"Because she doesn't want to hurt your feelings, whereas I don't give a shit. And I'm the one with the connections. Vela was happy to do me a favor."

"I bet she was." Billie emerged into the lobby and darted outside. The air was frigid and yet she was sweating profusely. Her body couldn't regulate its own temperature. What the hell was the point of a hypothalamus?

Jeremy grabbed her arm and gently swung her around. "Listen, you can't function without help. Panic attacks–"

Her breath stopped, and she glanced furiously around to see who could hear.

He lowered his voice, "Panic attacks are nothing to be ashamed of, but they need to be managed. You need to see someone. If it makes you feel better, I scheduled a therapy session too. After all the shit that went down in the Poconos, I needed to talk to someone. You're a very stressful person to know."

"It doesn't make me feel better." Billie's eyes darted to the parking deck entrance. She wondered if she could make a break for it. She was a fast runner, although Jeremy wasn't bogged down by a bag. His coat seemed lighter too.

Jeremy sensed her flight response. "Vela is very popular, and she's doing me a favor. She made room for you. Please just get your ass to that appointment, so Nicole leaves me alone."

She stared at him. "Her boyfriend has connections in HR. Did she promise to expunge your file in exchange for this favor?"

"No?"

"So convincing," she retorted.

"If you do this, we can be out of each other's lives. How does that sound?" Jeremy held up his hand like he was going to swear on a Bible. "Scout's honor."

"Were you even a Boy Scout?" She closed her eyes and sighed. "Of course you were."

He gently tugged on her coat sleeve and pushed her toward the psychology building. "Vela is getting a Ph.D in Clinical Psychology. She's nice and smart and can probably tolerate you in ways I won't."

"I can't afford therapy," said Billie, practically dragging her feet. She noted a few college kids giving her weird looks. She supposed she did look like a petulant child being dragged into the doctor's office.

"It's all done on a sliding scale. She gets in her clinical hours; you pay her $30 a session."

For several seconds, Billie said nothing, which Jeremy took as consent.

He deposited her in front of a door and stood back with his arms crossed. He tilted his chin as if to say, 'Go on, knock, you looney.'

She turned to him and grumbled, "Are you going to be here when I get out?"

"Absolutely not," he said. "I don't care about you that much." Then, more softly, he added, "You're a big girl. You got this. Also you're Gen Z. Why are you so opposed to getting help?"

"I don't like talking about my feelings," she said plainly.

"No one does," he said. "You're not special. But being a human being is fucking hard, and there's no manual, so you do what you gotta do to function. Now knock."

So Billie knocked. A beautiful woman, mid-20s with dark hair and brown skin – the same woman who had attended Jenn Herman's wedding as Jeremy's date – opened the door and said, "Welcome, Billie. I'm Vela. Why don't you come in?"

Smiling at Vela in response, Billie turned to Jeremy and flipped him off. Then she mouthed to him 'fuck you forever' as she shut the door in his face.

CHAPTER FIFTY-THREE

When Billie turned around, Vela was opening and closing several desk drawers. "I bought a new box of Sharpie pens, and now I can't find one. I swear if Gregory stole them, you can solve that murder because I will kill him."

Billie couldn't help herself; she laughed. She wanted to be mad at Jeremy and Nicole for their underhanded conspiracy to get her into this room, but Vela's charm was no match for Billie's temper. "Confessions don't usually come that easy for me," said Billie. "I gotta work at it a bit more."

Vela grinned and rattled a cardboard box. "Found it."

"Lucky for Gregory," said Billie as she scanned the office, deciding to take residence on the little floral sofa across from the club chair that Billie suspected was where the therapist sat and said things like, "And how did that make you feel?"

Vela grabbed a manila folder from a mostly empty bookshelf, some sheets of paper, and a bottle of water. She set everything on the side table next to the chair and plunked down in triumph.

Tucking a long, dark strand of hair behind her ear – Billie could see why Jeremy was smitten with her (friend, my ass) – Vela clicked the pen. "We weren't formally introduced at the wedding. Jeremy is shit with manners."

Understatement of the year.

"Anyway, it is lovely to meet you," said Vela, as her hand moved across the paper. "And just to be upfront, these notes are for me and me alone. Anything said in these sessions is super-duper confidential."

"Super-duper? Is that a psych term?" Billie asked.

"Yes. I'm presenting a paper on it at a conference." Vela grinned. "You're funny."

"Uh, thanks," said Billie. "So are you."

"Do you often use humor as a defense mechanism?" Vela asked.

"Well, I'm Jewish, so..."

Again, Vela grinned. "Let's talk about why you're here."

Billie exhaled long and slow.

"It's a lot, huh?" said Vela.

Billie rubbed her hands along her thighs, trying to dry the sweat blooming in her palms. "How long are these appointments?"

"An hour."

Billie raised her brows.

"It's meant to be one of many," said Vela. "Rome wasn't built in a day, neither is therapy. I like to think that taking care of your mental health is the same as seeing to your physical health. Right? You go to the gym to be healthy. You come to counseling to be mentally healthy. There's no shame in this game. There's no stigma to using the rowing machine for good cardio. So no stigma in coming here."

"Yeah, but the rowing machine doesn't make me cry," said Billie without thinking.

"Is that something you're concerned with? Being vulnerable in front of someone?"

Oof. Was Vela a carpenter? Because she hit that nail on the head.

"My job requires me to be strong, proactive, and clear-headed. I can't be those things if I'm crying or having a panic attack in a mini-mall parking lot after crashing my car."

"There's a doctoral student in our department who does a lot of work with law enforcement, and the PTSD is staggering. As a private eye, your work is dangerous, I presume."

"Lately, it has been." Billie sighed and again ran her palms across her thighs before shaking them out, something Vela noted.

"You get a lot of tingling sensations?"

Billie nodded; Vela wrote that down.

"Stomach upset?"

Billie nodded; Vela wrote that down.

"Ruminating thoughts? Intrusive thoughts?"

"Not intrusive, but my brain is actively trying to bring up things I had hoped to avoid thinking about."

"What kind of things?" said Vela.

"I don't know: everything I have to do. The laundry list of responsibilities. My mom has early-onset Alzheimer's disease, so I work to pay the bills and take care of her. My dad split years ago when the burden of her diagnosis was too big for him to handle."

"You're twenty-four?"

"Twenty-five in June."

"That's a lot for you to deal with at your age." Vela couldn't have been much older.

"I know, but shit still has to get done," said Billie. "I can't let my mom suffer. I can't make my father be a better person and send money to help. I can't sit by and let my boyfriend succumb to nefarious people who want to harm him. I have to earn a living. I have to food shop and clean and make sure my grandfather doesn't drink himself into oblivion. Although to be fair, he's been sobering up lately. I'm not in college anymore; I have to be an adult or we can't survive."

"Do you enjoy your career? Because investigative work of any kind sounds really stressful."

"It's stressful," said Billie. "But I'm good at it. I can help people, really help people, and I have. It's just, I can't seem to help myself."

Vela scribbled that down, and said, "What do you mean?"

"Well, for one thing, I don't know how to relax. I also let everything get to me. There's no reason for my father's words to hurt so much. I want to ignore him. Part of me never wants to talk to him again, and then I think about how sad that is. Like, this is my dad. I feel so guilty for how I feel about him. My boyfriend, Aaron, his father is a piece-of-shit, and I'm not just saying that; he has done heinous things. That's a man you ignore. But my dad…" Billie stared at the window. She could feel the tears building and burning her eyes. There would be no stoicism today. Vela plucked a tissue from a box on the shelf and reached over to hand it to Billie. "He wasn't always like this. He had good parenting moments. I wish…I wish things were different."

Vela put down her pen, shifted in the chair, and squared her shoulders. "Billie, you can only control what you can control. You do not need to do the emotional labor of others, particularly for your father. You can feel sad for how things have turned out; you can grieve for the loss of both your parents. I know they're still alive but you can grieve for them. They are different and you're now different, and we'll work on navigating that…together."

Billie sniffled and rubbed the tissue under her nose. She shucked off her boots and brought her feet up, settling into the couch as she did so. "How much time is left?"

Vela glanced at her watch. "Plenty."

"Ok, Vela, well buckle up, because we haven't even started talking about my mom."

Vela poised with her pen in the air. "Ready when you are."

CHAPTER FIFTY-FOUR

The next morning, Billie had been thinking about her therapy session with Vela – "It's called gray rock, being emotionally unresponsive to a toxic parent. We can explore that in another session." (Billie googled it for Aaron's sake, thinking that this could work with his father) – when Rabbi Schechter's secretary had called her from temple.

"You left a knit hat in the sanctuary. One of the women from the Sisterhood found it."

Billie winced, wondering oddly if she was in trouble with the rabbi, but that seemed ridiculous even to her. She wasn't a child. Adults didn't get angry with other adults for forgetting clothing items. This wasn't the fourth grade lost-and-found bin outside the school gymnasium.

The secretary insisted Billie come in before noon.

"Preschool's insane. Don't arrive then; there's no parking. And forget coming during Hebrew School. The moms don't leave. They sit in their cars until they spot the rabbi, then it's: 'Listen to my son practice his Torah portion again.' Best to come in around ten when it's quiet," she said.

And so Billie did, some time after her mother boarded the shuttle to Safe Horizons. Billie quickly found herself in the sanctuary again. For a second, she felt thirteen years old, anxious over reciting several lines of ancient Hebrew.

She was picking a rogue prayer book off the floor when Rabbi Schechter entered, looking every bit the part, in a yarmulke and green sweater vest. He was in his late fifties with thinning hair and a gleaming smile, and a heavy North Jersey accent. If a script called for a rabbi, casting would snap him off the street. He fit the role perfectly.

Especially when he said, "Belinda. I haven't seen you since your Bat Mitzvah. Ten years ago?"

"Roughly," she replied, mentally drafting an apology to Jews everywhere that yes, she hadn't made an effort to attend services.

He handed her the cap of multi-colored yarn. "Clearly made with love, didn't want you to lose it."

She thanked him and readied her departure when he gestured toward a door in the back. "Come. Let's go to the kitchen."

"Oh, I don't want to keep you." *I don't want to stay.*

"Nonsense. It's time for my third cup of coffee anyway."

Billie followed him to a room off the hallway with stainless steel countertops and industrial size appliances. The sinks were reflective and deep and had those faucets that could bathe an elephant. In the corner sat a Keurig which drew the rabbi's immediate attention.

"I know, I know, they're terrible for the environment." He popped a pod into the top of the machine and pressed down the lever. "But these kids in the afternoon are nuts, amped up for their toys. In my day, you got trinkets for Hanukkah. Socks. Baseball cards. The new U2 album, and that was a big present. Now it's Xboxes and PlayStations and something called a Squishmallow. You know about that?"

Billie shook her head.

"You know how many children asked me about Santa Claus?" he said.

She didn't.

"Five. And Rudolph this and Frosty that and how come Jews don't get an Elf on the Shelf? What are we doing?" He rolled his eyes – *kids today* – while the coffee brewed. Billie heard a hiss and then the steady stream of dark liquid. Once it was done, the rabbi removed his mug and toasted her. He sipped, winced, and frowned. "What's new?"

A lot.

"Not much."

"Come. Let's go to my office."

The rabbi sipped and talked and steered Billie toward a small room just a spit's distance from the kitchen. He set down his mug and dropped into a desk chair.

"I shouldn't get too comfortable," he said. "Preschool gets insane."

"So I heard." Billie glanced around the office, which was fairly standard as far as managerial spaces went, except for a framed print on the wall opposite the desk – a portrait of a man wearing a beige fedora and blue tie, his face decorated in a mustache and goatee.

The rabbi noted Billie's interest.

"You like? It's a Felix Nussbaum. A poster, but still. Means something."

"It's slightly haunting."

"Nussbaum was an incredibly talented artist, a German Jew who created his most powerful work when he and his wife were hiding from the Nazis in Belgium. Friends supplied him with art supplies and shelter. Even during the worst time of his life, he created."

"I'd ask what happened to him, but I feel like you're going to tell me he was murdered by the Nazis–"

"He was murdered by the Nazis. He and his wife were discovered, arrested, and sent to Auschwitz. His art, however, endures."

Billie tilted her head to examine the artwork closely. Although it was a copy, the textured brush strokes gave the work an almost living quality. Despite what those YouTube shrinks recited, the past mattered because the past endured.

For the first time in days, Billie wondered how Karl Sauer's daughter Christina was faring.

"You should come to services," Rabbi Schechter said abruptly, and Billie cynically questioned if he had just leveraged Felix

Nussbaum and concentration camps to get her back into shul. "Our Purim party is still quite the event."

"I don't know." She could've said, yeah, sure, in that noncommittal way most people agreed to things, but the rabbi would then expect her to show up. Billie wanted to stop disappointing people by rising to their expectations.

He then asked, "Is it the God thing?"

"Kinda. I mean I believe in being Jewish if that makes a difference."

"It probably does to God."

She sighed, a bit resigned. "God should do a better job of things. The way I see it, the world is crap."

"Oftentimes it is. But then, oftentimes, it is not. We live in a lot of gray area. As for God, well imagine God as a parent. Parents make you, breathe life into you, but then you grow up. And you're forced to sort yourself out on your own."

"Where does guilt and obligation come in?"

That got a weird look from him. "It doesn't. At least, it shouldn't." He rose from his chair, mug now empty, and perched himself on his desk. "I know things have been tough at home."

She snorted.

"But that's not your fault," he finished.

"I know that."

"The world can be crap, as you say, but it can also be beautiful, filled with natural wonders, love, pride in one's achievements. Life is not without struggles, but it is also not without joy." He pointed to the Nussbaum print. "Keep that in mind." The rabbi hefted up his mug. "Now time for the little rugrats. Glad we could catch up."

Billie nodded her appreciation, then headed for the door.

"Thanks, Rabbi Schechter," she said, turning to him and spinning Shari's knit cap on her finger. As she made her way down the hall, she heard him call after her, "Come to temple."

CHAPTER FIFTY-FIVE

When Billie returned home, she spent time on Wikipedia reading up on Felix Nussbaum, if only to satisfy her curiosity. Then she wondered how Derek was doing on the Cantor case. She could ask, but that would mean having to talk to him or Esha. It would also mean returning the painting, a task she had conveniently forgotten while trying to rescue Aaron. So now she sat on the living room carpet and sipped her third cup of coffee that day – something she and the rabbi had in common. She could feel the caffeine coursing through her veins as if a nurse had connected her to an IV bag full of Kirkland beans. She was antsy, slightly unfocused, but without the jolt, she feared she'd be comatose. Somehow this made her effective, but also slightly insane.

Jiggling her knee, Billie slopped a bit of liquid over the lip of her mug and onto her pajama bottoms. She kept glancing from the painting – the Fahrelnissa Zeid knockoff – to the images she had snapped with her phone of the concrete piece nestled in between the tarp and dirt.

The Cantor case would not leave her. As she had said to Vela, 'I can't seem to help myself.' This was probably one of those instances.

Return the painting; let the investigation go.

And yet, Billie wondered about the skeletal remains she had found in Karl's basement. She assumed that the cement chunk had been the murder weapon. It had felt hefty in her hands, like it could do some damage if wielded correctly.

There wasn't anything linking that and the painting aside from the artist signature: two letters: AS

So was AS the female skeleton Billie unearthed in Karl's basement?

And if so, why had Karl kept the woman's painting? Well, because Karl literally kept everything. But he then gifted it to his daughter. Why would he do that?

Because he didn't want to be reminded of his crime? Didn't want to see the evidence of his wrongdoing? Or because he loved art and hated people?

Art was not trash, but human beings were. Karl Sauer was a testament to that.

Now what? Now what? Now what?

She continued to stare at the canvas until her gaze blurred; the colors meshed into a bright blob of pinks, red, and oranges, like falling into a sunset.

Gramps stepped in front of her, disrupting the view. "Did you finish the pot?"

She peered around his legs. "Sorry. I thought you were done."

He huffed and glanced at his watch. "I wanted an afternoon cup."

"I can make another," she said, pushing gently on his legs, veiny with bruises that often appeared like magic, their origins completely unknown. "Can you move slightly? I'm trying to focus."

"Not sure how you can focus if you finished an entire pot of coffee," said Gramps.

"Jeez, I'll make more." Billie scrambled to her feet, spilling more coffee. "Shit."

"Language."

"I'm not five years old!" She bent down and sopped up the spill with the hem of her T-shirt.

David came running in, a toothbrush still lodged in his mouth. "What's with the yelling?"

"Your sister is jittery," said Gramps.

"I told her to lay off the caffeine," said David through a mess of toothpaste as he retreated toward the stairs.

"What the hell are you even doing anyway?" Gramps asked, looking down, before throwing up his hands and answering his own question. "I thought you were off this case. Can we have one week where we're not, I don't know, dealing with murderous art thieves?"

Billie ignored that remark. Aaron's rescue felt forever ago, and now she found herself stuck on this. "The person who painted this is the same person in Karl's basement." Then, with less surety: "I think."

Gramps sighed. "It goes without saying, but I'll say it anyway: stop going over to that Sauer place. Death trails you like skunk spray."

"Any ideas?" She shot him a look.

"Go back to serving deadbeats their court documents."

"If you can't be helpful," she said as she made her way back toward the kitchen.

Gramps groaned in defeat. "Fine!" He tempered his voice. "Fine. If you have little evidence to go on, then you need to work with assumptions."

Billie stopped and stared at him.

He continued, "You sure the skeleton is female?"

Billie nodded.

"And that Karl buried her?"

"If he didn't kill her, he definitely covered for whoever did."

"Let's reason for a second that a woman buried in his basement would've been someone he associated with. So this," he squinted at the painting signature, "AS person could've been a woman he was seeing. After all, who gifts other people art? It's a very personal thing to do."

"You think this is a crime of passion?" she asked, glancing from the canvas to Gramps, and back again.

"Maybe jealousy. Also the man was a racist jerk. Was he also an abusive jerk? Or did something happen that made him snap?"

Billie set down her empty mug and enlarged the image on her phone.

AS

'77

"Assume that the body you found was a woman Karl was involved with," said Gramps. "Who else would've been around then? To have seen him in the company of a woman who wasn't his ex-wife?"

"The long-time neighbor," Billie whispered.

Gladys.

"That's where I would go," said Gramps.

Billie darted for the kitchen. Gramps called after her, "Stay away from the coffee!" A grumble followed, "You've had more than enough already."

CHAPTER FIFTY-SIX

God bless old people, and their resistance to dumping their landlines. Using her laptop, Billie googled Gladys' phone number and called her from an old burner Gramps had bought. At some point, Billie was going to have to replace her cell.

After several rings, a man answered, and Billie momentarily panicked, assuming it was Gary, until the voice said, "Brah, anyone there?" Male teenager.

Billie softened her voice and added a bit of tremor, tried to sound elderly. "May I speak with Gladys please?"

She heard, "Grandma! It's for you."

Then several seconds of commotion, then Gladys got on the line.

"Hello."

"It's Billie. Um, Entenmann's girl."

"Oh, yes, dear. Any more on the neighbor's boneyard? Did the police find another body?"

That would've been something, and Billie suddenly was bummed she didn't have more interesting news to deliver. "Sadly, no. I mean, not sadly; it's good there isn't another dead person, but..." she was babbling. "No."

"Hmph."

Fearing she was losing her, Billie said, "You can help me in the investigation, though. Remember how we spoke about Karl Sauer and if he ever had any lady visitors?"

"I do," said Gladys, cautiously. "But I don't remember a girlfriend or anything."

"Do you remember, though, any woman or girl, any female at all who might've visited? Think late seventies. 1977, to be exact."

"Oh, well, now you're really testing my memory." There were several long seconds of quiet, and Billie wondered if they'd been disconnected, until she heard a long breath. "By 1977, he really was a hermit. I mean, how would he have met anyone? He only ever spoke to me, Joe, and the girl who delivered his groceries."

There was more commotion on the other line, and Billie worried that she was losing Gladys to the business of grandkids and the household.

"Wait," said Billie. "The person who delivered his groceries was a girl? A kid?"

"Oh, yes. Teenager. Chubby bunny. That's all I remember. Ran into her once because the station wagon was blocking my driveway, and I had to leave to pick up Patricia from preschool."

Billie's heart raced, and for once, it didn't suggest impending doom – caffeine notwithstanding. "Gladys, do you remember the supermarket that Karl got his groceries from?"

A snort, then a chuckle, then a: "Actually, I wonder if it was the old Grand Union."

"In Elmwood Park?"

"Of course."

"Gladys," said Billie. "Thank you so much for your help. You're a gem."

Another chuckle. "You're welcome, sweetheart. Don't be a stranger. I have plenty more Entenmann's to share."

"I won't," said Billie, and then she ended the call.

CHAPTER FIFTY-SEVEN

"Gramps!" Billie yelled from the kitchen.

"What?!" Gramps yelled back.

"Can you come in here a sec?! I need—"

He popped his face in and rubbed at his temples. "Let's not yell, ok? I got a burgeoning headache."

"Ok." She turned toward him and softened her voice. "Let's consider that the only interaction Karl ever had with a member of the opposite sex was with the girl who delivered his groceries."

Gramps frowned, then sighed. "I'm not going to like this, am I?"

Billie shrugged.

Another exhalation. "How old would this mystery girl have been back then?"

"Seventeen."

"And Karl?"

"Early forties, roughly."

"Son of a bitch." Gramps sawed away at his stubbly chin. "A teenage girl who delivered groceries would've been a local, I imagine. What supermarket?"

"Grand Union," she said.

"You could see if corporate has files on old staff, or...you could check local high schools. Start with Elmwood Park, and work outward from there. Call the office and see if they have any class lists or yearbooks on hand? They might. It's possible the painting," he pointed toward the living room, "was done in an art class. Maybe there's a way to identify it that way."

"Yes," she said, feeling a fluttering of excitement hit her. "Thanks."

As Gramps retreated from the doorway, Billie could hear him grumbling, "Why can't you just get the cheaters and insurance fraudsters? No, it's gotta be Nazi creeps. Again!"

Using her laptop, Billie googled the Elmwood Park Memorial High School phone number, and dialed the office on the kitchen cordless since the burner was about to run out of juice. A woman answered with a nasally voice and hurried delivery. Obviously, the call was an intrusion on her obligations.

Billie introduced herself but left out her profession, and she fudged the real reason for her call. The truth would not serve her here since she didn't live in Elmwood Park, thus why would she need access to the yearbook?

A story would suffice.

"So my aunt left me a piece of art, a gift given to her by an old high school chum. There's a signature on the canvas. I think the artist might've been a student at your high school."

"A signature?" asked the woman. "You need a signature? For what? A physical? Sports?"

In the background, Billie heard the commotion of high school. A voice over the loudspeaker. Phones ringing. Students asking for passes.

"No, I have a signature. Initials, really, on a painting that might've been done in an art class."

"Printing? Like tech ed? 3-D printing."

Billie found herself growing impatient and annoyed. "*Painting.* Art class. An oil painting from 1977."

"1977?" Now, it was the secretary's turn to get cranky. "You expect me to identify something from over forty years ago?"

"I just need a verification."

"What is this even for?"

"A genealogy project," said Billie without thinking.

"I thought you said your aunt left you art."

So *that* she heard correctly.

"It's both," said Billie quickly. "I'm putting together family heirlooms. I want to verify that it was made by a student at your high school. Would you happen to have a class list you can email me?"

There was a long beat, then a cackle, and another long pause. "No," she finally managed.

"Ok," said Billie, already feeling mightily defeated. "Do you have a yearbook I can look at from that year?"

Billie heard whispering and a mumbled conversation, and "this girl is calling about a yearbook." Then seconds of nothing before more mumbling. "We have all our yearbooks in the school library."

"Great—"

"But you'll need the principal's permission to access them. We don't just let anybody into the building. You could be a lunatic."

Theoretically, she supposed that was true. *Let's add in more lying:* "Well, I'm an alumnus. Mr W would let an alumnus look at an old yearbook to find her estranged aunt, right?"

"You were estranged? Then why did she leave you a painting?"

"As an apology," Billie said, trying to recover, but recover what, she didn't know. She was simply fumbling a play she had no chance of salvaging.

Now it was the secretary's turn to sound defeated. "Send me an email with the things you need, and someone will get in touch with you."

Billie was screwing this up. Exhaling, she grabbed a pen. "What's the best email address?"

"It's P Amato at Elmwood Park dot org. That's p as in pear, a as in apple, m—"

Billie's mouth went dry. P Amato? Patricia? As in Gary Amato's wife?

"You know what? Why don't I just patch you through to the school librarian? Let her sort this out."

"Uhhhh, ok," said Billie. "I appreciate–" the line went silent.

"Media center," said a voice. Again female, but younger, happier to help.

"Hi," Billie began, wondering how better she could explain her needs without confusing both herself and the person on the other end of the line, and then it just occurred to her to ask for what she wanted. Librarians were helpful creatures by nature: if you needed info, they were mostly inclined to get it for you. "Do you have a copy of the yearbook from 1977?"

"Let me check," said the woman.

Billie leaned back in the chair and sighed. She kicked her feet up on the adjoining seat and closed her eyes. A few moments later the woman came back. "We do."

"Great. I'm doing research, and I need something from the yearbook. Could you flip through and see if there is a photo of an art club or something?"

"All right. Just hold on a second."

See? Helpful. In Billie's dream utopia, everyone was a goddamn librarian.

The voice came back on the line. "I'm sorry, but the yearbook has been damaged."

"Damaged?" Billie dropped her legs and sat up.

"The page has been ripped out."

"That one page has been ripped out of the book?" she asked, slower this time.

"Yeah. I assume it's the art group. They're the only ones missing. Weird."

"Very," said Billie. The past five minutes had been odd indeed. Patty Amato answering the phone, and the specific yearbook page she needed had magically disappeared.

"You can try the local library," said the woman. "They should have a copy."

"I'll do that. Thank you." Billie muttered a *take care* and hung up.

But minutes later, when she called the Elmwood Park Public Library, the man at the desk put her on hold while he checked the reference books.

"It seems to be missing," he told her. Then: "Did you try the high school?"

Billie hung up, dejected, but also determined. Someone was trying real hard to obscure AS's identity.

Only Billie was going to try harder to uncover it.

CHAPTER FIFTY-EIGHT

Billie met the Safe Horizons shuttle bus as it rolled in front of the house.

The driver's aid, a very familiar gentleman she knew as Kevin – same dude she bribed at the morgue (how serendipitous) – escorted Shari down the steps, holding a paper bag that he passed off to Billie.

He pretended not to know her, so she, in turn, made it seem like they were best friends.

"Kevin! My dude. How's it going?"

He opened his mouth, but only sounds originating from the back of his throat managed to make their way to Billie's ears. She decided to prolong his misery and peeked inside the bag. "Another ceramic piece?"

He sputtered, "C-Came out of the kiln this morning." He dipped inside the bus and re-emerged, this time with a fake leather handbag in his clutches. "Don't forget this."

Billie sighed.

Kevin said, "She was worried about it the whole day." As he was about to climb onto the bus, Gramps opened the front door and yelled, "Kev!"

Kevin grimaced. "Oh, hey, Mr Levine."

Poor Kevin. He had Levines coming at him from both ends.

Gramps held up a finger and limped down the stairs, precariously holding Billie's laptop. She tensed as he approached the shuttle and showed Kevin the screen with an Excel spreadsheet. "Let me ask you some questions, if that's ok?"

Kevin shrank – all that bravado from outside the medical examiner's office evaporating under the heat lamp that was William Levine.

Billie looped her mom's purse around her own shoulder and escorted Shari inside the house. "Ma, you can't bring your purse to Safe Horizons anymore."

"I need it," said Shari as she shuffled inside.

"You don't, though." Billie helped her mom out of her coat and hung it up in the closet. Shrugging off her own jacket, she left the bag on the vestibule table. Billie considered hiding the damn thing, but realized that would create a whole new host of problems.

As Shari kicked off her shoes, Billie dug inside Shari's purse. There was a wallet with her driver's license and old loyalty cards for stores they no longer frequented. She found a set of reading glasses and a checkbook. Billie would definitely be taking that back. She also uncovered receipts from bills paid long ago. Aside from Shari's ID, there wasn't anything inside there that Shari couldn't afford to lose; only Shari didn't know that. She was simply holding on to the memory that her purse contained irreplaceable items like cash and credit cards – the relics of a life that was long gone.

Billie herded her mother into the kitchen for a snack. Plucking a banana from a bunch on the counter, she held it up. Shari shook her head. "There was lots of food at the place."

"At Safe Horizons?"

Shari nodded. "The people brought it in."

"The staff?"

Again, Shari nodded. "For-for a party."

"Holiday party."

It didn't go unnoticed that Shari was losing the specificity of her language.

Billie peeled the banana and ate it herself, hoping the chewing might distract her for a minute until Gramps entered the kitchen, securing Billie's computer in his armpit.

She swallowed and said, "Careful! Not everything is backed up on there."

Gramps glanced under his arm, rolled his eyes, and set the laptop on the kitchen table in a slow, exaggerated manner.

"Why can't you use your tablet?" she asked.

"The thing is so old. It closes windows on me without warning."

Sorta like Billie's phone.

"After this case is over, use your earnings to buy a new one."

Gramps gave that some thought. "Maybe I will."

"In the meantime..." Billie opened her laptop and changed the password.

"Nice," said Gramps as he retrieved a can of seltzer from the fridge. "Heads up, I put that abstract surrealist thing in the garage."

"Why?"

"It was blocking the television."

"You could've put it in the dining room."

"That's my temporary office for the Safe Horizons case. I don't want it cluttered with your stuff."

"I assume that Kevin guy is your number one suspect," she said. "In regard to the thefts."

"Number one, number two, and number three. How did you know?"

"Saw him wearing the stolen Bose headphones. With *Kareem* in Sharpie. Ha! That's what you get for shitting where you eat."

"Where was this?"

"Not important. Just don't get him canned yet. I may still need him."

"I'll give you a day or two," he said. "Then I go to Desiree."

"How did you get him?" she asked.

"Sneakers. Cameras caught a masked gentleman wearing all black, except for his Air Jordans. It's not ironclad, but it's enough."

"Impressive."

"Not bad for an old man," he said, grinning. "How's the yearbook thing going?"

"Hitting dead ends. Someone is waylaying me."

"Leave this to Esha or Malley," said Gramps before he brought the can to his mouth.

"You and I both know nothing will get tackled on a case this cold during the holidays." She typed away. "Besides, I'm close. I can feel it. If I can just get my hands on the Elmwood Park High School yearbook..."

"Maybe it's digitized," said Gramps, stifling a burp.

"That's what I'm checking now." Billie opened Google and entered her search string. There was a website with a whole directory of yearbooks, but she would need to register an account. Not a big deal. Annoying, but easy. She'd use one of her many Gmail throwaways for this to keep the spam at bay.

Gramps leaned over her shoulder. "I wonder if my old man's is on there. Search for Seward Park High School, Class of '32."

"Later," she said. "Or you can do it when you get your new computer."

Unfortunately, though, the 1977 yearbook for Elmwood Park had never been digitized.

"Tough luck," said Gramps.

"Motherfu—" She stopped herself and stood to stretch her legs. Then speaking of mothers. "Where's Ma?"

CHAPTER FIFTY-NINE

When Billie found her, Shari was precariously balancing on a step stool while hoisting a plastic tote off the garage shelf.

"Ma, you cannot disappear like that," said Billie breathlessly. "Remember last time?"

No, of course she didn't recall, but Billie had. The fear had been so visceral Billie could still taste its bitterness on her tongue. She shuddered against the cold. "What are you looking for?"

Shari rummaged through the bin and held up two yearbooks in triumph. "This. You need them."

"Elmwood Park," Billie clarified. "Not Teaneck, but I appreciate the effort." Nevermind that Shari couldn't remember if she had eaten breakfast that morning, she still recollected exactly where she stored her high school crap. Nothing about this disease would ever make sense to Billie. "Ma, let's go inside."

"You don't want to see?" Shari asked.

Billie glanced back at the side door, thinking of the mountains of work she had to do, the hours of crawling through internet archives, not to mention tracking deals on a new phone

Billie opened her mouth. "I can't–"

"What are you doing?" David asked, still dressed in scrubs and his coat. "I thought raccoons got in."

"Nope, just us." Billie helped Shari down and wiped off the yearbooks' dusty covers with her hands, before transferring the dust to her jeans.

Handing David their father's yearbook first, he flipped

through a few pages of staff photos – "The hair," David cooed – until he got to the senior portraits. There under L, they found Craig Levine.

"He looks so young," said Billie, almost in awe. Like seeing a ghost. She turned to David. "God, you look so much like him."

"Not a compliment," he said. Then he laughed and pointed to Craig's senior quote.

"'You give loyalty, you'll get it back. You give love; you'll get it back,'" Billie read aloud. "Tommy Lasorda."

"The irony!" cried David. "And he didn't even watch baseball! Let me see yours, Ma."

Billie handed over Shari's yearbook. Her maiden name was Baum, so she was quicker to find.

Shari had been a knockout in her youth. Blonde hair in Farrah Fawcett waves. A bright smile. She'd been in student council, Spanish club, and French club.

"You took French?" said Billie.

"I guess so, yeah. But I don't remember it," said Shari.

Billie couldn't blame Alzheimer's on that one. No one who took a couple of years of high school French remembered anything that wasn't *como ca va.*

"Ma, what's your senior quote?" asked David, his eyes skimming the page. "'If you're quiet, you're not living. You've got to be noisy and colorful and lively.'"

"Mel Brooks," Shari said, grinning.

David smiled, too, as he put the yearbooks back in the bin. He noted Shari's breath, visible in the frigid air. "Let's go inside. I gotta meet Matty. We're looking at another place."

Billie said, "So everything is good again between you and him?"

David nodded. "As I told you before, we can work things out. You don't need to worry. We agreed that there would be no guns in the house."

Sure, no guns in the house, but guns in Matty' car? Matty's office? Billie imagined the compromise stopped outside the apartment. Speaking of… "So another apartment tour? What was wrong with the others?"

David made a face. "Nothing feels right, yet. I want something that feels like us."

"What does that even mean?" she asked. "What kind of apartment represents a Jewish strip club owner and his boyfriend?"

"That's an oversimplification," he said drily. "I'm just saying. It's our first place together. It's a big deal. I want it to be right."

"Ohhhh," she said. "I get it. You're scared."

His voice hitched. "Don't be an asshole."

"I'm not the asshole who's stalling."

"No," he squeaked. He paused, composed himself. "I'm not stalling. I have standards."

"High standards apparently."

"Most places look like garbage."

"You're being picky because you're scared."

"I'm being picky because I want this to be perfect. I don't want to fuck things up again."

That stopped her as she struggled to put the bin back on the shelf. David wasn't stalling, or maybe he was, but clearly he feared his bipolar disorder haunting their new place.

"Give it more time, then," she said.

David nudged Billie out of the way as he hefted the plastic bin onto its spot on the storage shelf.

"I'm pushing thirty, Billie. I'm being thoughtful and deliberate. I don't want to set us up for failure."

"That's a lot of pressure to put on an apartment," she said.

David shrugged by way of response and herded Shari out of the cold garage. Billie followed only to hang back and stare at Christina Cantor's painting again. An idea needled her brain, poking at cerebral grooves, disrupting synapses. If only she could make the connection.

Hell, if her brain wasn't going to get her there, she knew someone who could. With the right persuasion.

CHAPTER SIXTY

In the dark, Billie glimpsed the embers of the cigarette before she saw his face, not that it mattered. He was dead meat anyway.

Ah, Kevin. You brought this on yourself.

She scrambled out of her car and darted toward him as if she was a shark who spotted a marlin. He took one look, dropped his cigarette, and grabbed for the door handle, but Billie anticipated this: she was already waving the cash in the air above her head.

"Don't!" she cried, reaching him moments before he slipped inside.

He took one look at the bills, this time crisp, new, and straight from the ATM. Sighing, Kevin said, "What do you want?"

"Information," she replied. "You selling because I'm buying."

"I don't trust you." He pointed at her with a fresh cigarette which he stuck in his mouth and lit.

Yeah, Billie was the untrustworthy one here. She played nice. "That was a misunderstanding. An accident."

"Aaron with you?" he asked as he inhaled.

"No, so don't worry." Aaron was still in the hospital recovering. Knowing him, he'd probably figured out how to establish a black-market medical device ring. She halted that thought. He was a changed man now.

Billie held out the wad of bills. Kevin stared at her palm for a beat, before grabbing the cash and shoving it in his underwear. Then he wagged his brows, a come and get it motion.

Billie forced a smile and said, "So the bones that arrived from the Sauer house. Hear anything?"

Kevin exhaled a gray cloud. "Female skeleton."

Billie gestured for him to keep going.

"The lady doc thinks the bones have been there for decades," he said, eyebrow cocked.

She had assumed all this. "More."

Kevin took another drag. "She also thinks the victim might've been pregnant at one point."

That was worth the cost of admission. "Really?"

"Something about the pelvis," he said, while gesturing around his groin.

Billie wanted to gag on her next question. "Were infant remains found with the body?"

Kevin shook his head. "That's the thing. No."

"So she had already given birth?" said Billie, musing more to herself than Kevin.

"That part I didn't hear."

"What about how she might've died?"

"Like the old man, crushed skull. Murder weapon was likely the hunk of concrete they found with her."

Billie remembered Gladys' words in reference to the girl: *chubby bunny.*

Chubby because she had been pregnant.

It would take eons for DNA to come back, if DNA could even be salvaged. This would have to do.

Billie patted Kevin's chest. "Thank you. This has been super helpful."

"Worth the money?"

"Sure," said Billie.

"You know? I could give you back your hundred bucks if you give me something in return." He jerked his head toward the building. "No one's in there."

"Kevin, Kevin, Kevin," she said. "I would rather sleep next to the skeleton than go anywhere with you."

Kevin shrugged. "Your loss."

"Definitely not."

"Well, if you don't need my information, you can fuck off."

"I will," she said, "once you give me back my cash."

That earned her a scoff. "Don't think so."

"Kevin, right now William Levine is combing through Safe Horizon's security camera footage."

"So?"

Billie took out her phone and snapped a photo of Kevin's Bose headphones, the same ones he'd been sporting the last time she interviewed him, as well as his sneakers. Gramps had already pegged Kevin as the Safe Horizons thief, but now she snatched the proof. Ooh. Her grandfather would owe her one. "He's re-examining the list of items reported stolen by Ms Hamilton, along with footage of you sporting these fancy kicks..." She showed him a still from the camera, then glanced from his feet to his pale face. "You know he's my roommate, right?"

Kevin shook his head. "Means nothing. Lots of people have these headphones."

"With Kareem written on them? In Sharpie?"

A lump bulged in Kevin's throat. "Those sneakers could belong to anyone."

"They could, but they don't." Billie held out her hand. Kevin dug around his boxer briefs for the cash and slapped it into her palm. She'd disinfect her skin the minute she returned to her car.

"Nice doing business with you," she said while heading out to the Oldsmobile.

"You won't tell him will ya?" he called after her. "Promise you won't tell him? Shit's expensive. I need both jobs."

"You need to get clean!" she called back. Then without turning around, Billie flipped him off.

CHAPTER SIXTY-ONE

Billie showed up at The Wagon, an Irish pub on Cedar Lane that catered to soccer enthusiasts and coppers who were soccer enthusiasts. Inside was nothing but wood paneling, flat-screen televisions, and club flags from cities Billie only recognized from Jane Austen novels.

Typically the crowd was too young for Gramps and too constabulary for Billie, but it was where the detectives from the BCDB hung out, so it was often where she headed when she needed to bend an ear.

Like now.

Detective Morales sat at the bar, sipping a pint and chatting with a blonde two barstools down. Every second or two, he would gesture to his arm in the sling. Was he aiming for a sympathy lay?

Billie slid in between him and the woman and said, "She was pregnant."

This elicited a choking sound from the blonde woman, who dribbled bits of Zinfandel down her blouse.

Seriously, who drank wine in a pub?

"Oh, sorry," said Billie to the woman. "I'm talking about a dead girl."

The woman immediately got up from the barstool and made her way to the pool table in the back where Detective Malley stood with other cops from the precinct.

"I love how you thought that clarification helped at all," said Morales, as he rubbed the tension from his forehead.

Billie frowned. "My apologies for cockblocking."

Morales tipped back the rest of his beer and then signaled to the bartender for another. "I hate that expression."

"Me too. Not sure why I used it." Billie leaned in. "The body I found in Karl's basement. Female. Likely a teenager. She'd been pregnant."

Morales slammed down his fresh beer on the cocktail napkin. "How in God's name do you know this?"

"Not important," she said dismissively.

"Oh, but it is. How you get your info is very important, Billie. Very. So I need to know how you know this because I don't even know this."

"Just because I have info that you don't have, doesn't make my info less credible."

Morales pounded his good fist on the bar top, startling her, and shaking his glass. Malley glanced their way.

Morales reigned in his temper. "Please go away. I'm begging you. My shoulder hurts, and no one prescribed me painkillers to deal with you."

Billie said, "The remains in the basement were a real person. And she had a baby at some point."

"Karl Sauer was a real piece of shit, Billie. I get it. A body was found, and Occam's Razor sorta suggests that the body was likely put there by Karl Sauer."

"Great, so–"

"Likely, but not definite. And unless the ghost of that woman murdered Karl, you're not in the ballpark where I'm batting." He went back to his beer. "Focus on your boyfriend's recovery. Not my cases."

She pushed off the bar. "You dismissed me last time and look where that got you."

Morales laughed. "Luck is no substitute for evidence."

"Luck!" She found herself lunging for him, just as Malley swooped in and grabbed her arm. "All right, tiger. Time to go."

Malley escorted her to the street and practically shoved her outside the door. She spun around and ran her hands through her hair. "He's ignoring evidence."

Malley held out his hands in that placating manner she found so patronizing, she wanted to take an ax to his limbs. "He's not ignoring evidence he doesn't have yet," said Malley. "You likely bribing some lackey for questionable information isn't proof of anything."

Billie stalked off, and Malley called after her. But she was on a mission. A mission for info, and if Malley, Morales or any one of the Bergen County detectives didn't want to play ball, that was fine. She would figure it out on her own. Because as she had told Vela, Billie was a damn good private eye.

CHAPTER SIXTY-TWO

That night Billie couldn't sleep. Her skin was too itchy; her bedcovers were too tight; her pajama bottoms gave her insistent wedgies. Her feet were too hot – she removed her socks – then too cold.

She tossed off the comforter like a lover she had grown tired of and headed downstairs for chamomile tea that would no doubt cause her to pee all night. There would be no victory.

She really needed to get to the Verizon store, but was stalling. With just a burner, Billie had been unreachable and that had its perks. Sadly that meant she could not text Jeremy, not because she thought of him as a friend, but because if his phone wasn't on do-not-disturb, she might disrupt his sleep. And what better way to settle her brain than to pester his.

She entered the kitchen, her hand searching for the light switch.

"Don't," said Gramps in the dark.

"Jesus!"

Billie pressed a hand to her chest to staunch her pounding heart. If she thought a cup of chamomile was going to help, she was more mistaken than a clown performing at a funeral.

"Why are you awake?" she asked.

"Can't sleep." Sipping a beer, he stared out into the yard.

"Why are you sitting in the dark?"

"What difference does light make at," he glanced at the clock on the stove, "two in the morning?"

"Can I turn on the light now?"

"Not yet."

"Weird." Billie went to the cupboard where they kept crap that barely saw use – extra duck sauce packets from the Chinese take-out, popcorn kernels, and dried fruit. She felt around blindly for herbal teabags.

"Why can't you sleep?" he asked.

"Got a lot on my mind." She dropped a teabag into a mug, filled it with water, and stuck it in the microwave. Somewhere a British person was having a cardiac event.

Gramps slipped his hand inside his sweatshirt pocket and placed a black object on the table. "Found this on your Hyundai."

Billie squinted at the roach-like form, until the microwave timer jolted her from reverie.

"It's a GPS tracker," said Gramps.

"I know what it is." Billie fetched her tea.

"Do you? If you had, you would've gotten it out of the wheel well instead of driving Ken's boat around Bergen County "

"Is that where you found it?"

"Yes. Why didn't you tell me you were being followed?"

She dunked the teabag several times, but inside she was forging a lie. "I didn't know I was."

Not her best.

"Billie, you can't be so goddamn secretive about everything."

"I don't want you worrying."

"Well, too damn late."

"Sorry. Jeez. The Roza case is over."

"You certain Roza did this?"

"Who else?" She sipped the tea. Needed sugar.

Finishing the beer, Gramps rose from the table and stood in front of the sink, his eyes scanning the backyard. "I don't know. Perhaps the person who was tracking your car is the same one currently casing the house."

She remained silent while her pupils adjusted to the shadows dancing along the garage wall. The mug slipped from her fingers. She clumsily caught it, inches before it could shatter against the sink basin.

"What?" she hissed, suddenly dropping to a crouch as if ducking for cover. "How do you know? Did you see a figure?"

"Relax," said Gramps in hushed tones. "I'm on it."

"Did you call the police?"

"No. I want to catch the bastard."

"Should I get my taser?" she asked.

"I'd get my gun but it's been eons since I was at the range, and–"

"You just answered your question," she whispered. Her hands gripped the countertop edge as she crouched below the window. "Get down! Should we wake Mom? David?"

"No."

Billie found his eerie calmness more terrifying than the potential home invasion.

He said, "You hear that?"

She did not.

Then glass shattering. But not inside the house.

"The garage!" said Gramps and Billie at the same time.

Billie went for her taser which was at the bottom of her messenger bag in the coat closet.

She shoved her feet into boots and tossed on David's jacket, which was the first thing she'd grabbed, and trudged in front of her grandfather as they sneaked out of the kitchen door and into the yard. Her taser was held out front, ready to strike like a cobra.

Gramps pointed to his eyes, then pointed to the side door of the garage, which was open, its window punctured as if peppered by gunfire.

Billie pushed herself ahead, but then Gramps shoved her out of the way so that he strode in front. She nudged him with her shoulder and took the lead, getting to the garage first.

Glass crunched under the soles of her boot. She flicked on the light, taser at the ready, and cried, "We got you, asshole!"

But the garage, from all appearances, was empty.

Gramps jumped in front of her and swore. "Son of a bitch! We missed him."

"This doesn't make sense," said Billie. "There's nothing in here to steal."

"Your stupid painting," said Gramps pointing to a dark void in front of the workbench.

Billie's hands immediately went to her hair. "The painting from the Cantor case! Godfuckingdammit."

CHAPTER SIXTY-THREE

The next morning, Christina Cantor called Billie on the Levine landline, and Billie stupidly picked up.

"I wondered if you'd still be willing to help me," Christina said.

Billie glanced at her laptop. Matty had shared his Hulu password and she had nearly finished binge-watching the first season of Veronica Mars (delightful, but unrealistic). Gramps had driven to Home Depot to repair the *goddamn garage door*. And Aaron was still in the hospital, although he had been moved to a private room where one of Nell Goff's flunkies stood guard like a member of the secret service.

In fact, Billie had overheard a nurse say that there hadn't been this level of protection when a New Jersey senator had his gallbladder removed and roamed the halls naked in an anesthesia fugue.

Billie was so ready to take back this case, she might've conjured Christina's phone call. Still, she played it cool, and conveniently left out the part where her place had been robbed of crucial evidence. That could be revealed later. "I'd love to help you, but Esha put Derek on the investigation."

"I'd rather it be you. I told Esha as much," Christina replied.

Derek might've been an excellent gumshoe but he was a slob, and Christina had suffered enough of her father's poor hygiene and ghoulish habits to last her a lifetime.

"I'll pay you off the books," said Christina.

Billie waited several seconds before responding, so as not to appear too eager. The truth was she could sink into her pillows and watch a pretty blonde girl solve crimes or she could just do it herself and get paid.

Also Gramps's ire at Billie for the break-in was justified. Not because Billie was to blame, but because someone was targeting her...again.

Billie said, "Give me a bit. I'll see what I can do."

Billie sensed she was close anyway. The case might've been as cold as the December frost, but frost thawed and grass eventually emerged.

She wondered if Malley would be willing to search missing persons cases from 1977. He owed her. He might not see it that way, but she sure did. Only she didn't know his cell phone number because it was stored in the crushed phone. Combing her Gmail for correspondence, she located his email signature, where he had included his many contact numbers. He couldn't escape her now

"Awesome detective work," she said aloud, before dialing.

"Malley," he barked into the phone.

"Levine," she responded.

"Jesus Christ." Billie could picture him rubbing his temples and smiled. Billie wondered if it was a perversion that she enjoyed how much she irritated other people. Best not to dwell on the psychology of it. Vela could unpack that for her next week.

"So I'm back on the case," she said.

"What case?"

"The Cantor case. The one Morales got me booted off of. Esha may not be aware, so don't mention this to her, ok?"

There was a loud sigh. "What do you want? I've got several vacation days coming to me, so whatever it is, please make it painless."

"The body from Karl's cellar," she began.

"I said *painless*."

"How long do you think it will take for DNA to come back?"

There was laughter on the other end, then coughing. All those cigarettes outside The Wagon were gonna catch up to him.

"If they get DNA," she said.

"It's not my case, Billie. And it'll take as long as it takes."

"Years," she replied.

"Possibly."

She sighed. "Can you, at least, as a favor to me, get me missing persons cases from 1977? We know we're looking for a teenage girl."

"Those files aren't digitized. That would require loads of time and paperwork."

"Ok–"

"And it's Christmas."

Billie tapped the phone against her forehead in frustration. Goyim and their inability to do anything during the winter holidays. Imagine if the world just stopped because it was Rosh Hashanah? Billie put her ear back to the receiver.

"Anything else?" asked Malley.

"Not sure," she said.

"What's really bothering you?"

"I don't know...the inertia of life during December. The injustice of the system for women in the 1970s. The fact that a teen got knocked up by a Nazi-adjacent middle-aged man and was murdered by him."

"All valid things."

She huffed.

"Anything else?"

"Yeah." She was quiet for a second as cerebral gears slowly clicked into place. "Fatima said she wasn't responsible for tipping off Roza to Karl's haul, and she was scared of whoever did it."

"Fatima is in the wind," said Malley. "But we'll get her."

"Maybe."

"Oh, there's another thing you should know while I have you here."

"Yeah?"

He coughed for several seconds. Billie heard a pause, a swallow, and a clearing of the throat.

For God's sakes, man, just spit it out.

"Gary Amato is dead."

Billie thumped back into the kitchen chair. "I didn't anticipate that. How?"

"Gunshot."

"Self-inflicted?"

"We don't know yet."

"When?"

"Last night. With Aaron in the hospital, I didn't want you thinking about this because I know you and you'll–"

"Where?"

He sighed. "His business in Carlstadt."

Figures.

She said, "He had kids." Poor Patricia. Poor Gladys. "Is that all?"

"That's all I'm at liberty to say right now."

"Thanks, Malley," said Billie.

"No problem, kiddo."

She was about to hang up when she remembered something. "Oh, and Malley? Merry Christmas."

CHAPTER SIXTY-FOUR

Gary Amato was dead.

The Feds had been on to Roza, evidently, so if one were playing Atlantic City odds, they'd been onto Gary. He'd leveraged his business to smuggle art and got caught. Perhaps Gary got spooked and anticipated that his freedom was limited. So he took himself out of the equation. Patty and the kids would just have to live without him.

However if one were playing Vegas odds – well, then Gary didn't kill himself. Someone erased him so he didn't sing in an interrogation room.

Why then was Fatima still alive? Because she hadn't been caught?

Billie sat back, listening to cars kicking up slush outside her house.

Focus, Levine, on something you can see.

She signed into her newspaper archives account and stared at the search bar.

Her job was to determine AS's identity. Maybe if she did that, everything else would fall into place.

Hell, it was Christmastime. Miracles could happen.

Billie decided to play around with several strings of search terms, starting with *missing teenage girl* and *pregnant*. She then limited the timeframe from 1977 (when she knew AS was alive) to 1980. The eggheads at the medical examiners had not determined the date of death so she just had to guesstimate, but if the supermarket delivery girl was *the* girl, then Billie was sure she would've been killed around '77 or '78.

Either way, she had no hits.

She then tried *missing girl* within the same timeframe and got very few entries – mostly children and no one matching the initials.

How did a missing teen not make any news back then?

The girl had been pregnant, although her remains indicated no infant was found with her. So where did the baby go?

Billie typed *abandoned infant* into the search bar and expanded the timeframe from 1977 to 1985.

And then she found it.

April 25, 1978 in *The Bergen Record*

Baby boy left for dead on River Road.

An Elmwood Park Police officer on patrol found a male infant, stuffed inside a garbage bag on the side of River Road. The baby was immediately brought to Hackensack Hospital. No word on the whereabouts of the mother. The infant should make a full recovery and will be placed into the care of family services.

She took a screenshot and emailed the article to Malley.

Billie tried to imagine this poor teenage girl had just given birth, and what did she do? She showed up at Karl Sauer's house, seeking help for her baby. *His* baby. And Karl killed her and dumped the baby like trash.

Billie's stomach soured as she considered this question: why not kill the infant? Maybe he couldn't bring himself to kill a baby. His son.

The girl had been a delivery driver, so if she had driven to his house, she'd had a car. A vehicle was a hard thing to hide.

River Road ran right alongside the Passaic River. So Karl killed AS, dumped her car in the river, and left the baby to its fate.

Back up, Levine.

What could Billie presume? That a teen girl who had been

pregnant with Karl Sauer's baby had been murdered in that house and buried in his basement. The medical examiner would determine that once he got back from Ft Lauderdale.

A teen girl who delivered groceries.

"A girl who might've worked at Grand Union," she said aloud to herself.

She opened a new tab and began googling. One of the first hits was a Facebook group dedicated to – get this – people who used to work at Grand Union.

She hated Facebook, but she loved this.

Billie searched the posts using the phrase "Elmwood Park" and "New Jersey." A few popped up.

I worked the deli counter.

I was a cashier!

I stocked produce.

My brother met his wife there.

So wholesome.

Do you know Ralph from the bakery?

No. What about Kelly? She was a manager.

One comment gave Billie goosebumps:

My sister was a cashier. She delivered groceries sometimes too.

Hold the phone.

I was wondering if anyone might remember whose homes the groceries were delivered to.

Well, what an interesting inquiry – Billie squinted – Faye Sydin Ahmad.

Billie's stomach plummeted.

Sydin.

What were the chances that was AS's surname?

Billie clicked on Faye's account and sent her a message, which was a gamble as they were not connected, and there were no mutual friends to link them together. Her message could easily be ignored, but it was worth a try.

Hi Faye, she wrote. *I'm Billie, a private eye, and I am looking into artwork* – she deleted that last bit – *into the disappearance of a girl who was murdered in 1977. A body was found in the basement in a house in Elmwood Park. Did you hear about that? Could it be your sister? I only have initials to go by: AS? Please call me at your soonest convenience. Number listed below.*

Take that Veronica Mars.

CHAPTER SIXTY-FIVE

Billie received a phone call later that evening, to which Gramps said, *since when are we using the house line,* and made arrangements to meet Faye at her home in Park Ridge the following morning.

Faye lived on DeGroff Place in a white split-level that ran perpendicular to the street, the only house to be positioned like that. Unlike the neighbors, there were no Christmas lights adorning the trim work, no lit tree in the window, although a wreath hung on the black door, signaling to Billie a celebration of winter rather than Jesus's birth. A Nissan sat in the driveway, parked below a basketball hoop.

There was no reason to knock as Faye was hovering inside the threshold while Billie parked her Hyundai.

Faye was in her mid-sixties with gray hair speckled with dark strands, cut in a stylish pixie. She wore black pants and a boxy lavender top, which didn't jive against the gray clouds, but rather seemed fitting for an Eileen Fisher Instagram ad.

As soon as Billie emerged into the overcast light, Faye was gesturing for her to hurry. "Get out of the cold."

There was an eagerness that beckoned Billie inside. Four decades of grief would be blissfully overshadowed by answers – answers Billie hoped to provide.

Without being asked, Billie removed her boots in the foyer and padded through the open living room to the dining area off the kitchen where a mahogany table was already set with tea and various plates of food.

Faye said, "I made the hummus, but couldn't be bothered with the baba ganoush. The baklava is also from Costco. The pita…from Shoprite. I was too anxious to cook."

Billie set her messenger bag beside the chair so as to have easy access to the photos she had printed out and a notepad. Her cell phone had yet to be replaced, so she was carrying the burner.

"You didn't have to go through the trouble." Billie wasn't sure how much of an appetite either of them would have once Billie mentioned unearthing the corpse of Faye's sister.

Faye sat down, but then jumped up as if bitten. "I forgot the sugar." Her voice called out from the kitchen, "My husband's in Istanbul right now, so it'll just be us. I'll FaceTime him later."

Billie couldn't imagine how that conversation would flow. "Honey, you'll never believe what? My sister's body has been found! She'd been murdered! There was a baby!"

Billie suddenly wished she had roped Detective Malley into coming with her, but the identity of the remains would take eons to be determined. And if she had told Malley what she was doing, he would've told her *no*, and Billie didn't do well with anything that wasn't blanket permission.

Sliding into the chair, Billie flipped through her notebook and clicked a pen. "Hope you don't mind if I write down some information."

Faye placed a bronze bowl in front of Billie and shook her head. She dropped a cloth napkin at Billie's place setting before situating herself at the head of the table. "I'm so glad to have people interested in the case again. I can't tell you how frustrating it was to deal with law enforcement when she went missing, jeez, forty-something years ago. The police told my parents that she had run away. 'Wild girls do that,' they had said. Her car had also gone missing, so naturally, they assumed she'd driven off." Her voice grew soft. "We all knew something bad had to have happened for her to disappear."

Billie felt like the interview was a train that had left the station without her. "Let's back up slightly. Can you spell your sister's name for me? You said on the phone that it was, I want to say Ashley, but I know that isn't it."

"Asli. A-S-L-I. It's Turkish. Means genuine and authentic, and that was definitely my sister."

"I'd love to hear about her," said Billie.

Faye shifted in the dining chair, wiggling herself into place, as if discussing Asli might unmoor her. "She was born in 1960. Summer. My mother said she was a baby born of fire because of all the heartburn, but that was Asli by design. She had her own ideas about things, particularly womanhood. She was independent, and she loved art. Her biggest inspiration was Turkish artist Fahrelnissa Zeid. Asli thought Zeid was revolutionary, and she wanted to be just like that. My father was old-fashioned, so he wanted Asli to find a nice Turkish boy and settle down, but that was never going to be her story. Not even before–" She stopped and inhaled a shaky breath. "You know after forty years, you'd think I'd stop crying."

"You don't have to."

Faye nodded while Billie flipped through the printed photos – courtesy of CVS – until she landed on the painting. She set the picture on the table and watched as Faye positioned reading glasses over her eyes, picked up the photo, examined it, and then removed those same glasses to wipe at the tears that had materialized from years of grief. There was grieving for the loss of a sister, but also for the loss of information. Malley often said that the not-knowing – the absence of a body – was harder on victims' families than a visit to the morgue. "Hope won't kill you," he had said. "It'll just wreck you from the inside out."

"That's her work," Faye said. "Looks like a copy of Fahrelnissa Zeid. She was learning from her. Eventually, she would've found her own style." She steeled herself, probably knowing that if she didn't dam up the tears, there would be a flood. "Where did you find this?"

Billie replied, "It was gifted to a woman by her father, Karl Sauer. Do you know that name? He was the old man who was found dead in his house in Elmwood Park."

Faye shook her head. "I hadn't until you mentioned him over Messenger; then I did some online sleuthing. So you think my sister is who they uncovered in his basement?"

"I do," Billie said. "I'm going to give you the name and number of the detective at the BCDB. He'll want to get in touch with you. Might be hard if they can't get DNA, but I did find this when I," Billie cleared her throat, "discovered her." Billie flipped through various images until she found the photos she had taken of the concrete piece, the one that had been found next to Asli's remains, and set them out like a hand of blackjack. Then for insurance, Billie said, "Just don't mention this part to the same detective. I wasn't exactly at liberty to..."

Faye nodded and repositioned her glasses. Leaning over the pictures, her mouth pinched. "That definitely looks like something she would've made."

"I can't really tell what it is," said Billie. "Is it abstract?"

"A woman," said Faye. "Hold on, a sec." Faye got up and disappeared.

Billie scrutinized the piece as she examined each photo, trying to discern a feminine shape. All she remembered was that it had been heavy in her hands, weighty.

Faye returned with a similar statuette, approximately two feet tall. Here the hour-glass figure presented more clearly Billie glanced from the statuette to the evidence on the table and back again. They seemed one of a piece.

"She called them phases of a woman; I think they were meant to mimic the moon or something. I'm not sure."

"Detective Morales will want to see it," said Billie.

Faye set down the statuette – together they reminded Billie more of Shabbat candles than women's bodies – but that was the thing about art, the interpretation mattered only to the viewer.

Billie said, "So I think Asli crossed paths with Karl when she delivered his groceries, and they must've connected over art, and it grew into a romance, I suppose."

That elicited a snort from Faye. "How romantic to seduce a teenage girl and then murder her."

"Touché."

Faye sat back in her chair. "She was happy that spring in 1977, like floating on air. I totally thought it was about a boy, but she wouldn't tell me, which was devastating at the time, as you can guess. But something happened in the winter and she fell apart. I work in mental health so I used to wonder if it was the onset of a mood disorder, but now, knowing that she'd secretly been seeing an older man, that must've been the reason. She'd gotten so depressed. Gained weight and dressed in bulky clothes. Cut herself off from friends. Quit the Grand Union."

Billie tapped the photos as if signaling to Asli's ghost that what she was about to say would be hard to hear. "There's something else, although it hasn't been confirmed by the medical examiner…" Billie waited for Faye's signal to continue.

"It's ok. This is what I've wanted. To know."

"It's possible that Karl got her pregnant."

Faye said nothing.

"It just occurred to me that perhaps Karl wasn't the father; that maybe Asli had gotten pregnant by another boy, and he got jealous, which–"

Faye cut in. "No, you were right the first time. Karl is German, right?"

"You're not surprised," said Billie. "But I admit that I am."

"Because you're not the first person to tell me this."

"I'm not?"

"About Asli's murder, yes, but about the baby, no."

Faye got up from the table and went into the kitchen for a moment before returning with her cell phone. "Months ago, I did one of those ancestry DNA tests. I knew I was Turkish, but there had been rumors of an Irish grandparent, and I wanted to know if it was true. Spoiler alert: it's not...Anyway, I got a message from an anonymous account because our matches showed that we were related. I can't even tell you what I thought at the time. I thought Asli was alive, but then this guy asked if we could get together. He said he represented a client who wanted to remain anonymous for now so as not to get his hopes dashed. Once this guy verified everything, he'd set up a meeting between me and the match. The client apparently had been looking for his birth parents for a long time."

Billie slammed back in her chair. "The baby had been adopted, of course."

"Right, that's what I figured. I knew then that Asli was dead. She wouldn't have let her baby go like that. Anyway, I saw the man's DNA profile, and half of him was of German descent, so, I definitely think he was Karl's son."

"A man?"

"Yes," said Faye.

"So what happened then?"

"Well I met with the investigator who said he was representing my nephew."

"Investigator?" Billie asked.

Faye scrolled through her phone until she came to a photo. "I took his picture without him knowing. He looked so much like my brother that I had to email my sister-in-law. I get why the man would pretend to be someone else, you know? He was probably worried what I would've thought, or perhaps he was ashamed of what Asli had done, but I realize I just have to give him time."

Billie glimpsed the photo before Faye pushed the phone across the table.

Trench coat, six-day stubble, a dejected spirit momentarily alight – shoulders squared, not hunched – and a smidgeon of serenity. He had gotten answers. Of course, this was before he had confronted Karl Sauer, and learned who his biological father had really been: a monster.

When Derek Campbell was a man who still had hope.

Everything slotted into place.

Billie bolted upright.

CHAPTER SIXTY-SIX

"Faye, we need to get you to a safe place," said Billie.

Dropping her notebook into her bag, Billie tried to mentally recall directions to the BCDB headquarters. The burner phone had no GPS and no Google Maps. If she could get to the Garden State Parkway, she could navigate her way from there.

"Do you have someone you can stay with?" Billie asked, suddenly wondering if a familiar place was the safest option. "Maybe a hotel instead."

Faye rose from the dining room chair, but she wasn't in a rush to move simply because Billie told her there was a reason to move. Then again, Billie hadn't told her the reason.

Corralling her thoughts, she said, "That investigator is Derek Campbell, I recognize him because I work with him. He's Asli's biological son, and–"

The military-style boots that Billie had seen on the man fleeing Karl's house were Derek's, issued to him from his short stint in the police academy.

The cadets used to call him 'Garbage Man.' Claimed he belonged in sanitation.

Malley had said that.

They knew Derek had been dumped as a baby.

So Derek had been the one who took photos of Billie asleep in her car to scare her off the Karl Sauer case. That's why Roza didn't cop to them. He had also begged off the stakeout, telling Esha he had his kid's basketball game, but according to his ex-wife, he'd never showed.

And he recently had come into money if his new clothes and condo were anything to go by.

Billie would bet her soul that Derek was the one who set up Roza with access to Karl's storage unit.

He broke into her garage, stole AS's painting, and he had planted evidence in Aaron's car. After all, he must have taken it with him after

"He killed Karl Sauer," said Billie.

Faye absorbed that piece of information, but remained unconvinced. "All right, but why do I have to leave my home?"

"Because you are the only link between Derek and your sister," said Billie. "He knows that, and he knows where you live. Once the police establish her identity, they're going to come knocking on your door. You'll mention Derek, ask to see the DNA results. They'll ask him for an alibi the night of Karl's murder. The point is, they'll come looking for him."

Faye stared at the table, the plates peppered about the surface, the dishes she so lovingly set out for Billie. "I should get containers." She reached out her hand, but Billie stopped her. "Trash it. We have to go."

Faye then jerked up her chin. "I gave him something. That Derek guy."

"What?"

Faye paced behind the chair. "The other statuette of the phases of a woman. There were three. I just showed you the one I kept. The other, I gave to him. The third was buried with Asli. Three pieces. Anyway, when he came to visit, I gave it to him as something to know her by."

"We really have to go," said Billie, reaching for the straps of her messenger bag.

"Go where?"

Faye and Billie whipped their heads toward the figure in the living room, standing with all the confidence of a man determined to get away with it. He was pointing a gun with a silencer at them.

Derek Campbell wore black sweats – a generic set, graying from detergent – that gave him the appearance of homelessness, and black boots, issued by a police academy he couldn't hack.

"Hello, Veronica Mars," he said.

Faye glanced into the kitchen where a back door opened to an outside deck. Derek noticed that too.

He waved the gun at them. "I wouldn't."

"Detective Morales knows I'm here," Billie lied.

"No, he doesn't. You would never tell a police officer what you're up to. I don't even think you're capable of it."

He probably had her there.

She said, "How are you going to play this? Shoot us both? Then what? Haul our bodies away?"

"Basically," said Derek. "You're not that heavy. I shoot," he pointed the gun at Faye, "take her cell phone, so it seems like she skipped out on her hubby while he's away, pack a bag probably. I kill you," he veered the gun toward Billie, "dump your body where no one will find it, make it seem like Roza Filipek came back for you, ooh, or better yet, you went off to join her squad. I bet I can manufacture that. Easy peasy."

"Seems messy," said Billie.

"I have the time," he said, before hefting up a black bag. "And I brought plastic and duct tape."

Billie heard Faye's labored breathing. She reached out a hand to steady her. They would not be going down this way. She didn't survive an FBI raid on Roza's compound in the Poconos to die in a suburban split-level in Park Ridge.

"They're going to run the DNA on Asli's remains," said Billie. "They're going to enter that DNA into databases and you're going to pop up. The police will link you to the untimely and weird disappearance of Asli's sister, not to mention your co-worker, a private investigator who was looking into the case. Then, there's your bestie, Gary Amato, whose recent death is super suspicious when detectives realize that you and he were on the same high school track team. You're standing next to him in the photo that's hanging up in his house. Then they'll realize that you used Patty Amato to get into the Elmwood Park Memorial High School library where you ripped out the yearbook page that showed Asli's photo. You can't tie up loose ends when they're this frayed."

"By then, I'll be gone," said Derek.

"Where ya gonna go? You have a kid," she said.

"I'll take him with me. I have a lot of money now."

"So I've heard. You cut out Gary and Fatima and gave Roza Filipek the entirety of Karl's storage unit. For a cut."

"It was my inheritance!" he cried. "I could do whatever I wanted with it. That's the least that asshole owed me after he left me to die."

"You got adopted," she said. "You didn't die."

"I was raised by alcoholics. My old man said he got a trash baby, said I lived up to my origins. I should've killed *him*, but liver failure got him instead." Derek scratched at his scalp with the tip of the silencer. "Funny thing was, I didn't even mean to kill Karl. After Fatima made the connection–"

"Fatima led you to Karl?" said Billie.

"I had worked with Mahmoud's before on another case, so I approached her for help. Thought maybe she could trace the artwork if Asli was still alive. So I showed Fatima the statuette and my half-German DNA profile. Mentioned a Turkish mother with Elmwood Park connections. Fatima drew a straight line from Asli to Karl Sauer. I had only gone to his house to find out if he was actually my father, and he admitted that he was. Said a whore showed up one day with a baby and he got rid of them both."

Faye winced.

"The old man didn't toss anything in the garbage, except for a day-old newborn. That piece of shit deserved to die. My only regret was using the statue Faye gave me. I brought it to him as proof – see? I'm your son. Let me in on that art haul you've got. But the kook came at me." Derek gave that some consideration. "Actually he laughed at me first. Then he lunged. So I clocked him over the head. He went down like dead wood. But I shouldn't have let my temper get the best of me. If I had given him a few more minutes, he might've exposed where he had buried Asli's body. You uncovering her really did catch me by surprise. Honestly, your whole investigative shtick would be refreshing if it wasn't also so goddamn inconvenient."

Derek waved the gun toward the steps. "Let's go upstairs to the bathroom. Get you in the tub. I think that'll be easier."

"I'm not making your life easier," said Billie.

"No shit," he replied.

"What else did Karl say about my sister?" Faye asked, her voice controlled and even, as if she was asking Derek about his hobbies or middle name.

"You don't want to know," said Derek.

"I do," Faye whispered.

He shook his head, dismissing an argument with himself, and redirected his attention to his boots. His features morphed from sadism to sorrow. "He said she meant nothing to him besides a good lay." He looked at Billie in a brief moment of earnestness, so quick Billie questioned whether it had appeared. "How do you walk away from someone like that? How do you let that go unpunished?" If he wasn't pointing a gun at her, this could have felt like a counseling session with her in the shrink's chair, pen poised to take notes.

"It might've gone unnoticed," said Billie, "if you had just left him there to rot and never involved Roza. But you tried to kill Fatima. You tracked my car and ran me off the road in your shitty sedan. You framed Aaron. You murdered Gary. And none of it mattered."

"I would've succeeded if it wasn't for your meddling," he sneered.

Billie approached him, but he raised the gun. "Not so close."

"If you kill us, your life is over," she said. "If you let us go, you get a head start."

Derek shook his head. "No."

Billie stared at his waist and hips.

The power comes from your legs and core. Fatima had turned to her friends while Billie stood there helplessly in the senior parking lot. "Watch this."

Without taking her gaze off him, Billie said to Faye, "Kitchen. Now."

"What?"

Billie lowered her shoulder and charged Derek. She slammed into him, her arms wrapped around his legs, and drove him into the coffee table.

The gun went off.

CHAPTER SIXTY-SEVEN

Derek Campbell had been read his rights while he lay shackled to a stretcher.

Detective Malley had said it was for his own good because Billie still had some fire left in her and with very little outlet, he couldn't be sure she wasn't still a danger to him.

Billie considered that a good summation of her mental state.

Granted, prison would be a nice staycation for good old Derek. The minute she tackled him, his head hit the coffee table which knocked him out. Billie and Faye managed to hogtie Derek with plastic cords found in the garage. And while Faye called the cops, Billie wrapped his gun in a towel and locked it in her trunk. At some point, he had peed himself.

It was a satisfying end to a traumatic case.

Although, it was possible that she had dislocated her shoulder. She sat on the bumper of the police cruiser with an ice pack pressed against her skin, the most futile of endeavors, while the EMTs checked out Faye. Despite the multiple bombs dropped on her, Faye was surprisingly all right. She stood at the end of her driveway, addressing the concerned neighbors who had showed up to her house with cake boxes.

Billie wondered what bakery provided goods for someone who had nearly been killed?

Doug Malley appeared and rested his bulk on the bumper, causing the entire cruiser to sink under his weight.

Billie said to him, "If Fatima ever turns up, I'm going to tell her that stupid rugby tackle came in handy."

"Cops found her hiding out at an empty house in Lavallette," he said.

"I feel bad for her," she said.

"You should feel bad for me," he said. "I'm supposed to be on vacation." Then he grew serious, and Billie waited for the inevitable speech that went alongside her ridiculous escapades. "You could've died. Again."

"A Hanukkah miracle," she said, but her attempt at humor was displaced by the tremor in her voice. There were only so many times that Billie could throw herself in front of a bus and not get squashed.

Malley put his beefy arm around her and squeezed. While the local coppers scampered about, carrying evidence bags, she and Malley sat in the cold, not even feeling it.

Snow would show up en masse after the new year when no one gave a shit about white Christmases anymore.

"Maybe as a holiday gift to Gramps," said Billie, "we can fail to mention this part of the investigation?"

Malley scoffed because they both knew there was no deceiving William Levine, even if that deception was by omission. And then to really drive the nail into Billie's coffin, Malley signaled to a Park Ridge police officer to come over.

Billie sighed, and without being asked, slapped her car keys in the officer's hand. She wanted to say she could drive herself, but when she stood, she wobbled like a newborn fawn.

Gramps would take one look at that police car, and he would know.

"Face your fire," said Malley as he opened up the Hyundai's passenger's-side door.

As if that wasn't what Billie did every single day of her life.

CHAPTER SIXTY-EIGHT

The next morning, Billie showed up at the Sauer house with a limp, sore shoulder, and bruised knuckles. She was still achy from tackling Derek to the floor, and could probably use another week's respite, but Christina had offered to pay her in cash, and Billie was a robot, powered mostly by money. Well, not mostly, but largely.

Sadly, that's what she and Derek had in common.

Christina had said she would be working at her father's home, trying to empty it out before a real estate agent arrived with an appraisal or the number for a demolition crew.

"I'm leaning toward the latter," she said.

And, yet, Christina had replaced the front door with a center glass-pane and curved brass fixtures. Billie hesitated, assuming the house had been buttoned up tight, but she must've been expecting Billie's arrival as the handle clicked easily. Fearing a trap, Billie stood on the threshold for two minutes until the rational part of her brain reminded her that the villains were gone.

Pushing open the door, Billie found the house dark.

Maybe they weren't all gone?

Her hand found a light switch but no illumination. She swiped her palm up and down several times but fared no better. Blown fuse? Possibly, but her stomach didn't seem sure.

"Christina?"

A response: "Basement."

Billie really had no interest in going down there, especially without bright yellow light to diminish the shadows. She swallowed a ball of phlegm that had taken root in her esophagus and grabbed a Louisville Slugger that had been propped up in the corner. Couldn't hurt, could it?

Her footfalls creaked as she descended the stairs and echoed off the concrete block walls, making her feel more ill at-ease than if she was entering a ghoulish dungeon brimming with forgotten prisoners.

And then Christina said, "Sorry, blown fuse."

There was a click and the sound of a switch being manually toggled. Then, light.

Billie dropped the bat. Christina popped her head between pillars of clear, plastic tubs. "Did I freak you out?"

"Yeah. You did."

Christina emerged into a pool of light emanating from a single bulb. She shoved her hand into the pocket of her overalls and withdrew a wad of cash. "Hope this makes up for it."

"Venmo would've worked too," said Billie, reaching for the bills that had been wrapped together in a rubber band.

"But now you don't have to claim it on taxes." Christina frowned. "I sound like my father." She leaned a shoulder against the plastic tub. Inside, Billie spotted a mishmash of colorful cloth. Dishtowels? Table linens? *Who cares?*

"Not gonna lie," said Christina. "I'd been regretting my decision to hire you. I kept thinking that if I had just kept my mouth shut, if I had just told myself to let it go, that I'd be no worse off. I wouldn't have known about my grandfather and father, or about Derek Campbell. I would've been ignorant of all of this."

Billie sensed a *but*, so she stayed silent, but internally she also wished Christina had just stayed home. But if she had, Asli would never have been found.

"Is it weird that I can't even blame Derek for what he did? How could I? My father tossed him out like trash, assuming he would die."

"I don't think it's weird at all," she said.

"Except he's my half-brother that I don't want anything to do with," said Christina. "I didn't even tell my boys about him, although I'm sure they'll find out from some jerks at school."

Family was more than DNA; it consisted of arguments over who got to light the menorah and ordering the low-sodium deli turkey that only one person ate and boxing up dusty beer steins. And in the Levine household, surprising a home invasion in progress.

Family meant more than a helix of atoms.

Christina asked, "Do you believe in generational curses?"

Billie sighed. If families were receiving curses, the Levines had mistakenly been first in line, thinking they were being handed pots of gold. "I believe in a string of bad luck influenced by a history of poor decisions, mostly made by other people," said Billie.

"You had that response at the ready."

"I've had a lot of time to think about it."

Christina moved around the towers of plastic bins as if she was dancing with a devil, until she stopped in front of one. "I need you to do me a favor." Without waiting for a response, she hefted up a box and withdrew a framed picture behind glass.

"It's a Felix Nussbaum," said Christina. "Not stolen," she added. Then flipping over the artwork, she noted a certificate attached to the back. "It's a numbered print, so likely my dad came across this legitimately – small mercy – but I was hoping you could give it to Rabbi Schechter. I know he's a fan."

Billie approached the picture, absorbed the muted colors, the profile of a man in a yarmulke, his face young, but haunted. Billie mentally questioned why Christina couldn't bring the painting to the rabbi herself until she remembered how shame overshadowed good intentions.

"Sure," said Billie. "I can do that."

Christina didn't utter a thanks, but Billie noted the gratitude all the same.

"Your boys are going to find out about their grandfather and Derek at some point. Wouldn't it be best coming from you instead of Kyle in homeroom?" said Billie.

Christina sniffled; her eyes dampened so quickly, Billie imagined the tears were sitting on those bottom lashes, just waiting for their time. "How?"

Billie swallowed her own emotions and said, "I hear therapy is doing wonders for people."

CHAPTER SIXTY-NINE

"Here, take this." Aaron winced as he reached into his coat pocket and withdrew a rectangular box that he pressed into her hand. They were sitting on Billie's bed, Billie careful not to disturb the mattress too much since Aaron's stitches were still so fresh. And as noted by his inability to reach for objects without grimacing, apparently they were also painful.

He gingerly reclined while she stared at the box that housed the newest iPhone. The reply, automatic and constant, was out of her mouth before she could stop herself: "I don't need you to buy me–"

Aaron cut her off, a tactic so expedient, it likely sat on his tongue waiting for moments like this. "It's a fucking phone, Billie, not a car. Also it'll be obsolete next year anyway. Just take it. I can't leave knowing you're resorting to tin cans linked with a piece of string. You need a decent phone for your business."

"Ok," she said, softly. "I'll take the phone." She laid down and tucked herself beside him.

A few days ago, Aaron had told her that he would leave New Jersey for a while. "Not forever," he'd said. And although Billie guessed that his lack of specificity on a return date was for her benefit, it was more likely he needed to pretend that this break was temporary.

Billie knew it was not.

Aaron was a mobster's kid. No matter how hard he tried to toe the line between law and criminality, he would always be in someone's crosshairs. Villains and heroes would exploit

323

Aaron's history for their own gain, thus making Billie his constant savior.

"It's only a matter of time before you do something for me that gets you arrested by your ex-boyfriend," he'd said. "And as much as I think you could become a Queenpin in a county jail, I don't want that for you."

"Again," she said. "Esteban Morales and I never dated."

He frowned, then laughed, then grimaced as he held a hand to his side.

Billie had tried to talk him out of it, begged really, only stopping herself when she realized that he was right. Years ago, Aaron had left for Israel for his own good, but now it seemed it would be for Billie's. It didn't matter if he walked the straight and narrow from here on out, someone would always try to knock him off the path.

Aaron tucked a strand of hair behind her ear. "I don't think you should give up on Levine Investigations, despite the insane circumstances you find yourself in."

She nodded, placatingly. Her body felt heavy, as if it was sinking into the mattress by the weight of her own guilt. Because with Aaron gone, Billie could manage her anxiety any which way she wanted, and sometimes that meant by dropping herself directly into the fire. Danger had an incredible ability to smother ruminations.

But Aaron only heard the silence, so he added, "Besides, you can be Gramps's boss. Imagine how fun that could be."

Billie shifted and chuckled into his armpit. "I don't know if fun is the word that comes to mind. Infuriating. Frustrating. Exhausting. Those seem like more accurate descriptors."

"Sounds like a blast to me," he said, before kissing the top of her head. She heard him sniffle, and her eyes burned. She had been doing such a great job keeping it together until this point. "I'm going to miss you so much, Billie."

She buried her face into his chest. "Will you let me know where you end up?"

He hugged her tighter, enveloping her in such a way as to suggest that this moment would indeed be the last they shared. She inhaled his cologne; memorized the sensation of her cheek pressed against his shirt. She committed to memory the shape of the buttons as she undid them one by one.

Finally, he said, "No."

"There's hardwood under here," said David as he cut into a section of stained living room carpet.

"I could've told you that," Gramps said from the kitchen. He held a bottle of Windex in one hand, a microfiber towel in another. He was giving the cabinets a once-over. Of course, by this point, it was really a thrice-over.

"Should I keep cutting?"

"Do what you want," said Gramps.

Billie, meanwhile, was tossing old copies of *TV Guide* and *Sports Illustrated* into a recycling bin. Matty had hauled out several already.

Gramps had thoughtfully posted some of Ken's least egregious furniture pieces on Facebook's freecycling groups, and a Hispanic man from Paramus had picked up the loveseat and Ken's old dinette set. When he arrived, he came without a winter coat, so Gramps insisted Billie translate while he showed the man Ken's closet.

"Tell him to take anything he wants," said Gramps.

Billie struggled for a minute while she tried to find the right phrases, but instead settled on "La ropa es suya." *The clothing is yours.*

The man nodded and said, "Sure?"

"Sure." Super sure. She wanted to add: "Esta casa es su casa," but really it would go to the highest bidder, once Gramps decided to put it on the market, which seemed how things were likely to go.

Billie handed the gentleman boxes to pack up Ken's wardrobe. Ken had been a packrat, which in this case turned out to be quite fruitful. Old Carhartt coats in great condition, leather Oxfords that only saw the inside of synagogue and funeral homes.

The man hauled out several boxes, saying thank you over and over again, but if Billie's Spanish was better, she would've explained that it was the Levines who were grateful. To have Ken's belongings find homes rather than a landfill made Gramps feel like he was doing right by his old friend. The generosity lessened the emotional burden.

Houses survived longer than their occupants. They took on new people who transformed the walls and floors into security and safety, or in Karl Sauer's case – a prison of his own making. Karl's home would hopefully be transformed by new owners. Actually, Billie thought, that place should just be leveled. There wasn't enough sage, paint, and new carpet to cleanse that hellspace.

Gramps grabbed a broom and began sweeping dirt into small piles while David rolled up the carpet remnants for garbage pick-up.

"I want more cases," said Gramps. "I had fun with Safe Horizons. It's fine if you're not going to continue with Levine Investigations. I mean I'm not going to nearly die in a Poconos warehouse," he narrowed his gaze at her, "but I'm still up for small assignments."

"I'm not letting go of the business," she said. "I'll manage it better, that's all."

"Oh," said Gramps, his smile returning. "Real good." Billie realized he had rehearsed an argument in his head that was just rendered moot.

While David hauled out the carpet, she said, "Let them rent this place." She jerked her chin toward the front door. "David and Matty."

Gramps sighed.

"They've put a lot of work into fixing up the house. It's the least you can do, even if it's for a few months while they save money for another place."

Gramps made a face and rolled his eyes, a performance only for Billie's benefit. "I already agreed that they could stay, but I'm charging rent. No freeloading."

"No one would ever dream of taking advantage of you." Billie went back to stacking Ken's books for the library donations drop.

When David returned, Billie whispered, "How much rent is Gramps charging you?"

David shrugged. "A grand a month to cover the property taxes."

"So you're doing it? You and Matty are moving in here?"

David nodded just as a truck pulled up.

"Another Facebook person?"

"No, that's our furniture being delivered. We bought a kitchen table, chairs, a new sofa, and a new bed."

Matty poked his head in with Brian Paretsky in tow. "Look who I wrangled to help me."

Billie nudged Brian's shoulder. "How are things?"

"Quiet," he said.

"You wanna hang out for New Year's? I'm going to be alone this year."

"Can't," he said.

"Oh?" She couldn't keep the surprise out of her voice.

"I met someone at Jenn Herman's wedding. A teacher. She's nice. I'm taking her into the city."

"Excellent, Brian."

"And you're not alone. You have Aaron."

Not anymore, but the only one who knew he had left was Matty, and they had both decided, without saying so aloud, that Aaron's absence was a subject never to be discussed. They were dandelions. The mention of his name would blow them to smithereens.

"And Gramps!" Brian added. "I bet he's a ton of fun on New Year's."

"He isn't," she said. "But you're right. I have Gramps."

And David and Matty and Shari and Nicole.

"Someone help me bring in these boxes," cried David.

Brian darted outside, and Billie took the moment to check an outstanding text message from earlier.

Her father had written: *The invitation to come out to Sedona will always be open if you and David want to take advantage. It's real pretty out here. Maybe that will entice you.*

Nope, Billie thought as she replied, *Congrats on your wedding.*

And that was it, because that was enough. She was an adult, and yeah maybe she was still his kid, but she was also her own person with her own trajectory. And she didn't need to make him feel like a good dad by attending his wedding if she didn't want to. And she didn't want to.

Forgiveness was one of those gifts you gave yourself.

As Gramps clamped David on the shoulder, maybe he was realizing that as well.

Billie said, "I'll carry in your stuff, but I'm not putting anything together."

"But you're the IKEA guru," David whined.

"Flattery will not get you a kitchen table," she said.

"How about fifty bucks?"

"That might do it."

"Save your money, David," Gramps cried. "For rent!"

Billie met Nicole for coffee in the Kentwell Student Center. The Starbucks inside was small, but well outfitted and provided enough café seating for conversation.

"Ramon should be here shortly," said Nicole as she swung her coat around the chair. "I'll introduce you, and then split. I don't like to hear about my co-workers' personal lives."

Billie frowned. "Why not? I imagine that kind of tea is good for the soul."

"You wouldn't say that if you worked in an office. You don't want people stopping by your desk to tell you how their boyfriend can't give them orgasms."

Billie immediately choked on her matcha latte. She coughed and sputtered for several seconds while Nicole looked on amused. "Yeah, how's that tea now?" She checked her watch. "Where is he? I have a meeting in ten on the far side of campus."

As if summoned, a lanky man with dark hair passed by. He had a rhythm to his gait and walked like ocean waves. Nicole clocked him immediately and called him over. "Ramon!"

Removing her purse from the nearby chair, Nicole pointed for him to sit, only Ramon didn't budge.

"Is he afraid of you?" whispered Billie.

Nicole pursed her lips. "He should be, wasting my time like this." She snapped her fingers and Ramon responded like a cocker spaniel. "This is Billie Levine, the private investigator I was telling you about."

Ramon immediately grew nervous. "Um, yeah, about that…"

Clearly, the dude had changed his mind about tailing his stepfather who might or might not have been stepping out on Ramon's mother. Fair enough; Billie could rustle up another client. "It's fine," she began.

"I hired someone else already," said Ramon.

"Who?" Billie and Nicole snapped together.

"Uh, uh, a Kentwell man," said Ramon. He whipped his head around until he spotted a face in the distance. A well put-together, Jordan-wearing teaching assistant with impeccable fashion taste but woefully poor people skills stood in front of the bookstore, making a show of examining his receipt while he sipped from some high-end insulated coffee mug.

Billie rose from the table and stared down Jeremy Yang, hoping that if looks could kill, he'd be face-down on the floor in a pool of his own insides.

"That son-of-a-bitch," she hissed, wondering why in all of their interactions, he hadn't told her that he was an investigator.

Because he's a coward, she thought, that's why.

But Nicole was more sensible. She had the wherewithal to ask the appropriate question which was "Professor Yang is a PI?"

Ramon reached for his wallet and withdrew a business card. Billie snatched it from him. Cream card stock. Gold embossed lettering.

JY Investigations

Jeremy Yang, Private Investigator

And then as if to personally offend her, it read *Licensed* underneath.

Jeremy caught Billie's eye and smirked. He then raised his tumbler, a toast of acknowledgement.

Billie would acknowledge him all right. She'd acknowledge him right to his ruin.

ACKNOWLEDGEMENTS

It was a dream to bring *Death of a Dancing Queen* to readers, so I am eternally grateful to the crew of publishing professionals who championed more Billie adventures.

First, a million thanks to my agent, Liza Fleissig, for her unwavering support and guidance. I would not want to do this business without her.

Thank you to my publisher, Eleanor Teasdale, who loves Billie as much as I do, and to my editor and book buddy, Desola Coker, who is truly a phenom in this business. Big hugs to Caroline Lambe and Amy Portsmouth and everyone else at Datura who work tirelessly on behalf of Billie.

Writing is often a lonely endeavor, but it's far less lonely working alongside friends and first-readers. They include Katrina Monroe, author of sensationally spooky stories; Elizabeth Buhmann, suspense maven; Jill Ratzan, grammarian, librarian, and eagle-eyed proofreader; Melinda Michaels, my drinking and drafting buddy (sometimes it's coffee; sometimes it's beer); and the national board (and our 4,000+ members) of Sisters in Crime. My involvement in the organization has made me a better writer and advocate. I feel so fortunate to have found my people.

I want to give a big hug to my Friday crew – the volunteers of the Ecumenical Food Pantry of Pike County – for buying copies of the book and for bragging about me even if it makes me blush.

My accomplishments wouldn't mean anything without the

love and support of my husband, Bob, and my three kids. I can't wait to embarrass my children at their schools' Career Day.

Finally, I want to thank you, dear readers. There would be no *Devil in Profile* without you. For everyone who bought a copy of *Death of a Dancing Queen*, shared the book with friends, and checked it out of the library, I am in your debt. There are so many stories you can choose to read; thank you for choosing mine.

ABOUT THE AUTHOR

Kimberly G. Giarratano is an author of mysteries for teens and adults. A former librarian, she is currently an instructor at SUNY Orange County Community College and the chapter liaison for Sisters in Crime. Born in New York and raised in New Jersey, Kim and her husband moved to the Poconos to raise their three kids amid black bears and wild turkeys. While she doesn't miss the Jersey traffic, she does miss a good bagel and lox.

Visit her at www.kimberlyggiarratano.com